VOTE FOR
PRISCILLA
VOTE FOR

Class of 95
Go, fight, win!
Luv, Priscilla

throwback

throwback

MAURENE GOO

zando
YOUNG
readers
NEW YORK

zando young readers

Zando
zandoprojects.com

First Edition: April 2023

Text design by Aubrey Khan, Neuwirth & Associates, Inc.
Cover design by Natalie C. Sousa
Cover illustrations by Kemi Mai Willan

Library of Congress Cataloging-in-Publication Data 2022945253

978-1-63893-020-4 (Hardcover)
978-1-63893-021-1 (ebook)

10 9 8 7 6 5 4 3 2 1
Manufactured in the United States of America

For my mother, obviously.

If the indebted Asian immigrant thinks they owe their life to America, the child thinks they owe their livelihood to their parents for their suffering. . . . I accept that the burden of history is solely on my shoulders.

—CATHY PARK HONG,
Minor Feelings

All right, okay, McFly. Get a grip on yourself. It's all a dream. Just a very intense dream.

—MARTY McFLY,
Back to the Future

throwback

prologue

prologue

My phone battery was at 7 percent and my dress was too small for me.

I resisted the urge to tug at the red sheath clinging to my butt and panic about the battery thing. *Concentrate on the task at hand.*

My eyes skimmed the crowd.

The homecoming dance may have been in the gym, but the dance committee had managed to transform it into something pretty dreamy. Metallic streamers were draped across the room, past the basketball hoops and framed jerseys, and silver balloons obscured the bleachers. Darkness shrouded everything else, the only illumination coming from flashing rainbow-colored lights. Every inch of the gleaming gym floor was already taken up by dancing bodies.

I spotted Priscilla—a vision in ice blue—one second before the lights shut off in the gym, and a few comical screams pierced the air. Everyone shifted excitedly in their formal wear, reveling in that perverse thrill edging on true fear.

But we weren't in the dark for long. Bright spotlights lit up the middle of the dance floor and Principal Barrett stood under them with a grin pasted on his face—his bushy eyebrows meeting his glasses, his suit baggy and misshapen.

Cypress Hill's "Insane in the Brain" started blasting, the lights started to strobe, and Principal Barrett moved his body in a bizarre way, arms lifted to chest level, feet shuffling in sync.

Oh my god. He was dancing.

The laughter in the gym was not kind. Goofy principals *actually* existed outside of bad teen movies? I didn't know why I was surprised, though. Everything about the past week had felt like a bad teen movie.

The music faded blessedly into the background.

"And now for the moment you've all been waiting for!" Principal Barrett bellowed.

"Kill yourself!" someone yelled back.

Everyone laughed. These freaking people.

Principal Barrett ignored the jeer bravely. "The announcement of homecoming king and queen!"

A current of excitement shot through the gym. Someone squealed in genuine excitement next to me.

I looked at Priscilla with those Shirley Temple ringlets—shiny and black and perfect. They brushed her shoulders bared by the strapless satin gown. A dusting of glitter on her skin made her sparkle. She was painfully pretty—a literal teen dream.

She caught me staring and made a face. "Take a picture, it'll last longer."

My smile turned into an unamused line. "I was noticing the concealer coming off your zit."

Her hand flew up to her chin. The microphone squawked and we both turned our attentions to Principal Barrett again.

Everything hinged on this one moment. Then this David Lynch fever dream of a week would be over. Hopefully.

I was ready to go home.

We reached for each other's hands at the same time.

And I waited to hear if my mother would be crowned homecoming queen.

one

one

There's this story that my mom loves to tell, about the day I was born. That year, Los Angeles was in the middle of a record-breaking drought. But when her water broke—"I swear to god, Samantha, I'm not lying"—the skies opened up and started pouring rain.

A decade-long drought was over in one day—that's how powerful the storm was. And when I was born eleven hours later, the power had gone out in the hospital, and her first look at my face was by the harsh light of a nurse's cell phone.

When I was little, this story made me feel special. Like my birth was a miracle, so much so that the natural world veered off course to welcome me in this spectacular way. And it was easy to feel special when I was small—when my mom's world revolved around me, shaping me into the best human I could be.

But as that changed, so did my perception of this birth story. Was it *actually* a way of telling me that I was a perpetual pain in the ass, from the second I was born?

SAMANTHA, WHERE ARE YOU?

A raindrop fell on my cell phone screen, obscuring the aggressive text from my mom. I looked up at the darkening sky just in time to see a flash of lightning.

"Shit-shit-shit." I slipped my phone into the pocket of my electric-blue knit dress and started to run from my car to the front steps of Oakwood Country Club. The drops immediately turned into a true downpour, and, within seconds, I was completely soaked. When I finally reached the covered entrance of the country club, my socks squished in my Docs. Guess they weren't actually waterproof. And my dress was a splotchy freak show—wet spots transforming the stretchy material into a piece of abstract art. Yeah, I was looking pretty sharp for my *country club interview.*

The things I'd rather do than go to a country club interview:

1) Eat glass
2) Dig a ditch
3) Argue with a white person about "All Lives Matter"

The rain came down in sheets as I squeezed water out of my hair. My phone buzzed again.

YOU BETTER BE ON YOUR WAY.

Again, I ignored the text. I didn't respond to all-caps texts from anyone but my best friend, Val, and only if it was because they were sending me a thirsty gif that needed my immediate attention. Also, there was something about the way my mom refused to *ever* use an exclamation point in texts, even when in all caps, that was a stealth power move. Not showing enthusiasm was my mom's tactic of keeping people in her life in check. So, no, I wasn't going to scramble to respond to her. Besides, I wasn't technically late for the interview. Mom just had zero chill.

I watched two luxury SUVs almost collide into each other in the parking lot. One of the drivers threw up his hands in exasperation, the windows fogged up with heat. As one car passed the other wildly, its tires created a giant wave of water that doused a woman running across the lot. She looked utterly shocked as she scrambled toward her own car.

The drama. On instinct, I pulled out my phone and started a voice note.

Hi, Halmoni.

Have you ever noticed that when it rains in Los Angeles, reality shifts?

Like, sunny pastel buildings suddenly look dirty—stains showing up against hideous stucco walls. Flowers that haven't existed for years bloom in the cracks of the center divider on freeways. You completely forget how to drive. What *is* driving? Water is touching my car!

A little boy with neatly cut dark hair pushed the country club doors open and bolted out, releasing a peal of laughter at the sight of the rain—a true rarity here in the fall. His parents tugged him back as he bolted straight toward it, hands reaching out eagerly.

There's also a part of it that's magical, right? We don't get real weather here. So, when we're reminded of these forces beyond our control—it feels otherworldly.

As if to punctuate that point, another flash of lightning lit up the sky. My body tensed as I waited for the rumble to come. And when it did, I felt it through my entire body—a roll of thunder that rattled my bones.

Where was I even going with this? It was a habit I picked up a couple years ago—narrating dumb stuff I was thinking for my grandma, who loved listening to the voice notes I sent as if they were her own personal podcast.

> When it rains here, you can kind of believe in something bigger than you. The possibility of something divine that could change your life in the time it takes for a crack of lightning to flash through the sky.

I stopped recording and pushed the doors open, the brass handles aged with a nice patina. Whatever genius revelation I was about to have evaporated as I walked into the lobby of Oakwood Country Club, across its plush, dark-green carpets, past a giant arrangement of fragrant lilies.

Each step I took toward my parents was punctuated by a squish.

Squish-squish. *Squish.*

"Hey."

My parents turned at the sound of my voice. My mom registered my bedraggled state—eyes sweeping over me from head to toe. "Oh my god."

I tried to smile. "Look, I'm on time!"

My dad looked baffled. "How in the world . . . ?" He waved his hand in the general direction of my ruined clothing. The image that my parents wanted me to project for this interview, I'm sure.

My mother, on the other hand, looked her part. A Burberry trench coat was cinched at her waist, a dusty rose skirt peeking out from the bottom. Her long, dark hair was perfectly blown out and balayaged. A raindrop wouldn't have dared to come within four feet of her.

"You *knew* the interview was today, what were you thinking?"

My mouth dropped open. "What? As if I could have predicted a downpour the second I parked the car?"

"Well, gosh, Samantha, there's this thing called the *weather report*." Mom was what businesswomen in Nora Ephron movies were like—acerbic. She had that quick wit and a sharpness that always cut to the bone.

I waved my hand through the air. "Who even checks that in LA? It's either you wear a sweatshirt or not."

Mom pinched the bridge of her nose. "Where were you after school?"

"I was helping Curren with his film for NYU."

My parents exchanged glances. Lickety-split, but I still saw it. They didn't hate my boyfriend, but they didn't love him.

"You spend so much time helping this guy with his college stuff," my mom said, her mouth set into a line. "Are you even getting anywhere with your own applications?"

This subject being brought up *here* of all places made my eye twitch. "Mom, I'm *fine*."

"What's 'fine' mean? You want to be on top of this so you're not *scrambling* to get it all done!" Mom's voice was raised and she glanced around, aware of her ruffled feathers.

"I'm not going to *scramble*." I dabbed under my eyes with my fingers, hoping to catch some mascara streaks.

"True, you're not a scrambler."

I let out a short laugh and my mom shook her head.

"My true dying wish would be for you to prioritize something important like this opportunity over helping your boyfriend."

The word "important" pinged against the walls of my skull as an elderly couple walked by us in matching pastel windbreakers. I gazed at the pale pink wallpaper, the floral-print curtains.

I couldn't help blurting out, "I just . . . why is this so important? I don't understand why I have to be here." My dad lurched away from us, suddenly fascinated by a watercolor painting of a French café hanging on the wall.

Mom drew close and pushed a strand of my damp hair behind my ear. "Because. They want to know our entire family. And, if we become members, you might have a place here for yourself in the future."

Sometimes I felt like I was on a hidden-camera TV show. Like, the time when my mother acted like joining a country club was a legacy she should proudly pass onto her daughter.

"What?" I asked, the word sounding stupid to my own ears. "Is this a . . . thing . . . that I'm supposed to want?"

But before my mom could respond, a white guy with a deep tan and a soft chin approached us. "Hi, are you all the Kang family?" he asked, glancing down at a clipboard.

Mom's face instantly transformed from irritated to sparkling. Her brow smoothed out, her eyes widened, and her smile was dazzling. "Yes, we are! I'm Mrs. Kang. But please call me Priscilla." She held out her hand and the guy took it eagerly, his face blushing a bit. When my mom turned on the charm, most men turned into sweaty, flushed pervos.

"Great! I'm Tate Green, the director of new memberships here. We can sit over in the great room for the interview."

He walked us over to a set of lemon-yellow striped sofas by a large picture window overlooking the golf course. We sat down on a long sofa and Tate took the armchair across from us.

Tate glanced down at his clipboard. "Well, let's just see here . . . Dr. Kang, you work at Valley View Hospital?"

My dad nodded. "Sure do." He was relaxed, his right foot propped over his left knee. In his navy suit and tortoise-shell eyeglasses, he and my mom looked like an attractive, wealthy Asian couple in a BMW commercial. The American Dream realized.

"And how long have you been a surgeon there?"

While they talked, I stared at Tate. I mean, how long does one need to be a *brain surgeon* before they were allowed in these hallowed, green-carpeted halls? He seemed to feel my gaze on him and shifted uncomfortably a few times, glancing at me every once in a while.

When he looked at his clipboard again, presumably to ask my mother what her LSAT scores were, I interrupted. "I have a question about Oakwood, Tate."

My parents' heads swiveled toward me, but I ignored them, leaning forward, a stream of water dripping off my collarbone and into my lap. I patted at it, absent-mindedly. "When did Oakwood Country Club have its first POC member?"

Without even looking at her, I could feel my mom's soul leave her body.

Tate blinked. "Oh. Um, POC . . ."

"Person of color."

He blinked again. "Yes, yeah, I knew that. Well, um, I wouldn't know off the top of my head . . ."

My mom's voice cut through his stammering. "Tate, what are your summer activities for teens?" She not so subtly placed a firm hand on my knee.

The relief was palpable when Tate straightened up and said, "We have several to choose from. Camps for golf, tennis, swim, and even arts and crafts. Is Samantha interested in any of those activities?"

I smiled blandly. "I'm graduating high school this spring. So, you will probably never see me again, Tater."

My mom let out a peal of musical laughter. "Samantha's the comedian of our family. We're very excited and proud of her for graduating."

Tate looked down at his file again. "Will she be joining her brother, Julian, at . . . oh, well, at Yale?" He grinned, an unspoken

"Good for *you*" relayed to my parents. Their smiles were wide, but I could tell they were a little forced.

Never in one million years would I ever get into Yale. Or UCLA. Or a state school with a party reputation that guaranteed an STD your freshman year.

Unlike my brother, Julian, whose childhood as a literal genius put him on a path of studying some kind of sciencey thing so niche that he was featured in the *New York Times*, I was a solid B- student who had to take summer school so that I could raise my GPA every year.

While they chatted about Julian's excellence some more, I stared out the window and had to squint against the blinding green of the grassy grounds.

"Samantha."

My mom's voice shook me out of my grass fugue state. "Tate wants to know about your activities at school." There was a hint of a plea in her voice—like, "Please act normal."

My activities. My mom knew I wasn't involved in any clubs or sports or anything. I threw her a *look*.

"Well, I go to class. Talk to friends. Eat lunch. Go to class again."

Nervous laughter all around. Tate scribbled something down on his clipboard, nodding his head. "Haha. Funny. So, are there hobbies or things you're interested in?"

I had agreed to this because it seemed to matter to my mom, and I didn't want to get into a fight. But this was really pushing it. What absolutely killed me, though, was that, yeah, if I weren't being interviewed by some preppy reject from a John Hughes movie, I could talk about the things I enjoyed. Like, genuinely. Movies, books, podcasts. That absurdly long article in the *New Yorker* about the history of bananas.

But that wasn't what Tater wanted to hear. Or my parents. They had tunnel vision—only seeing what they understood.

The green grass blinded me. "Yeah, I have interests. Like the climate."

The smile never left his face, but his body shrank back with trepidation. "Wonderful."

"Yeah, so that leads me to another question. Does Oakwood use greywater for its irrigation?"

Dismay crossed poor Tate's face. Before he could stammer out yet another non-answer, my mom looked at me with a deceptively serene expression. "Samantha, I know you're a budding activist"—*what?*—"but *we're* the ones being interviewed right now, so let's pull back a bit, okay?" The words were said lightly, good humor running beneath them. But I knew my mom was gonna straight-up murder me after this unless I smoothed it all over.

So, I smiled in response, knowing how to ease the room. "Haha. Sure. Just something to consider since I know that California has statewide water restrictions on golf courses and your lawns look incredibly green." Everyone held their breaths. "Anyway, I've really been into body-boarding lately."

The collective exhale from that room could have levitated the entire country club to the moon.

two

The TV was blasting in the family room while my parents made dinner that evening. I could hear snippets of the local news when I walked into the kitchen after my shower.

"... the most rain Los Angeles has seen in decades ... the last time LA had a storm this large was in 1995, when several people died in disastrous mudslides and flooding."

Mom had her back to me, searing salmon on the stove, the sizzle loud and satisfying. My dad was chopping some fennel on the island when he looked up at me, shooting me a grim look. A bit of a warning about Mom's mood, I would guess.

I padded over to a cupboard and grabbed a mug, filling it with tap water before popping it into the microwave.

"Why don't you use the kettle?" Mom pressed down on the salmon fillet with her spatula.

The cold marble countertop dug into my backside as I leaned against it. "Mother. How many times do I have to tell you that microwaves don't cause cancer? Don't listen to that bing-bong juice lady."

She cracked a smile then waved the spatula at me. "Gwyneth likes her."

"If Gwyneth told you to put a jade egg in your—"

"Sam!" my dad yelled.

Mom and I started laughing and I was pleased. Getting my mom to laugh had been a hard task lately. A beat of silence passed before I said, "So, let it out."

"Let what out?" Mom lowered the heat under the cast-iron skillet and turned on the range hood fan so that I had to raise my voice.

"I know you're mad about the interview!"

She finally turned to look at me, wiping her hands on her pin-striped apron. "Listen, I'm not mad. Just—"

"Let me guess! Disappointed."

"For the love of god, may I be allowed to finish?" Mom's voice was testy.

"*Okay.*"

"Like I was saying. No, I'm not mad. But I wish you wouldn't be so overwhelmingly *obvious* in not caring about something that I clearly do care about."

The microwave beeped but I ignored it. "It's a little hard for me to care about joining a country club. You must know how bizarre that is in this day and age."

"I *don't* know, actually." Mom turned on the oven. "Not everyone is as judgmental as you, Samantha."

I almost choked. The audacity of such a statement coming from *her*.

She continued, "Also, I felt sorry for that Tate kid with you asking all those inappropriate questions."

I spun around to grab the mug from the microwave, still hot to the touch. "It's only inappropriate to backwards-ass institutions like country clubs. Also, golf courses? Do you know how much water goes into maintaining those things in Southern California?"

Mom tossed the spatula into the sink. "While I'm ecstatic you're showing concern about the environment—"

"Well, yeah. I don't really have a choice, living here and all!" I interrupted.

"I can't also help but wonder, why don't you put that energy into joining the environmental club? It would be great on your college applications," Mom said.

"You know, not everything in life has to be mined for the glory of college apps." I reached for a chamomile tea bag to dunk into my mug. "Why can't I just have an interest in something without it being used to turn me into a dutiful little consumer-driven citizen?"

Dad let out a low whistle. "That's harsh, Sam."

I flushed. "Sorry, I don't mean—"

"To categorically insult us?" Mom asked, her voice steady.

An awkward silence settled in the kitchen. Dad busied himself with something in the fridge.

"I'm talking generally," I said. "The world could use less consumerism."

Mom laughed. "Okay. Well, enjoy that commune in the woods."

"Mom. Easing off on consumerism doesn't mean you become a doomsday prepper. There's, like, an in-between there."

Before she could answer, her phone buzzed, and she frowned down at it. "Why does this son of mine insist on texting questions that require an actual conversation?" she asked.

"Because he prefers machines to speak for him over any human interaction?" I asked dryly. Julian had truly thrived during lockdown like no one else on planet Earth.

She shook her head and tapped on her phone. The distinct digital jangling for FaceTime echoed in the kitchen.

"Hello?" Julian's calm voice rang out.

Mom's face broke out into a grin. "Julian! What exactly's going on with your tuition for next semester?" The two of them chatted about something money related and I popped my head into frame, behind Mom, making a face.

Julian squinted at the screen. "Hi, Sam."

"Hey, Julian," I said, scanning his face. It was so strange to go from seeing someone every day of your life to every few weeks via a screen. Whenever I saw Julian now, he looked a little different. Like today he had a light shadow of *stubble*. Weird. And his cheeks were more hollowed out than usual. But the changes were always subtle—he *was* Julian, after all. The short and tidy haircut always remained the same, as did his dark, serious eyes set under straight, serious eyebrows. Julian was fated to meet a flighty, artistic love interest one day, since he was clearly playing the role of the uptight, handsome scientist who needed to live a little.

My face inspection was interrupted by a flash of something colorful in the background. "Is that . . . are you playing *Breath of the Wild*?" I asked.

The phone shook as Julian reached for something hastily. The screen in the background turned black. "Yes. I had a break from studying tonight."

Julian acted like playing video games in his dorm room was the height of debauchery. Which was a bummer considering playing video games was the one overlap between us growing up. We never talked about our feelings, but we logged hundreds, maybe thousands, of hours playing games together. And because Julian couldn't even have a casual hobby, his interest in video games didn't just end with playing them. He became something of an antique video game collector—he owned all of the Nintendo consoles starting from the first Nintendo Entertainment System on. His old bedroom at home looked like a nostalgic shrine for former nerd Gen Xers.

Mom shot me a look. "Julian's allowed to relax once in a while, Samantha."

"I wasn't criticizing him!" I exclaimed.

Julian let out a short laugh. "You'd be criticizing the way I'm playing. Can't get past the Yiga Clan Hideout for some reason. My instinct is to blame the AI walk cycle, but I don't think it's that."

I shook my head. "It's not that complicated, dude. The Yiga Clan is just really hard. You can't just explode your way out—it requires finesse. And being observant. You know this game teaches you how to beat it each time you lose." Unsurprisingly, Julian overanalyzed video games, always taking them apart in his brain, dissecting what made everything work. "Took me an entire weekend of being holed up in my room to beat them." I glanced at Mom. "You didn't hear that, Mom. But isn't it so fun? The story is *so* good and stays with you for days."

"Being observant isn't my strong suit," Julian said.

Dad pushed between us to shove his face into view. "Hey, kid. How's biochem going? As brutal as I remember?" I took a step back, literally pushed out of frame.

Julian's answer was interrupted by a loud knock on the kitchen French doors. My aunt Grace was standing outside in a wet raincoat. She waved when we made eye contact.

When I opened the door, the sound of the pouring rain filled the kitchen and Aunt Grace slipped inside, wiping her boots on the indoor mat. "Wow, this rain!" she exclaimed. "I literally saw a car wipe out on the 2 just now. This feels *biblical*."

"Everyone's acting like it's the end times." I took her coat from her. "I didn't know you were coming over!"

She took off her boots and dropped her overnight bag on the floor. "I texted you!"

"What?" I checked my phone. It was dead. "Ugh, sorry. My phone battery lasts for like two hours these days. Even when it's not on. How is that even possible?"

Mom made a tsk sound. "You still haven't replaced it? Julian gave you that gift card."

Julian's disembodied voice asked, "You haven't used that yet?"

"Hi, Julian," Grace called out.

Dad held the phone out to face her. "Hi, Aunt Grace," said Julian.

She waved and grinned. "Look at that five o'clock shadow. So manly."

There was a beat of awkward silence and Julian didn't respond right away. When he did, it was with a strained laugh. "Yes."

But Aunt Grace answered smoothly, used to Julian. "Not that being manly matters. In any way at all. You do you."

I laughed while Julian replied with a stuffy "Thank you."

Mom took the phone back and wrapped up the FaceTime with Julian while Aunt Grace sniffed the air. "Mm, smells good in here. What's cooking, gang?"

"Salmon and roasted fennel," Dad said. "Did you bring any booze?"

Aunt Grace held up a canvas bag from a hipster wine shop on the east side. "Who do you think I am?" She walked over to put it in the fridge, landing a kiss on top of my head along the way. "It is *so* nice to be in this warm, dry suburban house."

Mom took the wine and inspected the label. "We need to get your landlord to fix that leak of yours."

Aunt Grace swiped a piece of bread off the counter and popped it into her mouth. "Might be time to use your lawyer flex to scare the cheap ass."

Mom shook her head and moved the bowl of sliced bread farther away from Aunt Grace's grasp. "Don't worry, I've already started drafting a letter. But I actually wish you'd just move out of that place already. You're probably being poisoned by black mold."

"Unni, not everyone can just up and leave their homes in LA," Aunt Grace said with a sigh. "The location is bananas, and I'll never find another rent-controlled place in Silver Lake for that price."

"Maybe it's time for a new job, too, then?" my mom hinted, turning to check on the salmon.

Aunt Grace slid into a stool at the kitchen island and ran a hand through her shoulder-length, bleached-blond hair. She was wearing giant neon-green hoops in her ears, an unexpected complement to her plum jumpsuit. "Before we have this conversation for the thousandth time, may I please be drunk?"

Mom was eleven years older than Aunt Grace and acted more like her mom than her older sister. The fact that they were almost opposite humans made the contrast sharper. In addition to her general hipness, Aunt Grace worked as a web designer for a women's shelter. Not that Mom wasn't charitable, but she sure as hell wouldn't be caught dead working for a nonprofit, living paycheck to paycheck.

It was a sore subject. Aunt Grace and I understood each other.

"Sam, can you put these in the oven for me?" Dad asked loudly, cutting the dreaded job discussion short.

I took the tray of fennel. "Hey, Aunt Grace. What do you think of country clubs?"

Both my parents groaned. I shot them defensive looks. "What?"

Aunt Grace took a sip of wine before answering. "Who even thinks about country clubs today?"

I closed the oven with triumphant finality. "Ha! There you go."

"A little unfair, don't you think, Sam?" Dad's tone registered a warning as he poured a glass of wine. He handed it to my mom, who set it down on the counter, her posture tense. She always got pulled a little tighter when Aunt Grace and I hung out.

"Why? What's this about?" Aunt Grace asked.

The kitchen filled with the pleasant scent of olive oil and caramelizing fennel. Mom started washing some pans in the sink and the sound was loud and disruptive. "We had an interview at Oakwood today. And surprise! Samantha doesn't approve of us trying to become members."

Aunt Grace met my eyes, and a silent message was exchanged. *Ew.* But then she leaned forward on the counter and looked at her wine glass thoughtfully. "You know what? I remember that country club. Your best friend had her sweet sixteen party there, right? What was that bitch's name?"

I choked. "OMG."

"Sorry." Aunt Grace grinned, not sorry at all. "But you had that terrible friend . . ."

"Deidre Buchanan," Mom said with a reluctant laugh. "And yeah, she had her party there."

"Sweet Sixteen?" I cringed. "Truly, you guys lived in wild times."

"Yeah, it was great growing up as a little lesbian then," Aunt Grace said with a scoff. "Country clubs and cotillions and me with my crush on Adela Brixton."

Mom smiled. "Oh, I forgot about her."

"I never did." Aunt Grace pretended to swoon. "That ponytail drove me wild."

Dad cleared his throat. "All right, I'm gonna go upstairs and change for dinner."

Aunt Grace patted his arm as he walked by her. "Yes, better have your valet put on your dinner tux."

He gave her a playful poke in the head. "Brat."

"Tell me more about Adela Brixton," I said, settling into a stool and taking a sip of my tea.

"Oh, Adela. She was softball captain and a teen dream."

I laughed. "Wow, you really had a type early on."

Aunt Grace's wine glass scraped on the marble counter when she set it down. "I did." Aunt Grace waggled her eyebrows at me. "Anyway, Adela was the one who got away."

I grinned. "I love your high school stories."

"Hey." Aunt Grace pointed her wine glass at me. "Don't go telling this story to Halmoni. On one of your voice notes to her."

The grin slid off my face. My mom looked between us. "What voice notes?"

"How do you know about those?" I asked, ignoring Mom.

"She was listening to one when I went over the other day." Aunt Grace paused, her brow furrowed with concern. "I didn't really hear anything if you're worried about that."

I shook my head. "No, it's fine. But yeah, it's . . . they're private messages."

"What notes?" Mom asked, exasperated.

"It's nothing," I said, running my finger over the rim of my mug. "Just—messages I send her so she can listen later."

"Why can't you just call her?" Mom asked. There was an edge to her voice.

"I *do* call her," I said. "This is just for fun. Halmoni likes it."

Was Mom actually curious about what I had to say?

She held up her hands as the timer went off. "Well, if it's another deep dive into the history of bananas, glad Halmoni's the recipient and not me."

Well, there you go.

Aunt Grace downed the rest of her wine. "How are things with Curren?" she asked, eager to change the subject.

Mom opened the oven and removed the baking sheet filled with fennel, making a ton of annoying clanging metal noises in the process. Subtle.

"He's good," I said. "We're almost done with his movie!"

"Oh, rad! Will I get to watch it one day? Aren't you the star?" Aunt Grace teased.

I dunked a piece of bread into my tea like a monster. "'Star' is a stretch."

"You've helped him so much, you should be co-director," Mom said while transferring the fennel to a platter.

"I didn't help *that* much."

When I reached for a piece of fennel, Mom slapped my hand away. "You practically spent your whole summer working on that movie instead of . . ." She trailed off.

"Instead of what?" I asked, managing to grab a piece of fennel.

Mom took a breath. She was probably having to do a mindfulness exercise just to talk to me right now. "I think you could have focused on something for yourself. Something that could add to *your* college applications, not just Curren's."

Everything always came back to this. I sighed. "Well, I guess I just had a fun summer, instead. Terrible."

Comically—cosmically—a roll of thunder shook the house. We all looked up at the ceiling for a second, and when I looked back at Mom, she recalibrated. Her irritation gone, her expression neutral. She had an uncanny knack for that—letting unpleasant things slide off of her like organic, cold-pressed coconut oil, never breaking the perfect facade. "Dinner's ready."

I slid off the stool and started to set the table. And I was hit with a startling sensation. For the first time ever, I was looking forward to the day when there would be one less place setting there.

three

Everyone was wearing pajamas at school the next day.

I opened my locker as a girl in a fuzzy lavender onesie walked by me, so casual. Michelle wasn't playing around. It was homecoming month at our school, which meant there was some sort of embarrassing themed activity every week. Apparently, today was Pajama Day.

"Hey, Sam," Michelle said with a wave. I waved back, hiding my horror. Her wave drooped when she registered my normal clothes.

"Love a onesie," I said, to make her feel less self-conscious.

She beamed. "*Right?*" There was a bounce to her step as she continued down the hall.

Someone else's accusatory voice asked, "Where are *your* PJs?"

I peered around my locker. My best friend, Val Caron-Le, was leaning against the row of lockers like a teen heartthrob—a silky eye mask pushed up on their curly brown hair.

"Wow, are you actually showing *school spirit*?" I asked. Val was not the type, but also, no one but the government kids really cared about homecoming all that much. Michelle-in-the-onesie was an outlier, for sure.

No one really cared about what anyone did at our school. If there ever was a post-high-school-bullshit era of socialization, our school was it. A social hierarchy just couldn't exist in this chaos. North Foothill was a racially diverse suburb of LA where everyone came from everywhere and everything was just kind of matter-of-factly accepted. Like if someone tried to Regina George–bully someone because of not having enough money or something, they'd get the crap kicked out of them by a gang of LARPers.

Val shrugged. "I love an excuse to dress up."

"Well, I wanted to spare everyone the sight of my sweats with a hole in the butt," I said with a grin. "Plus, my mom would have made me wear, like, something made of satin. That matched."

"Your mother is wasted on you."

I shifted my backpack onto my shoulder, and we started walking down the hall. "That's how she feels, too. She's annoyed because I messed up our country club interview yesterday."

Val walked alongside me in thermal leggings and a cozy cardigan. Their feet were tucked into tall, red rubber boots. For someone who exclusively consumed horror movies, Val always dressed for seasonal changes that happened in some fantasy rom-com they were starring in. "Oh, yeah, *that*. How did you even mess it up?"

"Well, first I got caught in the rain, and then Tate, our interviewer—"

"Tate?" Val made a face. "A name like that in *this* economy?"

"Right? So I'm sitting there, soaking wet with my Korean family in a place that, like, probably allowed its first Asian into the club ten whole years ago." My stack-heeled ankle boots sunk into the wet grass, and I cursed, unused to weather yet again.

Val wrinkled their nose. "They probably wouldn't let my family in *today*. Was there even a single Black person there that wasn't staff?" Val's mom was Black, and their dad was Vietnamese. They always joked that they would never age.

"Well, that's the thing! I asked about when they let in their first POC member."

"Amazing," Val said with a laugh. "Bet Priscilla *loved* it."

"I barely made it out of there with my life," I said, grinning. "They all just ignored me and started talking about colleges. How am I related to a person who wants to join a country club in this century?"

The sun peeked through some dark clouds and Val lifted their face up to its weak rays. "Your mother is an enigma." Val both loved and feared my mother. Mom had that effect on a lot of people.

"She was hung up about something else last night," I said. "Aunt Grace came over and mentioned my grandma voice notes."

"I love your HalmoNotes," said Val.

I shifted my backpack on my shoulders. "Well, my mom didn't feel the same way. She got all . . . weird about it."

"Weird, how?"

A pair of hands nipped my waist. "*Weird, how!*" Teasing and high-pitched.

I whipped around to punch Curren in the arm. "Hey!"

He flashed a smile, the sun coming down from the heavens to gild the contours of his face—his strong nose, crisp jawline. His messy black hair was tucked behind his ears, and I had an unobstructed view of his sleepy, gray-blue eyes. When I say my boyfriend is beautiful, I don't say that lightly. He looked like a dark angel in a goddamned painting.

"Rude," Valerie wrinkled their nose. "Thanks for interrupting us, Petrosian."

He threw his arm around me in that trash Edward Cullen way I loved. "You're welcome, Caron-Le. What, like, *amazing* convo was I interrupting?" His voice went high again. I pinched him.

"Nothing. Just another Mom rant." I pulled my sherpa-lined denim jacket tighter around me as a breeze whipped though the quad.

"Ignore her," Curren said, wrapping both his arms around me now, shielding me from the cold. "She considers *Real Housewives* prestige TV."

I shrugged. While I appreciated Curren taking my side, I never felt comfortable when he came in hot about my mom. He barely even knew her. I knew that was partially my fault—anything he ever heard about her was mostly complaining. But it also didn't help that my mom never invited him over for dinner or bothered to say more than two words to him. A very clear separation of church and state.

"Not everyone can be an auteur like you, Curren," Valerie said drily. They were one of very few people who gave Curren crap. He had a way of charming most people—like me. When we started dating last year, it almost felt like a tiny miracle. *Me?* We'd always run in similar circles and, like 99.9 percent of our student body, I thought he was hot. But at some point last year something shifted. His attention focused on me, and it was like a cloud had moved aside and I was soaking in the sun's rays.

Curren's arms stayed wrapped around me. "It's actually a scientific phenomenon—that you were birthed from your mother. You're the most chill human, I know. While she . . . I have never met a human being who should *literally* take a chill pill."

I feel like that was supposed to be a compliment, but it just was hitting me wrong this morning. Also? You couldn't literally take something that didn't exist. But whatever.

The second bell rang, and Val fluttered their fingers in a wave as they parted ways from me and Curren. We headed to homeroom together, a unit welded with laced limbs. When people said hi, it was to both of us. While popularity wasn't really a thing here,

Curren's almost universal appeal was the closest thing to it at our school.

While Mr. Finn was going though announcements for the day, Curren kicked at my feet. I reached over to press my index finger into the hollow at the base of his throat. I loved the access I had to all the weird parts to him. Felt like a secret, a privilege.

We kept poking at each other like real mature adults in love while Mr. Finn talked about all the sports happening this week, and the homecoming dance tickets going on sale.

"Okay, and now homecoming court nominations!"

A few loud boos shot through the class. People had been calling for a boycott of homecoming because of the incredibly gendered concept of homecoming court—especially the crowning of the king and queen. It was totally outdated and cringey and I couldn't believe it'd taken this long to even have the discussion.

"Everyone, calm down," Mr. Finn muttered as he pulled on his reading glasses. He peered closely at the sheet of paper in his hand. "Ah, let's see. The homecoming king nominees are Marcus Tsai, Curren Petrosian, Joshua Ford, and Zephyr Daud." Curren stood up and bowed while everyone clapped. I shot him a grin. Ham. It was proof of his charisma—despite the bad vibes about homecoming, people still liked him enough to nominate him.

Mr. Finn went on: "And the homecoming queen nominees are Isabelle Kim-Watson, Opal Turnham, Zella Sussman, and Samantha Kang."

Everyone looked over at me and clapped, some cheering. I smiled back at them, cheeks slightly flushed. I guess Curren's charisma spilled over to me.

He gave me a fist bump. "Power couple!" He said it playfully, but there was some truth to it. People loved us as a "couple"—and while I found the whole thing kind of embarrassing—the social validation felt nice, especially after dealing with yesterday's country club measure of mediocrity. It was the one thing I could always count on.

The bell rang to end homeroom and my phone buzzed with a text from Val: Congrats princess. Your mom is gonna love it.

Oh, god. She would.

I was grabbing my backpack when Mr. Finn called out my name. "I just need a second, Sam."

Curren leaned over and pecked me on the cheek. "See you at break, boo."

"What's up, Mr. Finn?" I asked, glancing down at my phone, which was buzzing with congratulatory texts from friends.

"You haven't turned in your senior project proposal." Ah, for English. Mr. Finn also happened to be my English teacher.

I frowned. "When was it due, again?"

He frowned back. "Last week."

Oh, oops. "Eep, sorry. I'll get it to you soon, I promise."

I flashed him a winning smile and spun on my heel to bail when Mr. Finn stopped me, again. "Not so fast."

"Yes?" I tried to keep the impatience out of my voice.

"Do you know what your proposal's going to be?"

I paused. "Well, I did think of something . . . ," my voice trailed off, wondering if my riff on those old people interviews in *When Harry Met Sally* was a complete enough idea to present to Mr. Finn. I thought it'd be fun to do it with friend groups as a sort of commentary on the relevance of marriage in the modern world.

"Well?" He looked at me expectantly.

Another deep dive into bananas—my mom's voice crept into my head.

"Um . . ." I stared at the wall behind Mr. Finn, my idea feeling stupid and small suddenly. "I still have to work out the details, actually."

"Okay. What's the format?" Mr. Finn crossed his arms.

Argh. "That's the surprise." Unable to help it, I winked at him. Like a sassy broad from the 1940s.

He was unamused. "The format is the surprise? What could it possibly be?"

The warning bell rang. "I have to run but I promise to get it to you!"

"By Friday, Sam!"

I was already out the door when I called out, "Sure thing, Finn!" I ran before I could get in trouble.

four

That evening, I drove over to Koreatown to have dinner with my grandma. It was a bit of a trek from the foothills to her senior assisted living community, but I was always happy to make the drive.

The front door to her apartment was ajar when I arrived. When I came over, Halmoni always kept it open in anticipation. The scent of food wafted over me and I was immediately hungry. Unzipping my boots as I hollered, "Halmoni! I'm here!"

"Okay! I'm just using bathroom!" Her voice sounded far away but she had clearly left the bathroom door open, too. Korean grandmas have no boundaries.

Just then, someone walked into the apartment behind me. An older Korean woman, her back stooped and her expression confused.

"Mrs. Jo?" I asked gently. This was the "Other Mrs. Jo" that lived down the hall. She had dementia, and often wandered into other people's apartments by accident. Halmoni tried to keep an eye on her, helping her with groceries and other errands.

Mrs. Jo looked at me blankly. "Why are you in my house?" she asked in Korean.

Familiar with the routine, I helped her back to her apartment, making sure she was settled before I called the front desk and let them know that Mrs. Jo might be having an episode. I left once a caretaker popped in, and I hoped she would be okay for the rest of night.

Back at Halmoni's, I walked through the small, cozy apartment—cluttered with photos of her children and grandchildren, piled high with Korean newspapers, filled with houseplants in varied stages of health and recuperation. A photo of my mom and me caught my eye. I was ten years old, and it was Easter. We were sitting in a rose garden at the Huntington Library, in *matching* floral dresses, surrounded by fat, pink-hued blooms. The sun was shining, the sky a soft blue. Mom was beaming, her eyes bright and her arms wrapped tightly around me. So easy in her physical affection with me. When I was little, we did things like that—wear matching clothes.

I walked over to see that the dining table was already set with bowls of rice, side dishes—banchan, and a small pot of a spicy beef soup that was one of my favorites.

Halmoni came in as I placed a couple of glasses down on the table. "Oh!" she exclaimed, as if surprised to see me. Her usual greeting.

I hugged her. "Hi, Halmoni."

"Sammy! Are you taller again?" she asked as she patted my head. My grandmother was actually pretty tall—almost as tall as me, and I was five eight. Her still fairly dark hair was pulled back into a French twist, her face clean and freshly scrubbed. My mom was always hassling her to put on some makeup. "You're not old enough to give up yet!" But my grandmother always pushed away the suggestion. "Why lie about truth?" was her usual response. After almost fifty years in the US, her English was still broken, but she was pretty damned good at joking in it, regardless.

She sat her slight frame into a chair and motioned for me to sit across from her. "Drive was okay? Not too much rain like yesterday?"

"Yeah, it was fine," I said as I sat down. "I think the worst has passed."

"I like your note yesterday," she said as she started placing the banchan onto my plate, like I was a toddler. I didn't mind. "Halmoni used to hate rain, but living here now I think it is magic, too."

"I'm glad you liked it," I said, pleased by Halmoni's praise. I pulled my right leg up onto the chair, resting my arm on it—like a total ajumma. "This looks so delicious. I'm *starved.* Mom's making us do keto."

"Mo?" Halmoni wrinkled her nose. "What is keto?"

"Just . . . a lot of meat and no rice and stuff," I said as I drizzled some soup into my bowl of rice, letting the liquid seep in.

"If she ever cook Korean food, she wouldn't need to diet all the time." Halmoni expertly dissected a piece of marinated brisket with her chopsticks, pulling it apart carefully then laying the strips on my bowl.

We hardly ever had Korean food at home even though Dad was also Korean American. It was a travesty, but my mom said that she didn't buy a Sub-Zero fridge so that it would smell like kimchi and dried anchovies year-round. Her priorities were amazing.

We ate under a framed photo of my grandfather—the formal portrait kind that was usually propped up at funerals. In fact, I was pretty sure this *was* from my grandfather's funeral. He had died before I was born, when my mom was in junior high.

Halmoni caught me looking at it. "Don't ever make me take one of those photographs, okay, Sammy?

"Um, *okay,*" I said with a nervous laugh. "This is a nonissue because you shall live forever."

She laughed but it didn't quite reach her eyes. "Yes, when you are young, the idea of death is so far away. Well, unless you are my children."

My chest pinched at that. I gave it a beat before I gently asked, "What was Halabuji's favorite food?"

A genuine smile lit up Halmoni's face. "Oh, he didn't have a favorite. He just eat everything. So much happiness at just eating."

I shoved a huge spoonful of rice into my mouth and nodded. "I get him."

"Chew before speak, Sammy," Halmoni said, but the scold was weak. "But yes, he loved every food. We saved a lot of money on groceries after he died." It was a dark joke, but Halmoni and I both appreciated dark jokes. We laughed like little gremlins as we continued to eat, but I felt a familiar gloom settle over me. It was the gloom that came with thinking about those first few years after Halabuji's death—what it had been like for Halmoni, suddenly a single mom raising two girls in a foreign country.

Halmoni interrupted my thoughts. "What fun things are you going to do this week, Sammy?"

I munched on some cold radish kimchi, the daikon crisp and tangy. "Fun? Hmm. Well, this is homecoming month at school. Which means, you know—"

"Oh yeah. Halmoni remembers. Your mom, she was really obsessed with that in high school," she said. "Homecoming this, homecoming that."

I rolled my eyes. We lived in the same suburb where my mom grew up, that's how much my mom loved high school. Mom had gone to North Foothill High, just like a billion years ago. "I don't even want to go. But you know Mom, she'll be pissed if I don't do all the typical high school nonsense."

"She won't really be mad."

"Yes, she will," I said. "You know how she can be."

My grandmother was quiet as she pushed a couple dishes closer to me. Her face took on a thoughtful expression. "You know, high school was emotional time for her. Halmoni didn't really know until much later. Homecoming was . . ." Her voice trailed off for a second before she smiled and shrugged. "Well, like most people, your mom has a reason for a lot of things."

I frowned. "Yeah, dictators often have their reasons."

Halmoni laughed, a sharp cackle that I shared with her. "Your mom is complicated person sometimes. She thinks she is helping your life. You know, you are similar in some ways," my grandma said while carefully wrapping her rice in a pickled perilla leaf.

"No way."

"Yes-euh way. You both do things . . . segeh. Strong." She pointed her metal chopsticks at me. "With very hard point of view."

"I am a *very* easy-going person," I said, my shoulders hunched in defense.

Halmoni laughed. "You are being segeh right now."

My shoulders dropped. "Maybe, I can be a *little* like that. Mom, on the other hand—she just thinks her word is law."

Another chuckle. "Yeah, she does."

"Exactly. I'm not like that."

She reached over then and patted my hand. I relaxed immediately. My grandmother was never stingy or self-conscious with affection, always doling out her love generously. She wore her emotions on her sleeve, like me. "You are not like that. But you both make a thought, or what is the word—decision? And then believe that is the best way. And when you both care about something, you care very much."

I patted Halmoni's hand back, the skin soft and thin over her strong bones. In my entire life I'd never seen her with nail polish on, but she always took care with her hands. They served her well, first as a seamstress in the garment district, then as the owner of a dry cleaner, and then as a grandmother knitting tiny, scratchy sweaters for my Barbies.

I thought back to the country club interview. "You're probably the only person in this family who thinks I care about anything."

"Maybe because you only show to me." Halmoni frowned. "In your notes to Halmoni, you always talk about so many things that are interesting! Very curious mind."

My face flushed with happiness. "You only find them interesting because you don't know how to stream podcasts yet."

"Halmoni knows podcast! I just don't care about anyone else's talking stuff. Yours is good. You know I'm right." She placed a piece of fish on my rice when I didn't answer. "Halmoni is also always right."

I laughed. "It's so weird how we're all always right in this family." She laughed, too, and our cackling filled the small apartment.

• • •

K-dramas played soothingly in the background as I did the dishes at Halmoni's sink.

When there was a knock on the door, I looked at Halmoni questioningly. She shrugged, not missing a beat of her drama. Before I could wipe my hands to answer, I heard a familiar voice.

"Hello?" Mom's head popped through the entry. Her eyes met mine. "Samantha? I didn't know you were here tonight."

"I texted Dad earlier," I said. Whenever I did Halmoni stuff, I found it easier to relay it to Dad.

She stepped inside, taking off her expensive clogs in a fluid motion that was born into every Asian person. She was carrying two bulging canvas bags. "I brought you some groceries, Umma."

Halmoni stood up comically fast, pausing the TV before walking over to Mom. "Oh! Good, good. What did you buy?" Speaking Korean, she took the bags like a greedy child and peered into them.

"Just some basics, in case you were running out. Rice, produce, tea," Mom responded in English. She stayed in the entryway—awkward and wary.

Mom always had presence in any room she entered, exuding poise and confidence. But at Halmoni's, she shrunk into herself a little bit. Like a grumpy teenager. There was always tension between my mother and Halmoni, and no matter how much Halmoni tried to ease it, it never went away. It'd been that way my entire life and one of those topics that, whenever I tried to broach with my mom, was always shut down. The topic seemed to pain Halmoni, so I never brought it up with her, either. But it was always easy between *me* and Halmoni.

Halmoni glanced up from the pear she was inspecting. "Why are you standing there?"

"I don't want to interrupt," Mom said. Testy.

This back and forth in Korean and English was the usual. Mom could speak Korean—she just never did. I would have killed to be fluent, but I only had Halmoni to practice with and I just never fully entered that sweet bilingual realm.

"What interruption?" Halmoni exclaimed. "Just come in, this is your family's home. Don't be so formal!"

Mom rolled her eyes and walked into the living room. She settled herself on a dining chair, her posture ramrod straight. Halmoni shuffled into the kitchen to put the food away.

I called out from the kitchen, "Do you want some water or anything?"

"No, I'm fine," Mom said. After a pause she said, "Oh, I have your dry cleaning in the car."

"What dry cleaning?" I asked as I shut off the faucet.

"I got your dress cleaned. You know, the wet rag you wore to the country club interview? I still can't believe you almost ruined it."

I plopped down onto the sofa and Halmoni joined me. "It was some random thing I found in a thrift store. Not one of your, like, couture *garments*."

She frowned. "It doesn't matter. They're *your* clothes. You need to take better care of them."

It wasn't that I didn't know that, but my mom literally acted like the world would end if you stained a sweater or shrunk a shirt.

"They're just *things*," I said. Halmoni patted my leg, a little signal from her. *Calm down, Sammy.*

Mom tapped her fingers on the dining room table. "Yes, well, unfortunately the world and life are made up of *things*. That cost *money* to buy."

Halmoni's voice was cheerful when she changed the subject. "Oh, what about the homecoming things? Is that this week, Sammy?"

Noooo.

An alertness came over Mom. "Oh, right, it's this week!"

"Yup," I said, picking at the nubby material of the sofa.

"Are you going to the dance this year?" she asked, her voice edged with hope. I hadn't gone the previous three years, much to Mom's disappointment.

Oh, god. I'd have to bring it up sooner or later.

"Actually," I glanced up at Mom, bracing myself, "I'll probably go this year."

"What?!" Her eyes lit up as if I had just told her Prince Harry had dumped Meghan Markle for me.

"Don't get so excited," I grumbled. "It's because I got on the court this year."

"*What?!*" Her voice took on a high-pitched screech that I had legit *never* in my life heard before. "Samantha, that is *so* great! Why didn't you tell me?"

Halmoni beamed between the both of us and patted my cheek. "Congratulations, Sammy!"

I tried not to smile, but Halmoni's pleasure and Mom's huge grin was kind of infectious and I felt my lips hitch up without my permission. "I just found out today. Chill."

"Oh, we have so much to do. Dress shopping, figuring out your hair since it's so short now. And, oh! Your campaign!"

I stilled. "My what?"

"Your campaign! For homecoming queen!" Mom's hands were actually clasped to her chest.

Dread pooled in my stomach. "Uh, I don't think I'm gonna do that."

"What do you mean? If you're a princess, you're in the running for queen."

Jesus. This had literally not occurred to me. "Mom, it's not a big deal. I just don't care that much."

The hands dropped from her chest and a look I was more familiar with came over her features: disappointment. "Well, what is it that you actually care about?"

I exchanged a glance with Halmoni, whose hands were tightly gripped together in her lap. Tense.

What did I care about? The answer was there, on the tip of my tongue, but with my mom, the words never came out as easily as they did for my grandma. Or Aunt Grace. Or Val. So instead, I just said, "Well, not *this*."

Halmoni cleared her throat. "Either way, exciting to be nominated right?"

Something about those words agitated Mom. She let out a scoff and looked away.

I took a breath and tried to ease the tension. "Mom, I don't know why you're so obsessed with homecoming queen anyway. You'd think it'd get me a scholarship to Harvard or something."

She grimaced. "In what universe would you even get *into* Harvard?"

"Mom!"

"Listen, I would have *died* to win homecoming queen. It meant something back then. I worked so hard for every bit of fun I had in high school. But even though I was one of the most popular girls in school, it never happened for me. And the one year I was actually nominated . . ."

I stared, waiting for her to finish. "What? What happened?"

Mom and Halmoni shared a look—a look heavy with so much baggage that I was surprised neither of them toppled over. Then, Mom stood up abruptly. "I have some laundry to finish at home. See you there, Samantha. Umma, don't forget to clean your rice cooker when you cook with this new rice. It's organic."

Halmoni took the bossiness in stride. "Okay. But you're going already?" There was desperation on the surface of her words.

Mom slipped back into her shoes. "Yes. Talk to you later."

Halmoni nudged me. "Sammy, you should go, too. It's getting late."

What? It was like eight. But something in Halmoni's eyes got me up off the sofa. "Okay. See you soon, Halmoni. Thank you for dinner."

"Of course," she said as she walked me to the door, where Mom was waiting for me. "Always welcome to eat here." Although she was saying it to me, she was looking at Mom. But Mom already had one foot out the door.

We walked down the carpeted corridor in silence, the popcorn walls, brown doors, and fluorescent lighting the perfect backdrop for our moods. Every time Mom rejected Halmoni like that, it felt a little tragic.

When we got to the parking lot, I thought of the look shared between Mom and Halmoni and couldn't handle my curiosity anymore. "Mom."

She stopped under a light, her skin and hair gilded by a greenish glow. "What?"

"What happened at homecoming?"

Her mouth formed a straight, hard line and I thought she wasn't going to answer. But after taking a deep breath, she said, "I didn't win, and I was so devastated about it. When I got home from the dance, instead of getting sympathy from Halmoni . . . well, she was her typical self and we got into a huge fight."

Something close to sympathy twisted my insides. The way my mom talked about high school stuff . . . that was probably a big deal to her.

"When was that?" I asked.

"Senior year." She looked at me. "That was kind of when everything fell apart between us."

Mom never talked about her Halmoni angst. I almost didn't want to move, afraid of scaring her off like a mongoose in the wild or something. But instead of elaborating, she pulled out her car keys. "So, that pea-brained Stephanie Camillo won, instead. Anyway, I give up on your homecoming queen aspirations, Samantha. Congrats on making the court."

Another rare moment: me feeling bad for my mother. She was showing an uncharacteristic moment of vulnerability and I felt like I should respond with something positive, to encourage such humanlike behavior in the future. Also, she was rarely proud of anything I did. I thought of roses and matching dresses and took a breath.

"Fine."

Mom looked at me, alert. "What?"

I sighed. "I'll do it. I'll campaign for homecoming queen if it means that much to you."

Her entire face brightened, her posture straightened. A witch's curse had been lifted off of her. "Really?"

Her happiness made me grumpier for some reason. "Yes, really. Geez." Was this all that it took to get Mom to be excited about something? An achievement involving a plastic *crown*?

She clapped her hands. "Ooh, this is going to be *so fun*. We can go shop for your dress this week." I could see the frothy designer dresses spinning in her mind already—an inventory of femininity that would make her proud, obscuring my physical flaws, while complementing my best features. It was a calculus that my mom had perfected. "You won't regret it, Samantha."

I kind of regretted it already.

five

A middle-aged man was playing a keyboard. Curren sat across from him, laptop propped on his lap and big, serious headphones on.

The bucket I was sitting on creaked, and when Curren glanced at me, I grimaced. *Sorry,* I mouthed. As soon as I did, though, I wanted to take it back. Why was *I* sorry when I agreed to spend a cold evening sitting on a bucket in Curren's damp garage, while he recorded music for his film with this rando he found on Craigslist?

I closed out of my crossword puzzle on my phone and checked the time. Man alive, I'd only been here for an hour?

The music stopped and I looked up hopefully.

Curren took his headphones off. "Hey, brother. So, I think that was great but maybe that bridge could be paused for just, like, a *bit* longer."

I frowned. "Really? I thought it was too delayed, actually."

"No, boo, we want maximum drama," Curren said with a wave of his hand.

"I think it might cross the line from drama to confusing, though."

Matt the keyboard player glanced between us, his pale hands stilled above the instrument. His skin looked like it hadn't seen sunlight in seventeen years.

Curren shrugged. "Music composition for a score is different from, like, a pop song, though."

I bit back "no shit." I didn't spend the entire summer helping to write and direct this movie without understanding the damn essence of a movie.

"I think you have to use drama sparingly," I said, persisting. "You don't want to lose the audience with too many repeated beats."

Before he could respond, my phone vibrated.

It was a text from my mom. I tensed immediately. She would not love me hanging out with Curren today instead of, like, working on whatever weird things you work on to win a homecoming campaign. (Plus, she called Curren "Jordan Catalano bad news," whatever that meant.)

When I opened the text, my heart seized. It was a link to a nearby hospital.

Your grandmother's hospitalized. Come over, quickly. Room 1028. It's serious.

A choked animal sound came out of me and Curren looked over. "What?" He was still annoyed.

"I have to go." I grabbed my bag and ran out of the garage, barely able to see straight.

Curren was at my heels. "Sam! What's going on? I thought you were going to stay."

His pouty expression just about sent me. "I'm sorry I can't hang around *waiting for my boyfriend* all goddamn day. My grandma's in the hospital!" My bag swung around with the fierceness of my movement.

"Oh, god. Sorry." He looked pained as he brushed a hand through his hair. But I didn't have time to worry about his emotions in reaction to *my* emotions.

"I'll talk to you later." I got into my car before he tried hugging me or anything.

The engine stalled. I jabbed the start button. "You piece of crap!" I let out a muffled scream while slamming my hands on the steering wheel. Then I took a deep breath and tried again, and this time, the stupid car finally turned on, and I accelerated toward the hospital.

After I grabbed a visitor's badge at the front desk, I waited impatiently for an elevator. Every passing second was killing me. I couldn't even check in with my parents because my stupid phone had died, *again*.

What could be wrong with Halmoni? I had *just* seen her. My grandmother had been healthy as a horse my entire life. Not a single thing wrong. Not even her teeth.

Tears filled my eyes as I choked down my sobs. I wished I could hold it together for once in my life. But I cried at the drop of a hat—at sad commercials or when people on HGTV shows won free houses. There was no way in hell I'd be able to keep it at bay now.

The elevator doors opened, and I stepped inside, wiping my face when I spotted the two nurses inside. They both smiled kindly at me before tactfully looking away. This wasn't their first rodeo.

I stared at the changing digital numbers. When I finally reached the tenth floor, I couldn't move my feet. I knew once I saw her, once I stepped into her room, I'd be entering an alternate reality I couldn't leave. Where every cell of everything I'd ever known would mutate into a scarier version of what was there before.

But this moment wouldn't stretch out to accommodate my feelings.

I entered her room, a beige and mauve cube. My grandmother was lying in the hospital bed, her eyes closed, hooked up to a billion tubes. Her mouth and nose were covered with a plastic mask, and I couldn't tell if the rattling noise was her or a machine.

Tears filled my eyes again. *Halmoni*.

My dad was sitting on a chair beside her, his hands holding one of hers. My mom wasn't there.

"Sam." My dad looked up at me with tired eyes. "You're here."

I stared at my grandma's still body. I reached for her other hand. "What happened? What's wrong with her?"

"She had a heart attack, honey."

"What?" My voice trembled. "But she's so healthy."

"Well," my dad threw a glance at Halmoni, "she actually had a bit of a heart condition."

I looked over at him in alarm. "What?" I didn't have any other words in my vocabulary, it seemed. "Since when?"

"For a couple years now. She didn't want you to know."

I gently squeezed Halmoni's hand. "Is she going to be okay? People get heart attacks all the time, right?" My voice was almost inaudible as I stroked the delicate skin of her hand. It was pierced with needles, bruised where her veins hadn't given way easily. It made me furious to see her body violated in this small way.

My dad got up and walked around the bed to hug me. Tight. His hand cupped the back of my head. "Sammy"—the nickname my grandmother used the most—"she's not doing well right now, but we have some hope."

I cried into his shoulder. There was no maneuvering around the awfulness of it all.

I heard the sound of measured, staccato footsteps and glanced up. My mom was standing in the doorway, two paper coffee cups in hand.

"Samantha." Her face was a little drawn but she was otherwise her usual impenetrable self. "You made it."

"What did the doctor say?" Dad asked as he stepped over to take one of the cups from her, his voice low.

She glanced at me for the briefest of seconds before looking back at my dad. "Mom went under this procedure, essentially coding her heart to bring it back. But they've had to induce a coma to spare blood to the brain. And because the attack was so severe . . ." She glanced at me again, hesitating. "They're not sure if she'll come out of it."

Not come out of it? My own heart was about to explode out of my body, and my eyes mined her face for more information. That wasn't as bad as it sounded, right? I looked for any emotional indication that I should be scared. Like really scared.

But her expression stayed maddeningly neutral. "I'll stay overnight. You guys go home. She's not going to regain consciousness anytime soon so there's no point in everyone staying here."

I reached for Halmoni's hand again, her skin cool against my warm palms. "I want to stay."

Both my parents looked at me. "Please," I said.

My mom shook her head. "I don't think so. You have homework and there's nothing you can do while you're here. Go home and I'll update you in the morning."

"*Homework?*" The offensive word echoed in the room. "Mom! I want to be here."

A loud noise in the hallway distracted all of us, and seconds later Aunt Grace burst into the room, her hair disheveled and her face pale. "How is she?" She let out a choked sob when her eyes landed on Halmoni. She stood there with her hands over her mouth, eyes welling up with tears. I felt a surge of relief to see someone react the way I felt. It made me tear up again, and Aunt Grace came over to give me a hug.

When we pulled apart, she crouched down and held Halmoni's other hand. "Umma? Can you hear me?" she choked out. Aunt Grace was close to Halmoni. They spent every Sunday at the farmer's market and marathoned K-dramas together. Whatever dysfunction was between Mom and Halmoni didn't seem to exist with Aunt Grace.

Mom explained what was happening in a low voice and Aunt Grace digested the info with glassy eyes. Finally, she asked, "Do you need me to do anything? Like get her things from home or . . ."

"We've got everything handled," Mom said. "Did you eat dinner yet?"

Aunt Grace shook her head, her voice hollow when she replied, "There's no way I can eat right now."

Mom looked up at Dad and there was a silent exchange. He said he'd check out the cafeteria while I stared at Halmoni, willing her to wake up.

"Samantha, you really should go home."

I looked up at my mom. "Are you serious right now?"

"This hospital room is cramped and Halmoni will be well taken care of, okay? She wouldn't want you here worrying," Mom said, her voice measured. In fact, everything about my mom was completely controlled, the slight slump in her shoulders the only sign anything was out of the ordinary. She was some sort of supercharged version of herself right now. It was confusing and kind of awful. The contrast between her and Aunt Grace couldn't have been clearer than in this moment, and I would have given anything to swap them as my mother and my aunt.

I swallowed the lump in my throat. "I want to be here when she wakes up. She needs me."

Aunt Grace glanced at my mom. "Maybe Sam can stay for just a little while longer?"

Mom looked over at my grandma and I saw something flicker in her features then. A half second of vulnerability, of fear and uncertainty. Hope flared through me.

Then it was gone, her expression resolute. "There's no point in all of us sitting here stressing out. When Dad gets back, you guys should go home together."

My eyes filled with disappointed, hot tears, and I couldn't manage a response. Instead, I leaned over Halmoni and pressed my forehead against hers.

"I love you," I whispered. "Wake up, soon."

As Aunt Grace cried next to me, my mom stayed quiet.

• • •

Something woke me up that night.

I blinked into the dark. Head full of cotton, eyes sticky with dried tears. A thin ray of light cut into my room.

"Mom?"

It was this thing I'd had since I was a kid: I could always feel my mom's presence before I saw her. My skin tingled and the air around me felt different. Because of this weird mom radar, I never got lost in groceries stores. She was never able to sneak up on me when I was on my phone instead of doing homework. Something in my body was always attuned to her location—our bodies orbiting the same central command center or something.

Her dark figure hovered by my bed for a second before I felt her weight press into the mattress.

There could only be one reason my mom was here.

"Mom?" I asked again, my voice garbled and small and full of fear.

"Shhh, go back to sleep. I just came home to grab a few things before going back to the hospital."

My heart was still pounding but I forced myself to ask, "Is she okay?"

Her silence made me look at her fearfully—a silhouette against the hallway light. Finally, she nodded. "Yeah. Still unconscious but nothing to be too worried about."

There was a slight movement, as if she was going to touch my hair, but she stopped. "Go back to sleep."

I watched my mom go, shutting the door behind her—leaving me alone in the dark. Why couldn't she just take another minute to tell me everything would be okay? To ask me how I was doing? She never seemed to really care about how I was feeling, but now, of all times, why couldn't she just step up and be my mom?

It all felt impossible to process, especially in this foggy state after having woken up from a crap sleep. I needed to talk to someone. I pulled out my phone.

Halmoni, right now you're in a coma. There's no nice way to put that. No sugarcoating. It seems pretty serious and all I can think about right now are those tubes coming out of your body. I know they're to keep you alive, but there's something so violating about them. They transform you from a human being with a life and interests and people you love—to a body in a hospital. I guess you can be both of those things. Everything in life seems to be different states of being, existing together. Like me going about life like normal when the person I love most in the world is struggling to stay alive.

The rain beat down on the window next to my bed.

I hate that I can't be with you. I know, I just *know*, that if I was there, you would pull out of this. Maybe that sounds delusional. But you and I have always had that thing, right? You get me and I get you. If I'm with you—nothing bad will happen. I won't ever let it.

Seconds of silence passed by, but there was nothing more I could say. So, I hit stop.

six

six

It was raining again the next morning and my car wouldn't start. At all.

"I'm going to turn you into scrap metal!" My voice cracked as I pushed the start button for the billionth time.

Thunder rolled overhead and I looked up into the dark clouds. Of course, my car had to break down during the rainiest week in LA's history. *Of! Course!* This was the worst possible time—not just because of the rain, but because I had planned to visit Halmoni during lunch break today. Every second I was away from her felt dire. I was still convinced that I needed to be there when she woke up. Being away from her just felt incredibly wrong.

After five more minutes of violent car abuse, I gave up and went inside, my shoes tracking water into the kitchen. My mom was in there packing a bento box of quinoa sushi or whatever it was she was into these days.

"Mom, can I get a ride to school? My car's not starting."

She didn't look up from her task of tucking cute food neatly into cute boxes. "What's wrong with it?"

I tugged at my backpack straps. "I don't know. It's been having trouble starting the past couple weeks."

"A *couple weeks*?" Mom looked up, aghast. She tapped the top of her bento box. "You know, if you told me something was wrong when it first started, we could have taken care of it *before* it broke down."

There was no gas in my tank to deal with this. Why was there even gas in *Mom's* tank to deal with this?

"Okay. Well, now it's broken down. Can you give me a ride?" My voice was short, my patience nonexistent.

For a second Mom looked like she was going to make me walk to school, but then she tossed the bento into her LV tote and grabbed her keys. "Okay. Let's go."

"Weirdo," I muttered under my breath as I followed her into the garage.

The rainy ride was tense, and I stared down at my phone to avoid any interaction. Our mutual disappointment in each other was stifling. I connected to the Bluetooth and started playing BLACKPINK.

Mom immediately lowered the volume. "Ugh, what is this noise?"

"Just the biggest girl K-pop group. You know, helping spread Korean culture around the world, but whatever."

"Yes, well, I would be much more celebratory if the music was actually *good*."

"Okay, Boomer."

Mom's lips quirked at that. We'd had a discussion once about how Mom somehow skipped being Gen X completely. I tried to make a TikTok about it, but she threatened to take my phone away.

"You think K-pop music is so fun and cool but when I was a kid, listening to Korean music would have been social suicide," she said as she squinted through the windshield wipers.

I made a face. "Well, you're an adult now. I think some serious examination over why you hate Korean stuff is in order."

Heat flashed through Mom's eyes. "I don't hate 'Korean stuff' and I don't appreciate being painted that way through the wisdom of a *teenager*."

It was a warning. She was using her lawyer voice. I was about to push back when I noticed us making a turn on Valley View Road. "Mom, we're not supposed to turn here."

"I know," she said casually. "We're going a different way."

"What way?" How many alternative routes were there to school? In fact, we were driving *away* from school and toward downtown.

She didn't answer me, and I looked at her suspiciously. "Mom?"

"Samantha."

"Where are we going?" But by the next turn, I knew. "The Gardens? We're going *shopping*?"

"Yes," she said, matter-of-fact as she carefully steered the car into the open-air parking lot of the Gardens, a sprawling outdoor mall complete with synchronized water fountains and hilarious topiaries.

"Are we running an errand or something?" I glanced at the clock. "I'm going to be late. And is the mall even open?"

"You know how during the pandemic I got my own personal shopper at the Gardens?"

"Uh . . . yes, I do remember that. Hard times for all."

Mom ignored the sarcasm. "Well, since I've been such a loyal customer, one of my perks is," she pulled into a parking spot marked VIP near the entrance, "shopping outside regular hours."

"O—kay. So, you want to go shopping? Right now? With me?"

She looked to me with a bright smile, the one she used with strangers to make them feel at ease. "Let's play hooky to get your homecoming dress!"

My brain was having a hard time following. "My dress?"

"Yes, for homecoming. You'll need one if you're on the court this year."

The absurdity of that statement hit me like a cartoon grand piano. "Are you . . . for real?"

Her cheeriness started to slip. "Why would I be not be 'for real'?"

I threw up my hands, feeling alone on the island of sanity. "Because Halmoni's in the hospital and I'm not running for homecoming queen anymore?"

Mom took off her seat belt. "That's why I brought you here. I thought getting your mind off Halmoni would be good. I thought homecoming would be something to look forward to."

"Something to look forward to?" All I could do was repeat the words my mother was saying, because it was like hearing a foreign language I didn't understand. Spoken by an alien.

I had to hold back the urge to cry. My disappointment in her since last night, a disappointment that had been building for years, turned into something different—something spiky and hot.

"You can't possibly think I care enough about homecoming to spend even a second thinking about it over, you know, my grandmother being in a *coma*?"

Mom flinched because I was yelling now. She put her seat belt back on with a vicious tug. The forced cheeriness was completely gone now. A car drove by us, sending a splash of water against Mom's BMW. There were actual shadows under her eyes, and I could tell that she hadn't put on any eye makeup. She looked tired. "You're not the only one being affected by Halmoni being sick, okay? Just because people don't show every emotion they have in *all caps* all the time, doesn't mean that they're not feeling them, too."

Part of me knew that was reasonable, but that part of me was being engulfed by a slowly growing rage. "Well, okay. Then not everyone can bottle up their emotions and set them aside conveniently to go about business as usual."

"That's what life *is*, Samantha. You can't just be waylaid by every single bad thing! By every emotion. You have to move on and keep surviving."

"I don't know, Mom. I think your grandma's life hanging in the balance is one of those things that can stall your life for, like, one second."

In a very uncharacteristic move, Mom dropped her head into her hands and tousled her hair, messing up the perfectly blown-out layers. "You have no idea how lucky you are to have this life. Your own car. A new dress for homecoming. But you never appreciate it. You don't take care of your things, you half-ass your commitments. You don't take anything seriously—like college, or your future. And then you expect *me* to do things for you. To fix it. Well, Samantha, I'm not fixing it for you this time. Figure out a way to get to school on your own."

Somehow Mom had turned this conversation about Halmoni into a review of all my shortcomings. Like I wasn't fully aware of them *at all times*.

I felt my entire body tighten like a screw. "First of all, I didn't let the car die *on purpose*. I don't know anything about cars! And homecoming wasn't *my* commitment. That's *your* thing. I only agreed to do it to make *you* happy!"

"*Do not do me any favors.*" The words were like bullets. She sat up and pulled the visor down to fix her hair, the moment of vulnerability gone as quickly as it came. "Go do whatever you want. Throw a tantrum that doesn't help anyone. Why would I expect you to rise to the occasion for once?"

Mom stilled, looking for a second like she regretted what she said.

Not giving her a chance to backpedal, I threw my car door open, grabbed my backpack and ran out—directly into the rain.

"Samantha!"

I turned to see Mom standing by her door, her hand shielding her eyes from the downpour. She looked furious. "Get back in the car!"

"That's a no from me," I said, my voice somehow calm. "I'm going to school."

"You are *so* ungrateful!"

I spun around, my eyes watering with anger. "Thanks, as always, for being such a loving and sensitive mother. I'm so lucky."

She dropped her hand, a small gesture of defeat. Water poured down her face. "I know you're worried about Halmoni, but you need to learn to take control of your emotions so that you can focus on what's actually important."

Something snapped. Hard.

"*Important?* Like, *homecoming*? Are you truly out of your mind?" My voice was raw and high-pitched. "I don't understand you! I will *never* understand you!"

Lightning lit up the sky for a second—and Mom straightened up again. "I know you don't understand me." Her voice was raised now, trying to be heard over the storm. "That's clear in almost every action and decision you make. I thought we could try and spend some time together today—have something to bond over. But, like always, I can't seem to do anything right with you."

I blinked against the rain. "Wow. You think I don't understand *you*? You think that I don't know how much I disappoint you and Dad because I don't have my whole life mapped out like Julian does? Or like you and Dad did? I'm just *not like that*. And why can't that be okay? Why can't I have the time to figure things out? When I'm the normal one! *This*," I gestured toward my body, "is normal!"

"You have it in you to be more than just normal, Samantha." Her hair was totally ruined now.

I shook my head. "It's unbelievable that somehow every argument comes back to this. Even when we're talking about the possibility of . . . of . . . Halmoni dying. How can you be so calm?"

"You think I'm cold. But I have a complicated relationship with your grandma. The Halmoni you know? That's not who I grew up with. And because you're so *close*, it's easy to see me as the bad guy."

"What could she have possibly been like to make you so . . ."

Mom looked directly at me then—a curtain of rain between us. "So what?"

"Fucked up."

And for a second, her face crumpled, and I felt my stomach drop, immediately regretting my words. But I didn't have what I needed in me to take them back. To apologize and try and fix whatever it was that was crumbling between us—a breaking down that was years in the making, almost completely erasing the relationship we had before, the one where I was my mom's entire world and she was mine and I could sense her presence by the vibrations in the air. Where our connection was something untouchable and special.

But then her expression went back to normal, and she was able to do the thing that I would never be capable of—recalibrating herself so that there was nothing complicated or upsetting left in her system. My mom threw her car door open. "Find your own way to get to school."

Every bone inside of me was trembling, rattling inside my skin. "I hate you."

My shaky words somehow crossed the distance between us, hitting her directly in the chest. But I didn't feel any relief. I felt sick.

She didn't respond. Instead, my mom got into the car and drove off, leaving me alone in the mall parking lot.

seven

I hate you.

I swallowed hard, willing the tears back into my eye sockets. All I'd been doing since seeing Halmoni yesterday was crying. I was *done*.

I stood under an awning in the mall entrance, resolutely not falling apart. I had to find a ride to school because my own mother had dumped my ass at the mall. Val had zero period like a freak so they couldn't pick me up, and my dad had already left for work. So, I texted Curren.

Hey, can I get a ride to school?

Seconds later: 😟 ah shit I'm grabbing donuts with Jon in Glendora rn

Glendora?! That was like forty minutes away. God, when Curren got a wild idea in his head he had to chase it like some impulsive, manic pixie dream boy. He texted again:

Everything ok?

I hesitated before texting back: Not really. Had huge fight with Mom.

The pause after that text was long. Too long. A pause that brought on a surge of panic in me. It was a familiar panic whenever I got too real with Curren, when I felt like I was being a downer. Curren had been sympathetic and sweet about Halmoni last night, but he was bad with serious stuff like this. He was someone whose life had never been touched by darkness. So, when bad things happened to other people, there was only so much empathy he could muster before he hit an inevitable wall. I felt like I had to perpetually be that "Sam is so chill" person on his arm, the one who got nominated to the homecoming court.

I was really good at playing that part. Usually.

As I drafted a few texts, scrambling to fill the silence and offset the emotions I had laid bare, an anger rose up from the pit of my stomach, burning in my throat. Anger at my mom, my dad . . . and now it was warping into anger at Curren.

I was just sick of acting so chill with everyone in my life all the time.

Don't hurt yourself responding or anything

The text was hasty and mean and I felt my heart thumping after I sent it. But I wasn't panicked anymore, I was raring for a fight.

After a few seconds: I was ordering my donuts.

And that was it. I stared, waiting for more. And when nothing came, the anger slid back into its dormant spot, and I felt stupid for even texting him.

So, a rideshare app it was.

In the app store, I clicked on the first one that popped up—Throwback Rides. It had like a billion positive reviews, so I downloaded it. It took me a second to set up the account; I had never needed to use one before. A text popped up after I requested a ride.

Your magical ride will be arriving in five minutes! ★

Okay, rideshare. Everything had to have a *personality* lately.

The five minutes gave me time to calm myself after the fight with Mom.

The image of my mom tired and trying to reason with me tugged at something low in my ribs. That feeling of sympathy again.

I can't seem to do anything right with you.

And yet, somehow Mom had centered this on her. That because my reaction wasn't what she wanted, it ruined everything. She was trying to make things right—but her way. There may have been a moment there, maybe an opportunity to try *not* to hate her, but for whatever reason I had let it slip by and just dug in my heels.

What was it about my mom that turned me into the worst version of myself?

I thought of her strained relationship with Halmoni and wondered if that was what was ahead for us, too. Like Halmoni said, both Mom and I were segeh in our beliefs. And when that belief was that we were *right,* and the other was wrong—where do you even go from there?

My phone vibrated with a notification just as a car pulled up to the curb and I looked at it skeptically. It was a rundown, old hatchback with chipped teal paint. Completely riddled with dents and scratches. "Throwback" was right.

I threw my windbreaker hood over my head and ran to the car, hoping to avoid getting completely soaked. The door opened with a velociraptor groan, and I slid inside.

It smelled medicinal. Weird.

"Hi there, Sam." The middle-aged white woman in the driver's seat turned and smiled. She was wearing a purple knit hat covered in sequins, and her straight brown hair was cut into a bob. "You headed to school?"

"Um, yup." I gave her a tight smile, a little weirded out by everything. I had created the account with my full name and didn't love a stranger calling me Sam. I glanced at my phone. Her name was Marge. Of course.

I felt something brush the back of my head, and when I swiveled around, I saw a pile of magazines teetering. The entire trunk was filled with *stuff. Oh, god.* I texted Val: I'm in a car with a potential serial killer in the form of a kOoKy lady FYI

"You look like crap."

My mouth dropped open. "Excuse me?"

"You look like crap, Sam." Marge steered us out of downtown, the rain coming down in sheets. Her wipers were limp and barely working—just kind of pushing water around. I squinted at the blurry windshield. *Hmm.*

Then I assessed the lock on my door, making a plan to roll out of the car if necessary.

"Something happen at home?"

I scooted closer to the door. "Nope. Everything's fine." Was I about to be straight-up kidnapped as a seventeen-year-old? Oh my god. Was this how human trafficking worked?

"You should let it out. Keeping that crap bottled up inside of you will turn you into an ugly old woman." She let out a burp to punctuate that point.

First, gross. Second, what in the hell? "I'm not bottling up anything."

"Your face says it all."

"*Excuse* me?" My patience was wearing thin. "Let's just get to school, please."

"Is it boy problems? Or girl problems?"

She made a hard right and I gripped the headrest in front of me. "None of your business!"

"A sibling? A dog, a cat?"

Silence.

"School? Sports?"

I snorted.

"BFF dramz?"

What?

"I know! You're saddled with the task of saving the world with a superpower that you've just begun to experiment with!"

I let out an exasperated breath. "It was just a fight with my mom, okay!"

"Ah," Marge said wisely. "Moms. More complicated than an origin story."

Even though she was a complete ding-dong, I couldn't help but laugh. "Yeah. I want to see Peter Parker dealing with his mother's impossible expectations and complete absence of emotional intelligence."

"I'm sure it's not as bad as that."

"Actually, Marge, it is." A flash of lightning lit up the sky and I startled, waiting for the crashing thunder. The storm had leveled up in the last five minutes. "I told her I hated her."

The thunder came then. Low and powerful, shaking the car. My heart leapt into my throat. *Please do not let me die in this weirdo's car.* Marge looked at me in the rearview mirror. "Do you regret it?"

The rain was coming down so hard now but instead of slowing down, Marge kept driving at top speed. I checked to make sure my seat belt was nice and tight. "If I say I don't, does that make me a bad person?"

"I don't think that's the right question," Marge said with a rattling cough. "Would you take it back if you could?"

I stared out the window. An obstinate feeling came over me—bringing with it all the unfairness of the past few years, spreading through my veins, poisoning whatever generosity or fair-mindedness I had left in me.

"No, I wouldn't. I wish *she* was different. I wish *she* could take back what she said. I wish *she* could understand *me*."

The car came to a halt, and I almost banged my head on the window.

"Jesus!" I yelped.

"We're here."

I shook my head. "Great." Longest ride to school *ever*.

As I fumbled with my seat belt, Marge turned to me. "Good luck, Sam."

The ominous words made me scramble out of the car faster. "Er, thanks."

I watched her drive away and looked up at the sky. It was still dark and roiling with movement, but the rain had stopped. Bizarre.

Stupid rain. Stupid storm. Stupid fight.

Weird car ride.

When I stepped inside school, I headed straight to my locker. My white Vans squeaked on the hallway floors as I dodged people. Someone bumped into me, and I turned to them in irritation, a scowl slashed across my face.

"Sorry!" A white girl I didn't recognize, with two buns on the top of her head speared through with chopsticks, waved at me before continuing down the hall.

What Chun-Li nonsense was *that*? When I approached my locker, I slowed down. The lockers had been repainted. Bright blue instead of puke yellow.

"An improvement," I muttered as I grabbed the lock and dialed my combination.

It didn't unlock. I tried again. Nothing.

"I'm gonna murder someone today." I gritted my teeth and tried again. Nothing. I slammed my hand against my locker and cursed.

"Uh, is there a reason you're beating up my locker?"

I looked at the tall red-headed guy standing next to me, his large shoulders shifting uneasily beneath his navy sweatshirt.

"Excuse me?"

He pointed at my locker. "This is mine."

I looked at the little metal plate with the familiar serial number on it and blinked. "No, it's my locker."

"No, it's not."

My eyes swept over him. "Who the hell are you anyway? Are you new? I think you might be confused."

He squinted at me. "I'm Neil. Who the hell are *you*? You're the one trying to break into *my* locker."

An icy trickle moved down my spine. Something felt really off. About everything. The lockers were repainted . . . but the paint didn't look fresh. In fact, they looked just as old and scratched up as they did before, when they were yellow.

"Wassup, Neil?" An Asian guy with spiky hair and insanely baggy jeans gave this Neil person a fist bump as he walked by. I stared after him. Who was *that*? And what in hell was he wearing?

In fact, what was *everyone* wearing?

I looked—like, *really* looked—around me then.

A couple of girls in tight baby tees walked by, their flared jeans covering their bubbly sneakers, hair twisted into small knots on their heads and their eyelids sparkling with glitter. A group of, well, dweebs walked in a pack with matching haircuts—straight bowl cuts parted in the middle. Then a bunch of Asian girls with long, straight hair and dark lipliner brushed by me, jeans slung low and cinched with hideous canvas belts. All of them glaring at me.

"Better watch who you're dogging, bitch," one of them said to me with a sneer.

What?

I shook my head. Right. It was still freaking homecoming month. We had these stupid themes. Today must have been nineties day or something. Everyone was *way* more into this theme than Pajama Day.

The bell rang and Neil stepped in front of me, grabbing the lock and opening my locker seconds later. He gave me a meaningful look, all *See, dumbass?*

My mouth dropped open. Maybe I was at the wrong locker after all. Did Marge somehow get me *high*?

Everyone was rushing to class, so I decided to do the same, locker be damned. I would deal with it later and just haul my books to homeroom. When I walked through the quad, I looked for Val but couldn't find them. We didn't see each other every morning so it wasn't that odd . . . but I still felt the strangeness of the car ride creeping through my body. Seeing Val would reset whatever weirdness was going on. And Curren . . . our testy text exchange was still bugging me.

I was about to text Val when the late bell rang. *Shit.* I ran to homeroom, slipping through the door as the bell was still clanging.

Mr. Finn was leaning over his desk, so he didn't notice that I was late. I jogged over to the back row where I usually sat . . .

. . . except . . .

The seats weren't arranged in rows. They were arranged in a circle. And the desks were different. The chairs were different.

And *the students* sitting in them were different.

I stopped in my tracks and stared at everyone. They stared back at me. All unfamiliar faces. Was I in the wrong class somehow? I turned to look at the teacher. Yeah, it was Mr. Finn. Same slouch, same disheveled hair.

I blinked. Way more hair. With none of the gray at the temples. My pulse picked up, and then he glanced at me from his desk. "Miss?"

What in the holy hell?

It was Mr. Finn, all right, but *younger*. And not wearing his tortoise-shell glasses. His skin was all . . . buoyant. Even his voice sounded different—higher and clearer. And dear god—it had to be said—Mr. Finn was *HOT*?

This was impossible. I felt the room spin slightly.

Before I could react, Hot Mr. Finn looked past me and said, "Priscilla? Do we have a new student?"

Priscilla.

And I felt it, then. The low electric buzz in my body. The kind you felt when a TV was turned on in a house. Subtle but the tiniest of signals that alerted me.

Every time my mom was near.

I turned around.

I stared into the face of a pretty Asian girl with flawless skin, thin arched eyebrows, and a pink-glossed mouth. Her high ponytail swished, and her eyebrow cocked while she assessed me. "No, we don't have a new student. Who are you?"

Oh.

My.

God.

eight

I used to look at old photos of my mom in high school and wonder if I was adopted.

There was no way that *I,* with my graceless limbs and unruly hair, was born from the body of a woman who once looked like a teen beauty queen.

My eyes scanned the girl standing in front of me: She was about my height with a slight, willowy frame. Her skin was lightly tanned and devoid of a single freckle, hair, or blemish. She had long, straight, dark brown hair that was pulled up into a high cheerleader pony, tied neatly with a giant blue bow. And I say cheerleader pony because she was wearing a cheerleading uniform—a turtleneck layered under a sweater vest, paired with a tiny, pleated skirt. Her feet were tucked into white high-top Reeboks that I would have killed to own. Except hers had blue puffy paint spelling out her name on them: PRIS

But it was her face that startled me into speechlessness. It was so familiar yet entirely foreign. If my mother was a babe at mom age, she was an absolute knockout in high school. The kind of girl who made every other girl her age feel like a bridge troll.

Because that's who I was looking at. There was no doubt in my mind. This was my MOM.

AS A TEENAGER.

My breathing grew shallow. Where was the air in this room? *Oh, god.* I reached for the closest thing next to me—someone's chair and a fistful of their hair.

"*Ow!*"

I barely noticed, my eyes still fixed on this person in front of me.

"*Hello?*" My mom frowned, a wrinkle forming between her eyes. "Did you hear me? Are you new or something?"

My mouth went dry. Was I even breathing right now?

"I'm . . . I'm Sam," I managed to rasp out.

She looked perplexed. "You don't go here."

I couldn't stop staring at her. How the *hell* was this possible?

Every movie ever made had conditioned me to know that this wasn't a dream. It didn't even feel like a dream. A dream was blurry around the edges. A little or a lot off. But everything I was seeing right now was scarily in focus: the familiar classroom with unfamiliar things in it, like the giant boxy TV bolted into a corner, a chalkboard with actual chalk, and an orange telephone hanging on the wall. And the glaring missing things—like a computer of any kind on Mr. Finn's desk, cell phones. In fact, I noticed several *pagers* hooked onto belt loops. Like, everyone in here was a surgeon.

This was definitely my school. That was Mr. Finn—hotness notwithstanding. And this was my mother as a teenager. Clear as day. If it was a dream, there'd be a random circus bear drinking from a water pump in the corner of the room. Or the classroom would actually be my house, but only if my house was an attic in a Victorian mansion. It'd be like that.

But everything about this felt and looked incredibly real. If real was a long time ago.

I was going to throw up. I needed to get out of there.

"I think I'm in the wrong class," I muttered before I turned and bolted from the room, my steps hurried and unsteady.

The Neil kid at the locker. *His* locker. Everyone's over-the-top clothes. Everything got blurry as I ran through the quad, heading for the side gate. I had to get out of there. Get home. If only I had my car . . .

Throwback Rides.

Throwback.

All the way back.

I stopped in my tracks.

No . . .

I fumbled through my pockets for my phone. When I unlocked the screen, a message was waiting for me.

Thank you for riding with us! We hope you find what you're looking for. Your ride will be waiting to take you home when you do. ★

They were words written in English, but my brain wasn't registering them. I read them again and again.

Did the rideshare do this to me?

Send me back in . . .

MOTHERFUCKING TIME?

I tried to respond to the messages but there was no option for that. I swiped through the app to no avail. Blinding rage took over and I was about to chuck my phone to the ground when it vibrated.

Another message popped up from the app: Be sure to keep your phone close. It's the only connection to your driver! Have a magical day! ★

What? WHAT?! I glanced at the battery level. *Jesus Christ.* It was at 90 percent. I immediately hit Val's number on speed dial.

Nothing. Not even ringing. It just . . . didn't do anything.

Right, right, right. It was . . . what, the nineties? There were no cell phone towers. My cell phone carrier didn't exist, and neither did smartphones. But I still shot Val a text just in case. Just in case by some miracle I hadn't been sent back in time. Like, this was some sort of elaborate prank.

Yeah. A prank. BY WHO? *GET A HOLD OF YOURSELF, SAMANTHA!*

I ran back into school, found the nearest bathroom, and locked myself into a stall. My phone was my only lifeline and I gripped it with both hands, staring at the screen with a magician's intensity. Val's text didn't go through, of course. I read the message from the Throwback app again.

We hope you find what you've been looking for.

What? Was I being given some kind of *mission*? A MISSION?!

I hit 9-1-1. Nothing. I called my parents. Val, again. Curren. Nothing worked. Nothing, nothing, nothing. My phone was about as useful as a flashlight. A calculator. A coaster.

I busted out of the bathroom, the door swinging hard. The empty hallway stretched out in front of me, and I took a long, hard look at everything around me. It was all just *slightly* off. The color of the lockers. The lighting. How did schools basically remain the same for like thirty years? That's when I noticed the banners plastered all over the hallway.

"Homecoming dance tickets on sale in ASB box office"

"Vote Priscilla for North Foothill High's Homecoming Queen!"

"GO COYOTES, BEAT THE TITANS!"

Oh. It was homecoming month here. Just like the future. And my mom was running for homecoming queen.

This was bananas.

I was startled by the sound of the school bell ringing, signaling the end of homeroom.

The only thing I knew at that moment was that I needed to get out of this school. To *not* see my teenage mom.

And there was only one place I knew I could run to.

• • •

The thing about Los Angeles was . . . you needed a car. Past, present, and most likely future, too.

I stared at the bus schedule in front of me. It was set behind a plastic screen and the laminate was all scratched up with graffiti scrawled on it. Right over the timetables. Thanks, degenerates!

But then a bus pulled up and I read the destination posted on the digital marquee: MacArthur Park.

Yes! That was near downtown. Very close to K-Town. From there, I could figure out the next bus situation.

I got on the bus and nervously looked at the driver, a young South Asian guy with a bored facial expression. "Hi, um, how much is the fare again?" I asked, clutching my wallet.

"A dollar thirty-five."

I blinked. "That's *it*?"

An elderly man stooped over in a front row seat scoffed. "Well, if it ain't Ivana Trump."

I flushed. *Ivana* Trump, what in the world? I quickly dug out some quarters and a dime and dropped them in. "From MacArthur Park, can I take another bus to Koreatown?"

"It's easier if you take the train at the MacArthur station. Red line, goes straight to K-Town," he said while moving the bus into traffic.

I grasped the pole next to me to avoid pitching forward. "Oh, okay. I've never taken the train. Do I need to buy a pass?"

"La di da. Never taken the train."

I glared at the old man. "Calm down, sir. There's a first time for everything!" Like *time travel.*

After the driver explained, very reluctantly, how to take the train, I found a secluded window seat in the back.

Okay, okay. You just have to make it to Halmoni's.

The thought of seeing my grandmother again was keeping me grounded right now. Maybe that's what I was sent here to do? To help her avoid getting a heart attack in the future? So many possibilities for missions ran through my head. Did I have something *bigger* to do? There was no way I had to, like, prevent 9/11 or something?! The pandemic? I was a teenage girl, not a trained agent with like, abs!

I watched the scenery pass, dread pooling in my stomach at the realization that I, most certainly, had traveled back in time. It was like one of those "Find ten differences between these photos," but in my brain. The post office looked the same except the palm trees that flanked the entrance weren't there and the name of the branch used different metal letters. There was a cigarette hut in the strip mall where my parents got their phones repaired. Cigarettes, really? Even subtle things, like the street signs, looked different to me. Entire city blocks were unfamiliar with buildings that were smaller, filled with signage for businesses that were completely foreign to me. And the people walking—they were mostly white. It was all just too weird.

Even though I knew I had to save my battery, I pulled out my phone, futilely trying to open various apps in the hopes that maybe one of them would work by some miracle. Unsurprisingly, nothing.

And so, I did something that I literally never do: I turned it off. The second the screen turned black, I felt the last connection to my real life disappear.

I was in the past. This was for real.

"Hey, what was that?"

My head snapped up. The obnoxious old man had moved into the seat across from mine and was now staring at me openly—or my phone, to be exact. I slipped it quickly into my jacket pocket. "What?"

"Don't play dumb," he said. "What is that?"

And maybe it was the wildness of it all, the hysteria that was threatening to push out of me—but I told him the truth.

"It's a phone. From the future. I'm from the future."

Seconds passed as the man stared at me, his dark eyes a little runny. Then, he finally asked, "How far into the future?"

There was a high probability that this man might have been a bit off, but I felt relief flood through my body—at being able to unburden myself of this spectacularly wild secret.

When I told him the year, he scoffed. "That ain't too far into the future. I thought you were gonna say about several hundred years—but you don't look that advanced, I guess."

A laugh bubbled out of me. "Thanks."

"So, what are you gonna do now?" He seemed mildly invested.

"I'm not sure. Because I have no idea why I was sent back in time. Or *how*. Like, I took this rideshare. Oh, a rideshare is like a taxi in the future. But I can't just sit around waiting to find out what to do. My grandma—what if she doesn't come out of her coma because I can't be there with her? And what if," my voice hitched here, "what if she dies while I'm gone, and I can never see her again?"

It's not like I expected this man to answer any of my questions. But he nodded and said, "Yeah, that's quite a pickle you're in. If I were you, I wouldn't waste your time complaining to an old coot like me. I'd go do something about it."

The driver yelled out the name of my stop. "I agree," I said, standing up. "Thanks for listening."

"Good luck, you need it, girlie."

You have no idea, weird, pushy Gramps.

nine

When I finally made it to my grandma's old folks' home, I had sweat through my sweatshirt. *Note to self: Sweatshirts don't really do the job one would assume.*

The train had been a nightmare. Total confusion at the machine to buy my ticket. I only had fifteen dollars in cash, which had also sent me into a panic. No one to accept Venmo here. Then, once I got on the train, a creepy-ass man followed me, and I had to keep switching cars. I deeply regretted leaving my pepper spray at home that morning. I felt so much more vulnerable in the past—without access to a quick text or phone call at all times.

After following a car through the parking lot gate at my grandma's place, I entered the lobby where a woman was sitting behind a desk, reading a magazine and looking incredibly bored. A radio droned in the background, the volume low and the sound staticky.

"Hi, I'm here to see Mrs. Jo in room 510." I took off my windbreaker, trying to cool off.

She put her magazine down and stared at me. "We have two Mrs. Jos, and neither are in room 510."

My stupidity hit me like a ton of bricks.

What the hell year was this? My mom was in high school, so . . . mid-nineties?

Of course my grandma wasn't here. She lived in an apartment with my mother. In North Foothill, where I had just come from.

And it was in this small moment of defeat, of reality hitting me, that I finally felt the full weight of what was happening—of the fact that I had inexplicably traveled back in time—and that I had no idea how I would get out of it. I was utterly alone.

A lump formed in my throat, and I turned away quickly so the woman wouldn't see me cry. When I looked up, I was met with a familiar face. An older woman was watching me, curiously, from a sofa in the lobby.

I blinked. "Mrs. Jo?" She was so much younger. Just a few strands of white hair and a straight back. But most noticeably—she looked at me with clear eyes. "It's you, Agasshi."

My breath caught. Was it possible that she recognized me? She had just called me the generic word for young lady, but there was recognition in her eyes.

She got up and waved her hand at the front desk woman. "She's my granddaughter. Okie dokie?"

The woman nodded and I gaped at Mrs. Jo, who was walking toward the bank of elevators. What? One, she spoke English? And two, did she have dementia already? But I followed her anyway, not sure what else to do, where else to go. This one familiar person felt like a piece of home, and I clung to the feeling like a life jacket.

We stepped into the elevator and Mrs. Jo tapped the fifth floor. The same floor where she and my grandmother lived in the future. I looked at her nervously. "Um, I don't know if . . ."

"Did you eat?"

Huh? She was definitely suffering from dementia. She must *actually* think that I was her granddaughter. I'd met her granddaughter before, in the future. She was married and a lot older than me. But, in the past, I was probably the same age as her.

Lord, the math.

I couldn't say no to a meal. And honestly, I *was* hungry. I shook my head and said no in Korean.

She nodded. "Okay, lunch time then." My Korean was so abysmal that she switched back to English.

It was ten-thirty in the morning but far be it from me to argue about lunch time with a grandma. We passed by Halmoni's door, and I felt my stomach clench. She was here, though, in this past. *She was here and not in a coma.* It was impossible to wrap my head around that. All I could see was her hooked up to all those tubes.

Mrs. Jo prepared some rice and fish for me as I sat on her leather sofa. Everything in her apartment was covered with a doily, like a storybook grandma. She had a few photos up but no plants like Halmoni's.

When lunch was ready, I sat down on the floor at her coffee table where she had laid out the food. Acting as if this was all normal when this was definitely weird. Really freaking weird.

She watched me eat in silence for a while, looking more and more content with each bite I took. Then she finally spoke, her voice clear. "Who are you?"

I almost choked.

A glass of water was handed to me, and she pounded my back. I took a gulp. "I'm Sam."

Mrs. Jo narrowed her eyes at me. "Oh, you are the niece of Eun-Ji Unni."

I was? When I didn't confirm or deny, she nodded, satisfied. "Eat more of the sengsung. I got fresh today."

The mix of Korean and English made me smile. Just like Halmoni. The Mrs. Jo I knew could barely speak in Korean, let alone English. The contrast made me sad, and I swallowed the lump in my throat, forcing more fish down.

"You stay here."

I looked up at her. "Excuse me?"

"Where are you staying? Hotel? Don't spend money. Stay here."

"Oh no, no. That's okay."

She kept her gaze on me. Steady and calm. "Sam. Before? You were crying. You need a place to stay."

It would be completely wrong to accept under false pretenses. Literally deceiving an old lady. An old lady with possible dementia. If not now, then in the future. But where would I go otherwise? What if I was here for days? Weeks? I tried not to think beyond weeks.

I finally nodded my head. "Okay. Okay, thank you so much."

But she only made a grumpy sound in response, clearly not needing the gratitude.

As she continued to eat, I tried not to tear up. The ticking of Mrs. Jo's old wood cuckoo clock filled in the silence, and its rhythm calmed me down—my breathing regulating to match. I felt calm for the first time since I had gotten here.

When Mrs. Jo cleared the table, I spotted something sticking out from a pile of magazines on the floor.

A newspaper.

I grabbed it and shook it out. It was a Korean paper, but the date was there, plain as day: October 12, 1995.

After the stars in my line of vision cleared, I took a deep breath. *Right.* I did the math. My mom would be seventeen years old. A senior, like me. And Thursday, October 12. The same exact day that I left my own time.

I had to get back home, and I was pretty sure that either Mom or Halmoni was key. My dad grew up in Illinois, so he definitely wasn't a part of this.

"Mrs. Jo?"

She looked up from the sink, where she was doing the dishes. "Mm?"

I walked into the kitchen and gently moved her aside. "Let me do the dishes."

"You don't know how."

I made a face. "What? Of course, I do, I'm not a child."

She laughed. "Yes, you are. Eggi." Baby. Lol.

"Well, I was raised to do the dishes so you're insulting my parents by not letting me do them."

Good tactic. She huffed and took off her pink rubber gloves. "Okay."

"Also . . . I have a question." I tried to keep my tone casual.

"Hmm?"

"Do you have a car?"

ten

Mrs. Jo's giant Volvo was a nightmare to steer through LA traffic. Despite the slog, I managed to get back to North Foothill in one piece. My mom grew up on a side of town that was crowded with large apartment complexes full of immigrant families. When I was very little, we used to visit Halmoni in the apartment. She moved out when I was around six years old, though, and had lived in senior housing ever since.

But I wasn't headed toward the apartment. I was headed to a different part of town, to a high-end strip mall nestled into the bottom of the hills.

I pulled into the parking lot and killed the engine. It was exactly the same as in my memories: Wedged between an Armenian bakery and a pharmacy, the dry cleaners had a large window with orange-striped awning. "Oak Glen Cleaners" was painted on it in cursive, bookended by an acorn and leaf.

It was hard to see inside, with the late afternoon sun glaring onto the windows. But I caught movement and squinted to get a better look.

A woman was moving briskly behind the long Formica counter. I could barely make out her profile—her hair in a familiar French twist, her posture imperious. *Holy shit.*

I pulled out my phone and turned it on.

Hi, Halmoni. Remember when Mom went back to work, and I used to spend days after school at the dry cleaners with you? My favorite part was drawing on the long butcher paper. Pressing the crayon hard into the paper because otherwise the colors wouldn't show up. It could have been boring for a kid to hang out at a dry cleaners all day, but you always made it so fun.

I stopped because my voice got garbled and strange. What kind of sick twist of fate was this—sending me back in time while my grandmother was in a coma?

Maybe that was the point.

Maybe if I talked to her, even briefly, everything would be illuminated. This would all feel ludicrous, except I traveled back in time in a magical hatchback, so . . .

I got out of the car, the door heavy and unwieldy as I opened it. A vintage car during an era that was vintage to me. Wild.

I looked down at my clothes. White Vans, jeans, rust sweatshirt, and lavender windbreaker. Nothing too weird that could alert Halmoni of my futureness. Not carrying my hoverboard or hologram glasses. My phone was tucked safely into my pocket, out of sight.

Why *didn't* I have hologram glasses?

When I entered the dry cleaners, a bell rang out. A familiar scent hit me—reminding me of those days after school, in the last few months of its being in business—cloying and chemical.

Everything looked almost exactly the same as in my smudgy memories. The orange counter, the wall of colorful spools of thread, the handwritten sign that said "Cash only." The whirr of the garment conveyer and the swish of the thin plastic bags covering the clothes rubbing against each other.

And the most familiar of all? Halmoni.

"Hello!" she called out, her back turned to me as she flipped through some coats. I stared at her back—a figure wearing a maroon cardigan and tan slacks, her hair black and shiny without even a hint of gray.

When she turned around, I expected swelling music—something. But instead, it was just her face, a face as familiar to me as anything else in the world. Smiling and questioning. "Can I help you?"

I swallowed and willed myself not to get emotional. For once.

"Uh, yes, I was wondering if you were hiring." I tapped on the counter nervously. She walked over, her flats making a clicking noise.

"Oh, no, we don't hire right now." Her voice was the same but quieter and more girlish, with a heavier accent, and an edge of formality and wariness that was unfamiliar to me.

I couldn't stop staring at her face. Unlined, smooth, free of makeup just like normal. Halmoni wasn't obviously gorgeous like my mom, but she was pretty in her own way. Strong features balanced by softness. People always said we looked alike.

Her brow furrowed. "Can I help with anything else?"

Right. Just staring at strangers. "Oh, uh . . ."

"Are you Korean?" she asked, assessing me curiously.

I gave a tight nod, like a Korean nod if it was possible. Respectful. "Yes."

She relaxed, something in her loosening—as if we were no longer strangers. "I wish I could have a job for you. But I have my daughter who helps already."

As if on cue, the bell rang behind me and I turned.

Shit.

My mom, Priscilla, stopped in her tracks. She wasn't wearing her cheerleading uniform anymore. Instead, she was in a short floral-print dress with a black crotchet vest draped over it. Her hair was still in its high pony, a backpack hanging from one shoulder.

Her eyes narrowed, trying to place me. "Hey, aren't you that new girl?"

Halmoni looked between us. "You know each other? School friend?"

"Not really." Priscilla shrugged. "We met today."

Being in the same room with younger versions of my mom and grandma was the trippiest shit I'd ever experienced. And I'd eaten 0.0002 grams of a shroom once when Val and I watched *Blue Velvet*.

"Yeah, I'm a new student. My name is—"

"Sam." A little nose wrinkle. "I remember."

"I wanted to see if, um, there was a job opening."

"No, we don't hire people we actually have to *pay*," Priscilla said, dry and flat. She walked past me, lifting a hinged part of the counter, entering the back of the cleaners. When I was little, I could just walk under it, the top of my head barely grazing the bottom.

Halmoni started speaking to Mom in Korean then—rapidly and with a light scolding tone. My Korean wasn't that great, but I was able to get the gist of it: "Be nicer." Halmoni glanced up at me, her expression forcefully serene.

Priscilla bit down on her bottom lip and inhaled through her nose. I watched this interaction with fascination. Huffy teenage Mom was brand new to me.

"Sam," Halmoni said, testing the name out in her mouth. It was brand new to her, too. "I think maybe lots of jobs at the Village Plaza. You can apply there." There was an apologetic tone to her voice as she suggested the giant mall, and I wanted to hug her.

"Thank you," I said. "I'll go check it out." I racked my brain, desperately trying to think of an excuse to stay when Halmoni dragged a plastic bin full of hangers to the counter.

"Why are you so late today?" Halmoni asked Priscilla, in Korean.

"You know I had cheerleading practice," Priscilla mumbled.

"Oh yeah, I forgot," she said absent-mindedly—but in a tone that I knew well. One that was joking around.

Priscilla tried not to smile. "Okay, *sure*, Umma. It only happens every day."

"I knew it would take up too much time." The criticism was there, even if mild.

Priscilla sighed. "It's good for my college applications."

Halmoni made a rude noise. "Sports would have been better. But you quit."

This was a small argument, a tiny bit of tension, but it felt so big to me. My mom had no idea that Halmoni would go into a coma in thirty years. And how useless it was to spend so much time arguing about dumb stuff.

I wanted to stop it but then Priscilla burst out with, "I hated swimming at six o'clock every morning!"

I looked at her in surprise. I guess it was just registering that this Priscilla was seventeen and *not* the mom I knew so well. The Priscilla of the future would never say she hated anything, let alone complain about doing something athletic and good for your body. "I don't hear complaining" was a mantra in our house.

"Yah, don't kid yourself," Halmoni said in a mix of Korean and English. "You didn't like the chlorine damaging your hair."

Priscilla looked like she was going to protest but she started laughing instead. "Yeah, that's true," she responded in Korean.

"What a bad reason, aren't you embarrassed?" Halmoni's Korean was sly, full of good humor.

The warmth between them was the most astonishing thing I'd witnessed since traveling back in time. Next to the fact that my mom was speaking Korean. Fluently. I kept thinking there was something so familiar about this interaction. And then I realized—it reminded me of me and Halmoni. I thought of how Mom talked about Halmoni ("She wasn't the grandma that you know"), and wondered what in the world could have changed this dynamic so dramatically, to go from warm and comfortable to where they were now—strained and cold.

When Priscilla's laugh turned into a snort, I let out a burst of laughter, too, before I could stop it.

The two of them seemed to realize I was just standing there like a creep and they both looked at me.

"So, Priscilla," I blurted out, "do you work here every day?" The question loud and stupid to my own ears.

"Yes. Why do you want to know?" Priscilla asked, looking down at the register. "Are you in love with me?"

Wow, gross. "Um, self-obsessed much? I've known you for zero point five hours of my life." The words came out before I could stop them, my Mom-response programming was so deeply entrenched.

She looked up then, startled. "*Um*, obviously it was a joke. You're a girl."

I tried to keep a straight face. Truly, the heteronormativity ran *deep*. "Yeah. I know."

Priscilla leaned forward, her expression growing suspicious. "Hey, where were you today? I didn't see you at lunch. Or anywhere."

"Oh. Uh, must have different lunch periods."

"What? We only have one."

Ugh. "Oh. I don't know then. Maybe you weren't paying attention."

There was a beat of silence, and I squirmed under Priscilla's probing gaze.

"Umma!" Her voice rang out suddenly and I jumped. "Did you fix my dress?"

She turned and walked away, forgetting about me.

I hemmed and hawed awkwardly, unsure of what to do. Stick around here just shooting the shit like some sad weirdo with nowhere to go? Leave now and have zero answers? I could practically feel the battery life draining from my phone, and with it, my only chance of getting back home to Halmoni.

"Is this going to be done in time for homecoming?" Even from the recesses of the cleaners, I could hear the concern in Priscilla's voice.

Halmoni made an irritated sound. "Unlike you, I have other things to focus on beside this homecoming thing."

"Well, it *is* important. Please don't mess this up for me."

"If you ask me one more time, Umma isn't going to fix this at all!"

Mom and Halmoni's muffled, bickering voices settled around me.

Wait.

I didn't win . . . when I got home from the dance we got into a huge fight.

Mom's words echoed in my mind. I remembered the signs in the hallway. It was still homecoming month here, in the past.

That was kind of when everything fell apart between us.

Scribbly math equations floated around me in slo-mo, the pieces coming together.

It couldn't have been a coincidence that I was sent back during homecoming week. The week that blew up Mom and Halmoni's relationship. With Halmoni in a coma, hanging on by a thread—I knew what I needed to do. Why I was sent back in time.

I needed to salvage the relationship between Halmoni and Mom.

And I needed to stop that fight before it happened. Which meant making sure Mom became homecoming queen. If she won, there would be nothing to fight about.

When Priscilla walked back over to me, a bundle of ice-blue satin in her arms, I stared hard at her. I had to befriend some stuck-up cheerleader from the 1990s? A person who had zero things in common with me, in the past or in the present? Someone who would probably *bully* me if given the chance? This was going to be straight-up torture. But it was a *plan*. The helplessness from earlier gave way to a glimmer of hope.

"So, when is homecoming, Priscilla?" Calling my mother by her first name was unnatural.

She spread the dress out onto the counter between us and bent over to examine it, running her fingers over the material, her touch feather-light and reverent. "It's next Saturday."

And today was Thursday. Okay, I had nine days. Nine days to make sure Priscilla won homecoming queen. Nine days to make sure the fight between Mom and Halmoni would never happen.

Could my phone battery even last nine days?

Only time would tell.

Ha ha.

"Oh, cool. Are you running for homecoming queen or something?" I asked, in the most hilariously casual voice I could manage.

Her eyes were sharp with suspicion. Reminding me once again that I could never outsmart my mother. Lying to her was never an option for me.

"Yeah?" She said it like a question.

This was going to be difficult every step of the way. But then, I remembered my mom's insistence on running a campaign to win. I could start there.

"Oh, great. Do you need help running your campaign? I've, uh, successfully won homecoming queen at my old school."

As if she couldn't sniff out *that* lie from a mile away.

"Wow." The word was so devoid of any actual awe. "I'm good, thanks."

My pride withered but I powered through. Yes, Mom in the future could instantly turn my confidence into a pile of ashes. But *this* Mom didn't know me—yet. I could prove my worth to this version of Mom. We were starting off with a blank slate. "I'm serious. I wasn't the obvious frontrunner"—Priscilla scoffed—"but I managed to persuade people to vote for me because I ran an airtight campaign."

She turned on the garment conveyer, the sound of the machinery speaking for her.

I spoke over it. "I heard Stephanie Camillo saying she's got this in the bag."

The machine stopped. *Gotcha.*

Priscilla walked over to me, pressing her hands into the counter. "What? How do you even know her? You've been here, like, five minutes."

"I overheard some girls talking about it in the bathroom." And then I tried to rack my brain for the most obvious, goading thing I could think of for someone like Priscilla. "Is she the most popular girl in school?" Wow. These were words I was saying.

But it was the right thing to say. Miniature fireballs lit up her eyes. "*She fucking wishes.*"

"Yah!" Halmoni yelled from a back room somewhere.

Priscilla lowered her voice. "Let me be real, new girl. Steph Camillo is *nasty* and she's lucky she even made the court."

Ba ha ha. I tried to hide my glee with a shrug. "Oh, well, maybe people know that already and won't vote for her, then."

"That's the thing, somehow, she's tricked everyone into thinking she's *actually* cool. Just because her dad's an entertainment lawyer and represents Zachery Ty Bryan."

I'm pretty sure I was supposed to know who that was. "Neat."

She scoffed. "Everyone in LA knows somebody who knows somebody. It's stupid and unprovable."

Actually, very true.

"Why is she nasty?" I asked.

"She gave, like, half the baseball team hand jobs."

I frowned. "How do you even know that? That's bullshit guys say to demean girls who reject them. It's gross."

Priscilla looked startled for a second. "Everyone just . . . knows."

"Wow, take, like, a *second* and think of how slut-shamey that is."

It was like I was speaking a foreign language. "What?" She stared at me. "I didn't call her a slut. Jeez."

Deep breaths. This was not the point. Making Mom woke and feminist in the future was a thankless task; I would *not* be attempting that here in 1995. "Never mind. Anyway, if you want to win homecoming queen, I can help."

There was half a second where I thought she might consider it. But then she seemed to come to her senses and realize that I was just some eager beaver bothering her at work.

"No offense, but I don't need help. I've got this." She turned her back to me, effectively ending the conversation.

A few minutes later, I got into Mrs. Jo's car with my tail between my legs. I sat back and stared up at the car ceiling. How would I ever pull this off? I always knew Mom and I were different—but now that we were the same age, that contrast was *sharp*. A girl like Priscilla would never want a friend like me.

She didn't even want a daughter like me.

When I glanced over at the cleaners for one last look, Halmoni was watching me through the window, a slight smile on her face. My throat tightened. I waved, maybe a little too vigorously, and she waved back, her hand halting and unsure. It was all the motivation I needed to figure this out.

I wasn't going to let Halmoni down—in the future or in any version of the world she existed in.

eleven

eleven

eight days to homecoming

Maybe it was weird that I was sleeping in a random grandmother's house.

But, technically, she wasn't random. I knew her. In the future. And, as far as I knew, Mrs. Jo never killed anyone?

When I was getting ready for bed, she had handed me a little travel kit. It was Hello Kitty themed and probably from the dollar store but made me tear up from the thoughtfulness of it all.

I lay there in the dark, the cotton sheet on the leather sofa slippery beneath me, and felt like bursting into tears for the millionth time, like a giant baby. But I had traveled back in time, for crying out loud! My grandmother wasn't in a coma! My mom was *my age* and I had to make her like me! I had to win a *homecoming campaign*. I tried to think of ways to do that, but I just kept spiraling about all the ways I could fail instead, and what disastrous path that would send me on.

I stared at my useless block of a phone. If only I could watch ASMR videos until I passed out.

But there was one thing I could still do with it.

Keeping my voice low, I hit record.

Hi, Halmoni. You know what's weird? How much I hated sleepovers as a kid. I mean, I always thought I loved them. But then the lights would go out, and everybody would fall asleep around me and there was nothing I wanted more than to go home.

The refrigerator hummed and I glanced at Mrs. Jo's open bedroom door. She insisted on it leaving it cracked open "just in case."

Because once the movies and pizza and gossiping were over, it was just me in the dark in some stranger's house. And everything was so different: The sounds of creaking floorboards. Or a ticking clock. The smell of the house. I would stick my nose into my sleeping bag so that I could remember what my house smelled like. I'm thinking about all this because at this very moment—and this is really embarrassing to admit—I'm somewhere that is making me feel that same stranger's-house feeling. And I just want to go home.

I did eventually fall asleep and woke up to the sound of clanking dishes and the smell of coffee. And for a couple of minutes, I stayed burrowed in my blankets, comfortable and warm.

But then I opened my eyes and saw the old TV across from me. Felt the scratchy acrylic of the blanket wrapped around me. Smelled the distinct smell of a house that wasn't mine.

And then it hit me all over again—I had traveled back in time. I had slept. It wasn't all just a dream. I was still here.

I sat up and saw Mrs. Jo at the kitchen counter facing the living room.

My heart sank. *Yeah, nope. Still not a dream.*

"Good morning, Mrs. Jo," I said, my voice creaky.

She nodded in response, pouring some coffee into a delicate teacup. "I made breakfast."

After I brushed my teeth and washed the sleep from my eyes, I stepped out to see buttered toast and a glass of orange juice laid out for me. I sat down, overcome with gratitude again. "Mrs. Jo, you didn't have to make me breakfast. I can help sometimes."

She pulled out a visor from her hall closet. "Help? What are you talking about? This is my house, and you are my guest."

Guilt tugged at me. She still thought I was some relative of hers. "Well, I can take out the trash or something before I go to school."

She paused as she put on a windbreaker. "School? You're not on vacation?"

Oh. Right. "Ah, no—I'm here to do a school exchange. Because the school here has a good, um, computer science program."

"Computer science?" Mrs. Jo asked, clearly puzzled by these two words. Oh, sweet Jesus, were computers not invented yet? No, no, they were. That much I knew about the nineties. Maybe it wasn't common yet, though.

I didn't need to worry. Mrs. Jo shrugged. "Okay, that is good that you are trying this new school. You can drive my car. I'm going on hike with hiking club now, bye-bye." And with that she was out the door. No further questions.

I loved Mrs. Jo.

While I got ready for school, I brainstormed. I needed a game plan for getting me back to . . . well, the future. I knew this all hinged on Mom winning homecoming queen, to make it to that finish line. Because that would mean the fight that messed up their relationship never happened, that Mom wouldn't blame Halmoni for it for literally the rest of her life. So here was the plan:

1. Convince Mom to let me help her with her campaign.
2. Once I'm in, spend time with her and Halmoni to keep things chill between them.
3. FIGURE OUT THE CAMPAIGN.
4. Mom wins homecoming queen.
5. Marge picks me the fuck up.

Okay, so yeah, I needed to figure out the campaign.

I thought about it as I showered and put on some of Mrs. Jo's makeup—the tamer stuff that didn't make me look like a senior citizen. Did people at my school run campaigns for homecoming? I tried to remember—it already felt like eons ago—but for the life of me, I couldn't even remember who had won homecoming queen at my school, *ever*. If the boycott was any indication, the tradition of the homecoming court was actually kind of dead.

I dabbed some peachy blush onto my cheekbones. I would have to look to the past for my plans. First—who else was on the court? So far, all I had was Steph Camillo. Once I figured out the rest, I could figure out how to knock out the competition. Or at least see how Priscilla was ranked next to them. After I knew that, I'd have a clearer idea of what kind of campaign needed to be run.

I pulled on a silky green blouse with gold buttons that Mrs. Jo had offered to let me borrow, which I did so I wouldn't hurt her feelings. Throwing my windbreaker on top of it, I hoped I looked intentionally alternative rather than unintentionally confused about clothes for young people.

On my drive to school, I flipped on the radio and moved the tuner to a station I recognized from the future, but instead of indie rock being played, a guy's voice blared out at me. "I miss when women liked smelling like fruit, you know? Now, it's all about natural oils and crap!" Another man and woman laughed uproariously in the background. *Ugh.* I changed the station, but it was more of the same thing. I missed my podcasts. Being at the mercy of what was on the radio was really its own kind of torture.

I eventually shut it off and thought about the task ahead. Before anything could start with the campaign, I needed to convince Mom to partner up with me. How? I had already struck out at the dry cleaner. Why would she listen to a rando like me? And not just a rando, but a rando who clearly was dorky and uncool by Priscilla standards.

I had to make myself undeniable.

When I got to school, I sat in Mrs. Jo's parked car for a beat. Not only did I have the monumental task of convincing Priscilla to let me help her, but I'd also have to bullshit my way into this school somehow, befriend people who were old as hell in the future, deal with nineties weirdness . . .

I had to be Marty fucking McFly.

It would've been funny if it weren't, you know, real. I had thought a lot about *Back to the Future* the night before. In the movie, there was a lot of fretting about changing the future in irrevocable ways if Marty didn't keep the past exactly the same. In my case, I was sent back for a *purpose*. I was *supposed* to change something. There was no way that the changes I created would make me, like, not be born. That would be a sick trick from this stupid magic rideshare . . . right?

Here goes . . . everything.

I pulled on my sunglasses and backpack and walked to school. Now that I wasn't so disoriented, I was able to actually register everything.

The parking lot was missing the solar panels and EV parking spots. The big shady trees in front of the school were only saplings. Everything was just cleaner and newer. In place of the electronic marquee was a lo-fi one with letters that you had to place by hand. An entire building was missing.

And the most glaring difference? No one was on their phones.

It was the most noticeable change, if I was being honest. Everyone kind of looked normal otherwise. It wasn't like *Back to the Future* when the kids dressed in, like, poodle skirts. In fact, everyone dressed almost the same. Mom was always complaining about how the nineties were back with a vengeance, and she was totally right.

But it wasn't just the nineties of it all. The school was practically bursting at the seams with homecoming school spirit. Streamers in our school colors—blue and white—were wrapped around poles and tree trunks and strung across the hallways. Every inch of the walls was covered with "BEAT THE TITANS!"—our rival high school. Our mascot, a coyote, was aggressively drawn on posters, teeth bared. Sometimes ripping out the entrails of a football player in Titan colors. Get a *grip*.

I walked into the administration office and approached the woman at the front desk, who was wearing a blue-and-white-striped sweater and a North Foothill baseball cap. "Hi. I'm a new student."

She stared at me expectantly. *Fake it 'til you make it, Sam.* I stared back.

"Do you need to enroll, sweetie?" she asked with a sharp air of annoyance.

"Sweetie" made me want to jab her with a pen, but I smiled widely instead. "Yes. I'm eighteen and my parents are working so I'm doing it myself."

"A lot of you Asian kids have that problem," she mumbled as she pulled out some paperwork.

"*Excuse me?*" My words came out in a screech.

She gave me a limp smile that was completely devoid of shame. "All your parents work around the clock."

I had no idea how in holy hell to respond to something like that. I wordlessly accepted the clipboard.

"Fill out the form and we'll get you all signed up."

I filled out the paperwork with shaking hands. For some reason I forgot traveling back in time meant dealing with some truly regressive, racist bullshit. Not just low-key racism but, like, *highly* high-key. I forced myself to tap into some tiny Zen part of myself—bypassing the 90 percent of me that was reactive and confrontational. *Just get through these next eight days.*

It was shockingly fast and easy to get a student ID, schedule, and locker assignment (one that was next to Priscilla's—wasn't hard to convince that particular woman that we were related, and I wanted to stay close to my "cousin"), and I was out of the office in time to swing by my locker before homeroom.

I stood at my locker and felt a rush of relief. This part, I understood. I unlocked it with my new combination and unloaded some of the stuff I had in my backpack. Textbooks from the future.

"Your locker's *here*?"

I peeked around the door. Priscilla, of course. Her glossy hair was down, parted on the side, falling perfectly around her face. Her white jeans were cinched at the waist with a black leather belt, and her forest-green, ribbed baby tee was scalloped on the bottom.

"Hey, Priscilla." I tried to be sunny. A person you couldn't hate.

She shut her locker. "Of all the lockers, you had to be next to mine?"

I held back from referencing *Casablanca*, knowing she wouldn't get it and would just think I was a giant dork. "Cool coincidence, huh?"

Her eyes swept through the hallway. "Uh, right." Then she focused her attention on me—her discerning gaze traveling from my hair to my dirty Vans. "Why are you wearing almost the same outfit as yesterday? And has anyone ever told you your hair makes you look like an Asian Jonathan Taylor Thomas?"

No beating around the bush with Priscilla. Past and present and future.

"Well, I just moved so my clothes are still in storage. I'm wearing what I have for now." I hoisted my backpack onto my shoulders.

She made a face. "Ew. Also, who wears their backpack like that?"

I made a face right back at her. "You mean, *on my back* like a freaking human being?"

"With both straps like a *nerd*."

Both straps? I glanced around me and noticed literally no one was else doing that. I begrudgingly slid off one strap. Had to conform to these stupid trends or else I'd stick out too much.

Priscilla was mollified. "Where's your homeroom?"

"Same as yours. Mr. Finn."

"Really? It's weird that Mr. Finn didn't know about it yesterday."

I shoved the schedule into my back pocket. "Yeah. I was confused, too."

She smirked. "My friends are going to be jealous you got into Finn's class."

"Why?"

A few seconds passed and she just stared at me expectantly.

"What?" I asked.

"Hello, do you have *eyes*?" she asked. "He's so hot. Everyone calls him Mr. *Fine*."

Mr. Fine? I tried to connect that name with the Mr. Finn in the future and my brain almost malfunctioned.

"Priscilla!" We turned to see three girls walking down the hall. Various types of pretty, similar outfits. I was surprised they weren't moving in slo-mo. They all glanced over at me.

Priscilla's face transformed—almost imperceptibly—but I noticed it. Every feature kind of relaxed into a cool, neutral state. "Guys, this is Sam. She's new."

"Hey," I said with a nod and friendly expression. Friendly but not trying too hard. My usual behavior when meeting new people. New people were my jam.

They assessed me with quick visual scans across my body. Then a shared thought bubble floated above them: *Yikes.*

Hmm.

They acknowledged me for about a second with awkward smiles then immediately stilled as a girl walked toward us, holding hands with a blond guy holding a skateboard. She was pretty in that cute, petite-girl way and made a big point of ignoring Priscilla and Co.'s blatant stares as she walked by.

They immediately closed in a tight circle around Priscilla. "God, is that Steph's *second* boyfriend this year? I hear he's a drug dealer," one of Priscilla's friends said with a snicker.

I looked back at the girl. So *that* was Steph Camillo. She walked up to another group of girls with her boyfriend—a group that I couldn't help but notice was not quite as aggressively perfect-looking as Priscilla's. I understood where she ranked in this school hierarchy immediately.

"And did you hear that she might be wearing a short dress to the dance? Anything to set herself apart like a totally obvious bitch," the girl with the Alicia Silverstone–blond hair said.

Priscilla made quick eye contact with me over their shoulders before responding to her. "Tacky. Who wears short dresses to dances?"

Who even DARES. I tried not to roll my eyes. I had to get these people to like me, after all—even if they were straight-up ignoring me at the moment. And imprisoned by their own internalized misogyny, but *whatever*.

And this was my chance to figure out who else was running for homecoming queen. "Are all the other girls on the court such obviously bad competition, too?" I asked in my best bratty drawl.

They exchanged glances, checking with each other first before deeming it okay to respond to me, I guess. It occurred to me suddenly that maybe some of *them* were running. "Unless you guys are also on the court?" I added hastily.

The brunette with her hair flipped out on the bottom replied. "We've all been on the court before. So, no." The other two girls confirmed this with smug silence.

Priscilla seemed to take pity on me. "There's me, Steph, Tessa Martin, and Alexandra Gunner. Steph and I are the only seniors—the rest are juniors."

"Do seniors always win?" I asked, since she said that as if they were immediately disqualified.

"Obviously," the Alicia Silverstone hair girl said with a snort.

"It wasn't like that at *my* school," I said, a defensive know-it-all tone edging into my voice. God, why was I letting these people get to me?

Priscilla turned then, her backpack foisted on one shoulder. And that's when I noticed it. At first, I felt secondhand mortification—then a flare of hope. This could be my chance.

I immediately stepped right behind her. "Priscilla," I whispered loudly.

She looked back, startled. "Close much?"

"Can you come to the bathroom with me?"

"What? Why?"

I widened my eyes, like, *trust me*. She continued to look suspicious. The rest of the girls were busy wrapped up in some petty observations, so I took off my jacket and shoved it at her. "You might want to wear this around your waist."

Understanding dawned on her face. Her cheeks turned red, and she immediately wrapped the windbreaker around her hips. "Yeah, let's go." She waved bye to her crappy gang, and we rushed to the bathroom.

She immediately booked it into a stall. After a few seconds she let out a muffled scream. "Oh my *god*. I can't believe I got my stupid period today. The day I wore *white jeans*."

"It's the Law of White Jeans," I said as I dug around my backpack, looking for a tampon.

Priscilla laughed, although it was a mortified kind of laugh. "So embarrassing. Hey, do you have—" I shoved a few tampons under the stall door before she could finish. She grabbed them. "Thanks. I can't believe I don't have any."

I couldn't either. The only reason I even had one was because Mom planted about a hundred little zip pouches full of tampons into every single bag I owned.

"I've never seen these kinds of tampons before," Priscilla said from the stall. "They're so cool!"

Oh. Crap. Right. Future tampons. Were they *that* different?

"Oh yeah—uh, my aunt works in pharmaceuticals and gets cool samples of future products." I tried not to laugh at the image of Aunt Grace working in pharmaceuticals. She owned a tote bag that said "BIG PHARMA, SMALL DICKS" on one side and "GUILLOTINE THE SACKLERS" on the other.

A few minutes later Priscilla came out wearing her cheerleading tracksuit. "People are going think I'm so weird wearing my tracksuit all day," she fretted as she took her jeans over to the sink. "Deidre's *definitely* going to say something."

I watched as she turned on the hot water. "You should use cold water."

Mom had taught me that. *Always rinse the stain in cold water immediately after. You don't even need soap if you get it in time.* I had joked that she had been a serial killer in her past, but she had just ignored me and said, *Trust me, you'll thank me one day.*

"What?" Priscilla glanced up at me, dubious.

I reached over and switched it to cold. "Trust me."

Lo and behold, the stain came out. Mostly. Priscilla held the jeans up and looked at them in wonder. "Whoa. That worked so well."

The open admiration in her expression was shocking. And felt good. I was never on the receiving end of that from Mom. She was the one who knew everything, I was the one who had to ask *her* for help constantly. But in 1995, Mom wasn't Mom yet. She was Priscilla. And I was her peer. She didn't have any of the hang-ups she had with me in the future—for all she knew, this new kid Sam was someone who had her life together. Who was confident, not just in social environments, but in school and also in her family.

This was my opportunity.

"Just one of my *many* tricks," I said as I pulled out some lip balm and dotted it on my lips. "You really should let me help you with your homecoming campaign."

She rolled the jeans up and put them into her backpack. "I don't know why you want to help me so badly."

Good point. I took a deep breath. "You just seem like you deserve it."

An awkward moment passed as Priscilla stared at me—looking into my soul, it felt like. Then she smiled. A slow, almost-shy smile. "Fine."

"Really?" I asked, in disbelief.

She rolled her eyes. "*Really*."

It was actually surprising to realize that I didn't need to trick Priscilla into working with me or throw around power moves to get my way. I just needed to be . . . nice. It made me wonder about what kind of friends she had.

I tried to look cool. "Well, get ready to win." Step one of the plan was *done* and we were full steam ahead.

"Geez." Priscilla opened the bathroom door. "Don't get too cocky."

Before I could respond with something *very* cocky, we bumped into a group of people who were stopped in the hall.

One of the girls burst out laughing. "Oh, god. Look, it's the new freak."

Who, *me*?

But when I followed her mocking stare, I found myself looking at a tall, lanky Latino guy with a mop of dark brown hair, wire-rimmed glasses, and an absent-minded expression. In fact, his head was so in the clouds that he smacked straight into someone—Neil, that locker dude from yesterday.

"*Watch it,* idiot," Neil said, so loudly that everyone in the hall quieted down to watch.

The guy looked at him for a second. "Yeah, all right."

He tried to walk past Neil, but Neil was *not* having it. He stuck his arm out like a barricade. "What did you say?"

The guy seemed to come back to Earth, looking at Neil, uneasily. "I just said, all right, man. It was an accident."

"I didn't hear an apology in there."

I scoffed. "Oh my *god.*"

Priscilla looked at me and hissed, "Sam!"

But no one was paying attention to us. All eyes were on the guy and Neil.

"Who is that?" I asked Priscilla.

She squinted. "Neil's the big guy. I'm kind of dating him." I looked at her in surprise. "The other one, I think his name is . . . Jamie? He's also new this year."

The Jamie guy laughed, low and drawn out. "All right. I'm sorry. Are we good?"

But something about that delivery didn't appease Neil. In fact, it seemed to further enrage the bozo. "The fuck are you laughing at? You think you can be on the football team and talk to me this way?"

That's when I noticed Neil wearing a literal letterman jacket. *This* was the guy Priscilla was dating? *Ew.*

Jamie shifted his backpack, clearly agitated. He opened his mouth but closed it, lips drawn in. As if physically holding back from responding. “Not sure what you want from me, Neil.”

The bell rang. Everyone started heading to homeroom, but Neil stood where he was. Then he did that thing that certain guys do—lunged toward Jamie then stopped inches away from him. His face close. “See you at practice, dipshit.”

Jamie just shook his head slightly.

When Neil walked by me, I blurted out, “Not if he doesn’t see *you* first, *dipshit*.”

“Oh my *god*,” Priscilla said under her breath. “Samantha, *shut up*.”

Neil halted. Jamie stared at me, his eyes narrowed, as if I had insulted *him* somehow, too.

“What?” Neil asked, looking astonished.

“You heard me,” I said. “What are you, seven years old? Who even *bullies* anymore?”

People scattered, laughing their asses off. Priscilla seemed frozen by my side.

Neil glared at me. “You’re that crazy bitch who tried to use my locker yesterday.”

“Hey!” Priscilla said sharply. “Knock it off.”

The two of them exchanged a look. Neil turned red but seemed chastened. He walked away, muttering.

I turned to Priscilla. “Whoa. Thanks.”

But she just spun around and walked off. Was she mad? At *moi*?

Another voice echoed across the hall. “You didn’t have to do that, you know.”

It was that Jamie guy, talking to me, his hands in his pockets.

“Uh, you’re welcome, I guess?” I said, irritated by everyone’s poor life choices this morning.

"I didn't need your help," he said testily before stalking off down the hall.

The second bell rang, and I stood there, alone in the hallway.

"*You are welcome!*" I yelled. Everyone in this damned school needed therapy.

twelve

twelve

eight days to homecoming

In homeroom, I sat next to Priscilla near the back of the class. Mr. Finn read the announcements and then went back to his desk, having given up on any other things to do.

"Okay, so let's talk campaign game plan," I started.

Priscilla interrupted me. "Before we get into any of this, we need to lay down some ground rules."

I nodded—eager and willing. "Sure!"

"What you pulled in the hallway? With Neil? You need to cut that kind of crap out." Priscilla leveled a serious gaze at me.

"What? Why?" My eagerness fizzled.

"Because—who do you think got me nominated?" Priscilla glanced around the classroom, her voice hushed. "Neil and his friends. And whatever you think of him, dating him helps us."

There were so many things I wanted to say in response, but I bit them back. Mom relied on this dude to get nominated? Wasn't she just popular? But by her deathly serious expression, I could tell she was actually worried about it. I took a moment before I responded. "Fine. But I still think he's a dick."

Her mouth twitched in a familiar smile—the Mom "trying not to admit that was funny" smile. "Well, your thoughts are your own, so go to town."

"Thanks for letting me have my own thoughts," I said dryly. "Any other ground rules?"

She thought about it. "Just don't be embarrassing."

"However will I deny my natural state?"

Her eyes narrowed. "Like that. Just be normal, please?"

"Okay, fine!" I flipped through my notebook viciously until I got to a blank page. "Let's get back to business. I think we need to do three main things to get you this crown. One, we need to blast your face and name across the school. Oversaturate it to a degree where people will get sick of you." I had thought of what worked on social media in the future—using the power of influencers as my guiding light for this campaign. What were influencers vying for if not popularity? Popularity was their currency.

"What?" Priscilla looked horrified. "That sounds like the *worst* idea."

"I know it does," I said patiently. "But trust me. People will forget you otherwise." Oversaturation of advertisements was why I owned a set of millennial pink luggage like every other sucker out there.

She tossed her hair like a weapon. "No one will forget me."

It was hard not to admire that insane confidence. "Okay, sure. But just in case, we will make fliers. And posters. And put them on every available wall space, and in everyone's lockers."

"Lockers? Isn't that kind of . . . ," her voice trailed off, trying to find the word.

"Spammy?" I offered.

"What? SPAM?"

Right. No email, no spam. "Like, junk mail? Who cares. People can toss it. What matters is that they will never forget for *even a second* that you are running for homecoming queen."

After a second of indecision, she nodded. "Fine. I'm just going to have to trust you on this one."

"Yes, you are," I said. Every kid in the future armed with social media knew that impressions were *it*. "Okay, number two: We need to make sure *everyone* feels a connection to you or feels like they know you. Who do you not know at this school?" Again, influencers thrived off parasocial relationships—making people feel like they *knew* you. Even if the image you presented was all fabricated.

A literal paper plane flew over my head. They *really* had to get creative in the analog world. Priscilla stared after it, deep in thought. "I mean, I obviously don't know any losers."

"Wow." I wrote that down in huge letters in my notebook. "Looh-ooh-sers. Got it."

She snorted. "I know how that sounds but it's true. I know everyone that needs to be known."

I took a deep breath through my nose, like Mom's yoga breathing. "While that may be true—the so-called losers outnumber you popular kids. By, like, a lot. Have you ever thought about that?"

Priscilla didn't answer, but she didn't argue with me.

"Okay. So—target unpopular kids. Next step . . . swag."

She just stared at me. "What?"

"What?" I stared at her staring at me. Then came the sinking feeling that I was using future slang, again. "Free stuff. We need to offer something to get people to vote for you. Even if people don't care about homecoming, they *do* care about getting free things."

Her voice was low, a whisper, when she asked, "You mean *bribe* people?" She was scandalized.

"More like an incentive," I said. "What can we offer?"

After a few seconds she sighed. "I don't know. I can't afford to buy anything. Steph's probably going to buy everyone pizza or something. But I don't have that option."

The bell rang and I put the notebook away. "It's okay. We have time to think on it. Homecoming is still eight days away. But I think we should figure it out by next week, that way we can give it out before everyone votes."

"All right."

"Oh!" I snapped my fingers. "Do you have any good photos of yourself for the flier?"

"Hmm . . ." She dug through her backpack and pulled out a glittery planner. She flipped through a few plastic sleeves full of photos. Wow. The OG photo library. "Here we go." She handed me a two-by-three-inch photo of her in her cheerleading outfit, posing on the field.

Everyone rushed around us to get out of class and Priscilla handed me the student government key card for the copy machine before we both headed out.

After second period, I headed to the copy room during our morning break. Perks of being friends with the class secretary.

As I got closer to the room, I heard a clanging echoing in the hallway.

I hovered in the doorway when I spotted a guy crouched over the copy machine, banging on it. Hard.

"Uh, is everything okay?" I asked.

He muttered, "This archaic piece of crap won't work." Then turned his head to look at me.

Nooooo.

It was Jamie.

We looked at each other awkwardly for a few seconds, then Jamie stood up, pushing his hair back from his face. He definitely remembered me from earlier. "I think it might be a paper jam."

I nodded. "Right. Can I take a look?" I didn't exactly feel like helping him out again, but the sooner I could get the fliers up, the better. I'd fixed many a paper jam for my grandma in the past. She loved printing out news stories from the internet unnecessarily.

He stepped aside and I pulled one of the paper trays open. This thing was definitely older and clunkier than copy machines I'd used in the future, but not that different. I was feeling around for the jammed paper when Jamie coughed. Nervously. "Hey. So about earlier this morning . . ."

My fingers grazed something. "What about it?" My voice was flat. I was still annoyed by the whole thing. Why couldn't some guys just accept help and be *grateful*?

"I don't need anyone fighting my battles for me."

I looked up at him. Incredulous. "Are you kidding me right now?"

He frowned. "No?"

God, this guy probably never joked around with a human being in his life. "Listen, I don't just stand around and let people be cruel to each other. It has nothing to do with you, personally. It's an affront to *me* to witness offensive crap like that. So, get over it." I couldn't reach the jammed paper beyond its edges and cursed.

Jamie was quiet, watching me. It was a little disconcerting. Then he blinked. "Annoying, isn't it?"

"What?"

"That shit machine."

I let out a little laugh. "I guess?" Suddenly something hot zapped me, and I pulled my hand out with a hiss and hit the machine instinctively. "Fucker!"

Jamie burst out laughing. "See?"

So, he *did* have a sense of humor. But his laughter vanished once he saw me grimace as I examined my hand, which actually hurt. "We should put this thing out of its misery."

I was startled when he dropped down next to me.

"Sorry for laughing. Is your hand okay?" While he didn't reach out to touch it or anything, he leaned in to take a closer look. I was suddenly very aware of the cramped quarters and how close we were.

"Yeah, it's fine," I said, my voice booming, standing up quickly.

Jamie stayed in a crouch and that's when I noticed a Band-Aid barely covering a big gash behind his ear. Some blood was seeping through it.

"Whoa. What happened to your head?"

His hand came up to touch the wound. "Oh. I got a little banged up in football practice."

Right. Football. That guy Neil was on the team with him.

"You don't really strike me as the football player type." The words came out before I could stop them, and I instantly felt like a huge jerk.

But Jamie just laughed, his disconcertedly elegant fingers still touching his Band-Aid. "Yeah. No, it's weird to other people, I'm sure. But, uh, a bit of a family obligation, I guess you could say."

Yikes. He probably came from a family with some macho dad who was pressuring him to play this dumb sport. Was everyone in the nineties just a big walking cliché? "Oh. That sucks."

He laughed. "Wow, you just . . . say things."

I flushed. "Not usually. Sorry, I'm just a little . . . I don't know. It's my first day here."

"Oh." He got up and brushed his hands off on his legs. "I'm actually new, too. Well, newish. I transferred for senior year."

I know.

"Guess I'll have to find a different way to make copies of this," I said, holding up the flier.

Jamie peered at it. "What is that?"

"A flier for Priscilla Jo. She's running for homecoming queen." I smiled my most persuasive smile. "You should vote for her."

He titled his head slightly, confused. "Priscilla . . ."

"Yes?"

Both of our heads spun to the door. Priscilla was standing there looking at us. Suspiciously.

"Hey!" I said, my voice poorly modulated again. "I was making copies of your flier."

"Yeah, I was coming to check in on that," she said, walking in. "What's taking so long?"

"It's broken," I said, pointing at the machine.

She pushed the copy button and it just sputtered, error lights flashing. "Oh, I know what it is."

"You do?" Jamie asked, surprised.

But I wasn't. The usual Mom wizardry. In sharp contrast to her prissy persona, my mom was the handiest person I knew. Toilet not working? Get Mom. Garbage disposal clogged? Mom. Internet down? Mom. And copy machines, too, I guess.

"See this?" Priscilla pointed at the error lights. "When these flash, it basically means this big ol' thing got overwhelmed. Overheated. So, you just have to unplug it and wait a few seconds." She did just that, reaching around the back to pull the cord out. The machine shut down with what sounded like a sigh. After a few seconds, she plugged it in again and it came back to life, shooting out copies.

"Are these yours?" Priscilla asked, grabbing the stack.

Jamie nodded and took them from her. "Yeah, they're copies of a quiz for Ms. Rivera." He lifted the top of the machine to grab the original quiz lying on the glass. "Thanks."

"No problem," Priscilla said, already busy setting our flier into the machine.

Jamie turned to leave but then paused and looked back, a lock of hair falling into his face. "See ya."

"Bye." It was the briefest moment of eye contact, but I felt it in my bones.

As soon as we were alone, Priscilla started laughing. "Wow, obvious much?"

"Huh? What do you mean?" I quickly grabbed the copies of her flier. "All right, let's go, we're done!" Priscilla followed me out the door.

"You're into that guy."

My face flushed. "No, I'm not."

"I walked in, and it felt like a porno."

I started laughing. "Shut *up*. No, it did *not*. He was mad at me for sticking up for him earlier."

"Oh, that. Yeah, that was weird." The hallway was empty because everyone was still at morning break. Priscilla stopped at a row of lockers, sticking a flier into each one.

I took some from her and started on the lockers across the hall. "How was that weird? What's *weird* is everyone just standing around letting some big dumb white guy shove Jamie around."

Priscilla's eyes grew wide. "Jeez. You don't have to call him *white*."

"In case you haven't noticed, that's what he is."

She cringed. "God, I guess. Feels rude to just, like, say it."

Was it rude? I guess this was when everyone was trying to be "color-blind." I slipped a flier into a locker. "Whatever! Either way, I don't see how you can just let people be such dicks around here. Even if you *are* dating one of them."

She let out a guffaw. "As if I have any control over that?"

"You have a lot of control. You're one of the most commanding people I know."

"What? You barely know me." She paused, a flier poised in midair.

Right. Gah. "I mean, you seem that way."

"If you say so. Anyway. Don't go off-topic. You like Jamie."

I let out a huge sigh. "I don't, dude. For real. I have a boyfriend."

She raised an eyebrow. "Yeah. Sure. In Canada?"

"No! At my old school." It wasn't a lie. I thought of how I left things with Curren, that tense text convo, and felt a little guilty at my clear momentary attraction to Jamie.

"Is he Korean?"

We moved to a new row of lockers, and I shook my head. "No, he's Armenian and Persian."

"Your parents don't care that you're dating a non-Korean?"

I chose my next words carefully. "No . . . that's not an issue. They don't love him, though. He's kind of like this artistic, beautiful slacker type."

Priscilla made a sound of disgust. Yup. Her feelings in the future, too. "I'm surprised they even let you date. Your parents must be super Americanized."

"They *were* born here." Again, I said that without thinking. Was it common for Korean parents in 1995 to be born in the US? The math!

"Oh, wow. Yeah, a totally different reality." There was wistfulness in her voice.

It never occurred to me that dating was easy for me. Mom and Dad were so tepid about Curren that I always felt caught in the middle. But they never had any rules about dating or anything—just, like, no sleeping over. They were still *Korean*.

We turned the corner into another hallway lined with lockers when the bell rang, and I pulled my schedule out of my back pocket.

"What do you have next?" Priscilla asked.

I glanced down. "Pre-calc."

"Let me see that," she reached for my schedule. Bossy. "Ooh, we have fourth period together—government. See you then!"

Something about her excitement made me feel *super* special, like a giant dork. The sheer power of mean girls. I would only put up with them for Halmoni. Also? I was starting to think that the mean-girl act was just that . . . an act.

Or maybe it was wishful thinking.

thirteen

thirteen

eight days to homecoming

I powered through pre-calc, truly amazed I was voluntarily taking an extra math class in my life. When the bell rang for fourth, I rushed to class, impatient to see Priscilla.

Scanning the US government classroom, I saw that a couple of Priscilla's friends from earlier were sitting with her, and I hung back, not sure if I was invited to sit with her, too. But she made a face like, "Come on." So, I plopped into a seat next to her. I remembered the other two girls from this morning.

"You guys remember Sam," she said. "Sam, this is Deidre and Haley."

Deidre. Why was that name so familiar?

"Hey," I said with a perfunctory nod.

Haley, the brunette, waved back then picked at her fingernails. Deidre, the blonde, shot me a quick, forced smile and opened her notebook like she had to get to work or something. That very negative vibe pinged something then. Deidre. The girl Aunt Grace talked about—the Sweet Sixteen party. Yeah. This all made sense now—why I'd never met any of Mom's old high school friends in the future. They all just clearly sucked.

After the bell rang, the teacher, Mrs. Worthington, took roll. The door opened and someone slipped in at the last moment, his head ducked as he beelined toward a seat in the back.

Jamie, of course. I refrained from watching him as he folded his long body into his seat.

I had to do the same thing I'd been doing all morning—stand up and introduce myself. I mumbled some nonsense about having moved from Boise (why not) and then sat down quickly. Lots of literal chuckles as I spoke. Rough. One thing I'd learned: The popularity ease I had in my timeline was nonexistent in this one.

Shortly after, we broke into small groups to discuss the process of getting a bill made into law. Priscilla and her gang immediately clustered into one and I eyed the rest of the class—resolutely ignoring Jamie—and noticed two Asian kids pushing their desks together.

I moved over to them. "Hi, can I join? I'm Sam."

The guy, his head shorn and wearing a baggy polo shirt, nodded. "Yeah. I'm Sung."

"And I'm Jennifer," the girl said. She had mocha-colored lips and was wearing a cream-colored turtleneck. Very aggressive neutral tones vibe.

As I sat down, I saw Priscilla giving me a *look*. I raised my eyebrows like "What?" She rolled her eyes and turned back to her group.

"Thanks for letting me join," I said, hoping that it came off sincere and not pathetic.

Jennifer was engrossed in picking out a pencil from her very cute Sanrio pencil case. "You're welcome?" I couldn't tell if it was a question or just the way she talked.

"Can I join you guys, too?"

I glanced up at Jamie's hovering figure. *There goes my plan to avoid him.* He seemed like he wanted to curl up and die, too. I guess new kids all had the same life dilemmas.

"Sure," I said, and we all moved our desks to make room for him.

Sung pulled out his notes and immediately got down to business. "So, first things first. A bill starts with a congressman introducing it to Congress."

I was impressed by his Virgo energy but—

"Congressman or congresswoman," Jamie said.

My head whipped over to him.

Sung scoffed. "Yeah. You know what I meant."

Jamie shrugged. "It's just not hard to say both."

There was an annoyed crackle in the air. "O—kay. Anyway."

Sung continued talking, mostly to Jennifer, clearly done with the two of us. I tried to pay attention but every part of me felt attuned to Jamie. Who *was* this guy? He was making it hard to ignore him and I *really* needed to ignore him—I had zero time for distractions during the few days I was here.

To avoid thinking about Jamie more than anything else, I tried to be somewhat engaged—school was boring enough when there actually *were* stakes. When it seemed like we had truly run out of boring bullet points about this process, I took advantage of the lull. Remembering why I was here in the first place. "Hey, so are you guys voting for Priscilla for homecoming queen?"

Jennifer shrugged. "Probably not."

"Why not?" I asked. "Where's the solidarity? She's the only Asian running."

Sung and Jennifer looked at each other—not exactly laughing but close to it.

"What?" My voice got defensive, embarrassed in front of Jamie.

"You're new so you don't know. But, like, Priscilla is so white-washed," Jennifer said with derision. "She doesn't have any Asian friends. Even at church where, like, everyone's Korean."

Sung snorted. "She's a banana."

"A what?" I felt uneasy—a banana didn't sound like a good thing.

"You know, yellow on the outside, white on the inside." Sung and Jessica erupted in laughs.

Jamie dropped his head into his hands. "Wow."

Miss Worthington looked up at us sharply and everyone shut up. I glanced back over at Priscilla and saw her through their eyes: Dressed the same as the two white girls sitting next to her, wearing the same hairstyle. Studiously ignoring us, the table o' Asians. Plus, Jamie.

Hmm. Maybe getting Priscilla elected would be harder than I thought. For some reason, she struck me as popular, overall—but it seemed to be with only a select group of people. Not the people that she had so summarily called losers. Yeah, easy to connect the dots there.

"I actually know her from before . . . we, uh . . . we had math tutoring together," I said, trying to pick an offensively stereotypical Asian kid activity. "We're friends."

If I was trying to build her Azn cred with that statement, it didn't work. Instead, they both looked at *me* more suspiciously. Jamie was unreadable, as ever.

"She's cool, you should vote for her." I was firm, determined to get these two votes if it killed me. If I couldn't even get *them* on board, how were we going to convince the rest of the students? "Plus, aren't you sick of the same old people winning these things?"

Now they looked *completely* done with me. "No one like us ever wins," Sung said. "And who even cares about homecoming court? That's white people shit."

I blinked. I didn't necessarily disagree, given how things were here, but it was still kind of shocking to hear. To witness the deep segregation in this school. A school that, in thirty years, would have gender-neutral restrooms and drag shows during pep rallies. An anti-racist committee. A K-pop dance troupe.

"Well, it doesn't have to *stay* white people shit," I said. "And voting for Priscilla would be one step closer to that. Even if you think she's a banana. She's Korean. She has a single Korean mom who immigrated here and works her ass off for her kids. I feel like that counts for something."

Sung shrugged while Jennifer looked down at her notebook. I caught a flicker of emotion—guilt. Maybe I actually got through to her? Jamie looked at me intently, his long fingers tapping on his notebook. I flipped open my notebook and pretended to write something down to avoid his gaze. This guy really didn't care about staring, I guess.

After a few minutes, Mrs. Worthington called the class to attention. "Okay, let's have some of you share what you've come up with."

I looked to Sung, as he was our unspoken captain and clearly knew this stuff. But he just kind of sat back. Mrs. Worthington looked straight at Priscilla's group. "Deidre? Haley?" They both looked expectantly at Priscilla, who sat up and spoke about the process of a bill becoming law.

Mrs. Worthington nodded when she was done. "Great job, girls." Priscilla looked pleased and Deidre and Haley gave her little high fives. Like they did anything. And why didn't she call out Priscilla's name? I tried not to make a thing of it when Mrs. Worthington called on another group of all white kids, but when it seemed like she was going to move on without calling on our group, I raised my hand.

Mrs. Worthington nodded. "Go on, Jennifer."

An awkward pause filled the room. I looked at Jennifer whose lips were set into a firm line, her gaze on some other plane of reality. "I'm Sam. That's Jennifer." Like—I was a *new student*. How could she mix me up with Jennifer?

I heard a snicker from the corner of the classroom and whipped my head around at the sound. Deidre. The hell? Was that directed at Mrs. Worthington or at *me*? But seeing a flash of irritation cross Priscilla's face and Sung and Jennifer's pissy expressions—I knew it was me. A familiar iciness crept down my back. That prickly awareness of racist crap. I'd never experienced it from a teacher before, however. I expected Mrs. Worthington to look embarrassed but she just flashed a quick "who cares" smile and said, "Okay?"

Stunned, I looked to Sung, who spoke up and gave his spiel. Mrs. Worthington moved on blithely, barely acknowledging him.

Not only did Priscilla have to deal with the bullshit coming from her fellow Asians, but she also had to deal with *this*, too?

The bell rang to end class and I was about to book it out of there but was stopped because Mrs. Worthington had some fresh hell in store for us. "Before you head out! Everyone, grab a partner for a project about the bill-to-law process!"

A collective "ugh" went through the classroom like a wave of despair. Mrs. Worthington ignored it. "Grab the instructions off my desk before you go. Each pair will select a law that you have to present as if you were in Congress trying to pass it as a bill first. Presentations are next Friday."

When everyone around us partnered up in record time, Jamie and I were left awkwardly looking at each other.

Well.

Since he already had to go through the painful task of asking to be a part of our group earlier, I asked him this time. "Do you want to partner up?"

Jamie looked slightly pained. "Sure."

A torturous beat passed. "Does Monday work for you?" he finally asked.

"Monday?" I echoed stupidly.

"Yeah, for working on the project? We could go to the library in the evening if that's okay. I have football practice."

Monday. Monday seemed a lifetime away. And did I *really* have to work on this project? But it would be suspicious if I didn't at least pretend to care. "Sure."

He pushed up his glasses again. "Great. Um, talk to you later, then."

"Yeah! Cool." I held up a hand. "See you then, bro!"

I walked away cringing.

Smooth, Samantha. Smooth. I tried to rush out before an anvil fell on my head or something, but I was stopped by Priscilla grabbing my arm.

"*Hey*. Sam."

I pulled my arm out of her grasp. "Ouch, dude."

"What were you saying to them?" She tilted her head in Sung's direction as he walked out of the classroom.

"Just trying to get you votes," I said. "Giving them a little personal history. Humanizing you."

She frowned. Deeply. "What? I don't want you telling them things about me."

"Well, too bad! You need to get their support. You know that the Asian kids call you a *banana*?" I whispered the last word, like it was a swear or something.

"So what?"

"*So what?* They're your community! The Asian vote should be yours, easy!"

"Oh my god. I don't want to be known as the *Asian* homecoming queen!" she said, her voice furiously hushed. "You see how Mrs. Worthington mixed you up with Jennifer? That's what happens when you clump yourself into an Asian group. You don't stand out."

"You can't be serious," I said, almost laughing. "You're blaming this on Sung and Jennifer? That was on Mrs. Worthington's racist ass. She only knows who you are because you hang out with a bunch of white girls."

Her features grew stony. "You just don't get it."

She stormed off away from me before I could respond. She was right. I didn't get it. At all.

fourteen

fourteen

eight days to homecoming

At lunch, I stood in the middle of the quad with my greasy pizza slice and realized I didn't have any friends. I could sit with Priscilla, but after our last interaction I was pretty sure she wouldn't want me to. Love how I was sent back to the nineties to prevent a fight and now here I was *in* one. *Love* this for me.

I surveyed the quad. I was lucky enough to never be the new kid in school. I'd never had to hover around tables or a cafeteria during lunch time, feeling like a complete outsider. Loneliness was a foreign concept to me.

It was fine. This wasn't my real life. I could endure some loserdom for a week. I had already lost all semblance of pride with Priscilla; what were hundreds of more pitiful looks?

Time was ticking and I wasn't going to waste time socializing anyway. I had to keep plugging away at this campaign.

What were the dynamics at this high school?

Close by was a table full of what I could only gather were the popular kids. Including my mother. They were all dressed fashionably, or at least, with a certain level of effort, since I really couldn't speak to how fashionable it all was. And it wasn't just how they looked (well-groomed, fairly rich), it was how they *acted*. Poised and practiced—as if they knew they were being watched. Admired. They actually reminded me of . . . influencers.

Priscilla was perched on top of the table, nibbling on a salad as she laughed at something Neil was saying. He looked downright smitten with her. Of course. They looked like the pastel cover of one of those old Sweet Valley High novels.

But it was more than that that made the tableau familiar to me. Priscilla was basking in his attention. Loving how it felt and looked.

It reminded me of how I felt around Curren.

The realization was deeply uncomfortable, and I reminded myself to get back on task. I needed to convince the people outside of that little popular group to vote for Priscilla.

Sung and Jennifer's comments reverberated in my mind: "She's whitewashed." Her lunch crowd was pretty white, I had to admit. But when I glanced around the campus, I noticed a lot of racial segregation, in general. Those old teen movies got that aspect of high school right. The Middle Eastern kids. The Asians. The Latinx. And then, it seemed like the rest were various kinds of white kids: nerds, jocks, and the beautiful and fashionable. White kids, allowed to contain multitudes!

My mom was one of the rare POC kids hanging with the white kids. As I watched her let out another peal of laughter, tossing her hair back, the whole thing just rang a little false.

Everything around me felt wrong, suddenly. I was standing on the same patch of earth that was home to me thirty years from now, but I might as well have been in another galaxy. I felt like an alien and my mom felt like a stranger.

I stared at the disparate lunch groups, with "she's whitewashed" ringing in my ears. I didn't have time to angst about time travel. Halmoni was depending on me. Let's get this campaign going.

I eyed the Middle Eastern group dispersed between a couple tables under the flagpole in the quad. A good a start as any. Wary expressions greeted me as I walked up. But I didn't let it bother me—I was social Teflon here. And if there was one thing I was good at, it was talking to people.

"Hey, guys! Just want to make sure you all remember to vote for homecoming queen and king this week!" I said, with what I hoped sounded like a normal amount of earnestness.

A drop-dead gorgeous girl with sunglasses propped on her head stared at me, her frosted lips pursed. "Homecoming?"

"Yeah, here." I handed her a flier. "You should vote for Priscilla for queen. I don't care about who you vote for king."

A couple of people laughed. *Noice.* "Anyway, hope you guys vote, and see you at the game!"

Someone snorted as I walked away, and I couldn't blame them, the wholesomeness of that statement was just too weird. I needed to figure out a way to be more persuasive.

I pushed on. My next group was a bunch of guys and a lone girl sitting around with . . . wait, were those Game Boys? I threw out a little prayer to Julian and his Nintendo museum. I stood over the shoulder of the girl and watched as she played . . .

The Legend of Zelda.

I almost threw my head back and laughed with triumph.

"Which dungeon are you in?" I asked.

The girl jumped in her seat and hit pause. "Excuse me?"

I stepped back and held up my hands. "Sorry to interrupt! It's just that, I got that game for my birthday and haven't been able to get past the Key Tavern." It was true, this level kicked my butt when Julian had let me play it. Wearing white gloves.

The girl, and the guys with her, all seemed to perk up, looking at me curiously. "Oh, yeah that's a hard one," she said kindly. "But I'm actually on Eagle's Tower now."

Inspiration struck. "Priscilla's way better than me at this game."

Everyone looked confused. I tried to sound natural when I clarified, "Priscilla Jo? She's running for homecoming queen." I handed them fliers before launching into details about the game. By the time I left, every one of them was ready to vote for a fellow gamer.

And so it went. I hit up the goth kids and talked about horror movies that I had watched with Val. The future of the internet with the nerds. Always dropping off fliers and mentioning Priscilla's connection to me or the topic at hand.

I did the nineties equivalent of a post on social media—putting Priscilla's face out there for as many impressions as possible.

When I was done, I still had time to eat so I grabbed a slice of pizza (which cost me *fifty-five cents*?! Things cost *cents* here!) and decided I'd use the rest of my lunch period to brush up on my nineties pop culture. I'd nearly messed up a few times when talking to people just now, which wasn't going to fly if I was going to continue this one-woman campaign for the next week.

I headed to the library. Before I grabbed a giant pile of magazines for my research, though, I located the last year's yearbook. Flipping through, I found pictures of all the other girls running for homecoming court. Unsurprisingly they were all white, thin, and pretty. Several of them were on sports teams and in various clubs. Kind of all-American and wholesome in the same vein as Priscilla. Hmm, senior or no, she definitely had stiff competition. I eventually headed out with a stack of magazines in tow. Without my best friend Google (*I shall never take you for granted ever again, Google bestie*), I had to resort to paper knowledge. I walked to the stands in the football field. In the future, that was a guaranteed introvert zone—where you knew you could be left alone.

I found a spot high in the back and spread the magazines out in front of me. It was time for my education.

Who even was the president? Hillary Clinton's husband?

Looking through a few magazines verified that for me. I flipped through to see the other headlines: A bombing by right-wing terrorists in Oklahoma City. Bosnian War still going. A massacre in Rwanda. A nerve gas attack in a Tokyo subway. O.J. Simpson acquittal. Geez, I couldn't tell if it was reassuring or depressing to know that the world had always been garbage.

"You like current events?"

I startled, almost dropping my slice of pizza on my lap.

Jamie stood in the stands below me, holding a pile of books. This guy! I wiped a pool of grease off a magazine with a napkin. "Do I like *current events*?"

He looked down, clearly embarrassed, then let out a huff of laughter. "Yeah. Sorry. Didn't know how else to greet you in a . . . pertinent way."

That made me smile. Smooth this guy was not.

"Do you mind if I sit with you?" he asked. He held up his stack of books, topped by a massive sandwich busting out of its wrapper. "Want to eat this bad boy with company."

That got a laugh from me. "Sure. I was just finishing up this delicious slice of grease."

"Yum." He sat down a row below me and carefully placed his books and sandwich next to him. "Are you doing research or something?"

"Yeah . . ." I glanced at the magazines. "Requires a lot of reading up on the news."

He nodded, unwrapping his sandwich, and chuckled. "So, you're popular like me."

A beat of silence passed, and he looked up at me, alarmed. "Sorry! I didn't mean—"

"Guy. I'm eating pizza alone by an empty football field. It's fine, I know who I am."

Relief and then amusement crossed his face. "So, not to be more awkward than I already am but I don't think we've been formally introduced. I'm Jamie."

What cute supreme awkwardness. "I'm Sam. Short for Samantha. Samantha Kang." Okay, how many versions of my name did I need to tell him?

"Hey, Sam. Jamie is short for James. James Mendoza." He looked right at me, into my eyes, when he said that, good humor peeking through his guarded expression. There was something about it that sent a flutter thorough my chest. *Whoa. Don't get fluttery about this future old man.*

"Hey, Jamie."

Something charged passed between us and I pulled a magazine toward me, trying to look absorbed.

He glanced at it. "What are you reading?"

"Uh," I flipped to the front, "*The Atlantic.*"

"Boring or fun?"

I looked at the spread—a feature on Americans visiting a Russian space station. "I think it's fun? Long-form journalism is a lost art." *Ack. Was it a lost art in the nineties?*

But it didn't seem to register with Jamie. "Yeah, most people just watch the news, I guess."

"Yeah." The news. Twitter. "I just like when someone gets really obsessed about something and talks about it in excruciating detail so that by the end, you're just as obsessed. Or at least, you can talk about it at a dinner party for more than five minutes."

"Dinner party?" He raised one eyebrow. One very nice, straight eyebrow. "You go to those a lot?"

My face got hot. "You know what I mean!"

"Yeah, I love dinner parties."

I swatted him with the magazine. "Shut up."

We both relaxed as a warmth settled between us. The kind that signaled a switch from strangers to friends. It was nice.

Jamie peeled the wrapper off his sandwich. "But, in all seriousness, that's cool. Are you interested in journalism? For college?"

I shrugged. "I don't know. Who knows what they want to be in high school?"

Jamie took a bite out of his sandwich and made a noncommittal noise.

"I think having to declare a major and pretend like you know your life path at the age of freaking eighteen is so stupid," I said, flipping through the magazine viciously.

"Yeah, what loser declares a major already?" he said, then pointed at himself.

I looked at him curiously. "What do you want to study?"

"Engineering." He took a second to wipe his mouth with a napkin. "Sexy, huh?"

What? Oh. The engineering thing. Right. "Yeah, I'm sure some people would find that very, uh, hot."

He smiled. "Good, I'm doing it for that reason and that reason only."

My smile mirrored his. "Well, listen, when the apocalypse happens, I'll be sure to find you so that you can build, like, civilization again."

Our smile-fest was interrupted by a football literally hitting Jamie on the side of his head.

"WHAT—" Jamie yelled as he jumped up and glared down at the football field. There was a very tall, very amused Latino guy standing below us, bent over in laughter.

I was ready to roll up my sleeves and fight yet another stupid football player when Jamie's face broke out into a grin. "You dick!" He tossed the ball back to him.

The guy caught it easily then waved it in the air as he ducked into the stands. "Enjoy your lunch date, James!"

Jamie flushed dark red as he brushed crumbs off his lap. "Uh . . ."

"Best friend?" I asked drily, picking up my magazines.

"Ha, kind of," he said with an embarrassed laugh. "That's Teddy. We're on the team together. He just likes to give me shit."

Lunch was almost over so I stood up, too. "Boys are so bad at friendship. I'll catch you later."

"Wait!" Jamie was awkwardly holding his pile of books again. "I was an asshole earlier. Thanks for trying to stick up for me." He said it with ease and sincerity, making that eye contact again.

"You're welcome," I said. Pleased and embarrassed, I left the field feeling less alone for the first time since I had gotten here.

fifteen

fifteen

seven days to homecoming

The next day was a Saturday, and Priscilla and I had agreed to meet up to work on making posters for her campaign, since we needed every minute we could get before homecoming.

Mrs. Jo had to use her car that day, so I waited at the bus stop in K-Town headed toward Priscilla's apartment. I sat on the cold concrete bench, the late morning sun warm on my face, when a silver Honda Civic came to a stop in front of me—abrupt and with a screech. A little Asian girl wearing a purple sweatshirt rolled down the passenger side window and stared at me.

I stared back uneasily. "Hello?"

"Grace, *move*," a familiar imperious voice commanded, and the little girl sat back in her seat so that Priscilla's face could pop into view. She frowned. "Sam?"

I held up a hand in greeting. "Oh! Hey."

"Are you taking the *bus*?" she asked in the tone she might have used to ask, "Are you torturing puppies?"

"Yeah," I said, closing my magazine. "Are you just here *coincidentally*?"

A car honked behind her, but Priscilla ignored it. "Yeah, I was running some errands for my mom. This is my sister, Grace."

Oh! *Oh.* Aunt Grace as a *child* was not something I was anticipating. I looked at the little girl with the shining, dark marble eyes, a heavy curtain of bangs sitting across her forehead. "Hi, Grace."

She continued to look at me curiously. "Hi." The car honked again, and Priscilla waved her arm out the window—bossily telling them to go around her. The car passed in an accelerated huff.

"Get in the car," Priscilla said. "We're going to the same place."

I scrambled to get in, paranoid of the passing traffic and the emanating road rage. "Thanks."

We peeled out into traffic, and I gasped, frantically grabbing for the seat belt. "Jesus!"

Priscilla glanced at me in her rearview mirror. "Okay, Halmoni."

I glared back at her. "There is a *child* in your vehicle, Speed Racer."

Said child popped her head over her headrest and stared at me. "Who are you?"

I couldn't help but stare. Traces of the Aunt Grace I knew were there in her features—her small snub nose, the curious eyes.

Priscilla made a sharp left turn. "She's someone from school." *Someone, not friend.* "Get back in your seat, Grace." Her voice was curt, impatient.

Aunt Grace moved in slow motion, avoiding turning around so she could still stare at me. She was undeniably cute.

"I'm Sam."

She wrinkled her nose. "Isn't that a boy's name?"

"Well, gender is a construct. So, no."

Priscilla made an exasperated sound. "What? Can you not be weird for like one second in front of a *child*?"

"People can choose whatever names they want, Grace. There are no rules."

"Oh my god," Priscilla muttered as we ran a yellow light.

Grace kicked the dashboard with her little Velcro-strap sneakers. "Hi, guess what?"

"What?" I asked.

"My teacher said today that dinosaurs went distinct because of a comet!"

Priscilla and I exchanged glances. Cute.

"Extinct, not distinct," Priscilla said crisply as she steered us onto a busy main road.

Priscilla Jo: Correcting Children since 1995.

"That's what I said!" Grace exclaimed. "Will we also be distinct because of a comet?"

I shook my head. "Probably not. More likely because of"—*was climate change a thing yet?*—"the overheating of our planet."

"Sam!" Priscilla threw her hand up in the air. "Way to freak her out!"

I looked at Grace, who looked back at me with wise eyes. I shrugged and she shrugged back.

We sped through the freeway to land back in North Foothill in record time. After parking in the underground garage of Priscilla's apartment, the three of us packed into an elevator. I hit the third floor, out of a habit I had for years of my life when Halmoni still lived in this apartment.

"Uh, how did you know that?" Priscilla asked as she raised a brow at me.

Shit. "Oh, sorry. I also live on the third floor! You do, too, huh? What a coincidence." The lie felt so obvious, but Priscilla and Grace didn't seem to think it was that odd and we rode the rest of the way in relative non-weirdness. The doors opened and we walked out onto the open-air hallway—the apartments bordering a courtyard filled with a fountain and leafy palms. Think *Melrose Place*, but immigrant families.

Grace reached for my hand as we walked to their apartment. A memory flashed through my mind—of a college-student-aged Aunt Grace holding on to my preschooler hand when we walked through the mall.

What a trip.

We stopped in front of a door with a quilted wreath hung over the peephole and a no-nonsense, dark-green doormat. Emotions rioted through me at the thought of entering this apartment, an apartment I vaguely remembered from my childhood. At seeing Halmoni, again. Priscilla was digging through her JanSport front pocket for her keys when the phone started to ring inside. The jangling landline echoed through the courtyard, and Priscilla quickly unlocked the door—leaving it wide open—and kicked her shoes off before sprinting to grab the phone. Before I could even step inside, I heard her exasperated voice: "But Sam and I were supposed to work on our posters together!" Grace and I hovered at the door—me out of politeness, Grace because she was staring at a snail crawling on the metal railing.

A few seconds later, Priscilla was in the entry, putting her Mary Janes back on. "Hey, sorry, Sam. But my mom needs help at the cleaners today, so I can't work on this anymore."

Gah, we only had so many days left. Panic crept up my back—freaking out that this wouldn't work, that I would be stuck back in the past forever. I needed to spend more time with Priscilla.

Actually, I needed to spend more time with Priscilla *and* Halmoni. That was step two of my plan, and I had been so focused on the campaign that I hadn't made any progress on this front. This was a stroke of luck.

"I wouldn't mind working on the posters at the dry cleaner," I said.

Priscilla shot me a dubious look. "You sure? I might have to work sometimes."

"Yeah, that's fine. I can help, too!"

Grace nodded. "You're very helpful."

I laughed—genuinely but also embarrassed. "Thank you."

"Well, okay. I guess that might work." Priscilla took her shoes off again. "I'll go get the supplies from inside."

Yes.

The drive to the dry cleaners was quick and I braced myself for Halmoni time again. I wanted to take advantage of it, but also act normal. How do you act around your beloved grandma who, in the future, is in a coma? Without scaring the hell out of her?

"We can use the big table in the back," Priscilla said as Grace let go of my hand and sprinted ahead, ducking under the counter like I did as a kid.

I nodded, distracted. Looking for Halmoni.

And there she was, on the phone, the receiver resting between her ear and shoulder as she flipped through a calendar hanging on the wall.

She hung up the phone and ran a hand over her face, looking tired and frustrated. I stepped forward, instinctively wanting to see what was wrong. But she looked up then, eyes focused past me, at Priscilla.

"Priscilla, I have to go talk with a vendor," she said in Korean, but saying "vendor" in English. No greeting, no smile. None of the warmth and attention I got when I stepped through her apartment door. "You have to watch the store alone for a little bit, okay?"

Priscilla sighed. "Umma, I brought Sam here so we could work on our project."

Halmoni registered me then. "Oh, good. Then you have help. Both of you watch Grace and the store, okay? Just two hours."

I nodded, wanting to be helpful. "Sure."

But Priscilla wasn't so sure. "*Umma.*"

Halmoni picked up her large, worn-out brown leather purse. On Halmoni's sixtieth birthday, Mom would buy her a hunter-green Prada tote that Halmoni would keep in its soft cloth pouch for years, never touching it. "You'll be fine. I'll be back soon."

She gave Grace's hair a ruffle and said, "Listen to Unni and be good." And then she was out the door in a rush. I felt disappointed. And nervous. How would I ever figure out what the issue was between Mom and Halmoni if I never spent time with them together?

Priscilla looked at me, defensively, preempting any embarrassment, it felt like. "You can leave if you want. I'm going to be stuck here."

But I wanted to stay. Spend more time with Grace, help out Halmoni. "It's fine. I can get started on the poster and watch Grace when you have customers."

As if on cue, the bell chimed and a tall, older man wearing a light blue dress shirt and khakis walked in. Priscilla sighed and plastered on a smile to face him. "Hi, Mr. Abranian! Here to pick up?"

While she helped him, I walked over to Grace who had seated herself in a chair and was staring expectantly at me. "So, what do you usually do here?" I asked.

"Homework," she said.

"First graders have homework?"

"Yes, it's real school now." She crawled up onto her knees and reached over the big table and grabbed the corner of the butcher paper roll that was nailed into one end of the table. "We can use this for the poster!"

"Good idea!" I helped her pull it out until it covered the entire expanse of the table. I found a roll of tape and taped down the edges so it wouldn't curl up. I found the paint markers in the bag of supplies Priscilla had brought and dug them out. "Okay, Grace. Don't get these on anything other than the paper. They're permanent."

Grace got a gleam in her eye that should have alarmed me. She grabbed the green marker and immediately smeared it on the surface of the table.

"Grace!" I stared at her, open-mouthed. What a *brat*.

In an instant, Priscilla was there, taking the marker from her hand. "*You're dead.*"

Grace squealed and bolted, but Priscilla grabbed her by the tail of her sweatshirt before she could get far. "You can't help with this anymore. Go sit at the sewing machine and do your homework."

I thought for sure that Grace would flip out and refuse. But Priscilla's voice was firm and scary, and Grace was only human. She hung her head down low and shuffled over to the smaller table behind me. Damn, that Mom power was strong in Priscilla from an early age.

"Sorry." I tried to wipe the marker off with my sleeve.

Priscilla waved her hand in the air. "Don't worry about it. Typical Grace." She pointed at her sister. "I've got my eye on you."

And then a second later Priscilla was ringing up Mr. Abranian and helping another customer who had come in during the scuffle.

She was good at this—multitasking, being in charge. She had to be. And she'd be good at this forever. I went back to Grace with my hands on my hips. "Don't make me sic your unni on you, Grace."

"I'm not scared," Grace said with a scoff. But a quick glance to her sister was all it took to get her butt back in her seat.

sixteen

sixteen

seven days to homecoming

I was working on the poster while sneaking peeks at Grace behind me. She was doing her homework with a forlorn expression. Poor, tortured child. I was writing "PRISCILLA JO FOR QUEEN" in huge block letters when Priscilla came over. "I don't want to use my last name."

My marker stopped in midair. "Why?"

"Who calls anyone by their full names? I'm the only Priscilla running."

She had a point but . . . I asked, "Is it because you don't like your full name? Your Korean last name?"

Priscilla's gaze was hard. "You are one of the most presumptuous people I have *ever* met in my life. Did you really have *any* friends at your old school?"

"*Yes*. I was popular enough to win homecoming queen."

She made a rude noise. "Your school must have been full of freaks."

I summoned patience from the depths of my soul. "Fine, let's nix the last name." I tore the paper off and started a new roll. There was a break in customers, so Pricilla was able to join me in making the sign. We were quiet as she painted the words, and I drew some crowns and flowers on the border. The rhythmic sounds of the washing machines ran in the background, and things were quiet until I broke the silence.

"Do you have to work here a lot?"

Priscilla slowly and meticulously painted a straight blue line. "Yeah. Pretty much every day."

"Oh. Wow."

"It saves my mom a lot of money to have me work here," she said. That note of defensiveness, again.

"No, I get it," I said. I did, on a theoretical level. Not on a solidarity level. I never had a job, actually. Whenever I had considered getting an after-school or summer job, my mom had been adamantly against it. She said I should focus on enjoying my youth, which I had laughed about at the time. But now . . .

She painted another straight line. "It does suck, though. I miss out on a lot of stuff."

"Like what?"

"Like . . . shopping after school with my friends. Or just, like, watching a movie or something," she said. "My mom thinks that stuff is, like, *insane* to do for a teenager. That all I should be doing is helping out the family or studying until blood pours out of my eyes."

I couldn't help but snort-laugh. "Would love to see that, not gonna lie."

She made an offended face then grinned. "It'd be like a very Korean drama moment, right?"

"You watch K-dramas?"

"K-dramas? Korean dramas?" She looked confused for a second. "Yeah, not like on purpose. It's my mom's only entertainment. It's so annoying. Don't your parents watch them?"

There was an opportunity for bonding here. I could feel it. "Yeah. They do. I like them, actually."

"You *do*?" She was so incredulous she almost messed up her writing. "Wow. I think they're really embarrassing. One of many reasons why I don't ever have my friends over at my house. Like the kimchi smell. How in the world does such a small jar stink up an entire apartment?" She was talking rapidly, and I didn't want to interrupt her Korean Seinfeld spiel. In fact, I had never heard Priscilla speak this many words before. Her whole demeanor had changed suddenly—she pulled her leg up so that her foot was resting on her chair, her arm draped over it. A slight slouch in her back. Like, straight Korean-ahjumma-gossiping style. "Also, my mom hates all my friends so what's the point? She's always pushing her Korean church friends' kids on me, and like, little does she know, that a lot of those kids are smoking after school and in *gangs* and stuff." Her voice hushed at the word "gangs." Haha.

"Yeah, I noticed you don't hang out with the Korean kids," I said, treading lightly given our last testy conversation about it.

Priscilla looked up at me. "What exactly did Sung and Jennifer say to you?"

"Nothing! I mean, other than the banana comment."

"Typical. I know they talk shit about me." She was acting like it didn't bother her, but I could tell it did.

I was suddenly *very* absorbed in painting a daisy. "I mean, it's dumb. Why do you have to hang out by ethnicity, anyway?"

"Right? I don't want to just be another one of the FOBs."

OMG. "Priscilla!"

"What?" She looked genuinely startled.

"That's not . . . just . . ." I wasn't even sure what to say. "It's rude and racist, to be honest."

"How is saying that about other Asians racist?" Priscilla was defensive, but also confused.

"Because why is it bad to be 'fresh off the boat'? Your parents were. Why is it bad to be 'just another one'?" My voice was getting louder, emotional. It made Priscilla pause.

"It's not *bad*. You just get treated a certain way when you are, okay? And I don't want to be treated that way."

I thought of Jennifer and Sung and what Priscilla said at the end of class. "Then do you *avoid* hanging out with Koreans or what?"

"Kind of," she admitted. "And not just because of the whole FO—uh, fresh-off-the-boat factor. I feel like they're really cliquey and judgmental of Koreans that aren't super Korean. They probably think I'm whitewashed because I don't listen to Korean pop music and, like, hang out in K-Town to karaoke."

I stayed conspicuously quiet. She raised an eyebrow. "See? Anyway. I don't want to just be 'the Korean homecoming queen.' I want to be . . ."

Her voice trailed off and I waited. She bit her lip and looked down.

"What do you want to be?"

"Normal."

I wasn't sure how to respond to that. How was being Korean American *not* normal? Why were the nineties like this? She was being vulnerable with me, and I knew it was because, in some way, she felt comfortable with me. Safe in sharing these things.

"I know what you mean," I said even though I didn't *really*. "But I think instead of seeing the 'Korean homecoming queen' as a bad thing—you can actually use that to your advantage."

"How?" Her brow was furrowed as she concentrated on her writing. Or maybe it was furrowed in dubiousness.

"Well, it helps you stand out!" I thought of the yearbook photos. "All the other candidates hang out in the same clique, and they're all popular, white . . ."

Again, me using the word "white" seemed to startle her. Priscilla nodded. "Yeah, so?"

"Well, okay, then in a lineup of girls who are practically identical, you'll stand out. In a *good* way. Don't you want that?"

Priscilla looked genuinely perplexed as she thought about it. "But I don't want to stand out because I *look* different. I just want to seem like everyone else—but the best version of everyone else. Does that make sense?"

I didn't know. Everyone in the future wanted to stand out—to make their mark in the world somehow. I thought of Curren and his movie, at how he once almost flipped a table when someone on TikTok had commented that he had "big Chalamet energy." He was so certain his whole sleepy-eyed, tousled-hair vibe was unique to him.

"Well, I just think you could make the only-Asian-on-the-homecoming-court thing work in your favor," I said. "You *do* stand out because of that, and maybe you'll be able to get support from other people who feel like they stand out, who also feel like it's impossible to blend in. Even if it kills you to do it, you should try and connect with them. The, what did you call them? 'Losers.'" I let the word land damningly.

But Priscilla was impervious to damnation. She rolled her eyes as she added some glitter to the dotted "i" in her name. "Okay, *fine*. What do you suggest?"

"Why don't you start with people you already know? Sung and Jennifer mentioned that you guys go to the same church. Why don't you try and befriend them there?"

"Ugh." But she didn't fight me.

Grace interrupted us with, "I hate math!"

I turned to her. "Me too, sister."

Priscilla rolled her eyes. "What is it, Grace?"

"Adding is stupid." She pushed back from the desk petulantly. Arms crossed and immovable.

I tried to hold back my laughter. Priscilla put her marker down and walked over to Grace. "Adding is not stupid. You're going to do it all the time as an adult and it's important."

The words were echoes from my childhood—my mom's endless patience sitting with me at the dining room table, going over multiplication tables, geometry theorems. She never let me leave the table without figuring it out. It drove me crazy.

Watching Grace squirm in her chair while Priscilla stood over her and helped, I knew Grace was feeling the same.

A customer came in then and Priscilla turned to them cheerfully. "Sorry, give me one second." And there was something about her face then—the strain around her smile, the tired eyes—that made me feel like a useless lump.

"I can help Grace," I said. "If you need to work."

She showed a hint of relief. "Okay, thanks." Then her mouth hitched up in the corner. "Are you sure you can handle addition?"

That made me laugh unexpectedly and she grinned, too, before walking up to the counter. I settled down next to Grace to help her attack 3 + 5.

We went through a few problems, and while she wrote down one of her answers, I asked, "Who's the better tutor? Me or Priscilla?"

She shot me a mischievous look. "Unni."

"How rude," I teased. "Fine, your unni or your umma?"

"Umma? She doesn't help me. She's too busy."

"Oh," I said, understanding in my voice but not understanding, really. Because my mother had always had time to help me. She made sure of it, even if it killed me. And when I glanced over at Priscilla, pinning receipts to a pile of cashmere sweaters and coats, I felt a tightness in my chest.

Something close to gratitude.

The woman who had come in, Asian and middle-aged, looked at us and clucked. "You poor things," she said in Korean.

I frowned, confused. But Priscilla seemed to understand who she was referring to. Her entire postured stiffened, her shoulders raised, her chin lifted. "Hi, Mrs. Lim."

"How's your mother? Looks like you have to help her out, again, huh? Terrible thing what happened with your dad." She wasn't even waiting for Priscilla to respond, just kind of going on her own journey of tragedy.

My hand clenched around the pencil I was using to help Grace with her worksheet. Grace wasn't paying attention, luckily. Just kicking the table legs and staring at her problem with angry concentration. Why was this rando talking about Halabuji with so much familiarity?

"We're doing fine, thank you. Can I have your order slip?" Priscilla's voice was clipped and formal as she held her hand out.

Mrs. Lim rummaged through her purse until she drew out a crumpled sheet of pale pink paper. "I can't imagine what it must be like for you girls. Losing a father and now having to work here. You should be studying at home, without a care in the world."

What in god's name? Priscilla turned on the garment conveyer with a hard slap onto the switch. Her body coiled with tension. Right, she didn't know I knew about her dad yet.

Not taking the hint, Mrs. Lim rambled on, "A woman having to raise her children alone, tsk. I hope your mother remarries one day. Every household needs a man. You girls need a father."

It was a miracle that I didn't just spontaneously combust. *What* was this woman going on about? I waited for Priscilla to rip her a new one, for the ice-cold assassin in her to end this woman.

But instead, she just pulled the garment bags off the conveyer. "Maybe one day. Your total is $21.75."

When Mrs. Lim finally left, the stink of pity still lingered. I shook my head as Priscilla noted the sale in a notebook. "Wow, how did you *not* karate-chop her in her big mouth?"

Grace giggled hysterically and I shot a guilty look at her. "You didn't hear that."

Priscilla walked back to the poster, picking up a marker. "She's just trying to be nice."

"Not really." I joined her at the table. "She was, like, reveling in her own feelings in reaction to something that literally had nothing to do with her. And every household needs a *man*? Are you serious, lady?"

"I know." Priscilla actually smiled for real this time. "So ridiculous."

"Why didn't you say anything to her?" I poked, still amazed at the casual sexism of it all.

"Because! What am I gonna do, make things all awkward and lose a customer because I'm annoyed by something she said? There's no point." She looked at me in that same baffled way she would in the future. "Why do you even care?"

I cared because I didn't like to see some rando make my family feel bad because my grandfather died. Because I physically recoiled at the idea of someone telling my grandmother she needed to have a man in the house. But I couldn't say any of this. Because it would be weird to care this much about Priscilla's life.

"I just hate when people are stupid and allowed to be happily stupid," I grumbled as I jabbed at a yellow happy face.

Priscilla smirked. "Yeah, I agree with you on that." We left the big dead-dad elephant in the room just . . . in the room.

Halmoni returned when we were finishing up the posters.

"Hi, Mrs. Jo," I greeted her brightly. Just happy to see her again.

"Hello," she said, taking off her coat. "Did everything go okay?"

"Yup," Priscilla said, rolling up the posters. "Sam helped a lot."

The power of my smile could have launched me to the moon. “Oh, not really.”

“Thank you so much, Sam,” Halmoni said, genuine in her gratitude. “Priscilla, you can take Grace home.”

Grace immediately started shoving her stuff into her little backpack. “Yes-yes-yes! I want to watch *Full House*.”

Halmoni laughed and ruffled her hair. “Only if you finished your homework.”

“I did! Because Sam helped me.”

“Wow, good thing Sam was here today,” Halmoni said warmly as she adjusted Grace’s backpack.

Inspiration struck. I could clinch step two right now.

“If you guys need help around here, I can just come by after school. For free,” I added quickly.

Halmoni looked taken aback. “Free? Oh no, we can’t do that.”

Priscilla looked mortified. “Sam, that’s totally not necessary.”

Shit. I was messing this up. “No, I was only looking for a job earlier because I wanted something to do after school. Um, my mom said I need real-world experience. We don’t need the money.”

Again, I knew immediately that was the wrong thing to say. Damn it! “I mean, we’re not rich or anything—”

“Sam,” Halmoni lifted a hand, stopping me from this horror show. “I can pay you. Actually, we *do* need some extra help. Can you work after school?”

“Really, Umma?” Priscilla looked at her mom in disbelief.

Halmoni nodded firmly. “Yes. You’ve been doing it too much.”

The pleased expression on Priscilla was the best thing I’d seen in days. But she still protested. “It’s okay, I don’t mind.”

“No, it might be getting in the way of your studies,” Halmoni said as she rummaged through her purse. Priscilla and I exchanged a look over her head. Studies. Yeah, or a homecoming campaign?

"So, Sam, can you work after school when Priscilla usually does? Four to six p.m.?"

I nodded vigorously. "Yes, that works!"

"Okay. I can pay minimum wage since you are still student, and I will pay you for today, too. Start Monday, okay?"

"Yes! Thank you!" I answered happily.

And the happiness on Priscilla's face? It was the best payment I could have asked for. Between this job and Priscilla letting me help her win homecoming queen, I was that much closer to mending this relationship, to getting back home.

seventeen

seventeen

six days to homecoming

The next morning, Mrs. Jo asked me if I wanted to go to church with her. It's not that I was against religion or anything. But I *was* against doing anything before noon on weekends. Mrs. Jo sensed my hesitation and shrugged. "If not, that is okay, too."

Sitting there, wearing Mrs. Jo's pajama pants, I was aware of her extreme generosity. And there wasn't much campaigning I could do on a Sunday anyway. Plus, everything was going so well—why not give Mrs. Jo this one nice thing?

"Sure, I'll go. Give me ten minutes!" After cobbling together an outfit with the help of Mrs. Jo's wardrobe again, we were out the door. On our drive there, it occurred to me that I had never been to church before. Any kind of church. Another point of contention between my mother and Halmoni. Halmoni was a devout Christian, but Mom went in the extreme other direction as a hard-core atheist. Julian and I always chalked it up to some bad bible camp experience or something. Also, the fact that Mom didn't have a spiritual bone in her body. Unless *Architectural Digest* was a religion.

"When we get to church, you follow other young people into smaller chapel," Mrs. Jo said as she steered us past MacArthur Park, the fountain in the man-made lake glittering in the sunshine. Our journey was just a couple miles farther east, close to downtown.

"What?" I looked at her in alarm. "I have to be alone?"

She made a sharp sound. "Not alone, many other young people your age with you. Church separate everyone by age—so, baby, bigger baby, and teenagers like you."

Great. More fun nineties teenagers.

The church was huge, taking up an entire block, beige and sprawling and completely devoid of any architectural intention. A man greeted me at the entrance, handing me a printed program.

"That's where you go," Mrs. Jo said with a nudge, pointing at a door leading to a smaller building off the main chapel, which was differentiated by its stained-glass windows and large cross hung beneath the A-frame eaves. "See you after service here, okay? They have lunch for us."

There were groups of teenagers streaming toward the entrance Mrs. Jo pointed to, and I followed them with dread-laced curiosity. All I knew about church was what I saw in movies and stuff—singing, droning sermons. But I had never seen a youth service before. *Oh, god, was some clean-cut dweeb going to play a guitar?*

Yet another program was handed to me as I entered—this one a printout of a few hymns and Bible passages—and as soon as I stepped in, my eyes had to adjust to the dim lighting. It was lively in there, groups of people chatting and goofing around. The girls were mostly wearing black pants and crisp white button-ups, but somehow, they looked cool and not extremely business casual. Maybe it was their various chunky black shoes, or long, streaming hair. The guys? Jeans and button-ups, their pants hanging low, their haircuts legitimately insane.

I felt incredibly alien in Mrs. Jo's floral-print, knee-length skirt and cardigan combo (it was cute, okay). At least I was wearing my Vans so that instead of looking like a culty 1950s sister wife, I looked like I had accidentally stumbled into a Korean church on my way to the vintage record store.

Because it was church, I guess I was expecting some nice overtures—the Christianly thing to do—but everyone was cloistered in their little cliques, and when they did look at me, it was with a quick appraisal and dismissal.

I felt a deep understanding of Priscilla then—why she hated everything about this. If she didn't fit in with the Korean kids at school, she *extremely* didn't fit in here.

The lights on stage switched on and off and it was the signal everyone needed to get into their seats—folding chairs set into neat rows—and quiet down. A few people in their twenties stepped up onto the stage, three girls and a young guy. The guy was clearly in charge, wearing black-rimmed glasses, acne scattered on the crest of his cheeks.

"Good morning, brothers and sisters," he said cheerfully. "Happy Sunday. As many of you know, I'm Pastor Paul." Music started to play on the speakers at a low volume. My body unclenched because nary a guitar could be seen. Paul did some church housekeeping—announcing upcoming events and other things. Then he said, "If there are any new brothers and sisters in Christ here today, we would love for you to stand up and wave hello."

Oh, god.

A couple people stood up—their backs hunched, their faces deeply uncomfortable. I was just going to lie low since it wasn't like I planned on coming to church in the nineties forever, but I felt a poke in my back.

"That's you," a laughing voice whispered.

I turned around to see Priscilla smirking at me, her arms folded in her floral-embroidered cardigan. *Of course!* She was wearing a white baby tee underneath, over an ankle-length black cotton skirt. Looking like everyone, but a little different.

"Shh," I hissed. But it was too late.

"Did I see another new face back there?" Paul called out, shading his eyes against the stage lights.

UGH!

I stood up and waved. The staring faces were in shadow, but I felt their eyeballs just the same.

"Welcome," Paul said amiably. "Please come up to me after the service so I can get to know each of you." I nodded in response and sat back down quickly.

With Priscilla sitting behind me, I couldn't talk to her, but we wouldn't have been able to anyway. The rest of the service was a bunch of singing (nightmare because you also had to do hand motions—which is why those three girls were up there, showing us the moves), a sermon that actually was kind of nice and not at all fire and brimstone, mostly about keeping faith in the modern world, and then some praying together.

It was over pretty quickly, and I was eager to talk to Priscilla. I was stoked that this random decision to go to church was actually going to help with homecoming. Sung and Jennifer were here, and probably other kids from school. It was a great opportunity to connect with them. "Where are you going now?" I asked her as she picked up her Bible and little black nylon purse.

"Bible study." She paused. "Have you never been to church before?"

I shook my head. "No. I'm just here with . . . an aunt. She asked me to come today. Can I go with you?"

"An LA Korean family who doesn't go to church," she murmured, turning the idea over in her head. "Interesting. Anyway, yeah, crash my class. Our teacher's pretty cool."

As we walked out of the building with everyone else, a lot of the teenagers were talking and laughing with each other, but I noticed that no one came over to chat with Priscilla. Unlike school, it was almost like she was invisible here.

"I see what you mean about this whole church crowd," I said in a low voice as I followed her into another building—one-story and carpeted in dark blue with soul-crushing fluorescent bulbs.

She walked at a brisk pace beside me. "Yeah." No elaboration and I didn't push her.

We walked into one of the rooms to find a couple people already seated around a conference table. A two-liter bottle of soda the color of neon vomit was sitting in the middle of the table, alongside a row of Styrofoam cups. The two guys in the room looked up at us briefly with quick nods.

We took our seats and soon after, everyone else trickled in—eight total, including the teacher who was, yet again, another young guy, probably in college? This one had good hair and a sparkling smile and made the girls fluttery.

"Hi, I'm Eric," he said to me directly. "Are you new?"

Priscilla spoke up for me. "Yeah, this is Sam. She goes to school with me." She shot a winning smile back at Eric. I raised my eyebrows at Priscilla when Eric turned around, mouthing, "*Hot.*" She tried not to laugh.

Bible study was, well, Bible study. Eric had us discuss some scriptures, but the tone was light, and Eric was—surprise!—very charming. Priscilla took notes in her little planner with her precise, pretty handwriting and I wondered what the hell she did with them after. Study them? It felt extremely unlikely given her future feelings about religion, but type A was gonna type A.

When it was over, Priscilla lingered, and I tried to look casual as I hovered by the door. She and Eric chatted for a little bit before she walked out with me. Before I could say anything, she shook her head, "Oh my god, please don't."

I grinned. "What do you mean? I was going to ask what we're eating for lunch."

We both laughed as we walked out into the afternoon sunshine. It felt nice to have a, I don't know, a real *girlfriend* moment with Priscilla. That unspoken language between friends about something stupid and fun.

The courtyard had transformed into an outdoor eating space. One side had long folding tables set up with a buffet of various Korean lunch items like rice, grilled meats, soups, and kimchi.

Mrs. Jo was working behind the table serving food and waved when she spotted me. "Oh, that's my aunt," I said to Priscilla, praying (for real, this time) that the two wouldn't need to talk to each other. Luckily, Grace came storming toward us before that could happen.

She threw her arms around my legs. "Hi, Sam! You go to our church, too?" Her excitement was unbearably sweet.

"Just visiting today," I said, careful not to make big promises to a little kid.

"Yay!" She pumped her arms in celebration anyway. "You get free food, isn't that so cool?"

It *was* cool and we got into line together. I was tense when we reached Mrs. Jo but she just quickly dumped rice on our plates. "Eat well," she said sternly before she moved onto the next people.

Priscilla wrangled Grace's plate and her own and then we looked for a spot to eat. I saw a table full of familiar faces—Sung and Jennifer with a few other people from school. They weren't just eating, though; it looked like they were assembling packages.

Another opportunity.

"Hey, let's go see what those guys are doing," I said to Grace loudly. Priscilla looked to where we were headed and stopped in her tracks. I looked back at her. "Homecoming queen, yay or nay?"

A tortured expression flashed across her face before she reluctantly followed. Using Grace as my cute shield, I walked up to the table. "Hey, guys."

Sung and Jennifer looked at me warily. "Hey."

"What are you guys doing?" I eyed the brown paper gift bags lined up next to packages of toothpaste and toothbrushes, rolls of white socks, combs, and bars of soap.

"We're making care packages for the homeless shelter down the street," Sung said.

"Oh, wow, that's cool," I said.

Grace put her plate of food down and reached out to touch the socks. Priscilla grabbed her hand. "Sorry," she mumbled.

"It's okay," Jennifer said. She looked at Grace with a smile. "Is that your sister?"

Priscilla nodded. "Yeah, Grace. Say hi—they go to school with me."

"Hi! I'm Grace and I am six years and three-quarters old," she said as she gripped Priscilla's hand.

Jennifer's expression softened. "Cool. I have a younger sister, too. She's eleven, though."

Taking advantage of this nice moment, I asked, "Could we help you guys?"

Sung and Jennifer exchanged a glance. Before they could waffle, I powered through. "Priscilla has a car, too, so we can drop these off."

"Oh," Sung said, surprised. "Actually, that would be really helpful. We're almost done putting this batch together if you want to drive them over after?"

I looked at Priscilla, sending her very intense "Say yes" vibes. She gave a tight smile. "Sure."

"Thanks," Jennifer said, real gratitude in her voice. "Um, you could join the volunteer group if you guys want? We do this every Sunday and then once a month we host a hot meal at the church."

"Oh, cool—" I started but Priscilla interrupted me.

"Yeah, I tried to join last time, but you guys said you had enough volunteers," Priscilla said, her voice light but laced with tension.

Jennifer flushed a little before shooting Sung a dirty look. "Oh, really?"

"We have room now," Sung said, clearly dying inside. "If you still want to join."

I watched this interaction with a neutral expression, but inwardly I was pumping my fists.

Priscilla made a plan to meet them in the parking lot and we sat down at a table to eat our lunch.

"Was that so bad?" I asked as I dug into my food.

Opening a can of Sprite with her manicured hands, Priscilla rolled her eyes. "I was just *waiting* for you to gloat."

"Didn't have to wait long." I winked at Grace who was munching on her lunch with gusto. "Let the bonding begin."

Priscilla's look of utter disdain made me take a different tack. "At the very least, you've got a couple more votes for homecoming queen?"

Priscilla tapped her chopsticks on the table. "Hmm. Maybe."

"If you can get through to Sung and Jennifer—who had made it *very* clear that they weren't your biggest fans—think of what might happen once you start reaching out to *other* losers."

"Shh! God, you're so *loud*," Priscilla said with a laugh. A beat later she looked sheepish. "I do feel bad that I called them that. It was a lot of assumptions being made, I think. By all of us."

"Well, I liked them!" Grace announced as she popped a kimbap into her mouth. "They're helping people. By giving *presents*."

I looked at Grace with affection. Sometimes, people showed themselves from day one. Later, as I was leaving with Mrs. Jo, as I watched Priscilla load her car with Sung and Jennifer, I also thought that maybe you weren't stuck as that person forever. That maybe you could change.

I just wondered if it would be enough to shift things in the future.

• • •

That evening, Mrs. Jo made me sujebi.

"This is my famous recipe," Mrs. Jo said as she placed a steaming bowl in front of me. "I only tell my best friends about it."

She didn't know it, but it was one of my favorites—an anchovy-based soup filled with torn-up pieces of dough, thinly sliced green onion, and so-soft-they-were-falling-apart potatoes. It was the ultimate comfort food. Halmoni always made it for me on rainy days.

At first bite, I stilled. It had the exact same flavor as Halmoni's. Did she get her recipe from Mrs. Jo? Tears unexpectedly sprang to my eyes and suddenly I wanted to drop everything and run and go see her.

In fact, ever since I had gotten here, it was taking an enormous amount of willpower not to ditch all my plans and hang out with her all day, soaking up every second of the six days I had left in case she wouldn't be in the future when I went back. It was both common sense and the instinct to get back home that kept me from doing that. That, and Priscilla potentially filing a restraining order against me.

"Taste okay?" Mrs. Jo looked at me with concern, picking up her spoon to take a taste from my bowl herself.

I tried to suck the tears back into my eyeballs. "Yes! It's delicious. Really good."

"Did you ever have before?" She pushed a small dish of fried tofu smothered in soy sauce and green onions my way. Then a small grilled fish. I dutifully reached for both, laying the pieces on top of my bowl of rice.

"Yes." It was all I could muster, and I shoved a spoonful of rice into my mouth to avoid elaborating.

She nodded, satisfied. "This used to be very common-people food in Korea, you know that?" I did, in fact, know that. Halmoni used to tell me the same thing. She grew up right after the Japanese occupation, when people were still struggling to scrape by and got pretty inventive with food. So, if they had a rice shortage, people started rolling out dough and making soups like this to fill their stomachs. It was the kind of life that felt a billion light years from my reality, even when the person who lived it was sitting right across from me.

"Yes, my grandmother told me," I said, careful in my words but wanting to give credit where credit was due. "She's also a good cook, like you."

Mrs. Jo nodded. "When you are our age and a woman, you had to cook. No other option. So, most of us get pretty good. *Most.*" Some memory of a horrible meal darkened her features for a second.

"Thank you, again. It's perfect for this cold weather."

"Yes, it is cold today." Mrs. Jo eyed me critically. "You wear the same sweater every day. I think you need new clothes. Even if only here short time."

I laughed. "No, I'm okay." Although, I did feel like maybe I had been smelling a little musty lately. Again, my mother's voice: *The best thing about being Korean is that we don't get B.O.* It was, like, her favorite fact in the world—said loudly in the Target aisle when I tried to get her to buy me my first stick of deodorant in seventh grade. I'd been mortified at the time, but it was true, I never got B.O.

But B.O. or no, I should probably wash my clothes. I spent the rest of the night doing exactly that, folding my clothes while watching K-dramas with Mrs. Jo and working on more campaign posters for Priscilla.

eighteen

eighteen

five days to homecoming

The next morning, I woke up to an empty apartment and a note from Mrs. Jo, scrawled on an envelope.

> *I am at swim class. Please take this for lunch, gas, and buy clothes after school today.*
>
> *Bye-bye*
>
> *Mrs. Jo*

My jaw dropped when I opened the envelope to find three, crisp hundred-dollar bills tucked inside. I made a note to future self, well, current self, to make sure I somehow paid Mrs. Jo back.

• • •

Later, at lunch, I beelined for Priscilla. I had woken up that morning with a brilliant idea.

I found her perched at her usual table, in a dark-red baby doll dress, her hair French-braided to the side, her feet in laced-up, camel-colored boots. *Hold up—were those* Timberlands?

W-i-l-d.

It was all very *Seventeen*-magazine-spread-on-breezy-teen-life, and I felt like a sweatshirt-wearing troll-person walking over to them. She was chatting with Deidre and a couple other girls I recognized, while a group of guys was off to the side, doing something stupid with their food and backpacks.

"Hey, Priscilla," I said.

Everyone looked up and I felt like I was naked. Priscilla smiled. "Hey, Sam."

"Do you have a sec to talk about homecoming stuff?" I asked, trying to ignore their stares and smirks. It was just so foreign to me—this open hostility, this underlying current of *competition*. As if there was some scarcity of attention at North Foothill High—this tiny, nothing place! I thought of my easy access to the entire world beyond this city—all the randos I followed on social to learn about their weird snacks, pets, and ways to get hard-water stains off stainless steel. I guess these guys only had crappy magazines selling them a very specific version of teenagerhood. I sent up a prayer to my loose-jeaned, middle-parted Gen Z gods.

Priscilla nodded. "Yeah, sure." Deidre shot her a look, and Priscilla, surprisingly, shot one back at her. Deidre looked taken aback before she closed off into a mini huddle with the other girls.

I sat down on the bench by her feet. "So, I had an idea for an incentive."

"What is it?"

"What about offering discounted dry cleaning for homecoming outfits after the dance if you win? I could talk to your mom about it today!" I looked at Priscilla with excitement. This was genius, in my opinion. She wouldn't have to spend money and it was tied to the whole homecoming theme.

But her reaction was *not* was I was hoping for. "What? No, I don't want to do that." She pulled on her sunglasses and took a sip of her Diet Coke.

I bristled. "Why not?"

"*Because.*"

It was taking all of my willpower not to flick her on the forehead. Her easy dismissal of this legit great idea was infuriating.

Her gaze drifted somewhere beyond my left shoulder, and she smiled—holding up her hand in an awkward wave. I turned to see who she was waving to and saw Jennifer. She flashed a quick smile back as she walked by.

"Before you say anything smug," Priscilla said with an eye roll, "let me eat some salad." She shoved a forkful of unappetizing-looking dry lettuce into her mouth.

"I wasn't going to say anything," I said, my face neutral. "But Jennifer's okay, right?"

She shrugged. "Yeah, she's been cool since I helped them out with the shelter stuff. And, I'm going to help again this week, too."

"Asians: They can be your friends, too," I said drily.

"Shut up." But Priscilla was laughing when she said it, holding up her fork like she was going to pitch it at me.

Then, I caught a whiff of intense Sunflowers perfume (a scent that would haunt me for the rest of my days, alongside CK One). Steph Camillo was standing over me, looking down at what I was writing. "A dry cleaning coupon?" She said "dry cleaning" like someone would say "vaginal discharge."

Steph had honey-brown hair, a golden tan, and some kind of vague light eye color. She was cute and, at the moment, extremely nosy.

Deidre and the others kind of glanced at her with smirks from across the table. I remembered how they talked about her that first time in the hall. Something about Steph flagged her as unworthy to them. Maybe it was her cropped and ruffled white top that showed an inch of skin above of her blue-striped shorts. Her platform clogs. All of it together was just . . . a lot. And if there was one thing mean girls could sense, it was the *trying*. The very fine balance between looking good and looking like you wanted to look good. Priscilla existed in the highest tier of the social order here. And Steph—cuteness withstanding—was in a lower tier.

"Is that for homecoming?" she asked, persistent and pushy, looking down at my notes. I covered it with my hand.

Priscilla drawled, "Can I help you?" in the most bored voice possible. It was the voice of someone who couldn't care less about you—a tone that was meant to make you feel incredibly stupid. And even though I found Steph obnoxious, I flinched at the mean-girl activation I sensed in Priscilla.

Steph wasn't deterred. "Do your parents own a dry cleaner or something?"

Something about this hit Priscilla's cold exterior—leaving an almost indiscernible dent in her armor. But I saw it. The lightning quick glance at Deidre and the others. Her lips drew in. "Why do you care?" The response was more defensive than aloof.

"Just . . . interesting. You don't *act* like your parents own a dry cleaners," she said with a giggle. Implying that Priscilla acted like she was better than that.

I shut my notebook. "Can we help you with something?"

"I'm not talking to you," she said, pointedly looking at Priscilla.

While I hated to side with Deidre and Co., I also found Steph annoying as hell.

"Well, *I'm* talking to her, so can you cut the passive-aggressive shit-talking and get to the point?"

Steph turned red, aware of all the eyes on her. "I was *just* coming over to talk to Priscilla about the country club brunch. Jesus," Steph said, her composure returned. "Didn't realize she had like, the Korean mafia behind her."

"What?" I stood up, puffing like a cat. "Say that again."

Priscilla was suddenly between us. "Okay, calm down, Sam." I glanced at her and she was giving me a *look* and I immediately depuffed. When I looked around, I noticed that her entire group was watching us with amusement. Deidre was covering her mouth with her baby blue nails, her eyes crinkled with laughter. Neil and some of the other guys were hooting into their fists. None of them stepping in, it had to be noted. God, Priscilla's friends really were the worst.

"Just say what you came here to say, *Steph*." Priscilla looked at her with irritation.

She threw up her hands. "This got so *dramatic*, god! I was just going to remind you about the brunch on Thursday and that it's semiformal attire." She paused and her lip curled. "I'm sure you can get something *cleaned* by then." At that *killer* burn, she flounced away.

"Did you catch that Korean mafia comment?" I said, facing Priscilla.

Priscilla shook her head. "Steph's not worth it. Ignore her."

"Wooooow. You guys were all like, *gangsta*."

I whipped my head around at the girl who said it—Haley. She and Deidre both cracked up.

"*Gangsta?*" I said, my voice high and heavily inflected with Valley Girl. "Did you learn that word on, like, MTV?"

Haley's features clouded and Deidre glared at me. "Wow, *relax*. What are you, Priscilla's bodyguard?" Something about the words suggested something salacious.

"Korean *pride*," one of the dudes hollered—a guy with a mop of curly blond hair, bleached by chlorine, if his swim parka was any indication.

A ripple of anger went through me, and I looked at Priscilla with an "Are these people for real?" expression. But before she could react, Neil came over and draped his arm over her.

"Man, shut the hell up," he barked at the blond guy. "Priscilla's not into all that. And I think it's cool her mom owns a dry cleaners."

I wanted to roll my eyes at the white knight-ness of it all, but Priscilla beamed—one of her big, special smiles. The one she used on Tate at the country club, a smile that she wielded like a weapon. "Right? I'm always cleaner than all your asses."

Everyone laughed, the tension in the air instantly lightened. I saw a spark of triumph in Priscilla's eyes.

Deidre glanced at a group of Asian girls walking by us. "Yeah, Priscilla's not like *that*. With that tragic bleach-blond hair and knockoff Calvin Klein."

Priscilla tossed her hair back—a gesture I'd seen her do a million times both in the past and present—and the dark, glossy texture caught the sun just so. But the practiced gesture, like a lot of things Priscilla projected about herself, felt so natural. Like she *was* that person who fit into this group.

Neil's eyes followed the movement—first her hand, then the strands of her silky hair, and finally the cheekbone they grazed. She let his arm stay on her shoulders, and when the bell rang, he whispered something into her ear, the picture of intimacy.

Her smile never left her face, but it felt like part of the mask, the costume, she was wearing. It occurred to me that her acceptance into this group was conditional—on her acting like one of the "cool ones," on her letting racist shit slide, but maybe it also depended on Neil's crush on her. After all, I'd just seen firsthand the effect Neil's obnoxious alpha energy had on these people.

God, that was dark.

The bell rang to end lunch and I shoved my notebook back into my backpack, feeling exhausted by everything that had happened.

"Hey, Sam." Priscilla grabbed her cheerleading duffel and backpack next to me.

I looked at her warily. "Yeah?"

She adjusted her bags on her shoulders, taking her time to respond. "Thanks for trying to, you know, with Steph."

I shrugged. "She needed a punch to the throat, but I guess being yelled at will have to do."

A smile, a real one, broke out on Priscilla's face. "She's the worst. Now you know why I have to beat her."

"Oh, don't *even* worry about that. I feel renewed with vengeance." I was only half kidding. Now that I knew that Steph Camillo was the toughest competition, it was even more important that everything go according to plan. Everything was riding on those votes.

As the second bell rang, I found myself almost alone in the empty quad—everyone had already rushed off to fifth period. I envied them their simple urgencies as I worried about making it back to my own world.

nineteen

nineteen

five days to homecoming

I'm not saying I was a natural-born dry cleaner employee . . . but maybe I was a natural-born dry cleaner employee.

"Thank you, please come again!" I chirped cheerfully as a customer in all-brown knitwear ducked out the door, a skinny scarf unnecessarily draped around her neck—the long tail almost getting caught in the doors as she left.

Halmoni closed the register with a resounding clang. "Very nice," she said with a nod of approval.

Also, I'm not saying I'm a sucker for Halmoni compliments . . . but maybe I was a sucker for Halmoni compliments.

We'd spent most of the afternoon going over the basic running of the cleaners (with me feeling guilty at wasting her time; I would, hopefully, be leaving in five days, after all). I'd shadowed for a bit, but then Halmoni threw me into the deep end by having me take care of a few orders, and it was weirdly great?

But maybe it was just great hanging out with Halmoni. Like in the future—things were just easy between us. I'd been worried that, since I was her daughter's friend, she would be reserved with me.

Instead, she'd been the Halmoni I knew. Warm, helpful, and funny. Something about her was relaxed when Priscilla wasn't around.

I didn't forget why I was there, though. "I hope I'm half as good as Priscilla." My tone was light as I poked an order slip onto a metal stand on the countertop, the last of a pile of order slips layered like a pastry.

"Oh, you have one day, Priscilla has many," Halmoni said in a non-answer kind of way. "It is not fair to compare, right?"

I nodded, never able to argue against Halmoni wisdom. "Thank you, again, for letting me work here. I'm glad I can help out; it seems like Priscilla's always really busy."

"I should be thanking *you*," Halmoni said as she turned on one of the dryers. She was never idle, hands and body constantly moving. "Priscilla . . . I know I ask too much of her."

There it was. My way into Priscilla talk. "She does a lot," I agreed. "But I understand—you have a lot on your plate, too."

Halmoni paused, then her voice grew more measured, thoughtful. "You know their father died four years ago?"

Obviously, I did know. But Sam of 1995 didn't know. I shook my head. "No, I'm so sorry."

Even though I'd lived my entire life without having known my grandfather, with knowing him only as part of my family history—something about Halmoni's mention of him made my throat tighten up. I nodded in response.

"It was a hard time for all of us. But it was very hard for Priscilla. Grace, she was so little. But Priscilla—she was her father's daughter. She always loved him the most." At my move to protest, Halmoni shook her head. "No, it's true. And that is okay. They had a special relationship. And to lose your father at that age . . ." Her voice trailed off as she kept her hands busy, always moving. Hands so familiar to me. "It's hard. And I worry about her, still."

The air felt dense—heavy with emotion. Halmoni's worry and heartbreak was palpable, and I wished I could be helpful. "Priscilla is doing so great," I managed to say. "You shouldn't worry too much."

Halmoni looked at me, her eyes both happy and sad. "Oh, I know at school she is doing great. She puts everything into school. Her friends. Then there's not much left for home, you know? And maybe she doesn't want to be home. Because it's not the same without her father. There is nothing for her here anymore." She said it lightly, like it was no big deal—but the words themselves, oof.

"But isn't that normal for a teenager?" I asked, trying to match the lightness in her tone. "In America, anyway." Wasn't that what I was always doing? Pushing against my mom? My dad and Julian? Defining myself by what they *weren't*.

I was totally aware of how weird it was to be defending my mother to Halmoni. What a trip. But I needed to figure this out, make things better between them. And then I had another thought—this strain between them. If it was the reason why she felt she had to hide her heart condition from us, maybe it had even indirectly led to Halmoni's heart attack.

Get Mom to win homecoming. Prevent fight. Fix their relationship forever. Maybe even prevent Halmoni from falling into a coma in the first place.

The connections were everywhere, and I was in my mind-mapping trance when Halmoni said, "Sam? Did you hear me?"

I snapped out of it. "Yes? Sorry! I was thinking about . . . homework."

Halmoni gave me a teasing look. "Don't lie."

My laughter made her laugh. She shook her head as she folded a sweater in tissue paper. "You are very easy to talk to, Sam."

While it made me happy to hear that, I realized it was also obvious: Other people's families were always easier to deal with than your own.

Your own? That was hard work. I spent the rest of the workday helping clean up, and Halmoni and I did it in amiable silence—the feelings between us easy and untarnished by any history. I relished every second.

I was alone on my bus ride back to school, so I took the risk of turning on my phone, hitting record.

> Halmoni, I wish you had told me about your heart condition. Did you think I wasn't strong enough to handle the news? Or was it not about me—but rather something you wanted to keep to yourself, to not make it the center of your life? Either way, we can't change the past, can we?

I paused. This would have been true a week ago. Now . . . now it was all different. I *could* change the past. If helping Mom and Halmoni's relationship in the past could possibly prevent the heart attack—well, that was all the motivation I needed to keep going. There was absolutely no turning back now. I hit record again.

> Even if we can't change the past—we can change the future. When you wake up, you'll see. You'll see how different it can be.

twenty

twenty

five days to homecoming

I had been both dreading and anticipating meeting Jamie for our project, and when I finished up at the cleaners, I had sweat through my sweatshirt again on the bus ride back to school.

When I got to school, it was quiet and empty. That meant I had a minute to collect myself before seeing Jamie. We had agreed to meet out in front, since he would be coming from football practice.

It was getting pretty obvious that I was kind of crushing on him. Which—okay, whatever. Human beings are gonna human. It's okay to be attracted to someone other than your boyfriend or *whoever*. But it was another thing to keep hanging out with this other person. Hours of alone time with this guy was *not good*. And there was the whole "in my timeline Jamie is a middle-aged man" aspect.

As I waited for Jamie, my fingers itched to reach for my phone, which I kept in my windbreaker pocket at all times. But last I checked, the battery was at 60 percent. The Halmoni notes were taking a toll on my dumb battery. Before I could waste another precious drop of battery power, I saw Jamie coming down the stairs.

"Hey," he said with a short wave, stopping in front of me. "Sorry if I kept you waiting."

Why was politeness so attractive? "I was barely waiting, no worries. So, where should we go to do this boring research?"

He pretended to think. "I don't know, how about this place called the public library?"

"Right," I said quickly. Hoping that he mistook my very real question for a joke.

We both stood there for a second. "Oh, uh, I don't have a car," I clarified.

"Neither do I," he said with a grimace. "I usually take the bus."

"Me, too!"

The excitement was a bit much for shared bus experiences, but he didn't seem to notice. "Cool. Let's do it."

We crossed the street to the bus stop and waited, the only people there. I tried to cool my feelings for Jamie off by doing the math to figure out his age in my time.

"You cold?" Jamie asked me suddenly. I realized I had visibly shuddered. At the thought of his future old-man face.

"No, I'm okay," I said, clapping my hands as if to affirm my robust health. "Do you know where the library is?"

He nodded. "Yeah, it's not that far. Just a few stops away. Next to the mall."

The bus pulled up and both of us dropped some quarters in before walking toward the back. I found us a couple seats and we plopped down next to each other, our shoulders almost touching. Why couldn't bus seats have a respectable space between them?

"It's your job to pull the thingy when our stop is near," I said. "It gives me massive anxiety."

"The anticipation of having to pull it?" he asked, his eyes serious and not teasing.

"Yes! Like, what if I forget? What if I do it too soon? What if I overlap with someone else and, like, it cancels each other out?"

The bus came to a stop, and we lurched forward slightly. Jamie looked up at the cord running along the wall of the bus and I felt embarrassed at having revealed this deeply boring paranoia of mine.

But Jamie just leaned over, his arm and shoulder brushing against me, and tapped the cord lightly with his finger. "All right. I got this. No worries, Samantha."

I wondered if he was being serious or sarcastic or what, but I realized he was just being . . . him. A little weird, reserved, but thoughtful.

After a moment, Jamie asked, "So, why did your family move here?"

I tapped my foot on the grimy, fuzzy bus floor. "My dad's job. He's a doctor." Staying close to the truth was best, right? "What about you? Why'd you guys move here?"

Late afternoon sun flashed on his face as he answered. "Family. My mom wanted to be closer to her family."

"Oh, is she from here?"

Jamie nodded. "Yeah, she grew up in LA. My grandparents, aunts, and uncles all live really close."

"That's nice."

It felt like such an obvious, non-thing to say. But he nodded and was quiet for a second before saying, "It is nice, actually. My mom . . . she's a single mom. She raised me pretty much all by herself after she divorced my dad. So, I think even if I'm, like, pretty much grown, it's good for her to have support."

There was loneliness in his words. I thought of Halmoni, raising two kids by herself. And while I had a billion questions (Where's your dad? Do you ever see him? Why did your mom leave LA? Why didn't she come back sooner?), I kept it to, "My mom says that your kids are always going to be your kids no matter how old they are. She said this when my older brother, Julian, left for college and was texting him every hour like a freak."

"You have a brother?" Jamie's attention was as laser-focused as always, and I resisted the urge to break eye contact.

"Yeah. He's my only sibling. He's only a couple years older than me but we're very different."

"How?"

There was no small talk with this guy. "Well, he's kind of a genius. Like, I don't say that lightly. He was a child prodigy, featured in the *New York Times* because he built a"—god, I had to be careful here—"robot thing. I don't even really understand it," I said with a laugh, breezing over the details of the miniature drone that could help pollinate flowers. "He's at Yale now."

"Whoa," Jamie said, leaning forward, propping his elbows onto his knees, which was no easy task in the small space. "So, how does that make you different?"

I leaned back. "Are you joking? He's a genius. I'm . . . not."

"So, yeah, he's really good at academics. But what else? Are your personalities different?"

I hesitated, not sure how to answer. "Well, yes, aside from the genius versus not-genius thing, we do have very different personalities. This is going to sound stereotypical or something, but it's true. He's really, um, introverted? Like, shy and not great in social situations."

"So, completely the opposite of you? I've seen the way you talk to people."

I was pleased and embarrassed. "I guess?"

"Um, not that I was watching you or anything." Very adorably, his high cheek bones turned pink. Like someone turned on the sweet blushing filter on his face. "It's just that, I've noticed how you seem to be comfortable around other people. In tune with them."

"Yeah." I shrugged. "It comes easier to me than Julian, that's for sure. He's definitely not really in tune with people's emotions. Very similar to my mom, actually."

"That must be hard," Jamie said quietly.

Something about the way Jamie immediately understood made my eyes water. I blinked rapidly, trying to make this cursed crying compulsion stop. "It can be."

He turned to me, on the verge of making some kind of sympathetic gesture that would *definitely* open the floodgates, but then he suddenly got to his feet and reached over me to pull the cord. The bell dinged.

"It's the next stop," he declared a little too proudly.

"My hero," I said with a grin, emotions-onslaught safely contained.

The library was busy in that hushed library way. Familiar and unfamiliar, like all the places I'd been visiting in the past. The carpet was a different color, the furniture more mid-century modern than its current depressing hospital-waiting-room vibe. But everything was laid out the same. The beautiful old clock in the center of the main room the same, the smell of books the same, the giant wall of windows letting in yellow afternoon light the same.

Because we weren't sure where to start, we decided to go to the experts. A nice librarian wearing a literal sweater vest and glasses chain led us to a reference section that had a few shelves full of bound records on congressional bills.

"Oh! And you'll also want to see the many ways bills can be both passed and thwarted. Let's go set you both up on some microfiche machines so you can read up on some news in the periodicals section," the librarian said. He started walking briskly toward a different room. I nodded my head like I knew what the hell that was.

We followed him to a bank of machines that looked like old-school PCs. There was a lone woman sitting in front of one, her face close to the screen as she used her right hand to turn a knob and the left to hold what looked like a small film reel she was feeding through the bottom. The film was then magnified on the screen, showing black-and-white photocopies of newspaper pages. Depending on how the woman turned the knob on her right, the film scrolled either slowly or quickly on the screen, the machine whirring loudly with each motion.

We were supposed to look through years of newspapers this way? PAGE BY PAGE? With no search function? This thing looked like something out of an eighties movie about the future, like *Blade Runner: Library Edition*.

"Let me grab you some pertinent film—some of the big newspapers the past couple years." When the librarian walked away, Jamie and I stared at the machines. Was this a normal thing that people just automatically knew how to use? Would it be like someone in my time not knowing how to use a cell phone? I started to sweat and deeply regretted this entire research trip.

Before I could have a full-blown panic attack, the librarian returned, handing me a plastic caddy full of little film reels before ambling away.

I quickly offered the box to Jamie. "Why don't you do the honors?"

He reached into the box and grabbed a reel. "Sure." I watched closely as he sat down at a machine and methodically set up the film. When he flipped a switch, the screen lit up and a newspaper page was illuminated, like the screen of the woman next to us.

"Cool!" I said without thinking. *Way to act like you're seeing electricity for the first time!*

Jamie looked pretty satisfied himself. "That's why I get paid the big bucks." He paused. "I don't know why I said that."

I placed the reels on the table and pulled up a chair next to him. "You deserve the big bucks, sir. I'm not, um, savvy with this thing."

"It's not the most advanced tech, that's for sure." *Oh. Oh, good.* Then I wasn't too much of a weirdo for not knowing how to use one.

"Should we start with the politics section?" I asked.

"Sure," he said, gripping the knob and turning it toward him. The pages started to fly by at light speed, whirring loudly, and I gasped.

"Oh, shit," he muttered, letting go of the knob like a hot potato.

We both took a second to look at where the microfiche landed—on the comics section. Marmaduke looked back at us mischievously. Laughter bubbled through my chest, and I pressed my lips together to keep it bottled up.

"Weird," Jamie said, his lips in a dissatisfied, straight line. "Didn't expect that." He touched the knob again, tentatively. He turned it by the tiniest of degrees, this time away from him. The pages "rewound" and we crept through the newspaper. "Crept" being the operative word.

I suggested, "Maybe, we can go a little faster?"

"Yeah, yup. Probably better," Jamie said, pushing up his glasses. He turned it a little less gently and the pages started scrolling by faster—but not so fast that we couldn't read the headlines and section headers.

Okay, great, we were getting the hang of it. I leaned forward to get a closer look and accidentally knocked my elbow into Jamie's arm. The pages started to fly by at a crazy speed again.

"Gah!" I yanked myself back. "Sorry!"

But Jamie wasn't paying attention because the film was flying through the machine so fast that the whirring became a high-pitched noise. The woman at the other machine turned to stare at us. Then, before we could stop it, the reel reached the end and *flew off*—slamming into the wall near the woman before dramatically clattering onto the floor.

I stared at the film as it spun around for what seemed like five hundred years. Jamie was completely silent next to me.

"How about we go check out those bound records?" I squeaked.

Jamie nodded quickly. "Yup."

We scurried off, holding back laughter, not able to get out of microfiche hell fast enough. Once we were far enough away, we ducked between some shelves in the biography section, catching our breaths. I looked up at Jamie with a grin. "Do you think the microfiche police will find us here?"

He grinned back, a slight sheen of sweat coating his forehead. "In this *incredible* hiding spot? No way."

Our laughter was muffled as we tried not to attract attention, but when we stopped, Jamie and I locked eyes. I straightened up and quickly walked past him. "Let's go find our Act of Congress!"

After a few minutes perusing the shelves, we landed on one that seemed interesting: the National Environmental Policy Act of 1970.

I read aloud from the act's description in the book: "After a century of rapid economic expansion, it was becoming clear that American progress had an environmental cost." *No shit.* "A congressional investigation revealed evidence of extreme mismanagement of the country's environment and resources. Lawmakers and the public alike called for an urgent and sweeping policy of environmental protection." I raised my eyebrows at Jamie. "This is juicy."

He laughed. "Would never have called a congressional act juicy, but yeah, I guess you're right."

"It's huge!" I said. "Hundreds of other countries would follow suit. It was the first time human beings would begin to consider the repercussions of all their consumption. I know how we can present this!"

Jamie and I spent the next couple hours figuring out the details. I didn't know if it was because Jamie was such a helpful partner or what, but it was the first time in a long time that I felt energized by a school project. I felt a responsibility to present this act in a way that would make an impression on the other students. Maybe environmental activism wasn't the actual reason I had been sent back in time, but since I was here, why not do some good? After all, Gen X was part of the problem, bro.

As I pored over my notes, I could imagine my mom's voice saying, "Can you put it on your college applications, though?" When I giggled, Jamie looked at me questioningly.

I said, "Ah, marching toward a warming planet, so funny."

He didn't miss a beat. "What's the deal with greenhouse gases?" The Seinfeld impression was so terrible that I started laughing harder. We were shushed by another librarian lurking around the corner and we both sank down into our seats.

I hid my smile behind my book. The trick to making school interesting? Time travel, I guess. Go figure.

twenty-one

twenty-one

four days to homecoming

When I got to homeroom, Priscilla was chatting with a group of people—*not* her usual pals, I noticed. Maybe she was actually taking my advice to mingle with the common folk to heart!

With her facial expression cool and her posture perfect, she felt so distant—like a different person from the girl I'd hung out with at the cleaners. It was almost like *this* Priscilla was a costume she put on. Armor, really. Not just to survive as one of the few Korean kids here, but to *thrive*. Mom never half-assed anything. Maybe I kind of understood her whole "don't want to be one of the Korean kids." And not just because they didn't seem to accept her.

To Priscilla, succeeding wasn't just getting into Harvard. It was the cheerleading uniform, the homecoming queen tiara. And in the future, it was the country club membership. There was a security to being seen as the all-American girl everyone envied at school.

But there *had* to be space for some overlap there—these two existences couldn't be as polarized as Priscilla thought. I just didn't know if that space existed in the nineties.

The bell rang and Mr. Finn read from the announcements. I zoned out until I heard him say, "Oh, and the homeroom channel is back up! Let's watch today's news."

Homeroom channel? He picked up a remote and turned on the boxy square TV bolted in a corner of the class.

On screen, three students were lined up in a low-budget "news studio," talking about homecoming. It was just all homecoming, all the time here. There was even a Homecoming Countdown Clock on the screen—"4 Days" flashed alarmingly. Thirsty for any distraction, everyone in class turned their heads to watch. It was probably mundane stuff to everyone else—but it was primo intel for me.

The news anchor, a girl with curly red hair and intense braces, looked seriously at the camera as she discussed the football team. "The Coyotes feel great about their chances of winning the game this year. Between new quarterback Joshua Enni and all-state champ Teddy Quintero, we're sure to have a great season."

Two images of football players posing in uniform flashed on screen—I recognized one of them as the guy who interrupted me and Jamie on the football field the other day.

"And now, let's move on to the homecoming court," the anchor continued. A shot of all the nominees standing for a corny group photo came up on screen. Priscilla, who was in front of me, sat up in her seat. "Our court this year is made up of princesses Stephanie Camillo, Alexandra Gunner, Priscilla Jo, and Tessa Martin. Our princes are Devin Connors, Eliot Bender, Neil Harper, and Jason Russell. Votes will be open to the entire school and cast during sixth period this Friday, and the king and queen will be announced at the dance. May the best man and woman win!"

I looked around and noticed the way everyone was glued to the screen. What they lacked in social media they had in a boring television channel. I had an idea.

I tapped Priscilla on the shoulder. "Hey."

She glanced over. "What?"

"Can you talk at morning break today?" I kept my voice low, but Deidre noticed me anyway and scowled. I smiled and flipped her off.

Priscilla pulled out her notebook, opening it up to some math equations. "Um, yeah, sure."

I smirked. "What, are you doing extra credit work in your spare time? Math fun just for giggles?"

She scoffed. "Spare time? No, this is my homework I couldn't get to yesterday. I had to make dinner because my mom ended up working late."

"Oh." Geez. *Not everything has to be a damn joke, Sam!* "Sorry."

"Why are you sorry?" she asked. "You didn't choose my life for me." It was said casually, not bitterly, but her words made me feel sludgy with emotion. I was actually regretful about not being able to *really* exist in this timeline for longer—to help Halmoni out after school for not just a few days, but a few months. While the monstrous concern-trolling by that Mrs. Lim lady the other day was completely unwelcome, things *were* hard for Halmoni. And it trickled down to Priscilla. Although, looking at her pristine, blown-out hair and fuzzy, baby-blue angora sweater—you'd never know it.

I realized that somehow, along the way, I really did want Priscilla to win homecoming queen. Not just for me to go home, but because it meant something to my mom.

She glanced up then. "Also? Seriously, why haven't you bought new clothes yet?" she whispered. "Are you poor or something?"

The feeling went away as quickly as it came. My lips pressed together, and I sat back in my seat to watch the rest of the newscast.

By the time break rolled around, I was feeling itchy in my skin. I was headed to the snack bar to meet Priscilla when I stopped in my tracks—frozen in front of one of the posters we had taped up early that morning, on the brick exterior of the cafeteria.

It said "VOTE PRISCILLA FOR HOMECOMING QUEEN!" bordered by hand-drawn tiaras and flowers. And now it had a giant red slash over the words—violent and ugly. On top of the words were "POSER SNOB." There were two other posters on either side of hers—one for Steph and the other for Eliot, one of the princes. And neither were defaced. Just Priscilla's.

My scalp was in danger of popping off from the steam building in my head. "Who the *hell*?" I yelled to no one in particular. People laughed as they walked by and caught a glimpse of the defaced sign.

A low whistle behind me turned my head. It was Teddy, that guy who had hit Jamie with the football the other day. Up close, he had severe but not unattractive features—knife-sharp cheekbones, a heavy brow. "That sucks, dude."

I clenched my jaw. "Yeah. I'm gonna *end* the person who did this."

He raised his eyebrows. "I believe you. Feel sorry for the chick who did this."

"Chick?" I asked, ignoring the stupid word. "Why do you think it's a girl?"

He looked at me like I must be joking. "You serious? Who the hell else would care about homecoming queen? No disrespect to your gender."

Hmm. He actually had a point, as annoying as it was to admit.

Another guy walked by and punched his shoulder, and Teddy grinned at him and walked away. "Priscilla's lucky to have a G like you have her back. Good luck with that!"

I flushed—embarrassed but also kind of pleased to be seen as protective of Priscilla. I stared hard at the poster. This would not deter me. Or Priscilla. The paper made a satisfying rip as I pulled the poster down and shoved it into a nearby trash can. I'd find out who did this. Teddy was onto something. This was probably not so much a random act of violence as someone who specifically didn't want Priscilla to win. Steph seemed like the obvious culprit, but I had no idea how Tessa and Alexandra felt about her, either. While Priscilla was popular, it was definitely possible that she could have several enemies.

My face managed to compose itself when I approached the snack bar where Priscilla was working.

"Hey!" I pushed my way to the front of the line, making a couple people swear at me. She glanced up as she grabbed a bag of Flamin' Hot Cheetos for someone. I waited patiently while she sold it to a tiny girl wearing baggy overalls and Adidas slides. (Some things just made a *complete* comeback, I guess.) Before she left, the girl hesitated and smiled shyly at Priscilla. "I'm excited to vote for you for homecoming queen!" Then she scurried off to her friends—a group of equally tiny freshmen who giggled with her.

I grinned and sauntered up to Priscilla. "Well, look at that!"

Priscilla tried not to look too pleased. "You are *so* smug."

"I know," I said, rapping my knuckles on the counter. "And I'm going to become insufferable when you actually win."

"I believe it. What's up?" Priscilla asked as she popped open the register.

I wasn't going to tell her about the poster yet. "I have an idea. Watching that news thingy this morning in homeroom made me think that you should do a segment as part of your campaign! Get you some publicity!"

Clearly, we had been making progress getting Priscilla's face and name out there, but with only four days left until the vote, we needed to ramp it up.

She wrinkled her nose as she tucked some bills into the tray. "Ew. That dorky show?"

"OMG, Priscilla. Get over the dorks for a minute."

"What? 'OMG'? What are you *talking* about?"

A world without "OMG." OMG.

"Uh, just my shorthand for 'oh my god.'"

The register clanged shut. "That is so . . . unnecessary. It's the same amount of syllables."

Hmm. She was absolutely correct. "Whatever. Let's go approach the news 'dorks' about it so we can get it on air before the dance!"

I heard a throat clear behind me.

It was Jamie, of course. What the *hell*, how was this guy everywhere? I instantly felt my cheeks get hot.

"Hi, I'm one of the news dorks," he said. "I'm the camera guy."

"Really?!" I grabbed his arm. "Ooh, can you help us? We need to film something."

He looked down at my hand, quick as lightning, then said, "Sure. I'm headed there at lunch, have to go film a few things in the studio. It's in the green building, room forty-five."

"Cool, we'll see you there!" I let go of his arm and let him buy his peanut butter crackers before waving bye to him when he left.

I was grinning when I turned back to Priscilla, until I saw her sly expression.

"What's with you two, anyway?"

Heat rushed through me. "Nothing!"

She smirked. "Okay."

"I have a boyfriend." I said it so loudly that two people near us stared. "See you at lunch, okay? Don't ditch me for your douchebag friends!"

"You're really making this fun!" she called out when I walked away.

Then I ran back to the trash can and dug the poster out. After carefully folding it up into a neat rectangle, I slid it into my backpack.

• • •

I got to the news studio before Priscilla did and found Jamie in there, alone. He was sitting on the edge of the news desk, fiddling with a piece of camera equipment. It was dark except for a spotlight right on him.

Way to be subtle, universe.

"Hey."

He looked up at me, that floppy curl falling into his face again. His nose wrinkled a bit as he pushed up his glasses. "Hey, Samantha."

Samantha. No one called me that but my mom, and there was something about the way he said it that made me forget for a second why I was there.

"What did you need to film?" he asked as I walked up. He placed the camera thingamajig next to him and brushed his hands off on his jeans—jeans that actually fit him, by the way, unlike the giant ones falling off every guy's ass in 1995.

"I wanted to interview Priscilla for a segment. For homecoming stuff. Do you think the news kids would air it?"

"I think so. You could talk to Taylor, who's in charge of the programing. I can introduce you after school if you want."

"Oh, awesome, that would be great. Thanks!"

He looked at me in that unnervingly focused way. "You know, I wouldn't have thought that you and Priscilla would already be such good friends. Didn't you just move here?"

"Well . . . I wouldn't call us *good* friends. Yet."

"Which is weirder, right?" he asked, tapping his fingers on the news desk. My eyes were immediately drawn to this movement. He had really nice hands.

"Why is that weird?"

"Well, why would you help someone this much who *wasn't* your friend? What's in it for you?" It wasn't accusatory exactly, just genuinely curious. I couldn't blame him. None of this made any freaking sense if anyone took five minutes to pay attention. And I really didn't need Jamie paying attention.

I wished I had something to do with *my* hands. "Um, well. Like you said, I'm new. Priscilla's popular, and I thought maybe she would introduce me to her friends."

"No offense, but I think you could make better friends. She hangs out with some real shitheads."

My shoulders pulled back a little. "She's not as bad as most of them. Once you get past her . . . exterior."

He didn't argue with me. "All right."

"But correct, her friends seriously suck." I slid a glance at him. "It's not easy being the new kid."

He laughed, looking down at his feet. "Yeah, I guess not."

A moment of silence passed between us, and I felt the need to fill it.

"Speaking of the campaign, I found this today." I pulled the poster out of my backpack and unfolded it on the table.

Jamie leaned over it, bracing his hands on the edge of the table. "Whoa. Sick burn."

I laughed. "Yeah, I know it's a weak attempt at sabotage but—"

"It's still bad." He glanced up at me. "Do you know who did it?"

"No, but I am going to find out. Mark." I tapped the poster. "My." *Tap*. "Words." *Tap*.

His shoulders shook with silent laughter, and I hit him in the arm. "I'm serious!"

"Yeah, I know. That's why it's funny." His eyes were sparkling. *Sparkling*. "Do you have any leads?"

"No." I stared down at the poster. "But look at that handwriting. It's a girl's, right? I know it's stupid to say that, because it's not like handwriting is indicative of anything. But no guy would be caught dead with this writing." In 1995, anyway. "Also, your friend Teddy made the point that only a girl would care enough about homecoming queen to deface this poster."

Jamie gave the handwriting the same focused, unhurried attention he seemed to give everything else. His eyes carefully traced the path of the half cursive "N" with its flourish on the end. "Yeah, I think you're right," he said.

"So, obviously, the most likely culprit is one of the other girls on the homecoming court." I stood back. "But which one? Do you think it's someone who hates her? Or just wants to beat her?"

He shrugged. "Honestly, I have no idea why anyone would do something so stupid and obvious as this, but maybe both?"

Before I could respond, the door to the studio flew open.

"What's up, dorks," Priscilla's voice boomed. I hurried to hide the poster, but her eagle eyes landed right on it.

"What's that?" She walked over, her Mary Janes clacking with each step.

"Uh . . . one of your posters. Or it was." I reluctantly moved aside so she could see it.

She paused for about two seconds to take it all in before smoothing her hair back. "So immature." Then she glanced over at me and Jamie, both of us hovering anxiously. "Why do you guys even have this here? Throw it out."

"I want to figure out who did it," I said, folding it back up.

"Why?" Priscilla crossed her arms. Everything about her closed up.

"Because . . ." I zipped my backpack, the poster safely back inside. "It's messed up. I want to bring them to justice."

"Oh my god." Priscilla threw her arms up in the air. "Who cares? Just leave it alone. Clearly, some bored creep went around messing up everyone's posters."

"I didn't see any other posters with this crap on it," I said, refusing to budge.

"Let it go," Priscilla said, her voice firm and no-nonsense. Very reminiscent of Mom Voice. "Why focus on something I can't control?"

Jamie coughed then. "Um, we don't have much time to use this room, so . . ."

"Right." I turned to him, apologetic for wasting his time with our Veronica Mars antics.

"Thanks for helping," Priscilla said to Jamie, her good manners kicking in. "So, what are we doing?" she asked, fluffing up her hair. "Should I put on more makeup?"

This immediate switch into professionalism after seeing her posters defaced, ignoring my thirst for vengeance—it reminded me of Mom brushing off my concerns about Oakwood Country Club and its (probable) racist history. I always chalked up Mom's compartmentalizing as a sort of cowardice or lack of fire. Kind of like Gen X immigrant-kid-assimilation lizard brain.

But now, I wasn't sure. Maybe it was just a form of survival, picking her battles in a life full of them. I swallowed the knot in my throat.

"I thought I'd ask you a few questions off camera and then Jamie would record you answering them." I pulled out my notebook where I had written down some questions. "He can handle the setup and all that."

Jamie steered Priscilla by her elbow, toward the news desk. "I think we'll just have you stand here. I'll film you close-up, so we don't get the desk or anything else in the shot."

"Great, but do *I* look okay?" Priscilla asked with exasperation.

He grinned. "Yeah, you always look great."

She flushed and I frowned. *Um, no, thank you.*

Once Jamie had the camera and lighting set up the way he wanted it, I stood next to him with my questions in hand.

"All right, here we go!" I clapped my hands. "Please introduce yourself first—name, grade, all that."

She gave a hair toss then smiled radiantly into the camera. "Hi, I'm Priscilla. I'm a senior and I'm running for homecoming queen."

What a natural. I nodded approvingly. "Why should people vote for you for homecoming queen? Answer it in a complete sentence so you don't need to hear the question to understand what you're talking about."

Jamie looked at me in surprise. "Nice."

Priscilla took a second, looking up at the ceiling, silently mouthing some words. Then she cleared her throat and smiled into the camera again. "You should all vote for me for homecoming queen because I'm a great representative for this school. I'm cheer captain, class secretary, and a straight-A student. I've got school spirit in spades and would look great in a crown, too." With that she gave a little wink.

I laughed. "That was great. Okay, now, why does winning homecoming queen mean so much to you?"

She nodded then took another beat before speaking, "Winning homecoming queen means a lot because it means you all care about wanting only the best for North Foothill High. See you at the game!"

It was said perfectly, and Jamie stopped filming. But it wasn't what I was hoping for. "That was good. But let's make it more personal."

It was like I had given her a B-plus. She crossed her arms. "Personal, how?"

I thought about my own perplexed reactions to Mom in the future about homecoming. About all the stuff that mattered to her. "Why don't you explain what homecoming means to you? All these American traditions? Because that's what sets you apart from everyone else—you're a child of an immigrant. This means something different for you."

There was a flicker of emotion in her eyes. Vulnerability. "That feels . . . I don't know, *too* personal."

"It's not. Trust me. People need to get to know you—the *real* you—to vote for you."

She put her hands on her hips and stared down at the floor. I worried she was going to refuse, but then she looked up, straightened her posture, and tossed her hair. "Okay, I'm ready."

I looked to Jamie who started recording.

Priscilla looked straight into the camera and softened her features. "Winning homecoming queen is meaningful to me because it's a step closer to my parents' American dream. That's why they came here—to give me every opportunity. I want to represent our school with your support. And, besides, what's more American than homecoming queen?" And with that, she gave a knowing smile.

When Jamie and I were silent, Priscilla looked between us with trepidation. "Oh, no, was it that bad?"

I shook my head, trying to keep my voice measured and not give away how deeply touched I actually was. "No, that was so good. Perfect."

She looked pleased. "Really? It wasn't too cheesy?"

"No way," said Jamie, leaning against the camera. "It was great. And you're great on camera."

"Is there a way to make sure they'd air this for us by Friday?" I asked Jamie, annoyed by him complimenting Priscilla again. "We need to make sure everyone sees it before they vote."

"I'll ask the producer today."

"You mean Taylor?" Priscilla interrupted. "Don't worry, I'll talk to him." The assurance was steel in her voice, and honestly, I believed that anyone would do anything for her. Like when my mom would ask if a new discount could be applied to a previous purchase. Like when she told my seventh-grade tennis instructor that she'd prefer if he didn't raise his voice to motivate me. People just listened to my mother. And hopefully, with this amazing spot, we just gave my mom a megaphone.

"Thanks for your help," I said to Jamie.

He looked up from fiddling around with camcorder, dark eyes barely visible through his hair. "Anytime, Samantha."

Again. *Samantha*. I felt warm all over.

Priscilla interrupted the tension, "Thanks, both of you." She squinted at me. "What are you doing after work today?"

"Um, a whole lot of nothing."

"Do you want to go shopping?"

"Huh? Shopping?"

"Yeah." Priscilla pursed her lips. "It's just that you've been wearing the same clothes for many days in a row."

Right. "Are we going to partake in a *makeover*? Like, at the mall?" I took my Valley girl drawl to new heights.

"Just stop. I'll pick you up at the cleaners."

"Will the mall still be open that late?"

"Yeah, you've never been to the mall in the evening?"

"No, have never partaken—partook?—in such wonders."

"Why are you like this?" She fluttered a hand goodbye before closing the door behind her.

"Well, maybe you're not such an odd pairing after all," Jamie said, shaking his head. "Something just makes sense with you guys. I see it, now."

The pleasure at hearing that caught me off guard and I hid it by hitting him on the arm. Way too jovially—all, "Hey, friend-o!"

The studio felt way too intimate suddenly. I held up a hand. "See you later, bro!"

I walked away cringing, yet again.

twenty-two

twenty-two

four days to homecoming

"Sam, are you busy tomorrow evening?"

I looked up from stapling some invoices together. "Tomorrow?"

Halmoni nodded. "Yes. I thought you could have dinner with us at home?"

Warmth spread through me. "Oh, sure!"

She looked at me sternly. "You don't have to check with parents?"

Oh. "I mean, yes, after I ask them. But I'm sure it'll be okay."

"Oh, yes, because we're Korean." Halmoni nodded sagely.

I laughed. "Yes, that's why."

We were still laughing when Priscilla walked in. She looked at us, a smile hovering on her face. But it was one of those "confused and annoyed by my confusion" smiles that didn't quite reach her eyes. "What's going on?" she asked.

Halmoni's laughter faded and something about her expression closed up, too. I grabbed my backpack from under the counter. "Oh, just talking about dinner tomorrow," I said.

"Dinner?" A tiny line appeared between Priscilla's eyes.

Halmoni briskly answered, "Yes, I ask Sam to join us tomorrow. Going to make galbi jjim."

"Great," Priscilla said breezily—but her light tone was covering up something else, I was sure of it. "Hope my mom hasn't been running you ragged already."

Halmoni frowned as she pressed some slacks, the steaming sound loud and satisfying. My back was sweaty under my backpack as I tried to navigate the unease. "Ha! No way, it's been fun."

"Okay, see you tomorrow," Halmoni said. "Priscilla, you going home?"

"No, actually, I'm taking Sam shopping," she said. "If that's okay." That made me pause. Did I *ever* have to ask my mom's permission to go to the *mall*?

"Shopping?" Halmoni's tone was critical, but then she relented, maybe because I was involved. "Okay. Just be home by nine, okay?"

"Okay, bye!" Priscilla was already halfway out the door and I waved goodbye before I was at her heels.

"Thank you!" I called out. And Halmoni nodded, smiling. The trust in it filling me with warmth.

* * *

It was amazing what a difference thirty years made for malls. The Garden—the big, sprawling outdoor one that dominated North Foothill—didn't exist yet. Instead, Priscilla drove us to the bricked relic that no one ever shopped at anymore. Well, at least they didn't in my time.

In 1995? It was *bumping*.

The food court barely had any available seats, the smell of Orange Julius permeated the air, and there were actual people in the Sharper Image store, testing out massage chairs.

"You don't have to watch Grace tonight?" I asked Priscilla as we walked by a giant fountain with pennies piled up on the bottom.

She shook her head. "My aunt takes her to swim classes Tuesdays and then she hangs with the cousins until my mom picks her up."

"Do you have to watch her a lot?"

"Yeah, because my mom works all day." Priscilla paused. "As you've probably noticed by now, my dad died a few years ago."

The din of the mall crowd felt really loud when I responded with a quiet, "I'm sorry."

I had wondered if Priscilla would bring up my grandfather. I thought of my talk with Halmoni yesterday, and about that awful run-in with Mrs. Lim over the weekend.

She looked straight ahead, not breaking her purposeful stride. "It's okay. I mean, it's not, but you know. It is what it is."

The nothing-phrase felt practiced. It was the nonchalant ease with which she said it. I didn't respond, hoping she'd say more. But she didn't and I didn't want to press any further. We continued to walk through the crowds, and I soaked in the nineties of it all, registering every single thing—the fashion, the pay phones, the horrible typography on stores I'd never heard of. But some of the stores in the mall hadn't changed at all and I stopped when I recognized one. "Should we go in there?"

Priscilla glanced up. "Banana? Do you have a lot of money with you? It's nice stuff."

I blinked. Going into a Banana Republic would be the absolute last resort store for my mom if we were in a fashion wasteland. She never shopped at chain stores anymore.

I thought of the cash Mrs. Jo had given me. "Oh, I got money from . . . my parents this morning."

"Must be nice. Fine, let's go in."

The bitterness in her voice was just as surprising as Priscilla willingly shopping at a Banana Republic. Mom would never let anyone catch her feeling jealous or petty. If a neighbor remodeled their kitchen with a killer Viking stove, my mom would be generous in her praise, never letting on that it was her dream stove. Nothing won out over Mom's pride—it made her confidence foolproof.

We walked into the store and Priscilla immediately went to a rack. Even at seventeen years old, Priscilla had precision in her shopping. Focused, with a discerning eye that dismissed most of the things she looked at—her hands flipping through hangers decisively. It's not like I wasn't aware that my mom hadn't grow up with money, but at school, it was hard to remember that about her. Steph's bitch-ass words echoed in my head: "You don't *act* like someone whose parents own a dry cleaner." It was meant to be an insult, but it was true. It actually made me wonder if that was the first time *anyone* at school knew about the cleaners before that day. She was so good at projecting who she wanted to be.

I was glad she was starting to let her guard down a little with me. "What do you think of this?" I asked, holding up a striped long-sleeve shirt.

She made a face. "Horizontal stripes add pounds."

I made a face back. "First of all, who cares. Second, that's just toxic crap women's magazines feed you to make you feel insecure so you keep buying their magazines in the hopes of fixing all your 'flaws.'"

She held up a dark red cardigan. "I don't even understand what you're saying. Try this on. And a few other things." Her arms were full of her selections.

In the dressing room, I pulled on some denim overalls over a cream-colored baby tee. If the legs hadn't pooled at my feet, it would have been an okay outfit. I stepped outside to where Priscilla was waiting for me by a three-way mirror.

She adjusted the overalls straps. "Why are you wearing this so high and tight?" When she was done, the bib of the overalls hung so baggily over my chest that my boobs were halfway out.

"Really?" I stared at my reflection. "I look like a reject backup dancer."

She went back into the dressing room to grab the cardigan from earlier. "Wear this over it."

As I pulled it on, I shot Priscilla a glance. "Why are you being so nice to me?"

She concentrated on pushing up my cardigan sleeves halfway up my forearms. "You're helping me with this campaign, and also—you stuck up for me the other day, and, well . . . no one really does that."

My chest tightened with the loneliness of that statement. "Well, I'm gonna make you work for that favor today," I said to lighten the mood.

She snorted in response. It felt like a nice, friendly moment, so I decided to risk bringing up something that I knew she'd get annoyed by. "But I have a question. Why are all your friends assholes?"

Priscilla stepped back from me, as if to focus on my outfit, but her jaw was set, her posture defensive. "Why don't you go try on the corduroy pants and denim shirt?" Completely ignoring my question. Whatever good will I earned had its limits, I guess.

I went into the dressing room but pressed on; it was easier now that we were separated by a door. "I'm serious. None of your friends stepped up when Steph was saying all that crap, and everyone said *more* dumb crap after!"

Mulish silence. "You don't know them. Or me. At all."

The corduroy pants were too small. I wriggled into them, willing it to happen. "I mean, I've met your family. We've gone to church together. And you're taking me shopping right now. I think I do know you a little." I pulled on the denim shirt and stepped outside.

Her arms were crossed. "Well, you sure don't know how to dress like me."

“These pants are too small,” I said. “My hips are about to bust the seams.”

“I also have wide hips,” she said, untucking my denim top. *Yeah, I got them from you, Mother*. “Why are you tucking this in? Gross.”

I wouldn’t let her off the hook that easily. “I just think you should hang out with non-assholes.”

A long-suffering sigh escaped from her. *Oh, Mom, you have no idea how many times that sigh would define our relationship.* “Here’s what you don’t seem to get, Sam. Clearly, you don’t care about being popular. Am I wrong?”

I shook my head. She grabbed a vest from the fitting room and handed it to me. It was embroidered in earth tones and truly hideous.

“So, if you don’t care about being popular, all of this seems stupid to you. Like, who cares about having girls like Deidre like you? Or guys like Neil? But for me, it *matters*.”

The vest fit me, but now I looked like a rodeo fangirl with too-tight pants. I looked at Priscilla’s reflection in the mirror, exasperated. “*Why?*”

I knew this conversation would push all of Priscilla’s buttons. It was just a little too earnest to have with someone you barely knew.

But she answered. Staring at my ugly outfit, not meeting my eyes. “Because. Didn’t you hear what I said in my campaign ad? I want to be *accepted*.” She paused and the words hit me hard when she finally made eye contact with me.

She continued, her eyes steely and her voice full of conviction bordering on anger. “And they’ll never accept me if I’m just some Korean kid who sits with other Korean kids eating ramen. Whose social life revolves around church. Who lets people walk all over her and make fun of her kimchi sack lunch. I don’t give them the chance to reject me—I have to be the one with power. *That’s* why my parents came here. *That's* why my mom works like a dog doing people's dry cleaning for them every freaking day. She's worked too hard for me *not* to excel on their terms."

I was speechless. In my entire seventeen years of living with my mother, I had never heard her talk about the pressures she dealt with as the kid of immigrants. She had always seemed so removed from Halmoni, from her own upbringing. As if she were above it all. But you couldn't be above it all when you were a child of immigrants. That pressure, that feeling of indebtedness to your parents, it was woven into you like a fine thread.

My silence made Priscilla fidget. "You probably don't get it. For some reason, you don't seem to have that pressure." She busied herself with stuffing me into more outfits. But her words stuck with me all the way to the cash register, as I paid for the clothes Priscilla had meticulously picked out for me, so that I could blend in, so that I could have a chance at surviving high school. It wasn't that different from what my mom did for me in the future. Except, she didn't realize we lived two different high school realities. Completely different worlds. The armor she needed—it was for a battle that didn't exist for me.

"I don't have that exact kind of pressure because my parents *were* born here, so I guess that accounts for some of this." I gestured toward myself as the cashier handed me a large plastic shopping bag filled with my neatly folded clothes. Such thick, luxurious plastic. "But you're wrong about me not having any pressures. I do. They're just different."

"How?" Priscilla asked as she led the way again.

I tried to figure out how to explain this to Priscilla since I was essentially talking about *her* in the future. "Well. My mom wants me to be more like her. Really driven and," I glanced at her, "kind of all-American."

Maybe I expected that to land or something, but Priscilla just scoffed. "You're complaining about that? My mom thinks Americans are all poorly raised underachievers and doesn't get why I hang out with them."

"Hal—I mean, your mom doesn't think that," I said defensively.

Another sidelong glance at me, this time a little annoyed. "Yeah, she does. She's very judgmental about all my friends, everything I do. Sometimes I wonder why she even came to this country if she didn't want her kids growing up to be American."

I bit back from saying that it was natural to want to preserve your own culture. That maybe the American dream was a scam sold to us with Hershey bars after the Korean War. But, also, what Priscilla was saying just wasn't adding up to the Halmoni I knew. She was never that critical of how Americanized I was—whatever that even meant. In fact, one of the reasons why I loved her so much was because of how, unlike my mom, she never judged me or scrutinized my choices. She was just happy to see me happy.

But I also knew that wasn't Priscilla's experience with her. And at this moment, while she was being generous and open, I believed her. I believed that Halmoni made her feel that way. Because the anger simmering under the surface, the hurt I heard in her voice—it was all familiar to me. And I wondered if I was finally getting to the real issue between my mom and my grandmother, what led to the homecoming fight.

"Even though my parents are pretty, I don't know, 'Americanized,' I still have, like, ridiculously high expectations put on me, too," I said. "I just stopped meeting them so they kind of gave up."

"Gave up?" She looked incredulous. "Lucky you. My mom would literally starve me if I didn't get into Harvard."

"Harvard?" I looked at her in surprise. Mom graduated from Berkeley and Halmoni was always so proud of that.

"So stereotypical, right? But that's what's expected of me." A sullen expression came over her, a clear look into my mother's emotions that I never got in the future. Priscilla of 1995 was definitely aloof, but there were still glimpses of vulnerability through her armor.

"Is that where you want to go?" I asked, eager to keep her talking.

She laughed. "As if what I want matters!"

She said it weirdly devoid of any bitterness. Just a fact of life.

Just when I thought our makeover montage was over, my mom stopped in front of a Claire's Accessories. Wild. "Can we stop in here really quick?"

"Sure." We stepped into the brightly lit, jam-packed little jewelry store. Like Claire's in my time, it was trinkets overload and full of girls browsing the racks, trying on rings and bracelets as Ace of Base blasted so loudly that I was afraid we'd get seizures.

I sorted through an alarming number of chokers before I found a pair of amazing earrings—giant plastic cherries. So outrageous and perfect.

I held them up to my ear as Priscilla walked over to me. "Really?" she deadpanned.

"These are for *me*," I said, glancing at the staggeringly low price tag. I found a pair of eggplants next to the cherries and picked them up with a wicked grin. "What about these?"

"Eggplants? So what?"

Oh. No emojis yet. Damn. "Never mind."

"I don't have my ears pierced anyway," she said smoothly. "My mom won't let me."

Right. She got them pierced as an adult. When I was eight my mom took me to pierce my ears at a dermatologist to make sure that nothing went wrong. I hadn't really wanted to do it, but she assured me that I'd want pierced ears one day. When I had fussed with the gold studs so much that they had gotten infected, my mom made me *re-pierce* them.

I looked at the way Priscilla eyed the rack of endless plastic earrings with a furtive wistfulness. It was one thing to hear about all the things my mom didn't get to experience, and another thing to witness it.

"Did you find anything you like?" I asked, placing the cherry earrings back on the rack out of guilt.

She sighed. "Oh, I really wanted to get this necklace for the dance. But, I don't know."

"Which one?"

We walked to the corner of the store where a wall of bejeweled necklaces sparkled before me. They were over-the-top feminine and princessy, but I could see the appeal. They were just so *shiny*.

"This." Pricilla reached up and picked up a delicate silver chain dotted with various pastel stones, each one irregular in shape and size. The way my mom held the necklace made it look expensive and precious.

It wasn't what I would've picked for myself, but it was one hundo Priscilla. "It's really pretty. You should get it."

She put it on, and it sparkled on her neck. Her eyes lit up just looking at her reflection. "It's kind of expensive."

I looked down at the tag. It was $30, which wasn't that expensive. For me. It wasn't that expensive for me. I still had $80 left of the cash Mrs. Jo gave me. But there was no way Priscilla would let me buy this for her. She'd rather let vultures eat her entrails live.

Then a determined look crossed Priscilla's face—jaw set, eyes narrowed. "You know what? I've worked hard. I deserve this necklace."

The number one job of girlfriends was to agree with statements like these. "Hell yeah," I said.

A few seconds passed as Priscilla looked at the necklace, running her finger along the glimmering chain. "I'm getting this!"

After she paid for it, in cash with exact change, she readjusted the necklace in its silver jewelry box, tucking the ends into the cotton padding, making sure nothing got twisted or damaged. And on the walk to the mall exit, she kept peeking at the box. The satisfied smile on her face widening with every step.

Nothing I had ever owned made me as happy as that necklace made Priscilla. I felt a tiny squeeze in my chest. Oof.

We walked by the food court and a familiar scent wafted over me—a very specific combo of oil, meat, and sugar. My stomach immediately grumbled. "Want to grab Hot Dog on a Stick?" I asked.

She feigned gagging. "Do you know how fatty that stuff is? I'm going to break out."

"Fine." I squashed the disappointment.

"But I can get a smoothie while you eat that calorie bomb."

We grabbed our food and sat at a chrome-edged table in the food court. I dipped my golden-brown corn dog into a swirled mass of mustard and ketchup.

Priscilla grimaced. "You must have good metabolism."

Luckily, I was accustomed to my mother's fine art of paying too much attention to what I ate. "You know, it's rude to comment on people's weight and eating habits."

"Jeez. I was complimenting you. Excuse me for living." She pushed a shiny strand of hair behind her ear, her pinky held out like she was at high tea.

"It's not a compliment because it's assuming that I want to be thin." I wiped mustard off my chin. "And it's letting *me* know that you're paying attention to my weight."

"Okay, please," she scoffed. "Are you telling me that you *don't* pay attention to people's weight? Like, if you saw someone you wouldn't think *skinny* or *overweight*?"

This conversation never got me anywhere with Future Mom, and I wasn't about to get into how problematic the word "overweight" was with her right now in a nineties food court. I took a sip of my lemonade. "The takeaway is just this: Can women not focus on our bodies so much?"

She waved her smoothie in the air. "It's not like I *want* to. Who wants to? We all wanna eat pizzas, but no one wants less than perfect for homecoming queen."

"You literally look perfect."

Her laugh startled me. It came from deep in her chest—a laugh I'd only heard a few times. "You're so weird, you know that?"

"How could I not? You say it pretty much every five minutes."

She grinned and sat back. "So, do you think I can actually win homecoming queen?"

"Do I *think*? I *know*." I started ticking things off with my fingers. "People you don't know have adorably told you they're voting for you. You're probably getting the church kids to vote for you. We're going to think of a cool incentive even if it kills me to give up the dry cleaning coupon idea. And the news segment is going to air tomorrow and it's going to blow everyone else out of the water—defaced posters or no."

Priscilla grinned. "Why are you talking like a CEO or something, god." But her tone wasn't critical. She seemed happy and relaxed—I could tell that winning seemed possible to her now. And a large part of that was because of me.

"Speaking of, who are you taking to the homecoming dance?" Priscilla asked.

I took a monster bite of my corn dog. "No one. I'm going solo, baby."

"No way. You have to go with a date."

I stopped eating. "Wait, that reminds me. Who's *your* date?"

"Neil, obviously. Since we're hoping to win king and queen."

I kept the distaste off my face, trying to be nice since she was being nice. "Oh. Cool."

But she missed nothing. "I know you don't like him. He's no *Jamie*." She said his name in a sing-song voice that rang out into the entire food court, almost drowning out the Gin Blossoms blaring in the background.

"God, Priscilla!" I yelped, nearly throwing my body across the table to shut her up. Her name came so easily to me now. "Could you be any more *embarrassing*?"

"Ooooh, you're finally embarrassed by something?" she said with a laugh. So gleeful at tormenting me. "You must really like him."

I shook my head. "We're just friends. I told you, I have a boyfriend."

"Well, you don't act like it. I see the way you are with him. He likes you, too, I think."

I felt my ears get hot. "I don't act any way with him." Guilt sludged through me, Curren's face flashing in my mind. "And Jamie doesn't like me."

"Seriously? You are *terrible* at picking up on signals," she said. "He's so into you."

My entire face was on fire. "He is?"

"See? You care!"

I couldn't not be real with Priscilla anymore. I dropped my head into my heads. "Ugh! Okay, yes, I know! We have all this *chemistry*. But it's not like I'm gonna *cheat* on my boyfriend. It's just that we got into this fight recently and now it's making me rethink everything . . ."

Priscilla folded her hands neatly under her chin. "I was actually just teasing but I guess you really do like Jamie?"

"Obviously!"

"What's wrong with that, though?" she asked. "If you like him, you like him. It's not like you can just flip that off like a switch because you're dating someone else."

I looked up at her in surprise. "Wait. What?"

"You're in *high school*," she emphasized the words with a dramatic hand gesture. "It's not like you're *married*. It's okay for your feelings to change."

This time *I* sat back in my seat. "Whoa. You're right." I brushed off Mom's boy advice in the future because, the whole Mom of it all, but right now? Priscilla was actually making a good point. We were having, like, a real friendship talk about relationships. Without any judgment or any notions of who I was as her daughter. I was just . . . maybe her friend?

"Yeah, you can break up with your boyfriend. Duh," she said with a shake of her head. "Do it before homecoming so you can take Jamie."

I laughed. "Okay, let's not get ahead of ourselves."

"Go see this boyfriend tomorrow. It's classier to do it in person," she said with a final slurp of her smoothie.

"I can't!" I said, laughing again.

"Why not?"

I told the truth. "He lives far away."

"*Sure.*" She drew the word out into multiple syllables before her expression brightened. "Oh, you know what else is going on tomorrow?" Priscilla asked, taking another sip of her smoothie.

"What?"

"That country club brunch Steph was talking about yesterday," she said. "They're throwing it for the homecoming court, during second and third period. We're allowed to bring a friend . . . um, did you want to come with?" She asked me with a Priscilla level of nonchalance, but something in her voice revealed a bit of insecurity.

"Oh, sure! Country club, huh? It's not Oakwood, is it?"

"Yeah!" She looked at me curiously. "Are your parents members or something?"

"They're trying to be." Even in the past, Mom still found a way to make me go to this dumb country club.

A muscle in her jaw twitched. "Hmm. Good luck with that." It wasn't said bitterly, but cagily, as if she were holding something back. "Oh, and it's a little formal. Wear that floral dress we bought."

"Oh, instead of my dominatrix outfit?"

The smoothie almost shot out of her nose and our hysterical laughter echoed throughout the food court. It was in that moment I realized that I was going to miss this friendship. And—if I was being real with myself—Jamie. It was the first time I was sad about going back home. Of leaving two people who, against all odds, I'd grown to care about.

twenty-three

twenty-three

three days to homecoming

When Mr. Finn turned on the TV in homeroom the next morning, my stomach flipped in anticipation. Priscilla had assured me that she talked to the news segment guy, Taylor, and everything was all squared away. I was so proud of this segment—with two days left until we voted, it was going to seal the deal, I just knew it.

On TV, two students sat behind a desk, awkward under the bright studio lights. One of the news anchors started talking, and his name popped up on screen: Taylor Swift.

I burst out laughing. "His name is *Taylor Swift*?" Everyone turned to stare at me.

"Just, uh, never mind," I said with a cough, slumping into my seat.

The two anchors went through their daily announcements, including one about the ticket sales for the homecoming dance.

"Speaking of homecoming," Taylor said (*Taylor Swift* said), "we have a special homecoming court segment with one of the court nominees." People in the class shifted in their seats, interest piqued.

The interview started rolling, Priscilla smiling into the camera. Her spiel wasn't new to me, but what caught me off guard was how well the segment came out. Jamie had some skills. He had added a filter or something to make all the colors pop. The camera closed in on Priscilla at optimal times and he even added in some music for optimal emotional pull. At the very end, the words "PRISCILLA JO IS RUNNING FOR HOMECOMING QUEEN" splashed across the screen in a hilariously aggressive font. It was TikTok worthy.

I clapped my hands, and everyone turned to stare at me again. Priscilla smiled at me from her seat. But as I looked around to see everyone's reactions, I realized we seemed to be the only people who were happy.

"Is that *allowed*?" a guy wearing a beanie asked.

A girl in a swim parka turned to Priscilla. "Hey, did you have to pay to do that?"

Priscilla shot her a cool look. "No, I didn't pay."

"So, they just let you run what was basically a commercial for free? What about all the other nominees?"

Other people in the class started grumbling similar opinions.

For the first time since I met her, Priscilla looked flustered. She made eye contact with me, and I saw a kindling of resentment in there. It filled me with a familiar anxiety, and I knew I had to do something.

"The interview was my idea." I stood up on my desk. Dramatique but definitely attention-grabbing. It worked. Everyone looked at me instead of Priscilla.

"Who the hell is that?" The muttering wasn't unkind as much as confused.

"Oh, that new girl," another person said, dismissive and annoyed. "Bob or something."

BOB? I powered through, "I'm *Sam* and I'm helping Priscilla run for homecoming court. This segment just shows how much she wants to win this thing! It's a sign of her enthusiasm and creativity and you should all vote for her! Priscilla for homecoming queen!"

I smiled and shot up a peace sign at the startled class before the bell rang. Mr. Finn tutted at me before he went back to his tattered paperback copy of *Misery*.

When I scrambled back down, Priscilla was standing by my desk. Something close to admiration in her gaze. "You're really ridiculous, you know that?"

I slid my backpack on. "Ridiculous gets the work done."

She grinned. "Well, no one's going to forget that segment now. Meet you at my car for the brunch, okay?"

There was something messed up about me trying to please my teenage mother, but Priscilla was Priscilla, and I had to admit her happiness made me feel validated. Despite this little bump, I still had a good feeling she was on her way to winning homecoming queen.

• • •

Well.

I was wrong.

People were in a freaking *outrage* over Priscilla's commercial. They thought it was unfair and typical popular-kid favoritism. There were even gross rumors circulating about what Priscilla did to get Taylor Swift to air the commercial that made me seethe with rage. By morning break, unrest permeated the air—like the feeling before a revolution. Or, what I imagined it would feel like before a revolution. And now, thanks to my stunt in homeroom, people definitely knew who I was.

"Priscilla's bitch," someone yelled at me as I walked through the quad, heading out to meet Priscilla for the country club brunch.

I spun around. "*What* did you just say?"

The guy who said it snickered behind his fist, his two bozo pals at his side. His cap was turned backwards, his baggy pants falling off his hips under his green-and-gold color-blocked shirt.

Common sense told me to turn around, ignore this worm. But I had been dealing with everyone's dumbassery all morning and I was at my freaking limit. Everything turned red. I stormed toward him, both fists clenched. I caught his fearful expression for one very satisfying moment—

And then someone grabbed me from behind. Their arms wrapped around my waist, basically lifting me off my feet.

Then, a voice at my ear. "Not worth it." I twisted around to see Jamie with a grim expression on his face.

He set me down then, gentle but quick. I was so shocked that I didn't care that the guy and his friends scrambled away.

"*Excuse* me," I said, adjusting my dress, the anger leaving me so quickly that I was left feeling slightly drunk. "I can handle myself."

"Sorry," he said immediately, his hands held up. "I didn't know what else to do. You were about to smash that guy's face in."

Oh. He hadn't been protecting me. He was protecting that jackass. "I think you overestimate these fists."

He laughed, dropping his hands to his sides. "I doubt it."

"Sorry you had to see that," I said. "I've been dealing with some crap this morning."

"The segment, right?"

I nodded. "Totally backfired. Two days left until the vote, and we're totally screwed."

"I don't know," he said, running a hand through that sweet AF hair. His green sweatshirt fit so well I had to look away. "All publicity is good publicity, right?"

"She's been working hard to get her name out there, and I'm worried people are now going to vote *against* her."

He was quiet for a second. "Maybe she could take this opportunity to revamp her image?"

"What do you mean?"

"Well, she's kind of . . . you know . . ."

Taking pity on him, I finished the sentence: "She can be a snob."

"Yeah. So maybe she can try to win hearts and minds with the two days she has left."

I tried to appear encouraged by Jamie suggesting the plan that I had already been trying to execute for days. But maybe Priscilla needed to take it further. Do something less subtle.

"SAM!"

I prickled at that voice. Priscilla was charging toward me. She ignored Jamie, her furious eyes on me.

"Why did I listen to you?! That interview isn't just going to make me lose homecoming queen, it's going to make everyone *hate* me." She looked completely panicked as she held up a ripped poster. "People are even tearing down my posters now!"

I looked at the pieces in her hands, her jumpy expression. *Shit.* "I have a plan!" I didn't. I actually had no plan. But I would think of one.

"No! No more plans! I'm already screwed because of your *great* ideas!"

I made eye contact with Jamie, who lifted a hand in a gesture of "peace out" and ran for it. *Great.*

I kept my tone upbeat. "Can you give me one last chance to help?"

Before she could respond, a couple of people walked by and threw us dirty looks. Priscilla's face paled.

"Ignore them," I told her.

"No, it's not that. Did you see what they're eating?"

I squinted. "Ice cream?"

"Look at the cups."

I walked over to them. "Let me see that," I said, swiping the cup from one guy.

"What the hell—?" The guy was too surprised to do anything as I stared at the Barbie-pink cup. The words "VOTE FOR STEPH" were printed on them with an illustration of a crown.

"Where did you get this?" I demanded—a total rude monster now.

He yanked it back from me. "In the small quad, freak." The two scurried away from me as Priscilla walked over.

"Was that what I thought it was?" I could tell Priscilla was trying to stay calm.

I nodded. "Yeah. She's giving out free ice cream." All around us, people were holding the pink ice cream cups.

Cursing under her breath, Priscilla ran her hands through her hair. "That *biter*. She heard us planning yesterday!"

"Yup." My heart was pounding in my chest from rage adrenaline. "The other day, when she came up to us at lunch."

I was almost certain now that Steph was behind the vandalized posters, too. The scrawled words "SNOB POSER" flashed in neon letters through my mind. I thought of her place in the social hierarchy—how Priscilla's friends treated her. "That's okay, we'll deal with her later. For now, we have to work on spinning your commercial."

"Forget it, Sam." Priscilla crushed the poster pieces in her fists, her eyes glazed as if she were holding back tears. "Why did I even try? I knew I wouldn't win."

It was shocking to hear those words of defeat coming from her, but more shocking to see Priscilla about to *cry*. In that moment, I felt the same way I did once when a saleswoman followed Val around a fancy store—ready to absolutely *destroy* in fierce loyalty and love for my friend. Because even though we had a complicated relationship in the future, right now things weren't complicated at all. It was very clear. I had to help my friend.

"Since I'm coming over for dinner tonight, we'll come up with a plan then," I said. "Don't worry. We've got this, okay? For now, let's survive this country club thing."

Priscilla nodded, even though I could tell she didn't believe me. But I also knew I would do everything in my power to make her believe again. Priscilla wasn't as tough as her future self yet, so I had to rise to the occasion.

twenty-four

twenty-four

three days to homecoming

"What exactly is this event going to be?" I asked as I buckled into Priscilla's car.

Still looking rattled, Priscilla backed the car out of the parking spot. "It's just, like, the country club being nice to us because we're on the homecoming court. I think they're doing this because Deidre's dad is some bigwig there and she was on the court last year."

"Deidre, huh?" I couldn't hide the distaste in my voice.

We exited the school grounds and turned onto a main thoroughfare. "She's not that bad," Priscilla said. "Can you stop being judgmental for one afternoon?"

"*Me?*" The incredulity was genuine.

"Yeah, you." She made a turn onto a more residential street. "I don't need more people hating me."

She had a point, and I vowed to keep my mouth shut so I wouldn't somehow insult someone again. Really easy to do with these people, unfortunately. My focus should be on how to fix the interview fiasco. This event might help, actually. It would be the first time I would see all of the homecoming princesses in the same room. I could suss out their feelings about Priscilla—take a temperature check on their dynamics, and confirm whether or not Steph was actually trying to sabotage us.

"I'll be polite, but I'll still hate Deidre. She acts like a bad TV villain," I said with a huff.

Priscilla looked at me with a conflicted expression, then broke into a grin. "I promised I wouldn't tell anyone but . . . speaking of TV and Deidre. She was in a laxative commercial. Like, running to a toilet because she just 'had to go.'"

I howled with laughter. "What?!"

Priscilla did a bad job of hiding her own laughter. "I know. She tried acting in middle school and that was the only thing that came out of it."

My hands flew up to my mouth. "You mean, diarrhea?" We both laughed hysterically. I held onto this little nugget like a treasure. I knew Priscilla had only offered it up because there was no one else she could tell.

We arrived at Oakwood and it felt very, very trippy. The last time I was there was just a few days ago, caught in pouring rain. It looked, expectedly, exactly the same. It was the same carpet, the same potted ferns, the same oil paintings on the wall. Talk about frozen in time.

When we walked down the hall toward the ballroom where we'd be having brunch, led by little placard signs tied with balloons in our school colors, people openly stared at us.

"Cool crowd," I muttered to Priscilla as we passed a woman wearing a pale-yellow tennis dress and a sour expression.

Priscilla smiled resolutely then tossed her hair. Armor initiated. And for once, I was relieved to see it. It made me straighten my own spine. I wasn't going to be cowed by a bunch of tragically tanned snobs, either.

The ballroom was comically large for the number of tables that were set up for the brunch, but it was beautiful—a bank of windows overlooking the evergreen of the golf course, dotted with weeping cedars and leafy sycamores. Each table topped with a white tablecloth, an arrangement of blue-purple hydrangeas, and silverware polished to gleaming levels. Fake doves held up a large banner draped across the stage in the front of the room: "Congratulations to the 1995 North Foothill High Homecoming Court."

I eyed the room, searching out the homecoming court but noticing a lot of others as well.

"Who are all these old people?" I asked Priscilla, in a kind-of whisper.

Her eyes were also scanning the room, doing some kind of calculation. "Some of them work at Oakwood, but a lot are parents of the nominees."

Oh, that made sense. The family resemblances became clear as I spotted a tall woman with dark hair near Eliot Bender on the basketball team, and a pair of bespectacled red-haired business types next to Neil. If this was a family thing, Halmoni's absence felt conspicuous. I glanced at Priscilla, who was as composed as ever, though I could sense she had also noticed. The guilt over the commercial rushed through me and I knew I had to start fixing things *now*.

"Can you introduce me to the other girls on the court?" I tried my best to sound innocuous. Priscilla didn't want me obsessing over the defaced posters, so I had to hide my plan.

For a second, she looked like she didn't want to do anything but sulk in a corner. But then that inner Mom "suck it up" thing happened. She pushed her shoulders back and walked toward the groups of people.

Everyone was mingling comfortably, as if all the other families knew each other. Did none of these adults feel the need to make us non–country club members feel welcome?

Yeah. Probably not as per the definition of "elitism" and all.

We went up to where two of the princesses, Alexandra and Tessa, were pouring orange juice for themselves. Their parents appeared to be busy talking to other people.

"Hey, guys," Priscilla said in a warm but confident greeting.

They looked over and smiled. "Hey, Priscilla. And you're Sam, right?" Alexandra asked me.

"Yeah," I said, astonished that anyone remembered my name after I'd attended this school for an entire 0.5 seconds.

"Are you guys sisters?" Tessa asked, innocently enough. We *were* related. But—I also knew we barely looked alike. I took after my dad and Halmoni, and Priscilla looked like her dad.

Priscilla and I exchanged a glance. That glance that all Asian girls everywhere share when they're mistaken for each other. I decided to take a page from the Priscilla Handbook of Dealing with Shit and just let out a laugh. "No, we're not sisters."

Tessa had the grace to look embarrassed. "Oh, sorry. I guess that wouldn't make sense unless you were twins since you're in the same grade." She paused and looked further mortified. "And you're new here, so . . ."

"You guys just hang out a lot," Alexandra said to fill the silence.

Priscilla maintained a cool exterior. "I guess." The curtness of the response made it clear that they had to just live with their stupidity for a second.

Stupid or not—they seemed pretty harmless. And not threatened by Priscilla in any way. In fact, Tessa looked downright starry-eyed to be talking to her. Popular-senior-girl status and all.

I decided to do a little digging. "Did you guys see the ice cream Steph was handing out yesterday?" I asked, feeling bold because she wasn't there yet.

They both nodded.

"And did you think Priscilla's interview was any more unfair than the free ice cream?" I pressed. Priscilla widened her eyes at me, willing me to shut up.

Alexandra shrugged. "Not really. It doesn't matter much to me. There's no way I'm gonna beat either of you guys." She gave a self-deprecating grimace before taking a sip of her juice.

"We wouldn't win anyway," Tessa said. "Seniors always win." She paused, clutching her glass. "You should definitely win, though. It's not your fault that none of us had the idea to use the news show."

Priscilla's posture relaxed, just slightly. "Oh. Thanks. A lot of people are pissed, though."

As if on cue, Steph walked in with her parents, wearing a form-fitting seersucker dress under a white cardigan. Looking like she was cosplaying country club. I drew a red circle around her in my mind. *You're dead meat.*

A woman walked up to the stage and clapped her hands to get everyone's attention—her long nails tipped with a French manicure, her hair highlighted blond, her eyebrows dark. "There are assigned seats, so please everyone find their tables so we can begin brunch!"

Priscilla and I found our names written on little placards on a table by a window and sat down. I peered at the cards next to me to see who we were sitting next to.

"For crying out loud." It was Steph and her family. They came over to sit down seconds later. Steph's mom with a bold lip and an ecru business suit, and her dad with dark hair and a surly expression, like he'd rather be hand-waxing his Mercedes than be here.

I was somewhat sympathetic.

"Hello," Priscilla said politely as we sat down. "I'm Priscilla and this is Sam." So well-mannered and poised compared to every other teenager in this room. Including my own slouched self.

Steph ignored her and took a sip of coffee, leaning back in her seat. Her mother nodded with a tight smile. "Hello, we're Steph's parents." No names, just that.

Her dad wagged a finger between the two of us. "You sisters?"

Deep yoga breath.

Priscilla smoothly answered, "Nope. Just friends."

Steph, unlike the other girls, didn't look embarrassed. She let out a snort of laughter instead. My head whipped toward her, and she flinched at my expression.

"Your parents couldn't make it?" Steph's mom asked.

Deep breath.

Priscilla shook her head. "No, unfortunately. But I thought it would be fun to bring Sam."

"What do your parents do?" Steph's dad asked, clearly still skeptical that we weren't sisters by the way he was studying our faces.

Jesus, just shut up, man!

I placed my napkin in my lap so that I would have something to do besides physically stopping this man from talking. Priscilla watched the movement, then clocked everyone else's missing napkins, and instantly put hers on her lap. It was basic table manners, the kind she'd taught me when I was a kid, but I could tell the etiquette was unfamiliar to her in this moment. She ran her hands over the napkin. "My mother owns a dry cleaner. My father passed away."

A flicker of sympathy crossed Steph's mom's face. "Oh. Well, I'm sorry, dear." Steph looked startled, too, for a second.

That's right, bitch! Feel bad!

Suddenly Steph's dad snapped his fingers. "That's where I recognize you from! Oak Glen Cleaners, right? On the bottom of Greenbriar?"

Priscilla nodded and her expression was the most carefully composed mask. A server came by with toast, blessedly interrupting this conversation from hell.

But it wasn't over. "Your mom runs a fantastic business," Steph's dad said. "Always gets my hemming right. Must be those delicate, small hands, right?"

I almost choked on my white bread.

"Dad," Steph said, her voice low and embarrassed.

He continued, ignoring her. "Well, good to see a hardworking immigrant family making it in North Foothill. My great-grandparents immigrated here from Italy, you know." As if he could relate to Priscilla. As if he knew anything about what she was feeling right now.

I felt like I had bugs buzzing in my mouth. Like they needed to be let out or I was gonna die. But I knew verbally eviscerating this middle-aged loser would do nothing to help Priscilla. That, for now, making these kinds of people think they were well-meaning was the way to survive.

"Your mother must be very proud of you for making the court," Steph's mom said, kindly but also totally oblivious to her husband's complete jackassery.

Only I noticed the strain around Priscilla's eyes. "Yes, she is. She's sorry to miss this event."

We ate the rest of brunch without much more talk. Steph's family kind of ignored each other while eating. I tried not to be too obvious as I observed them. Sometimes you meet crappy people's families and it all kind of makes sense. Steph's did, too, kind of. She seemed to be as horrified by the brunch situation as we were.

More coffee and tea were being served when the same woman from earlier stood up on stage again. "I hope you all enjoyed lunch. My name is Julie Keener and I run the high school programming at Oakwood. So, I can say with full confidence, that we are so immensely proud of all of you for making the homecoming court. What an honor! Give yourselves a round of applause."

Everyone clapped, and I slapped my palms together limply for Priscilla's sake.

"Here at Oakwood, we have a long tradition of our members being some of the most prominent figures of the community, and you are all well on your way to becoming the same," Julie said with a giant smile. "To spotlight each of the nominees, we've prepared a lovely slideshow."

The lights dimmed and the curtains were drawn as a screen was pulled down behind the stage, and a projector rolled out. I felt like I was at a sales conference or a wedding, neither of which I'd been to but had seen on sitcoms.

Classical music started playing, and a baby picture of a cherubic, pink-cheeked baby projected on-screen. Everyone laughed and cooed. Tessa sunk into her seat and groaned audibly. Her parents looked at the screen adoringly.

Julie spoke, "Tessa Martin was born in France—ooh la la!—and moved to North Foothill when she was seven for her dad's job at the Jet Propulsion Laboratory." We flipped through a few more childhood photos—of Tessa playing soccer, cute Halloween costumes, and so on—as Julie narrated. God, what was this, a funeral?

I was about to make fun of it to Priscilla when I noticed that she had stiffened up, her hands in her lap clutching her skirt in tight fists. "You okay?" I whispered. "Are you dreading your baby photos coming up?"

But she only shook her head tightly and I backed off, getting seriously strange vibes from her. We went through a couple more people—more adorable baby photos, family vacation pictures in the snow, tales of how well-rounded and wonderful these kids were—when it was Priscilla's turn. Which I knew because the first photo that came up was an older yearbook photo.

"Priscilla Jo is a senior at North Foothill and has worked incredibly hard to be here today," Julie said, her voice taking on a weird gravitas. I frowned. Where was her baby photo? The photos that came on screen were mostly school and yearbook photos, and from the past couple years. Julie rattled off Priscilla's academic accomplishments but didn't say anything cute or detailed about her hobbies and interests like she had with the other nominees. I started to get a sinking feeling in my stomach.

When Priscilla's section was over, there was polite but kind of confused applause. Julie paused. "Oh, it should be noted that we couldn't include Priscilla's childhood photos as they were left behind in Korea." Everyone made murmuring understanding noises, but I stared at her. *Korea? What nonsense?*

But I didn't get any explanation from Priscilla until the slideshow was over and everyone was getting up to leave.

"What was that?" I asked. "Your family photos are in Korea?"

She shook her head, clearly agitated. "That's not what I told her. She just . . . turned it into that."

"Why is every incident here so embarrassingly racist?"

But she wasn't really paying attention to me because she was so upset. "I didn't know they were going to do this. Or I would have tried to get some photos." Her lower lip trembled. "My mom—after Appa died—she . . . she put all our photo albums in storage because it was hard for her to have them around. And I didn't want to ask her to take them out just for this. I thought it was going to be for a poster or something, but not *this*."

I felt alarmed as I realized she was on the verge of doing something Future Priscilla would never do—crying in public. I knew that if I reached out to hug her, she might actually burst into tears. And I knew that if she cried here today, in front of all these people, she would never forgive herself.

"Well, you're the only one leaving here with even a shred of dignity. My god! Did we *even* need to see Devin's *bare toddler ass crack* in Aspen?"

Priscilla's brimming eyes suddenly crinkled, and she laughed. "Sam!"

Relief rushed through me. This, *this*, I knew how to do. "And freaking Steph's insane bedroom with the *dolls*? Like, yeah, thanks for confirming you're a future serial killer."

Priscilla was laughing so hard now that I relaxed. All signs of tears were gone. We walked toward the exit where Julie Keener was saying bye to everyone. I could overhear her gushing to Steph's parents, "We are *so* excited to have you all apply for memberships next week! I hear from your sponsors, the Johnsons, that your tennis game is killer, Liz."

Steph's mom, or Liz, I guess, demurred with a wave of her hand. "Please. Anyway, this was just fabulous, thank you so much for setting this up. We'll be sure to keep you all in mind for Steph's graduation party."

I'm sure.

Priscilla held out a hand to Julie. "Thank you so much, Ms. Keener, for such a special brunch. It was an honor to have Oakwood host us today." I saw Steph pause in the doorway while she watched this interaction. And I saw what she saw: the incredible poise and graciousness. The perfect homecoming queen. Steph's eyes narrowed, jealousy twisting her features. Whatever shred of sympathy she might have had for Priscilla enduring her embarrassing dad earlier was totally gone.

Julie Keener smiled this kind of wide, unsure smile. "Of course, dear! You should be *very* proud of yourself for making it here."

Pardon? "Here" meaning, the homecoming court? Or . . . the freaking vanilla American dream of being inside a country club?

There was no talk of "your family should join" like there was with the other families. Its absence was so heavy I felt its weight as we walked through the club, passing the great room where, in thirty years, Priscilla would be sitting to interview for membership. There was no doubt in my mind that this brunch had something to do with it.

Julie snapped her fingers, as if she just remembered something. "Oh, one more thing, Priscilla!"

Hope sparked in Priscilla's eyes. "Yes?"

"By any chance, are you in need of an after-school job? We're hiring salesgirls for the pro shop and thought you'd be perfect! Such good people skills." Julie clapped her hands, that's how great her excitement was.

Priscilla kept her smile on her face but the spark in her eyes was instantly extinguished. "Oh, um, I actually help my mom out at work . . ."

I looked at her because that wasn't true anymore. But if there was one empirical truth about Priscilla, it was that she was proud.

Julie dropped her hands. "Oh, drat! Well, thought it was worth asking. Reach out to me if you are, in the future, though!" She turned to talk to another family, unaware of the hope-crushing that had just occurred.

I wondered if Priscilla was understanding what I was understanding: that all the popularity and posturing with the right people in the world couldn't earn you real acceptance in a place set up to make it impossible for you to join.

We walked out into the parking lot in silence, me giving Priscilla the space to deal with her feelings. When we reached her car, Steph was getting into hers, just across the way from us. "Wait for me a sec," I said to Priscilla before I walked over to Steph.

"Hey, Steph."

Steph sat in the driver's seat, about to close the door. I grabbed it with my hand. "You're the one who's been messing up our posters, right?"

The worst actor in the world, she widened her eyes in confusion. "What?"

After having witnessed Priscilla's humiliations today, I was not having it. I leaned in close. "If you try *anything* else, I'm going to end you."

Her mouth dropped open. "You're insane." She grabbed the door and slammed it shut. But I saw the moment of panic, again, and knew my hunch was correct. I felt a brief punch of power before I felt a little bad. It's not like I relished being some kind of bully. But sometimes—especially being Asian, being a girl—it felt good when you saw that flash of fear when people have realized they've underestimated you. And now Steph knew she needed to watch her back.

The drive to school was pretty subdued—the bitter taste of brunch lingering. But when Mariah Carey came on the radio, I couldn't help it. As the chorus started, I sang along, and was eventually joined by Priscilla. Mariah heals all wounds.

The light turned green, and Priscilla hit the gas so hard it would have made Vin Diesel's neck snap. I braced in time—I was getting used to her style of driving. She looked over at me. "So, I've been thinking about it. And I think we should do the dry cleaning coupon idea."

"What? Are you serious?"

She nodded, her jaw clenched. "Yes, we need to offset the fallout from the segment. And . . . why *do* I care so much about what these people think of me?"

I held my breath. *Whoa. Really?*

"They either vote for me knowing who I am, or I don't need them," she said with resolve. "So yeah, I'll make copies of the coupon, and we'll give them out tomorrow."

I pumped my fist in the air. "Yeah, bitch!"

"Oh my god." But it was said with affection, and for the first time since I had gotten here, and maybe ever, I felt like we were on the same team. It was us in this car and no one could touch us. Our dreams, our hopes—it had nothing to do with the world outside these windows. And I would do everything to protect the things Priscilla wanted.

twenty-five

twenty-five

three days to homecoming

At the cleaners that afternoon, I brainstormed nonstop, trying to figure out how to get Priscilla out of the interview mess. The brunch only further fueled me—Priscilla *was* the underdog now. While the coupons would help, she needed to acknowledge the scandal directly.

Oblivious to my turmoil, Halmoni had a lightness to her while we worked, clearly looking forward to our dinner. It made me happy—no easy feat while I was staving off panic attacks.

While she drove us to their apartment after work, we listened to some Korean radio. I thought of all the ways people communicated with each other in the nineties without social media. TV, radio . . .

Inspiration struck—I had an idea. I just had to convince Priscilla to believe in me, again.

When we got to the apartment, Priscilla and Grace were already there, SWV playing, and the apartment already cozy with the smell of cooking rice.

"We're home!" Halmoni called out in Korean as she took off her shoes in the entryway. I leaned over and untied the laces on my sneakers. Before I could straighten up, a small body hurled itself into me.

"Sammy!" Grace screeched, clutching my legs.

I balanced myself and laughed. "Hey, Grace." Aunt Grace maintained this enthusiasm for greetings well into her thirties. Her fierce hugs often sucked the air out of my lungs.

A less enthusiastic greeting came from Priscilla, who was in the kitchen chopping up some scallions. "Hey," she said when I walked in. She looked tired, and I felt bad for making her do this dinner tonight.

Halmoni walked in and immediately scrutinized the scallions. "Do it at more of an angle, not straight like coins."

Priscilla's shoulders seized up and irritation came off her in waves. "You're welcome."

Halmoni paused and glanced at me. "I'll get the rest of dinner ready. Sam, you go relax."

"Oh, no, I can help," I said, already going over to the sink to wash my hands.

"No, you're our guest!" Halmoni insisted. "You can be with Grace in the living room."

I kept washing my hands. "I insist."

Priscilla stopped chopping. "Why are you washing your hands for so long?"

Ah, the days before singing "Happy Birthday" twice while you furiously scrubbed your hands to ward off a deadly virus.

"Um, daughter of a surgeon," I said as I wiped them dry.

Despite Halmoni's disapproval, I helped a bit in the kitchen. Cracking then beating eggs for the squash jun, chopping more raw veggies to serve with ssamjang. Halmoni would kindly help me out here and there. There was a moment when I caught a strange expression cross Priscilla's face as she watched us.

We cooked in amiable silence, with the sound of Grace watching TV coming through from the other room. And, while this should have felt routine, it sadly didn't. There weren't many evenings spent in the kitchen with Mom and Halmoni in the future. I swallowed the lump that formed in my throat and willed myself to hold it together. *Jesus!* Suddenly, this dinner felt so significant. A rare opportunity to share a meal with Halmoni, Mom, and Grace before all the complications of the future.

Before we sat down to eat, I popped into the bathroom. After I washed my hands, I stood at the sink, looking at the little jar of potpourri, the Keroppi toothbrush that I could only assume belonged to Grace. Priscilla's drugstore makeup meticulously organized in the corner.

I pulled out my phone, ignoring the alarming "52 percent." I was willing to risk some battery drainage.

> Hi, Halmoni. It's so strange to be near you and still miss you. You're one of the few people who believes in me, unconditionally. And right now, I could use some of that faith. I'm worried I'm going to fail at something really important. I guess in the past, I've been okay with failure. What doesn't kill you makes you stronger, and all that crap you read on inspirational posters. Or at, like, Home Goods. But I can't fail this. And I'm really, really worried. You would know what to say right now. You always do.

I turned my phone off and went out into the dining area, sinking into the floral seat cushion on the dining room chair. The dinner spread on the glass-topped table was so familiar it hurt. Small porcelain bowls of fluffy white rice, metal utensils, various banchan in familiar floral-patterned dishes, a red potholder used as a trivet under the pot of galbi jjim—a stewed short rib as sweet as candy.

"I hope you like it, Sam," Halmoni said as she took off her apron.

"This looks delicious, thank you."

"Do you eat Korean food at home?" she asked as she leaned over and started placing bits of the perfectly stewed meat onto Grace's bowl.

I resisted looking at my mom. "Um, not really. I wish we did. I love Korean food."

Priscilla snorted. "What a butt kisser."

"It's true!" I gulped down a huge scoop of rice to prove my point, then reached for a large portion of soybeans sautéed in sesame oil and chili flakes. "My parents just don't know how to cook it very well."

Halmoni nodded her head. "Ah, they are born here?"

"Yes." I busied myself with tearing off a piece of fish.

Halmoni pushed my chopsticks aside with her own and expertly pushed fish meat off the bone. She made a small pile of meat on the plate and gestured for me to grab some. It was an echo of our last dinner together and my throat tightened with emotion.

When I ladled some of the galbi jjim sauce onto my rice, Halmoni watched with a curious expression. "How funny. You do that just like Priscilla and her dad."

Priscilla's spoon stilled above her rice, which was also soaked with sauce. We smiled at each other awkwardly.

"Strange. Sometimes I just very much feel like I know you, Sammy," Halmoni said. My heart skipped a beat.

"Her name's Sam, not Sammy," Priscilla said, embarrassed. She glanced at me. "Sorry."

I shook my head. "Oh, no, it's fine. My grandma calls me that, too." *Crap.*

But no one found it odd. And why would they? Even if Halmoni thought I looked familiar, through some weird blip of time and space, she could never make the connection. And hopefully she never would.

"That's nice. Does your halmoni live near you?" Halmoni asked.

"Yes." I squeaked out as I pulled a rib out of the pot.

"Priscilla and Grace's grandparents live in Korea, so it's very sad for them," Halmoni said. "We only visited them once."

"You've been to Korea?" I asked Priscilla with surprise. My mom had *never, ever* talked about visiting Korea before. I'd only gone once with Halmoni as a little kid. Our family had traveled to Europe and Southeast Asia, but never Korea.

She shrugged. "When I was little. Grace wasn't even born then."

"Yeah, so it was *boring*," Grace said, holding up her spoon. Like a little dictator.

Halmoni pushed the tofu closer to me. "Priscilla complained the entire trip. She didn't appreciate it."

The mood shifted and I looked down at my food, not wanting to get too involved. This testy, antagonistic attitude from Halmoni was startling to me. She never acted like this with me or Julian. Or even with Mom. When I witnessed their squabbles, it was always my mom who was the aggressor, the one who snapped first.

"Sorry if I thought hanging out with strange family members I didn't know was boring," Priscilla said. "We didn't even do anything fun!"

"Appa and I took you to Lotte World!" Halmoni said, putting her spoon down, annoyed.

"Umma. We live in *Southern California*. Home to Disneyland."

It was hard not to jump in and stop the argument, like I would if Mom and Halmoni got snippy in the future. But I couldn't do that here—it would be totally inappropriate and overstepping.

"Our appa is dead," Grace said matter-of-factly, reaching for a large lettuce leaf and then shoving it into her mouth, barely fitting all of it inside.

Everyone got quiet. I wanted to disappear into a hedge like that Homer Simpson gif.

"She knows that," Priscilla said finally, her voice prim—an echo of a tone she'd use whenever she wanted a subject dropped.

Suddenly it felt like Grace had tugged on some thread in the conversation, upending the balance of things. Priscilla poked at her food, her head dropped, and I got the horrible feeling she was holding back tears. I glanced over at Halmoni, hoping she'd say something, but she just cleared her throat and got up from the table to head into the kitchen. Dishes clattered loudly and it sounded conspicuously artificial.

You always know what to say. The words I'd spoken to my grandmother into my phone earlier echoed in my mind as I now watched Halmoni avoid saying anything at all.

Grace looked so small at the table, her round, black eyes not missing anything. Her bottom lip wavered as she looked at Priscilla. "Sorry, Unni." The whispered words were swallowed up by Halmoni's noise in the kitchen.

But Priscilla heard them, and her shoulders straightened. She lifted her head and smoothed her hair back. The only sign of any tears was some redness on the tip of her nose. "You don't have to be sorry. Hey! Is that a fly?" She bonked her playfully over the head with her chopsticks and Grace burst into giggles.

I laughed, too, to help ease the tension. But I felt like crying myself, to be honest. After dealing with everything else today—Priscilla had to be a good daughter and sister, too. There seemed to be zero space for her to feel *anything* about the death of her father. Which was only a few years ago. She just . . . carried so much. Alone.

I nervously kept an eye on the kitchen, waiting for Halmoni to come back. Why wasn't she the one smoothing things over? She always did that with me. She eventually appeared with a pitcher of water, as if that was what demanded her attention in the kitchen.

"This is warm water, better for digestion," she said to me, smiling. But she avoided looking at her daughters and I felt the chasm between her and Priscilla then. How could I possibly help close it? I was just some rando barging into their lives. It felt impossible.

But so did time travel. Right.

I accepted the water and took a deep breath. "Thank you. Oh, did you know that Priscilla is running for homecoming queen?"

Priscilla's head whipped toward me, her eyes wide.

Halmoni took a sip of water. "What is that?"

I thought of how supportive Halmoni was of everything I ever tried. Maybe *I* could convince her of the importance of homecoming and what it meant to Priscilla. "It's an honor bestowed on you for homecoming if enough people vote for you."

"Vote based on what? Good grades or something?"

"Oh, no, um," I stammered, "just if people like you."

Priscilla made a frustrated noise from across the table. This wasn't going the way I'd hoped, but I couldn't take it back now.

She rolled her eyes. "It's a big deal, Umma."

"Winning a contest about how many people like you?" Halmoni scoffed. "What a waste of time. You always care too much about what other people think of you, Priscilla. If you put that much care into your own family, then we'd be the happiest family in the world."

It was meant to be a joke, her light tone indicated that. But I took it the way I knew Priscilla did. So, the weight of the family's happiness was *on Priscilla*? The unfairness of that almost took my breath away.

For the first time in my life, I was totally and utterly *not* on Halmoni's side. Mom had been right. The mom she grew up with was not the Halmoni I knew in the future. And it was actually a different person from who I worked with in the cleaners, too. This was full-on Tiger Mom nonsense.

"Well, I'm helping Priscilla with her campaign so she can win," I said with a confidence I wasn't sure I had anymore. "It's been really fun."

Halmoni nodded with a tight smile, clearly battling her real feelings and being polite to a guest. "Well, she is lucky to have you as her friend."

I glanced at Priscilla's proud profile, her chin held up high despite feeling miserable, and said, "Actually, I'm lucky to have her as a friend."

Priscilla looked at me, surprised. Grace clapped her hands. "Can I also be your friend?"

I laughed. "You already are."

Grace gave a satisfied little nod and happily dug into her food.

Although Priscilla shot me a small grateful smile, we finished dinner with all the unspoken words hanging over us like a ghost. I felt my determination to fix all the things between Halmoni and Mom wilt. This dinner just highlighted how deep the rift actually was—and how it felt so much bigger than homecoming. Where did that leave me now?

twenty-six

twenty-six

three days to homecoming

Our moods subdued and contemplative after dinner, Priscilla and I made quick work of the dishes, then ducked into her room to work on Operation Salvage Homecoming Queen Campaign.

I stepped into her bedroom and took in the pale pink walls, floral curtains, posters of random blond teenyboppers, and a school pennant hung next to a bulletin board full of magazine cutouts. It was like *Full House* threw up in here.

But what stood out to me was a corner of her room that was set up like a mini laundry room: a drying rack full of neatly hanging clothes and underwear. And an iron resting in its own little home base, a clothes steamer, and a small shelf holding various accessories like a lint roller and static-cling spray.

"Good god, your family *does* own a dry cleaner." I realized I was witnessing the origin story of my mom's obsession with keeping clothes clean.

"Ha ha." She flopped down onto her bed and sighed heavily.

I tried to change up the general defeated vibes permeating the air. "Hey, thanks a lot for letting me crash your family dinner. It was really delicious."

She crossed her arms across her torso, like a corpse. "It's not a big deal."

I knew it was, though. She had told me she never had friends over. I tried to imagine Neil or Deidre with their shoes all over the pristine carpet and shuddered.

"My mom really likes you," she said.

And then I understood—the expression I saw on her face earlier when Halmoni and I were cooking was jealousy. Even in the past, Halmoni and I had a connection that was clear to everyone around us.

"It's easy to be likable to moms when you're not their daughter," I said, thinking of how my mother doted on Val.

Priscilla sat up and looked at me, tentatively relieved as she sensed this thing we had in common. "When I have kids, especially a daughter, I'm not going to make life so difficult for her."

I coughed to cover up my laugh. "Okay, so let's talk homecoming," I said, sitting down in her white ladder-back desk chair.

"Do we have to?" The exhaustion was palpable.

"Yes, we do. I have an idea."

"Great." The sarcasm oozed.

I kicked her foot. "Hey! You said you'd give me another chance."

"Fine."

"We've done the TV route, now let's go to print."

"What do you mean?"

"You should write an op-ed apology in the school paper." I was brisk, no-nonsense, not giving her room to argue. Priscilla leaned back on her elbows. "An apology? For *what*?"

"The fact that you took advantage of your connection with Taylor to have an edge during the homecoming election."

"What? That's bull."

"You and I know that, but it's the only way to calm people down." My mom was essentially being canceled in 1995. And everyone knew that the only thing canceled people could do was apologize. Anything else just added fuel to the fire.

Priscilla considered it. "Fine."

I scribbled down words as I read them out loud. "I know a lot of you are mad at me right now, and I get it. I'd like to begin by apologizing for the interview aired on North Foothill News the other day. It was a move that gave me an unfair advantage in the homecoming race. Although I didn't intend to do anything against the rules, I realize that it's not about rules, but rather good sportsmanship."

I glanced over at Priscilla to see her reaction to what I wrote. She looked skeptical. "I feel like this isn't really 'spinning' it. Shouldn't we try to defend ourselves?"

"No way," I said. "Being defensive is the *worst*. We need to be genuine."

"Well, I'm not *genuinely* all that sorry."

I snorted. "Well, for the purposes of this speech, you *are*. You are trying to validate everyone's feelings right now."

"Good lord," she muttered. "Okay, but can we make it sound more like me and less like an old nerd?"

"Fine. Less old nerd."

In that spirit, we hammered out the rest of the speech together with only a bit of push and pull. When we finished, I had her read it out loud and clapped at the end.

"Great, perfect." I felt a little relief at having possibly solved this one problem. Between this and the coupons, she still had a shot at winning.

Even Priscilla looked a little less worried, if still skeptical. "You're pretty good at this."

"At public apologies?" I said with a laugh.

"No, at writing. You're a good writer." Her back was turned to me as she said this, taking off her cardigan. She stopped to inspect it. "Drat. I must have snagged this on something, there's a hole now. I'll have to sew it up."

I felt warm from the inside out at what she said about my writing. For once in my life, I didn't have a ready quip. A joke to bounce off a compliment in self-deprecation. It had been a long time since Mom had said anything like that to me. As a kid, "Good job!" was a common phrase thrown at me—when I made a soccer goal, when I got straight A's. But it had been years since I had last felt the glow from praise.

"You know how to sew?" I asked when I finally managed to get over myself.

"Hello, my mom is a seamstress," Priscilla said as she placed the cardigan on her ironing board. "I'm guessing your family can afford to get this kind of stuff done for you?"

I took a second before nodding. "Yeah."

"Lucky." There was wistfulness there, not jealousy.

In fact, Priscilla's entire room felt like a dollhouse of Americana teen wistfulness. But if you looked carefully, you'd see the yellowed blinds under the floral curtains and the slightly DIY quality of the pale pink furniture—a paint color my mom had clearly brushed on carefully over some secondhand nightstands.

"Hey, what are you wearing to the dance?" Priscilla asked suddenly.

Shit. I had completely forgotten about that part.

Priscilla understood immediately. "Oh my god. You don't have a dress?"

"Well, not exactly. I guess I can go shopping again tomorrow?" My money, though, was running low. And I really, really didn't want to ask Mrs. Jo for any more.

Priscilla walked over to her closet. "Forget shopping. You can wear something of mine."

She opened the mirrored sliding door. "I don't have a ton of options, but honestly I don't trust you to find anything better than what's already in here." She sifted through the dresses, each one in a clear plastic dry cleaning bag, knotted on the bottom.

"Thanks," I said with an eye roll.

She pulled out a dress, the plastic swishing. "You know, real friends tell each other the truth. They don't just blow smoke up each other's asses all the time."

"Are you saying . . . we're *friends*?" I dragged the word out as obnoxiously as possible, and she laughed again.

"Why are you such a dork?"

I laughed, too, but I was actually serious. The idea of Priscilla considering me her friend gave me an intense rush of satisfaction. "Let's see the dress."

Priscilla hung the dress up on a heart-shaped hook hanging by her closet and carefully untied the knot at the bottom. Then she removed the dress from the plastic and held it up for me. It was a short, sleeveless, red sheath dress with a square neckline. It looked awfully *tight*.

She turned away tactfully so I could change. "Try it on before you say anything."

"Fine." Once I slipped it on, I had to yank on the bottom to get it over my butt. "I don't think we're the same size," I grumbled.

Turning back to face me, Priscilla took a long, scrutinizing look, her hand in her chin. "Hmm, I actually think it fits you fine."

"Do you really think it looks okay?" I asked, glancing at my reflection in the mirror. I felt like Cher from *Clueless*. All I needed was a white feather boa. I wasn't sure that movie was out yet, so I kept that observation to myself.

"Yes. Wear it," she held up her hand. "Don't fight me."

I had to admit I looked pretty good. A voice slid into my thoughts: *Too bad Jamie won't see me in this.* A devil whisper.

"Hello?" Priscilla's voice interrupted me. "Earth to Sam!"

"I like it, thanks for letting me borrow it," I said quickly.

She looked satisfied. "Good! Just don't ruin it or I'll kill you."

"Yes, I'm aware," I said, sweeping my hands toward her clothes station.

It was late so Priscilla offered me a ride home. I was about to follow her out of her room when I noticed three glass jars sitting on her desk filled with various amounts of cash and coins. Each had a label made by a label maker: "Big Bear," "Samantha," and "Discman."

Samantha?! What in the world . . . ?

In the elevator back down to the garage, I asked, "What's with the 'Samantha' jar in your room? Are you saving up to buy me more clothes?"

She paused in confusion, then wrinkled her nose at me. "What? Oh. That. It's the money I'm saving for a Samantha doll. For Grace."

"Samantha doll?"

She looked at me like I had sprouted a third eye. "Yeah, you know, the American Girl doll?"

Ohhhh. Right. American Girl dolls. "Oh, yeah. Cool."

"It's so expensive," she said. "But Grace wants one. I remember when all my friends had the dolls, and I would have to go over to their houses to play with them. There was no way my mom would ever get me one, so I would collect all those catalogs as if they were, like, the *New Yorker*. Anyway, Samantha's the best one, we all know this. She had the fancy clothes, tea sets, and cutest bedroom." Priscilla grew animated as she spoke, using her hands, her eyes lit up with enthusiasm. I realized how rarely she let her guard down this way—showing earnest interest in something. A genuine desire.

She glanced at me, a little embarrassed. "Anyway. You probably don't get it. I bet your parents got you all the dolls."

As a kid, my mom got me a custom-made American Girl doll that looked like me-ish—Asian with long brown hair. I was obsessed for about five minutes before tossing it onto the pile of other toys I had in my room. I remembered what Mom said to me during our last fight: "You have no idea what your dad and I do so that you can have this life . . . But you never appreciate it. You don't take care of your things . . ."

"I wasn't big into dolls," I said, smiling weakly. "But I'm sure Grace will love it."

"My god, did you really think the label was about you?" Priscilla cracked up. "You're conceited."

"Ha, yeah." As we made our way downstairs, my brain tried to absorb the fact that I was almost 100 percent sure my mother named me after a doll she had always wanted. A doll that represented an intense girlhood desire that never left her.

It wasn't a lot to live up to or anything.

twenty-seven

twenty-seven

two days to homecoming

I was a ball of nerves the next day, counting down until the morning break. That was when the school newspaper featuring Priscilla's op-ed would be distributed. As soon as the bell rang, I ran outside to grab an issue from one of the many newsstands scattered across campus. I flipped through it quickly to the opinion section. But the op-ed wasn't there. *What the hell?*

Someone punched me in the arm. Priscilla. Grinning.

"Where's the piece?" I asked, panicking as I scanned through the newspaper.

"I didn't publish it," she said.

"What? Why?" That had been our last chance. The vote was *tomorrow*. God, typical Mom to ignore my suggestions and do whatever she wanted instead. Now we really were screwed.

Priscilla trotted away from me, backwards, on the balls of her feet, bouncy and graceful in her cheerleading uniform. "Come out to the quad and see!"

I swear to god, this better be good, or I will give up this entire mission right now. I followed her into the quad, my feet dragging with trepidation.

The quad was filled with people eating their snacks and talking, as usual. I searched for any signs of . . . something. *Where did she go?*

"Hey."

The speed at which my panic turned into anticipation on hearing that voice was alarming.

"Hey, Jamie," I said, hoping I didn't sound *breathless.*

He was watching me with a half smile. "Who are you looking for?"

"Oh, Priscilla. She said that—"

A squawking, feedback noise interrupted me, and my head swiveled toward it. A group of cheerleaders was on the small stage set into the quad. I spotted Priscilla in the middle, holding a mic.

What was she up to?

"Hey, North Foothill, I'm Priscilla Jo." She paused, giving people a second to stop what they were doing and look at her onstage. "I know a lot of you are mad at me right now. And I get it."

I looked at Jamie with wide eyes. "I think this is the op-ed we wrote yesterday!"

She continued as her cheerleaders lined up behind her like her school spirit entourage. "I'd like to begin by apologizing for the interview aired on NFH News the other day. It was a move that gave me an unfair advantage in the homecoming race. Although I didn't intend to do anything against the rules, I realize that it's not about rules, but rather good sportsmanship. When I made the decision to do it, I was just thinking about one thing: I want to win and maybe this will help. It's not an excuse, but an explanation. And this desire to win? It's something that drives a lot of what I do."

She paused while the cheerleaders waved their pompoms and shouted, "GO! FIGHT! WIN!"

Laughter rippled through the crowd, and Priscilla gave the audience a knowing smile. "And sometimes when I aim for winning, some of you get caught in the crosshairs."

The cheerleaders all pointed fingers at the crowd and said, "Bang-bang!"

OMG. My mouth opened in shock, but everyone else around me laughed. *Sweet summer children.*

"So, I'm doing the obvious thing and saying I'm sorry while wanting you to vote for me for homecoming queen. I know how that comes off."

"Dear god, please don't strip," I whispered. Jamie raised his eyebrows and hid a smile.

They didn't strip. Priscilla continued, her ponytail lifting up slightly in the breeze. "It feels disingenuous and fake. You're allowed to think that and not believe me. I don't know if I would believe me. But here's something real, something I can promise you: I'm working hard to win because I love our school."

"Be true to your school!" A wave of pompoms, arms outstretched.

Priscilla took a deep breath, as if the next words would be hard for her. "I get excited to come here every day. To cheer for our football team. To represent our school. Because I'm grateful for it—I'm grateful for all of you."

And then the cheerleaders did throw off their jackets, turning their backs to the audience. Letters were pinned on the back of their uniforms that spelled out "THANK YOU." Priscilla whistled and two of them came to her side and squatted low, then hoisted her up onto their hands.

She bounced up high, did this crazy spin thing in midair, and was caught neatly. When she landed, she yelled, "I know I can't give you free ice cream, but I would still love it if you could make me your homecoming queen! Go, fight, WIN!"

I couldn't help it, I held my arms up and yelled, "*Fuck yes!*" And I wasn't the only one—people were cheering all around me, whistling and whooping. Priscilla had pulled this off, in a way I would never have thought of. I had written the op-ed armed with all the lessons of social media and the future, but she had tweaked it for a 1995 audience—and had made it so much better with her natural charisma.

In the crowd, I spotted the goth kids actually stepping out into the sun to clap for Priscilla. The Zelda questers looking up from their Game Boys to cheer. The Asian church crew. The Middle Eastern kids. Everyone I had approached about Priscilla. I felt renewed hope surge through me.

Jamie let out a low whistle. "Well, holy shit, that was awesome. Did you write that?"

I flushed. "Yeah. But I mean, it was all in the execution. Only Priscilla could pull off a stunt like that."

He looked at me with this calm intensity that I had somehow gotten used to in just a few days. "It wasn't just Priscilla, you gave her something great to work with."

I was hit with a sudden blast of sadness at having to leave him. At going back to Curren. I was reminded of the time I had gotten an A-plus, like an actual *A-plus,* on an English essay I wrote on *Beloved* junior year. I had enjoyed writing it because *Beloved* was obviously amazing, but I was shocked that I had gotten an A-plus. My English teacher at the time, Ms. Anderson, had written so much praise that I had felt a physical thrill reading her notes. I had re-read the essay through the lens of knowing it was good and it had warmed me from the inside out seeing it that way. The first person I wanted to share the news with was Curren. He had given me a little spin in the air and a "Good job, babe," but didn't ask to read it. I left it in his bag so that he could read it later, but he never did. I never brought it up again. And because he never returned the paper, I hadn't shared it with my parents or anything. At the time, I had brushed it off. *Who wants to read an English essay for fun?*

But now standing here with Jamie beaming at me, I felt sad and angry at my past self for letting Curren's disinterest slide. For that, and for so many other things.

"Thank you," I said too earnestly, meaning it with every fiber of my being. Then, because I was overcome with the monumental feeling of it all—the potential forever goodbye—I threw my arms around him and gave him a fierce hug.

He was absolutely still for a second. I knew it was probably weird, but what was there to lose? Before I pulled away, his arms wrapped around me—slow and firm, and warm. "You're welcome." Then I felt a soft chuckle on the top of my head. "I'm pretty sure you won hearts and minds. Yes, you *did*, Obama."

I froze. And I felt him freeze, too. Neither of us breathed.

When I pulled back, I stared into his face. "What did you say?"

His expression of discomfort immediately adjusted to ease. "Oh, haha. You probably don't know him, he's—"

"Barack Obama?" My voice was almost a whisper.

Jamie's grin slid off his face. The air in my lungs zipped right out. It was the tiniest sign of confirmation I needed. The entire world tilted and became a blur. The sounds of the quad turned into a loud buzzing, bordering on nightmarish.

His eyes pierced through my skull. "What?"

My heart was pounding so hard I thought it was going to propel me into space. "Barack Obama. *Future* President of the United States of America."

Jamie rubbed his hand across his face. "Holy shit."

twenty-eight

twenty-eight

two days to homecoming

The only people who existed on Earth at that exact moment were me and Jamie. The entire quad could have caught on fire, and we'd still be here, staring at each other, trying to make sense of the reality we were suddenly facing.

As I stood there, memories of our microfiche disaster flashed through my mind: Jamie's fumbling of the machine. How he didn't necessarily say he knew how to use it. His use of the word "tech," which had felt a little off to me at the time. But why, *why* would I ever assume he was also from the future? That he had also traveled through time?

Before I could react, before either of us could do a single thing, Priscilla came over. She was out of breath, her cheeks flushed with excitement. "I think I did it!"

I shook my head, trying to clear it, and blurted out, "What?"

She laughed and rolled her eyes. "I mean, *we* did it. Don't worry, I am giving you credit where credit is due."

Right. The speech. "That was awesome, Priscilla." I looked at Jamie while I spoke, trying to dig into his brain with my eyeballs. Who *was* this guy?

She paused, then looked between both of us. "Uh, am I interrupting something?"

I knew I was here to resolve Mom stuff, but honestly, I wanted the earth to swallow her up at this moment. Unfortunately, every single part of the universe was conspiring against us, because just then the bell rang.

Priscilla grabbed me. "Hey, I got you a pass to help work on the homecoming float with me during next period. I want your opinion on it!"

Fuck!

"Oh, okay. Hey, Jamie, *want to join us*?" My eyeballs were literally going to dry out and shrink into pinpricks with how long and intensely they'd been staring at him.

He glanced down at his watch. "Oh, actually, I can't. Have to run—bye!"

I watched him book it across the quad. *What the hell?*

Priscilla shook her head. "*Anyway*, let's go! Ooh, and I have the dry cleaning coupons. We can give them out at lunch today!"

I nodded reflexively and she dragged me by the arm toward the football field as I took one last glance behind me. But Jamie was nowhere to be seen.

. . .

It was impossible to concentrate on this absolutely ludicrous task of building a homecoming float when all I could think about was Jamie. Could it be possible that he was also a time traveler? And if so, why did he run? Did he secretly work for *Marge* and get caught?

Was he spying on me? Was all of this chemistry between us just a sham?

I tried my best to stay present with Priscilla, who was riding the high of her successful speech.

"I saw people who I *know* hate me actually smiling, you know?" she said happily, gluing some metallic streamers onto the side of the float. Our float was essentially a flatbed truck decorated with the dance theme: (inexplicably) "tropical." A chair was bolted in the middle for Priscilla's throne. Each homecoming candidate got one, which I found absolutely bonkers. She paused in her gluing. "Maybe I have a chance of winning. Which I have *you* to thank for. A lot of these people wouldn't have been won over if you hadn't done a lot of the legwork first of talking me up."

I looked up from the sign I was making—"Priscilla Jo, Class of '95"—completely shocked by the naked gratitude. "Oh. Well . . . you're welcome! But your speech really cinched it. You have a good chance of winning, Priscilla."

Priscilla got a gleam in her eye. "Yeah, who's gonna care about ice cream today, right? Especially once we give out the coupons as one last push. I owe you, Sam."

"Don't worry about it," I said with a grin. "Just win!"

I was gluing a cardboard crown onto the throne when Priscilla jumped out of the truck to grab a pair of scissors from our supply box. She squinted at something across the field. "Hey, there's Jamie. Why is he hopping the fence?"

I whipped around. Indeed, Jamie's tall, lanky form was jumping down from the chain-link fence bordering the football field. He landed, clumsily, on the sidewalk on the other side.

As I watched him begin to run, something took over me. An intense need to find out what the hell was going on. Exhilaration. A sort of mania born out of *traveling in time* and discovering that I might not be the only one.

I dropped the glue gun and climbed into the cab of the truck. "I just heard the truck make a weird noise . . ."

"What?" Priscilla watched me as I jumped into the driver's seat. "Sam—"

"Just checking on something!" I called out. I turned on the ignition, the keys having been left dangling there already. *Here goes nothing.* I pushed on the gas pedal and crept the truck forward. "Oh no, the accelerator is stuck!"

"Are you kidding me?" I heard Priscilla's shouting behind me. But for once I didn't care about Priscilla. Or homecoming queen. I needed to get to Jamie. I drove through the field—people diving away and screaming.

"Oh, calm down!" I cried out. "I'm going like three miles an hour!" I had my eyes on Jamie as he bolted down the sidewalk. He was still close.

What I didn't anticipate was the locked gate.

"Oh, shit." It was too late now. I slammed my foot down on the accelerator—putting the pedal to the literal metal as the truck rammed through the low gate.

I cleared it easily and let out a whoop of victory. "Yes!"

The crash caught the attention of Jamie, who turned and stopped in his tracks as I careened toward him. The look of shock on his face was so extreme that I knew I would remember it forever.

When I caught up to him, he threw his arms up in the air. "What in the ever-loving hell?" His voice was hoarse.

"Hello, Jamie." I hit the brakes, then opened the passenger side door. "Come with me if you want to live."

He continued to stare at me. "*What?*"

"Get in, before I run you over, too."

And, whether it was from shock or fear, he did, putting his seat belt on immediately.

"We need to talk, buddy." I drove us through the quiet back streets of school, full of houses and shady camphor trees.

He was quiet.

"You're from the future, too," I prompted, the words sounding absolutely bananas.

Finally, he nodded. Quick and terse—if a nod could be terse. It was all the confirmation I needed.

My voice shook. "Were you sent here to spy on me? Or sabotage me?"

That got his attention. "*What?* No! I mean, were *you* sent to sabotage *me*?"

I almost ran into a parked car. "Absolutely *not*. Who are you? What year are you from?"

Please don't let him be, like, thirty years old. Or a spy.

"2023."

A buzzing sensation of relief and excitement coursed through me. He was only two years older than me. Not decades. The enormity of what we were talking about seemed to hit him. He sat back in his seat, dazed. And then after a second, he glanced over at me, nervous. "What about you?"

"2025."

The year seemed to echo in the cab of the truck. We stared at each other. I imagined he was feeling what I was feeling. A relief so profound that he wanted to burst into tears.

I wasn't alone. I wasn't the only one. My body sagged from the release. My hands unclenched the steering wheel.

"So why the *hell* were you running away?" I finally asked.

He grimaced. "Honestly? I don't really know, it was instinct. I've been hiding this secret for so long—I've been so focused on getting out of this mess that I just . . . I just freaked *out*. I thought I blew it. And like I said, I also wondered if Marge sent you here to sabotage me. I wasn't sure if I could trust you."

"Freaking Marge." I took a deep breath. "Throwback Rides?"

He let out a sharp laugh. "Yup, Throwback Rides. Oh my god. This is legitimately the wildest shit ever." A thoughtful expression came over his face. "You know what, though, there were a few signs you were from the future."

"There were?" I asked.

"Yeah." Jamie smiled. "Something about your clothes. And just the way you reacted to things. Also, some of your references . . ."

"That's it?" I blurted out. "No way. You didn't know from those subtle clues, give me a break!"

He pointed at me, realization dawning over him. "No! The big one . . . the big one was when you said your mom *texted* your brother in college. It didn't occur to me until, like, right now. But when you said it, something felt off that entire afternoon. And not just because you've clearly never been in a library before."

I laughed so hard I almost dislodged a rib. "Oh. Oh my god. I *did* say 'texting.' How did you not know then?"

"Because!" His voice went high. "Because texting is so *normal*, so obviously a part of our lives. Why would I notice it just because I've spent a few weeks out of the eighteen years of my life in 1995?"

It was true. Because no one assumes anyone else is a time traveler.

I took a shaky breath and looked at him. "Wait, so when did you get here?"

"Six weeks ago, Samantha. *Six weeks*. Two days into the school year."

"How have you even . . . *why* have you been here so long?" I asked out of fear for myself, not just concern for Jamie. Was I going to be stuck here, too? I realized I had just been operating off the assumption that once I finished my mission, I'd be zapped back into my own time.

He rubbed his hands over his face. "I have a vague theory. You know that guy Teddy Quintero?"

I was shaking my head when I remembered. The guy who threw the football at us—the one who witnessed the defaced poster. "Oh yeah, your friend on the football team?"

A huff of laughter. "Well, he's not just my friend. Teddy's my . . . uncle."

He paused dramatically, waiting for me to respond.

I burst out laughing. Again. Laughing so hard I started crying. I had to pull the float over and catch my breath.

"What? What's so funny?"

When I recovered, Jamie looked confused and a little hurt. "Sorry, my reaction is because—dude. Teddy's your uncle? Guess who my mom is?"

"Your *mom*?" His mouth dropped open. "I mean, I don't know . . . oh, *shit*."

I wiped a tear from the corner of my eye. He gaped at me. "*Priscilla?*"

I nodded furiously, and he fell back against his seat. "Wow. I mean. *Wow*."

It felt so good. So, so good to have someone else know the truth about me. To know that I wasn't alone. And that it was *Jamie*.

"So . . . we've been sent back in time to hang out with our teen-aged family members," he said, his voice taking on an edge of con-fusion. "Why, though?"

"Wait." I sat up. "You don't know why yet?"

A car drove by the truck and honked, startling us. We probably did look weird, sitting in a random half-finished homecoming float.

Jamie took a few seconds before he answered, his fingers pulling on a loose piece of thread on his sweatshirt. "I *might* know why. It has to do with Teddy, right? My uncle Teddy . . . he's a freaking mess in the future." A darkness settled into the words, and I didn't say anything.

"He gets into a lot of trouble," he finally said. "I . . . sorry, not sure I want to get into it."

"Of course," I said quickly. "No worries. It's not my business."

"Thanks." He rolled down his truck window, cranking it jerkily. "So, I *think* it has something to do with the homecoming game."

"Oh my god!" I shrieked. "Me, too. Me, *too*. At least, homecoming, not necessarily the game. I think Priscilla has to win homecoming queen."

Understanding dawned on his face. "That makes . . . *so much more sense*." He let out a bark of laughter. "Do you know how confused I've been by your intense drive to help Priscilla win this random thing?"

"Listen, you really threw a wrench into everything by questioning my friendship with her!"

His smile could have lit up the entire city of Los Angeles. "Knowing you're from the future, too . . . this changes a lot of things."

I blinked. It was the first time I'd seen Jamie smile like this. It was like seeing a glimpse of something precious and borderline miraculous.

Also, was he insinuating what I think he was insinuating? Excitement thrummed inside of me—subtle at first, and then through my entire body, reaching my fingertips and my toes. My eyelashes.

Curren. That hadn't changed. Yet.

"Where have you been living for six weeks?" I asked abruptly. Really, the first of many questions, and also the safest one.

He chewed on his bottom lip. "Uh. The football team's supply closet."

"*What?*" Aghast, my eyes swept over him—looking for signs of neglect and general ill health. "Are you allowed to do that?"

"No way," he said. "But Coach let me have the keys since I'm also the assistant equipment manager. So, I have my stuff hidden in there." My expression must have been extremely pitying because he said, "I'm fine! It's actually really private and cozy."

"Hmm. If you say so." I didn't like the idea of him sleeping in some damp locker-adjacent closet. Alone.

Jamie's brow furrowed. "What about you? You've only been here a few days, right?"

I nodded. "Yeah, I got here last Thursday. After a huge fight with my mom. Uh, Priscilla in the future. There was a rainstorm and then suddenly the car dropped me off in freaking 1995."

Jamie ran a hand over his face. "When I found out, I had a panic attack in a bathroom stall."

Heart tug. "I also had a dark bathroom stall moment." I had so many questions. "How are you even surviving? Don't you need money?" There probably wasn't a Mrs. Jo in Jamie's life.

"It's the biggest damn coincidence. That morning my mom had given me the cash from the store—she owns a boutique in Echo Park—and had asked me to deposit it before I went to school. But Marge dropped me off at school. So, I have all this *cash*."

"No one thinks it's weird you have money from the future?" I asked. "Aren't the bills different?"

"Some are," he said. "But I washed and wrinkled them like hell so that it's hard to tell. And it's not like I've been shopping anywhere fancy. All the clothes I've been wearing are from Goodwill." He looked at me. "So, wait, where have *you* been living?"

I filled him in on the Mrs. Jo situation and he shook his head, looking dazed. "Unreal. Completely unreal. Don't you think all these coincidences are . . . *not coincidences*?"

"Jamie." I put my hand on his knee. "We traveled back in time. *Nothing is a coincidence*."

He looked at my hand then back up at me. I was about to pull my hand away when I heard shouting. I turned to see a teacher running toward us from the broken gate.

"Shit." I racked my brain for some excuse for why I stole the float, until I locked eyes with Jamie and was hit with something. Adrenaline.

It rushed through me, barreling through my veins, buzzing on the surface of my skin. Maybe it was finding out about Jamie. Maybe it was crashing through a fence in a homecoming float. Either way, I wasn't ready to let go of this feeling yet.

"Hey. Want to go for a ride?"

Jamie looked hesitant for about a second before he grinned. "Hell yeah."

I put the truck back into drive and sped down the quiet street, the shouts of the teacher fading away. "Where to?"

Jamie tilted his head back, warming his face in the afternoon sun. "Wherever your heart desires."

Stomach clench. I laughed. Nervously. "Let's find a spot to park this thing where we can't be found. I think I know of a place."

I steered the float around the neighborhood until we reached the edge of a park tucked into a canyon.

Jamie looked around with a smile. "I used to have my birthday parties in this park."

"Cute." I whispered it creepily, but he heard me anyway and we both flushed.

I found the small back road off the park that I was looking for, which wound up a hillside and ended in a parking lot surrounded by a grove of sycamores. There were markers for a hiking trail but, as I suspected, it was completely empty this time of day. I parked the truck and we got out.

"Are you in deep shit with Priscilla because of this float?" Jamie asked as he shut the door.

I looked at the half-decorated truck. "Very likely." Then I noticed the strewn supplies in the truck bed. "Do you want to finish decorating this thing while we talk? Maybe then she won't murder us."

He nodded. "Sure, I'm a crafting wizard." His delivery had the usual Jamie gravity, but his eyes were sparkling.

"I'm excited to see your skills, bro." We climbed into the truck bed and got started. We sat in companionable silence for a while—gluing construction paper palm trees together, dousing everything in glitter—all the things we wanted to say hovering over us.

We were close enough for me to catch a hint of a crisp, piney deodorant scent mixed with sweaty-ish boy scent. Why was that attractive? This thing, whatever it was, needed to stop before it started.

I cleared my throat and held up a paper palm leaf. "Palm trees are not native to California, did you know that? They're so synonymous with LA, though—it's a pet peeve of my boyfriend's."

A beat of silence. "Oh. Yeah, they're more tropical than desert."

I slowly let out a body-shuddering breath. Relief or something close to it passed through me. The truth was out there now. "Yeah, so haha to this dance theme, right?"

"So much about this stuff doesn't make sense, Samantha." Somehow whenever Jamie said "Samantha," everything had an undercurrent of intensity that made me want to splash my face with cold water. Or dump it on my body like that scene in *Flashdance*.

"So," I said quickly, trying to dispel the intimacy. "What exactly do you think you have to do for the game and Teddy?"

Jamie carefully applied a frond onto his tree. "I think we have to win the homecoming game. Which we didn't in the, I don't even really know what to call it, the other timeline? The *real* timeline?"

"Let's call it Norm Times."

He laughed. "Okay, during Norm Times, North Foothill lost the game. And the reason why, or so Uncle Teddy claims, is because he dropped a game-winning touchdown pass. They were only down by three points, so one touchdown would have won it. But he dropped it and they lost. And the *reason* he might have dropped it is because he started to drink his senior year, just to loosen up and be celebratory about graduating. He was all set to have his pick of colleges with a football scholarship. But he messed up the big game, and because he was so upset, he and some of his teammates decided to act like complete clowns and got wasted afterwards. Then they drove around town and . . . well, they hit another car and killed an elderly couple."

I sucked in a breath. "Jesus. That's awful."

"Yeah. The guilt and the shame broke something in Teddy. Like, he didn't graduate, let alone get into any colleges. Then he couldn't really get work. Still hung out with his football buddies on weekends, getting wasted."

"I'm sorry."

His eyes met mine, sad but also finally unburdened. "Thanks."

Something was bugging me, though. "Why were you sent back so early, then? Why six weeks before the game? Seems excessive."

He tapped on his palm tree, making the fronds shake. I glanced at his fingers. He caught me looking and stilled, then pushed his glasses up his very nice nose. "Well, probably because I needed more than a few days to learn how to play football."

I almost spilled glitter all over my lap. "Oh my god! You didn't know how to play football before you got here?"

"I mean . . . look at me."

I didn't need to look at him. It had only been a few days that I'd known Jamie and yet I could picture him so clearly in my mind. That thick lock of hair that always fell in front of his glasses. The languid way he moved his long limbs. Confident, but quietly so. The way his mouth quirked up as he tried to bite back a smile.

Flashdance cold bucket of water.

He laughed at how long it was taking me to respond. "Exactly. It's been the most hellish six weeks of my life."

The image of Neil throwing his weight around in the hallway flashed through my mind. "So, you've had to spend time with those asses even when you *don't enjoy the sport of football*?"

"Yes. A fun challenge, right?" Again, the lighthearted tone. But one look at his face and you could see the exhaustion there. This trip was way harder on him than it was on me.

"No offense, but if you're not good at football, how did you make the team?" I imagined all that body slamming and winced at the thought of Jamie getting knocked over by someone as big and dumb as Neil.

"I didn't actually plan on joining the team. I signed up to be their assistant equipment manager, but their punter hurt his back the week I traveled back here and so they needed me to join their special teams squad—basically it's like a bunch of randos who focus on kickoffs, field goals, and punts and stuff," he explained, going off my confused expression. "Literally all I ever do is practice a trick play where I pretend to hold the ball and then stand up to throw it to the receiver. Because I'm tall, not because of my innate skills," he said with a laugh.

"Whoa. That's pretty lucky, because you get to be teammates with Teddy?" I said, relieved that he wasn't on the field that much.

"Right. So, since then, I've been following Teddy around like a seriously unhinged lapdog, all under the guise of wanting a 'mentor.' Just keeping an eye on him, making sure he's not drinking or doing dumb shit instead of showing up for practice. And I figure, if we lose the game, then I'll have to be here afterwards to stop him from getting into that car."

I let out a low whistle. "That's so much. How has it been?" I asked. "Hanging with Teddy, I mean?" Dappled sunlight bounced across his features.

"Fine? I think he's confused about this weird kid following him around. But, again, Teddy's always been so good-natured and chill.

He's been real cool to me." He said the last sentence quietly. "It's actually been really nice to be with this version of Teddy—the Teddy whose life hasn't been ruined. The one with so much potential."

"Yeah. I understand that feeling well." My situation with Mom was different, but familiar in this one way.

Jamie's eyes snapped over to mine. "My turn to ask questions. First of all—what's it like having Priscilla Jo as your *mother*?"

I propped up my finished palm tree. "Here's the wildest thing: The Priscilla *you* know is the chill version. Like with Teddy, whatever issues she's dealing with right now get way worse in the future."

"Because of . . . *losing homecoming queen*??" Jamie was uncharacteristically incredulous.

"Kind of. Not really? Basically, in the Norm Times she loses and gets into a huge fight with her mom, my grandmother, over it. The fight messes up her relationship with my grandmother forever. And in my opinion, it ruins her personality, too." It all came tumbling out, each word lightening the load.

Jamie was quiet. He was always kind of quiet. It was something I liked about him. He didn't rush to fill in silences, to make things easier and more comfortable for everyone.

Finally, he asked, "Are you close to her? Your grandmother?"

I sat back against the edge of the truck and looked up. The leaves of a sycamore swayed in the breeze above us. "Yes." I paused, wondering if I wanted to go on. I did. "So, the other factor in all of this—that makes it feel so much more urgent than it should be—is that my grandmother's in a coma."

Jamie's hand reached out for a second before retreating back to his side. "Oh, shit."

"Yeah. She had a heart attack the day before my fight with my mom. And our fight had something to do with that. So here I am stuck in the past, not knowing whether my grandmother's going to pull out of this thing or not." And because it was still so fresh, still so awful every time I thought about it, my eyes filled with tears. I turned my head, completely mortified. He let me wipe my tears away without saying anything, without acting uncomfortable. I tried to control my voice so that it wouldn't waver. "Yeah, it's really scary. It's also kind of torturous because, you know, I get to see her again here."

A soft curse. Then a long exhale that seemed like it came from the depths of his soul.

I nodded. "Yup."

Jamie ran a hand over his face. "I feel dumb about being so torn up about Teddy when you've got Grandmother in a Coma."

I paused for a brief second, and Jamie looked horrified. "God, I'm sorry. I have the worst sense of humor."

But he didn't. I laughed. It was exactly right for the moment. When everything felt so dire and absurd. "Yeah, the worst. Do you also dance at funerals?"

He nodded, straight-faced. "I do a mean Macarena."

"OMG, Macarena! What even? You've spent too long in the nineties."

"Has Macarena even happened yet?"

"OMG." Then I laughed. "I said 'OMG' to Priscilla the other day and she thought I was having a stroke."

His grin absolutely blinded me with its rare beauty. "I used the word 'hashtag' in class one day."

"Excuse me, what about the news anchor, *Taylor Swift*?"

We both laughed so hard that the float was in danger of falling apart. This was the most normal I'd felt in days. Maybe longer than that. Because something about Jamie's quiet intensity, of paying attention, made me feel seen in a way that was completely new to me. And I didn't know it was something I needed until I finally experienced it.

"OMG, how's your phone holding up?" I asked, digging mine out of my windbreaker pocket. "Mine has been losing battery power by the day—I'm almost at forty percent. I should have listened to my mom and replaced this but how did I know I was going to *travel back in time*?"

Jamie's entire body straightened, alert as hell. "*Oh*, I actually figured out a way to charge it."

"*What?*" I yelped. "Show me!"

He reached into his backpack and pulled out his phone, which was attached to some sort of battery pack and cable. Everything was duct taped together like a Frankenstein tech monster, but I didn't care.

"Oh my *god*," I said, excited beyond belief, my hands almost shaking. "Could I possibly get some of that sweet battery power?"

"Of course," he said with a laugh, very pleased with himself. He unplugged the battery from his phone and handed it to me, our fingers brushing against each other, lingering a little longer than necessary.

Giddy with relief, I eagerly took the end of the cable and inserted it into my phone's charger port. Or I tried to. It wouldn't go in. I tried again. And then it occurred to me . . .

"Crap," I muttered.

"What?" Jamie peered over my shoulder at the phone.

I held up my phone, so the port was facing him. "The charger ports on these stupid phones get changed up every couple years. I forgot. I can't use this."

Jamie's mouth dropped open. "What? No way." He took it from me to see for himself. But after a second of examining my phone, his shoulders dropped. "*Sonofabitch*," he said under his breath.

I smiled at the uncharacteristic swear. His frustration was sweet. "It's all right, it only has to last for two more days."

Placing the makeshift charger back into his bag, Jamie looked sullen. "Yeah, I guess you're right." The perfectionist in him was really jumping out at that moment. It was incredibly endearing, like everything else.

"Hey," Jamie said suddenly, looking straight at me again. "Have we ever met at school? I mean, in Norm Times."

I did some hard math. "I don't think so." *I would have remembered you.* "And you graduated when I was a sophomore. You probably thought I was some freshman pipsqueak."

"I doubt it."

It was said very sincerely, and I tried to laugh it off. "Believe it or not, it took me awhile to grow into the spectacular specimen before you."

This time, his silence was disconcerting. His eyes slid down from my face to the rest of my body, before quickly looking up again. But then he did that thing he did, speaking as if we hadn't just shared a sexually charged moment of weirdness. "Well, not like I'm that visible in school, either."

It was true. Jamie was the kind of person you didn't notice right away, but when you did you realized he deserved a nice, long second look. *Flashdance, Sam.*

A current of fuzzy static passed between us and I had to turn away to avoid getting completely singed. I busied myself with another palm tree. "Better get this float finished or Priscilla will murder us both and we'll never get back to Norm Times."

He guffawed. "I do not doubt it."

"And hey," I said, my hands stilling over the construction paper. "Thanks so much for helping me with this."

"Of course," he said, genuinely surprised.

"I owe you one," I said. "I might not play football but maybe I can sabotage the other team or something. Isn't that what they do on TV?"

"Please don't," he said, laughing. "At this point it's just a matter of Teddy staying out of trouble. But you know—*I* can still help *you.* I'll make sure I get the football team to vote for Priscilla. Shouldn't be hard with her dating Neil and all."

"Really?"

"Really."

We exchanged pleased little smiles before getting back to making the truck look like a tropical paradise. A little less burdened and a lot less alone.

twenty-nine

twenty-nine

two days to homecoming

We got back to the football field by lunch with the finished float. I managed to convince Priscilla that the truck had malfunctioned, and Jamie had helped me fix it. She seemed *highly* skeptical of the whole thing but the float was safe and sound and she didn't have time to interrogate me further—we had to pass out the dry cleaning coupons.

She handed me a stack of paper slips that said: "If Priscilla Jo wins homecoming queen, bring this into Oak Glen Cleaners for 30% off dry-cleaning your homecoming dress or suit!" Little doodles of suits, flowers, crowns, and dresses floated around the words.

Adorably, Jamie offered to help and the three of us split up with very specific targets. Jamie had the football team and journalism kids. I had the church crowd since they were already warming up to Priscilla. As for Priscilla, I made her approach the goth kids, the gamers, and all the other not-popular students we had been campaigning to for the past week. The vote was tomorrow and I was hoping this personal outreach, paired with the success of yesterday's speech, would seal the deal with the fringe groups.

By the time school was over, and the adrenaline of the day had left me, I was barely able to concentrate at the cleaners. My mind kept going incessantly back to everything that Jamie told me.

"Are you okay, Sammy?" Halmoni asked me as I stared blankly out the windows into the parking lot. The lights had just flickered on with the sun setting.

I snapped out of it. "Oh, yeah, I'm okay. Sorry. Just tired."

She frowned and her hand reached out to feel my forehead. It was so Halmoni-ish I had to smile. "I'm not sick, I promise."

But she still looked concerned. "I don't know, maybe you should go home today. Not necessary for you to work when sick."

I was going to keep arguing when I saw a flash of green outside of the window. Jamie's sweatshirt. With Jamie in it. In the parking lot. He waved. Keeping my hand low to my waist, I waved back. He darted away.

"Um, you know, maybe you're right. Maybe I should rest and not get you sick, too."

Halmoni practically pushed me out the door and Jamie was waiting for me around the corner, behind a dense hedge.

"Sorry to be all, *subterfuge*," Jamie greeted me, looking sheepish.

I grinned. "Your subterfuge could use a little work."

He stuck his hands into his pockets and rocked back onto his heels. "I just thought—I mean, I was getting *killed* in practice because I couldn't concentrate."

"Same, same. I mean, minus getting killed in football."

His expression shifted into something more nervous. "Would you want to, I don't know? Hang out or get dinner or something?"

My nod was probably too vigorous. "Sure, yes!"

He laughed at my enthusiasm, but he looked down when doing it, and I saw his cheeks flush. *Come on, now.*

We decided to book it out of North Foothill to more adventurous waters. One long bus ride later, we landed on Olvera Street downtown.

"I can't believe you've never been here." Jamie's eyes reflected a string of lights, sparkling like a manga character's. Olvera Street was kind of a tourist trap, but it was also a legit historic street in LA that dated back to the nineteenth century. We were standing in a brick-paved alley lined on both sides with small shops and restaurants, the center filled with stalls selling various leather goods, souvenirs, and other knickknacks.

I shrugged. "You know how you never see all the iconic things in your own city?"

"Yeah. I've never been to the Hollywood sign."

"So passé," I said with a drawl. "Is this what Olvera Street is like in, you know, Norm Times?" I asked.

Looking around him thoughtfully, Jamie answered, "Yeah, actually. So much is different in downtown but this, this has stayed the same." It was Jamie's idea to come here—not mine, that would be embarrassing, all "Hello, Jamie *Mendoza,* ever heard of the famous Olvera Street?" For him, the familiarity was soothing. For me, the newness was exciting.

"So," I said, "do you think the football team has a chance at winning the homecoming game?" When you thought about it, it was so clean, so symmetrical. Me: Help Mom win homecoming queen crown. Him: Help uncle win homecoming game. It couldn't have been a coincidence that we were sent back in time to live out the same week.

"I think so. Honestly, I can't really contemplate the alternative."

"I know what you mean," I said as we perused a shelf of tiny leather sandals dyed in bright colors. I had zero backup plans. If none of this worked out, I'd have to start from scratch with almost no battery power.

Jamie picked up a turquoise pair of sandals and pretended to try them on, shoving his large sneakers into the tiny shoes. The shopkeeper tsked at him. "Lo siento," Jamie said with a sheepish laugh. *Cute-cute-cute.*

We left the stall, and I sniffed the air, suddenly ravenous. "Do you smell tamales?" There was an order window on the corner of a building with a line and we stood at the end of it.

"Hey, Samantha." Jamie poked me lightly in the arm. "Who's your president? I won't be able to handle it if—"

My hand shot up over his mouth. "Nope. No telling you about the future."

He shook his head free, his lips grazing my palm. He caught my wrist and then let it go—so quick. "Why not?"

I needed a second before I could respond. "Haven't you ever watched any time travel movies? You're not supposed to know stuff about the future. It's going to mess you up in some twisted way."

"I'm not asking about how I *die*. Just who the president is."

He was grinning and I felt myself grinning and at that moment I heard a whisper in the back of my mind: *I really like him.* I almost stumbled when the person in front of us moved in line.

I pulled my jacket tighter over my flannel dress. "No. No president knowledge. Or like, who won the World Series." I paused. "I wouldn't know that anyway."

We ordered our tamales and ate them as we walked through the rest of Olvera Street. At the end of the rambling street, in an open courtyard flanked by giant fig trees, a mariachi band was playing in a gazebo, and people were dancing. We sat along a low retaining wall and watched, finishing up our tamales, surrounded by neon-orange birds of paradise.

Jamie gazed out at an older couple dancing—the woman wearing Nikes and a floral skirt, the man's white chest hair poking out in tufts through his unbuttoned shirt. "Do you ever worry if we're messing things up because Priscilla and Teddy are going to remember us? Imagine when we zap forward in time and they're, like, I don't know, doing the dishes, then you show up and then it's like, *drops glass plate on the tile, 'You're that kid I knew from high school!'*"

I laughed. "I'm sure it'll happen just like that."

He shrugged, but seemed glad to have made me laugh. "I do worry about that. My mom and my grandparents live in Hollywood, so I don't have to worry about bumping into them. But they're all tight with Teddy, so I wonder, you know? What if they show up to the football game or something?"

It was cute, this stream of consciousness. He had been stuck here *so much* longer than me. He must be absolutely exploding with the things he could finally talk to someone about.

The sun had set, and it was getting cold. We watched as the mariachi band started to pack up.

"Well, and what's going to happen to us?" I asked. "Do you think . . . we'll remember each other when we get back? That we'll remember what we went through?"

Jamie let out a huge breath. "Man, that would be *messed up* if we didn't."

"But we might forget, right?" I was suddenly sick at the idea of not remembering any of this. Jamie.

He stood up, suddenly. "We don't know what's going to happen to us. So, let's make the most of tonight." He held out his hand and I grabbed it.

We ended up across the street at Union Station, a Spanish-style building constructed in the 1930s. Even people who have never been to LA have probably seen Union Station and its circular drive, lined with palm trees. It's been in a billion movies and TV shows, because it's beautiful and timeless in a city where things are discarded at a neck-snapping speed in pursuit of the next big thing. Union Station was like the best postcard version of Los Angeles.

Inside, the high ceilings were made of beautiful old wood, painted with Spanish flower motifs, the floors were tiled and the leather seats were deep.

Being in there was like . . . well. Traveling back in time.

And the best thing about train stations was that they were open twenty-four hours. During the day, it was crowded with travelers and commuters, but right now, it was quiet, almost empty, just a few people curled up in the cathedral-like waiting room, sleeping.

Jamie and I settled into a pair of chairs and leaned our heads back, looking up at the intricate ceilings.

"Hey. Do you think anyone else is doing what we're doing? Like, we can't possibly be the only *time travelers*." I whispered the last two words.

"I thought about that, but I kind of had to shut it down. It's just a little too mind-blowing."

I nodded. "Yeah, like that overwhelming feeling when you're at a planetarium and they start telling you about how small you are on Earth, and then Earth to the sun, and then like the sun to the solar system, and then—"

"I'm about to have a panic attack." But he laughed, this loose, open laugh that probably purified the air around us. "But yeah. Exactly that feeling."

The sound of a train coming in was loud in the quiet space. Jamie looked at me. "I don't think we have much time for like, wonder."

I shook my head. "No. We have less than forty-eight hours until votes are counted. *If* Priscilla's speech today did the job."

"I think it did," Jamie said, with a confidence I didn't quite share. "I think it showed that Priscilla is, like, human."

Our eyes met. "Why? Does she really seem that perfect?" I asked.

Without even the slightest hesitation, he said, "Yeah."

A surge of jealousy rushed through me, completely unwelcome. "Well, let me tell you, buddy, as her daughter, I can assure you that she's *not*."

He struggled to keep a straight face at my irritation. "I *know* she's not perfect. She just seems that way."

"Yeah, she does." I sighed. "I'm hoping that if she wins this thing, she'll chill the *hell* out and, like, I don't know, become someone who's not obsessed with being the poster child for American teens. And then maybe she'll stop pursuing that same exact ambition as an adult, making my life a whole lot easier!"

"Do you think that's the source of all the problems between you two?" He looked at me seriously.

Something about the way he asked it made a seed of doubt that had been bouncing around in the back of my mind the past few days start to really take root. "I really don't know anymore. I don't think it all comes down to the homecoming competition itself, but what the win means to Priscilla. I mean, our big fight was about me not running for homecoming queen anymore."

"*You* were going to run for homecoming queen?"

I poked him. "Don't look so skeptical!"

He laughed, holding up his hands. "I mean, up until today I believed that you won it already at your old school. Good cover story, by the way."

"God, all the stories I've had to make up!"

"Same. Uh-uh." He ran a hand through his hair. "Let's see, I said I used to intern for Bill Gates and that's why I'm so good with these dinosaur computers."

My laugh rang out in this beautiful space that had somewhat been frozen in time. It was tempting to pretend that we were, too—that our lives in the future were far away.

"Is that the fight that summoned Throwback? The fight about homecoming?" Jamie asked.

The memory of that fight in the parking lot—the things we both said to each other—came back to me in a painful wash of feelings.

"Yes and no." Again, courteous silence. I settled into the quiet, letting myself think before continuing. "It was also about my grandma."

Jamie made a sympathetic sound. I let myself look at him and take comfort in that patient, calm expression. "My mom can be such a . . . how do I say this?" Just a few days ago, I would have said something like "cold, unfeeling robot." But now, those words felt wrong. "She's just really bad at processing her emotions. Like, her *mother is in a coma* and she just went back to business as usual. She wanted to take me shopping the next morning. Anyway, I called her out on it. We fought and she left me in the rain."

Jamie was leaning the side of his head on his arm, looking at me. His voice was muffled into the crook of his arm when he said, "I'm sorry, Sam."

"Thanks," I said, tucking my own face into my arm. We looked at each other this way—our arms protecting the bottom halves of our faces, our eyes peeking out. "Imagine Priscilla being your mother when you're like me."

"What's that supposed to mean? When you're like you?"

"You know." I darted my eyes away, uncomfortable.

"I don't know."

My cheeks got hot. "Imperfect."

His silence this time was terrible. I stared at my fingers as I tapped on the wood armrest, feeling time pass by in some warped, slow-motion way and wanting to die. This was the kind of sad sack talk that would make Curren break out in hives.

"Perfect is boring."

It was the right answer. He always had the right answer, somehow. I relaxed and shot him a smile. "So, I'm not boring you?" It was teasing and blatantly flirtatious and I felt myself wince.

"I spend my thrilling evenings in an equipment closet, remember?" His eyes crinkled in the corners with amusement. "And no, you're not boring. At all. I'm happy to talk to you about all this. It's nice to finally have someone to talk to."

I couldn't even imagine the loneliness of being here for weeks, and I reached out, instinctively, to touch his arm. "Same, I'm glad we found out about each other."

He lifted his head, sitting up. "I can't believe I slipped with an Obama reference."

I snickered. "Dork."

"Nerd."

Someone coughed in the distance. I said, "Aren't the social hierarchies here so nuts? Like, I always thought nineties movies were exaggerating with all that stuff. But my mom is a straight-up *mean girl.*"

"Try being a football player. I have a cheerleader *assigned to me*. To bake me cookies."

I pulled at his letterman jacket playfully. "Regressive and gross, man."

"Agreed, man."

We smiled, not quite at each other, but warmth settled between us.

"When I go back—you'll be . . . what, in college?" I asked.

He nodded. "I hope. I'm applying to a few schools."

"Oh, wow. I'm also in the middle of apps. So weird."

"Yeah, college apps are the weird part of all of this. For sure."

I laughed. "Shut up."

"What schools?"

I pressed my lips together. My list of schools was nothing impressive, and I didn't *really* care but suddenly I did. When did I become a college snob like Mom? I rattled off the short list of colleges in an offhand way. "And yeah, like I mentioned, I have no idea what I'm majoring in, so I'm undeclared."

"Does that bother you?"

I felt instantly defensive, but he hadn't asked with any judgment, just a genuine, quiet curiosity. And I was about to say, "No, of course not," but there was something about Jamie that made me want to peel off this version of myself like a zip-up onesie—a version for my parents, for my teachers, even for Curren.

A onesie. Not that different from Priscilla's armor. Maybe. I thought of Neil—I thought of Curren. Why both Priscilla and I decided to date these guys. What they gave us. What we gave up in return.

Traveling back in time had made me realize that wearing this onesie *did* bother me. I thought of Halmoni in her coma, and the possibility that she might never wake up, never having known how things would work out for me, never seeing me graduate high school, go to college, get my first job.

"I don't know," I finally said. It was the truth. "I really do think it's kind of ridiculous to expect high school kids to declare what they want to study for four years and commit to a life path that early. Not everyone"—I waved my hand at him—"knows what they're into that early."

He nodded. "Yeah, that's true. But you'll figure it out."

"Do you have a girlfriend?" I blurted it out so fast, so loudly, that a flock of pigeons comically flew out of the rafters. "Oh gosh. Or boyfriend? Sorry to be so nineties."

The hand slid off my shoulder, slow and deliberate. I refrained from slithering like a little snake along with it.

He let out a huff of laughter. "Nope. And, uh, it would be girlfriend."

"Sorry. That was random."

"Not really."

"Yeah, I guess not. I do, though. Have a boyfriend."

"Yeah, you mentioned it earlier. Subtle." A literal twinkle in his eye.

I laughed. "I know. I just . . . I wanted to be fair to Curren."

"Curren." He said it like he was testing out the name in his mouth, as if it was the first time Jamie had ever heard such a strange word.

"Just so you don't think I'm a total time-traveling flooz"—he laughed—"things are weird with me and Curren, and this entire time traveling thing has made it all the clearer that I'm not sure why we're together. So. It's not like I'm madly in love with Curren and then just talking to you all the time, like, *oh this is so innocent.* And okay, I need to just stop." I ran my hands over my face and fake-screamed into them.

Jamie's laughter rang out through the station. "Samantha, it's okay. Don't worry about it. Any of it. Things are strange, this is unprecedented stuff we're experiencing. And besides, we need to keep our eyes on the prize, right? We've got this."

And even though it had the tone of a corny football pep talk, it worked. Because something about Jamie was steadfast and right. I trusted him—whatever was making me feel unsure and unfocused was finely calibrated in him.

Our conversation had opened an entire can of worms but, for now, I kept it locked tight. Together, we walked out of Union Station into the Los Angeles night.

thirty

thirty

one day to homecoming

It was homecoming court election day and all I wanted to do was run around yelling at people to vote for Priscilla, making it rain with dry cleaning coupons. But first I had to actually give the government presentation that Jamie and I had been working on.

We sat next to each other in class, both of us fidgeting—the air between us crackling with our shared secret.

A couple groups went up before us, presenting their bills. One pair just shared a speech that droned on and on about why we should pass the Civil Rights Act of 1964—a true disservice to one of the most important acts of Congress. If they got anything above a C-minus, there would be no justice in the world.

Then, Jennifer and Sung presented the Anti–Drug Abuse Act of 1988. They were both wearing black D.A.R.E. T-shirts and had visual aids with poster boards, one of which featured Nancy Reagan's face and her now infamous slogan, "Just say no." I tried to keep my own face straight as they made their case earnestly.

Some things just aged poorly.

Mrs. Worthington called me and Jamie up next. Jamie bent his head toward mine, his voice low. "Ready?" My stomach flipped.

"Yup!" I said, bouncing up from my chair. Jamie lurched back a bit to avoid getting impaled by my elbow. We both reached into our backpacks and pulled out tight velvet blazers we had scored at Goodwill. A few titters as we put them on over our regular clothes—I could hear Priscilla, specifically, groan. Jamie also pulled out a cassette tape player, borrowed from the football locker room. He hit play and the upbeat tempo of "Bad Moon Rising" by Creedence Clearwater Revival filled the classroom.

I clasped my hands in front of me. "Let me set the scene. It's 1969, the Beatles have their last performance on the roof of Apple Records. Three hundred fifty thousand music fans descend on Woodstock. We land on the moon. Richard Nixon wins the presidential election. The US starts withdrawing troops from Vietnam. Also happening is the bulldozing of entire communities and ecosystems during the construction of the Interstate Highway System."

I stopped to look at Jamie then. He looked down at his index cards, his hands shaking a bit. It was very cute. He said, "This bulldozing, along with a myriad of other environmental related events, has made American citizens angry and distressed at the impact of industrialism on our environment."

"It's time for a change," I said. I paused for dramatic effect. Priscilla made eye contact with me and rolled her eyes, but I ignored her. "So, Representative Mendoza and I, Representative Kang, would like to introduce to our esteemed members of Congress, the National Environmental Policy Act."

Jamie changed the cassette tape. I never appreciated digital music as much as I did in that painful twenty seconds of clattering tapes being removed and then placed into the stereo. At last the music started—this time Marvin Gaye's "Mercy Mercy Me." I let the smooth and mournful voice set the mood before I launched into the details of the bill. Both Jamie and I took turns making our case, while Marvin Gaye reiterated the urgency of the issue at hand.

When we finished (to enthusiastic applause, even from Priscilla), we handed out a sheet that gave a rundown of the biggest climate issues and the ways in which we could make small changes in our daily lives to help. Jamie and I shared a giant grin. We were hoping to incept a better world.

The rest of the presentations were *fine*, but I was buzzing from the success of ours and could barely pay attention. Although Priscilla and Deidre's was pretty good—it was an immigration bill—even if, at one point, I expected Deidre to say there was no "RSVP" on the Statue of Liberty.

While we watched the rest of the presentations, Jamie's hand brushed against mine, that was how close our seats were. It felt nice to be a part of a team. I felt a flash of guilt at thinking that—especially having spent all of my summer helping Curren with his film. But I had to admit it now, my mother had been right when she said I had spent too much time working on *his* thing. This was different. This was *our* thing. And not only that, Jamie had happily let me take the lead, but still pulled his own weight.

Class ended and as we headed out, Mrs. Worthington smiled at me and Jamie and said, "Great job, guys." It was such a little thing—a compliment from a teacher—but I'd forgotten what that felt like. To really work hard on something and be validated for it.

God, what was happening to me? I was becoming a corny school dork. And for something I wouldn't even get a grade for!

Priscilla said bye to me before running off to her next class when I felt someone touch my arm.

Jamie. "Hey. Remember what we talked about yesterday?" he asked.

"I don't know. We talked about a lot of things, one of which included *time travel*," I said, my voice hushed again at the last bit.

He smiled. "Yeah, we did. But I'm talking about the whole 'not knowing what your life path is' part."

"Oh, right," I said, confused as to where this was going. "Is my life path to be a . . . senator?"

His smile got bigger, his dark brown eyes literally twinkling with laughter. "Oh, well, yes, sure, if you want. But what I was going to say is that, well, you're a storyteller."

My cheeks felt hot at his conviction. "What makes you . . ."

"That speech you wrote for Priscilla. The way you tell me things about yourself. The way you look at everything through a specific point of view. You have something to say. And you know how to do it in an interesting way. To get people to listen. Like our presentation just now. It was like a podcast come to life." He paused and looked genuinely surprised. "Has no one ever told you that before?"

I looked away so I wouldn't tear up. "Yeah, I guess my grandmother."

He looked like he wanted to hug me or something, but instead he just chewed on his bottom lip. He kept his unwavering gaze on mine. "She sounds like a smart lady."

I needed to change the subject before I started full-on sobbing. "Hey, at least we learned how to use micro-freaking-fiche."

He threw his head back with laughter. "Oh, god. Did we, though? *Did we?*"

"You know, I actually believed that you knew how to use that thing," I teased. "You were very persuasive with all your silent confidence."

He blushed. "I mean, it didn't look that complicated. I watched that one lady and copied her exactly. Or so I thought!"

"Yeah, you could have pulled it off if the film reel didn't *launch into space.*"

Jamie laughed so hard he snorted. "Legit launched."

That made me laugh. It was really nice to hear familiar slang from this specific person.

The bell rang then, and we parted ways, headed off to our respective classes in 1995, Jamie's words lingering on my mind.

I had thought that outside of Mom stuff, nothing I did here would impact my future. But maybe I was wrong.

Before I could skip down the hall in my heel-kicking good mood, someone grabbed me by the arm and turned me around. Hard.

"Priscilla?" I pulled my arm out of her grip and rubbed it where she had grabbed me. "What the hell?" Her face was pale, her eyes wide with panic.

"Sam, we're screwed."

thirty-one

thirty-one

one day to homecoming

This was the first time in my life that I had ever been called into the principal's office. In fact, I thought that a principal's office was just a fantasy place that existed in teen movies. But no, there we were, sitting in front of the mahogany desk of Principal Barrett. The office was small and dark, its only window shuttered with blinds. The fluorescent lighting made me feel like we were being interrogated.

"Do you girls know why you were brought in here?" We sat silently on the hard plastic chairs. I looked to Priscilla, not wanting to say anything to jeopardize her. Also, I *hated* power trip questions like that. *Just tell us already!*

"I believe it was about the coupons," Priscilla said, her voice beyond polite.

"Exactly, young lady," he said, not using her name, infuriatingly, when there was no way he didn't know who Priscilla Jo was. He sighed and sat back in his leather chair, as if he were dealing with a nuclear crisis instead of some trivial high school drama. "It was brought to my attention that you are bribing the student body for homecoming votes with your coupons."

A shocked silence dropped between us.

"Well? What do you have to say for yourselves?"

Finally, Priscilla seemed to regain speech. "We're not! I mean, we're just offering an incentive—"

"A bribe," he interrupted. Rude and patronizing. It made me furious.

"This is ridiculous." My voice was loud, but steady. "We're not giving out coupons if people vote for her. We're giving them out as a promise if she wins. Like Priscilla said, it's an *incentive*."

He looked at me. "I don't really know you, young lady. But here at North Foothill, we hold everyone to the highest standards of fairness. No one gets special treatment."

I held back from laughing. What a load of utter bullshit. This high school was all about certain people receiving special treatment. He must have seen the derision on my face because he frowned deeply.

"I am seriously considering disqualifying you, Priscilla."

"What?!" I almost jumped out of my chair. "That's completely unfair! Steph Camillo's been giving out free ice cream all week!"

"*Sam.*" Priscilla's voice was clear and firm. It was Mom Voice. "Stop." She took a deep breath, her hands shaking in her lap. "Principal Barrett. I apologize, I had no idea this was going against the rules somehow. Please don't disqualify me. I can just tell everyone that the coupons don't apply anymore. Please."

She was pleading with him, but her spine stayed straight, her gaze clear and focused.

He thought about it then shook his head. "I don't know. This isn't the behavior one expects from the homecoming queen. You're supposed to set an example."

Her chin trembled as she nodded, the first sign of emotion breaking through. "I understand. But please, I've always been an example at this school. This is . . . the only . . . ," she swallowed, trying to keep her feelings in check, "the only time I've messed up."

He seemed to soften. "I'm going to think on it."

Think on it?! "But we have to vote during sixth period," I reminded him.

"I am well aware." He swiveled his chair to pick up some files, already dismissing us. "I'll let you know by the end of next period, Priscilla."

We were dismissed. When we stepped out into the administrative office, the bell was ringing to end lunch, and everyone was bustling around already. Priscilla was staring blankly in front of her, her posture completely slumped and defeated.

"There's no way you'll be disqualified," I said.

She looked at me with teary eyes. "How can you know that? Why do you act like you're so certain about everything all the time? You made me think I could win this thing. Now I might not be able to be on the *court*."

The truth of it punched me in the gut. All of this was my idea. It was my fault. I had somehow messed everything up, way worse than before. Priscilla might not win, and she'd get into the fight with Halmoni anyway, and I'd be stuck here in the past forever. Not able to reach Halmoni in the future. My family. Val. My entire life.

"I'm going to class," Priscilla said. When I made a motion to follow her, she held up a hand. "I don't want to talk about this anymore."

She walked out and I stood there, completely at a loss. Completely without a plan.

That was when I saw Steph Camillo slip into Principal Barrett's office.

What. The. Hell.

I thought of how I had talked to her at lunch that one day, and in the parking lot at Oakwood. How she knew about our coupon plan. How she'd clearly been threatened by Priscilla since day one.

Oh my god. This really was my fault.

All the air left my lungs and I slid into a nearby chair. Everything around me turned into a blur; I felt like I was going to pass out.

I needed to fix this. I needed to get home.

I looked to see if anyone was around, but the office was blessedly empty. I pulled out my phone. When I turned it on, the battery level made me cringe: 34 percent. This was worth it, though.

I opened the Throwback app and frantically looked for a contact link even though I already knew, from my frantic searching that first day, that one didn't exist.

In desperation, I said, "Siri, call Marge."

Siri basically LOL-ed.

Then, out of pure blinding frustration, I tried summoning another car. Even though there was no Wi-Fi. I hit "Request Ride" and watched the pinwheel of death spiral for eternity.

Damn it. I dropped my head between my legs, closing my eyes.

"Sam?" I opened my eyes and saw a pair of mismatched socks tucked into a pair of hiking boots. *What?*

I sat up straight and found myself looking at Marge.

MARGE.

"You!" I stood up immediately. "Send me back! *Now!*"

She grabbed my arm. "Follow me." People looked at us curiously as she pushed me into a nearby supply closet.

"What are you doing?" I watched Marge shut the door and turn on the light. We were surrounded by shelves of office supplies. In a small space. "Oh my god, I have *so much* to say to you."

Marge glanced at her wrist. Her bare wrist. "Well, you have five minutes."

"What?"

Her voice a monotonous drone, she said, "As per the fine print in your agreement with Throwback Rides, you are allowed one five-minute emergency advice session by your driver. That starts . . . now."

"Are you kidding me?" I asked her. "No. Nope. You're taking me back."

Marge looked at me then, her expression serious. "You haven't finished what it is you need to do here, Sam."

My eyes filled with tears. "I know. In fact, I messed it all up."

Her eyes never left mine. "Maybe. Maybe not. You still have an hour to fix things. How will you do that?"

"I don't know," I said with a hiccup. "I'm out of ideas. And I'm so tired."

Marge put her hands on my shoulders. "You're doing great. Do you think you could use what you've learned here to figure out a way to solve this?"

It was a patronizing question, but it got to the heart of the matter. The entire reason why I was here, right? I was supposed to solve this.

I thought of Steph going into Principal Barrett's office, of what that implied and how I could use that, of what my part was in all of this.

I thought I knew what I had to do.

Slowly, ever so slowly, I nodded my head. "Okay. Yeah, I think I can."

She clapped her hands so loudly I jumped back. "Great!"

"May I repeat for the millionth time, *what the hell*?"

She held up her empty wrist again. "Beep beep! Time's up."

With that, she whipped open the door and strode down the hall. I was at her heels. "Wait! Marge! That's it? Can you let me know if I'm on the right track? Is there a version of this where I might be stuck here forever?"

But she didn't stop, and when she turned a corner, she was gone. *Great!*

I didn't have time to think of how or what just happened and what the implications were. Fifth period was creeping along, and I needed to fix this.

Principal Barrett's door was still closed, so I paced in front of it, reliving my "triumphant" moment with Steph. That flash of fear in her eyes. *God damn it.*

The door finally opened, and Steph started when she saw me.

I held up my hands. "I just want to talk."

She worked her jaw, her eyes narrowed, not believing a word I said.

"Please."

We walked outside, the skies cloudy and the campus empty with everyone in class.

"What is it?" Steph asked in a clipped voice. "I have to get to class."

"Did you tell Barrett about our coupon?"

A tiny spark of that fear from earlier. She didn't answer right away.

"Listen, I'm not going to, like, beat you up, okay? I'm just trying to figure a way out of this!"

She sighed. "Yeah, okay? I didn't think it was fair."

"Did you not think it was fair, or did you not want Priscilla to win?"

"God, who cares *why* I did it, okay?" She pulled at a long strand of hair, looking down at it, as if it were the most fascinating thing in the world.

"I care!" I tried not to lose my temper. "It sucks that Priscilla might be disqualified because you got mad at *me*."

She looked up with confusion. "What? That's not why I did that."

"It's not? What the hell, then, Steph?"

"Because!" Her voice echoed in between the buildings. "Priscilla, Deidre, that whole group, they're *assholes*. They all treat me like shit, and I want her to *lose*. Do you know the stuff they say about me?"

Oh. *Oh*. I immediately cooled down. "Steph, I know. I hate those guys, too. But Priscilla? She's not really like them."

"*Okay*." Steph let out an incredulous scoff.

"I know, I know. I'm not saying she's perfect. Or, like, very nice to you. But—she's just trying to do her best here. You know, she's an outsider in that group, too, and she's only kind of accepted by them. Do you see *them* helping her campaign?"

Steph was quiet as she digested my words. She looked somewhere past my shoulder, her face impassive. "Well, they've always been such jerks to me since junior high. I don't know what I ever did to make all of them hate me. And Priscilla? Somehow, she knows how to make them like her."

"Yeah, but she pays for it," I said firmly. "It's hard on her."

"You wouldn't know it," she said with a scoff.

"I know. Because she . . . ," and my voice wavered then, "she's really good at keeping her emotions locked up."

Something buckled in Steph then. She looked down at her feet. "Yeah . . . I didn't know her dad died."

"I don't think she likes to talk about it."

Neither of us said anything for a while. Finally, Steph sighed, an epic sigh reserved for selling her soul to the devil. "Okay. What do you want me to do about it now?"

I looked at her hopefully. "For real?"

She scowled in agreement. I tried not to jump with joy. "Barrett said he would 'think on it' before sixth period. Can you go with me to tell him you're okay with the coupons and she should stay on the ballot?"

A long pause again before she rolled her eyes. "Fine." I tried to refrain from hugging her as we walked back to the office.

• • •

After it was all sorted out (Priscilla had taken the news stoically, but I saw the relief in her face), we all cast our votes during sixth period. A literal box was passed around the class for tossing in our handwritten selections. I held on to my piece of paper tightly when the box reached me. *Please, please, please.* I dropped it in and felt a weight lifted. It was all up to the election gods now. I had done all that I could do. I ran to Jamie's locker after school, excited to fill him in on my surprise Marge visit. He was grabbing his duffel when I reached him.

"You'll *never, ever* guess who I saw today," I said, gripping his arm.

He glanced down at my hand, then moved away.

"What? Are you scared of my cooties?" I teased. But his serious expression immediately sobered me. "What . . . what's up?"

Unable to look me in the eye, he said, "Teddy almost got kicked off the team today."

"What? Why?"

"Because he got drunk after practice last night." Jamie slammed his locker shut. "The practice that I ditched."

The pieces came together. He had missed practice because he had been hanging out with *me*. "Jamie, you can't—"

"Sam." His tone was hard, unyielding. "I'm not blaming you, it was my decision to skip, but I can't mess this up at the eleventh hour. I've been here for *six weeks*."

My heart sank. "I know. And you *won't* mess it up."

Jamie's jaw clenched as he shouldered his duffel. "You're right. I won't. Because I won't let myself be distracted." His voice softened. "I'm sorry, Sam." And then he walked away, without ever once looking at me.

thirty-two

thirty-two

homecoming day

I woke up the next day with a hard jolt, fully bouncing up into a sitting position. Today was the day. Either everything was going to go as planned, or I was going to be stuck in 1995 and live a life of fraud and maybe even be kidnapped and experimented on by the government when they realized that I had no social security number, or fingerprints or birth records on file.

No big deal.

And then there was Jamie. I still felt a gut punch when I replayed our last conversation. I understood where he was coming from, but it still hurt. Did the past week mean so little that he could walk away from it all so easily? Was I the stupid one for feeling so strongly about someone I just met? For wanting to break up with my boyfriend over him? I screamed into a throw pillow.

Mrs. Jo wasn't awake yet, so I pulled out my phone and started recording.

> Hi, Halmoni. I love the story of how you and Halabuji met. How he walked into your parents' restaurant on the day you were

supposed to take your passport photo. So, you were wearing your prettiest dress and had your hair done. It was like *the* moment for Halabuji to walk in while you were serving tables. And that you always felt like you "tricked" him because you normally didn't look like that. I'm not sure why I'm thinking about this story except—do you think that if people meet under extraordinary circumstances, that whatever feelings they have for each other might not endure? That it was only that specific cocktail of events that made it all happen?

. . . asking for a friend.

Yesterday had been my last day working at the dry cleaners—and possibly the last time I would see Halmoni. *At this age*. I had to keep saying that to myself. Halmoni would wake up in the future. I would make it back and be there for it. I had to be.

When I had said goodbye to her, I'd surprised her and gone in for a hug.

"Are you okay, Sammy?" she had asked with concern between her brows. Koreans didn't just *hug* each other.

I had brushed it off as excitement for homecoming and tried not to bawl as I walked away.

Today was going to be full of goodbyes. Next up: Mrs. Jo. I decided to spend a bit of quality time with her on our last day and we went to her favorite place—the Korean grocery store. I wanted to help her in some way after the inexplicable help she'd given me.

"This is too expensive for ppa," Mrs. Jo muttered.

I looked at the sign above the pile of green onions she was sifting through. They were like ten cents a bunch, lol. Korean grandmas gonna grandma.

After the produce section—where Mrs. Jo meticulously picked out soybeans, daikon radishes, and lettuce—we headed to the butcher counter. As she leaned over and checked out the fish and beef, I surreptitiously took out my phone, which I had already turned on a few minutes ago. I snapped a quick photo.

I just wanted something to remember Mrs. Jo by. Because future Mrs. Jo wasn't quite the same. But then I saw the battery level was at 20 percent, and that sent me spiraling so I turned it off before slipping it back into my pocket.

She haggled with the butcher until she got the cut of meat at the price she wanted, and we moved on to the frozen foods section. There was someone handing out samples of dumplings and I grabbed two for us.

Blowing on it to cool it off, I said, "I think mandoo is one of my top five favorite foods."

"Do you know how to make it from scratch?" Mrs. Jo asked as she scrutinized the dumpling before popping it in her mouth.

I nodded. "Yes, we do it for New Year's." Halmoni always made sure we made them, no matter how misshapen the dumplings became.

"Definitely better made from scratch," she said with a sniff. The lady giving out samples looked unamused. We moved on to the dried food aisle. "So, you're really ready to leave tonight?" I had already told her that I would be leaving that day.

"Yeah, I think I'm ready."

"Good. I'm sure your family misses you." Mrs. Jo grabbed a pack of kelp. I watched her efficient movements with fondness.

"Mrs. Jo, I don't know how to thank you for everything you've done for me."

She waved a hand and pushed the cart farther down the aisle. "It's nothing."

"No, it's not. I'm nearly a complete stranger and you—"

"You're not a stranger."

"Yes, I know we're family—"

She got down on her haunches and poked through bags of dried anchovies. "No, no. Not that. I know you from a previous life."

Oh boy.

"Yes, I know I'm a Christian. But when I was a little girl, I was raised Buddhist. And some of those things never left me, even if I now know that Jesus Christ died for our sins." She handed me a bag of anchovies and I placed it in the cart. "Reincarnation . . . I have always known that I had a previous life. I was a girl then, too. And so were you."

All I could do was follow her silently down the aisle, smiling widely at passersby. *Don't mind us, just talking about previous lives and Jesus.*

"When I saw you in the lobby that first day—something told me we had crossed paths before." And then she turned to me, her eyes raised to look at me directly. "And you knew me, too."

I couldn't deny it. I *did* know her. She must have picked up on that and thought it was because we were, like, courtesans from the Joseon era or something. I just didn't have it in me to argue with her, after all she'd done for me.

"Yes, I do think we've known each other before." It wasn't a lie. Suddenly I knew how I might pay Mrs. Jo back. It went against all the time traveling rules . . .

The aisle we were in was empty, so I drew in close and said, "So if you think we've met in a previous life, you trust me, right, Mrs. Jo?"

Her eyes scanned the row of chili paste in front of her and she made a noncommittal grunting noise.

I took out a pen and one of Priscilla's fliers from my backpack and scribbled something on it. "I am writing down a note for you to keep with you and read every day until you do it, okay?"

"What?"

"Just trust me. I'm writing down some Korean record labels and entertainment companies for you to invest in. Some exist now, and more will exist later, okay? Invest however much is comfortable for you—but do not forget to do it. And *do not* forget to invest in Big Hit when they become a company."

Without lifting her gaze from the chili paste, she held out her hand.

"Don't lose it!" I said firmly, placing the folded-up piece of paper in her palm and wrapping her fingers tightly around it.

"Okay, okay."

"Don't forget!" I held back tears at that. Dementia would eventually come for her, but until then she could be filthy rich.

Mrs. Jo triumphantly held up the paste she was looking for. Way more excited about that than the stock tips I had just handed her. "Yah, Sam. You nag too much. Let's go pay now."

I followed her to the registers, my step lighter than before, willing my desires into reality.

· · ·

With only a few hours left before the game, I joined Priscilla on the football field to help her put the finishing touches on her float. What I didn't expect to see was the football team practicing on the other side of the field. I tried not to be obvious, but my eyes were on Jamie. I was keeping my distance, but not feeling great about it.

He was tall and slender compared to most of the players, but counter to his self-deprecating description of his athletic skills, he wasn't bad. He definitely wasn't *great*, but he had a grace to his movements. It wasn't awkward at all.

Suddenly, my vision was blocked by Priscilla's face. "Wow." She shook her head. "Did you break up with your ugly boyfriend yet?"

I thought of Curren's dreamy gray-blue eyes, the way his lip curled when someone told a joke. "No. And he's *not* ugly. In fact," I looked at her slyly, "some would call him Jordan Catalano bad news."

She groaned. "Of *course,* you'd like that kind of guy."

I let that one slide. "As opposed to what? What kind of guys do *you* like?" In the future, I knew her type. Guys like my dad. Reliable, a little old-fashioned, smart, and hard-working. A lover of dad jokes. That last quality might have been something she endured rather than sought out. But Neil really threw me for a loop.

"I don't know. Cute ones?"

"Wow, truly original," I said flatly. "What else?"

She stared out into the football field. "Well, I like guys who aren't full of themselves."

"You mean like Neil?" I asked pointedly as he spiked the football into the field aggressively then literally pounded his chest in celebration.

"Neil's whatever," she said with an eye roll. "I'm just going to homecoming with him, not *marrying* him. It's just high school nonsense. I'm waiting for the right guy once I graduate, when you can actually get serious."

This shouldn't have surprised me. My mom's pragmatism was really at the beating heart of all her decisions. I watched Jamie as he loped between cones while others sped through. There was something about his lack of urgency that made my lips curve up into a smile.

She followed my line of vision and rolled her eyes but smiled, too. "Although . . . sometimes high school guys can be fun to watch, too."

The two of us stood there, leaning against the chain-link fence, and kind of perved out for a minute watching the football players. Jamie was kneeling on one knee, his other leg stretched out behind him. He held the football and another player stood by, looking like he was about to kick it. But, at the last minute, he stopped, and Jamie stood up, ball still in hand. Then he tossed it across the field. Ah, this was that trick play he was telling me about. The ball kind of wobbled as it arced through the air. They did this play a few more times, Jamie crouching down each time to set up the play.

"Do you think," I mused, "that when they invented football, they called a position 'tight end' just to make us focus on the best part of this sport?"

"Sam!" But the chiding was mixed with a burst of laughter. A full-bodied laugh that made Priscilla throw her head back and close her eyes. It made me incredibly pleased with myself. When I was little, I often cracked my mom up by doing silly things—like wearing her bra on my face or pretending to trip and fall into the swimming pool. But over the years, the instances I made her laugh grew fewer. Pretty much nonexistent now.

So, I let myself bask in this A-plus level of laughter from her. I was going to miss this.

And then, because it felt like one of the nicest moments I'd had with Priscilla, and because this might be one of my last chances to get her to talk about this specific topic, I decided to ask, "What's it like to lose your dad?"

As expected, she was completely caught off guard by this random and very intrusive question. But I let the awkward and shocked silence continue, a trick used by interviewers—letting silences linger because people always rushed to fill them.

Priscilla turned to the field, her arms folded across the top of the fence. "It's shitty." She let out a laugh. "Like, duh, right? But it's *really* shitty. He was sick but died really quickly after his diagnosis. Stomach cancer. I guess he was in pain for months and hadn't gone to the doctor because we don't have health insurance."

I sucked in a breath. They didn't? I knew enough about health care in this country to know that living without insurance was basically being a walking time bomb. Which I guess exploded on Priscilla and her family four years ago.

"So, yeah. He got sick and was in the hospital for a couple months and then he just . . . died." Her voice was quiet, a whisper at that last word. "Some family helped us by running the cleaners and taking care of Grace—she was only two, but my mom and I were at the hospital every day. It was really terrible . . . this is going to sound so bad." She glanced up at me, worried about my reaction. "But I really hated being there. I wanted to be anywhere but there. I didn't want to see my dad like that. It made me want to scream having to watch strangers change his diapers, feed him through a tube. And while I'm grateful for everyone who tried to help him get better, I never want to step foot into a hospital again for as long as I live."

I thought of my mom practically pushing me out the door of Halmoni's hospital room, what it had felt like at the time. And how different it felt now.

It was hard for me to hold back tears. "I'm so sorry, Priscilla."

She sensed it in my voice and glanced at me, her own eyes glassy. "Thanks. I don't . . . I don't really have anyone to talk to about this."

"What about your mom?" I asked, kind of knowing the answer already.

"My mom?" Priscilla stared back out onto the field. "She . . . she's the one person who was sadder than me. She was so sad that it filled up our entire family. The apartment. There was no space for me to be sad."

The words landed between us with such rawness that I was completely speechless. So, my arms just reached out and brought her in for a hug. She was quiet for a second before saying, voice muffled in my jacket, "Thanks."

When we pulled away, Priscilla wiped her eyes and I looked away to give her some privacy. Getting a handle on my own emotions. My eyes were eventually drawn to Jamie as he guzzled a bottle of water on the sidelines.

"So, did you ask him yet?" Priscilla asked, her composure back as she swiped at the smeared mascara under her eyes.

"Huh?" I tried to cover up my embarrassment at having been caught looking at him.

"To the dance!" Priscilla leaned into the fence and openly stared at Jamie. He must have felt our eyeballs on him because he turned toward us.

"Oh my god," I muttered as I swiftly dropped my head. "Priscilla!"

She waved at him. "I bet he would die happy if you asked him."

Thinking about how I would have agreed with her just a day before made me sad, so I just laughed it off. "Can you stop with the matchmaking, ahjumma?"

"Well, time's ticking!" Priscilla said, tapping her watch.

She had no idea.

thirty-three

thirty-three

homecoming day

On homecoming night, the lights of the football stadium were blazing.

I clutched my backpack straps like my life depended on it. It had Priscilla's red dress in it, and I knew that if it got even one wrinkle, she'd murder me. And I'd decided to keep my books and school stuff in the backpack, too. I was feeling optimistic about making it back to Norm Times and going about my life like nothing happened. Although I had no idea how I'd be able to do that, really. How does one recover from time travel? Wish Marty McFly had written a manual after his travels.

I walked into the stadium, past the filled bleachers and onto the blindingly bright football field. The grass was green, freshly cut and fragrant, and the cheerleaders from both schools were stretching near the bleachers. Low-vibrating strains of wind instruments and the occasional honk came from one side of the field, the marching bands warming up. A current of excitement ran through it all, and for a second, I understood why people loved high school. Something about tonight felt like it could last forever.

I walked all the way down to the sidelines looking for Priscilla. When I spotted her, chatting with the cheerleading squad, I waved. She just nodded in greeting, but there was warmth in her expression.

After I found a seat close to the sidelines on the North Foothill side, the football players streamed out onto the field—in dramatic, overly rah-rah fashion, of course. Jamie was one of the last ones. I spotted him by his height and movements. When he took a seat on the bench, I willed Jamie to look behind him, but he stared resolutely ahead. I swallowed the hurt creeping through me.

As far as football games go, this was probably the most exciting one I had ever seen. My investment level was so intense that the people sitting behind me moved seats. Every time the linebacker on the rival team, the Lone Pine High Titans, plowed into Teddy, I yelled, "I'm gonna murder you in your sleep, you shithead!"

The game was going well so far. In the first quarter, both teams had scored touchdowns, so we were tied 7–7. Then in the second quarter, the Coyotes scored another touchdown, but then the Titans made a field goal. (I made this random woman next to me explain it all, not wanting to miss a single, potentially life-altering thing.) So, we were up by four points, 14–10, by the end of the second quarter. Teddy was playing well. Really well. I hoped Jamie was feeling good. Less stressed. I wished I could help, but at this point it was just all up to Teddy.

It was also the first time I saw Priscilla in her element: cheerleading. Watching her now, I realized she was *good*. Not just at smiling and being peppy, but she was athletic as hell. Even though they were expected to be sideline accessories for these giant guys hitting each other, Priscilla took the job seriously, giving it her all as she executed perfect kicks, flipped in the air, and balanced girls on her shoulders. And more importantly, she enjoyed it. I saw the gleam of pride, the joy in her eyes, as she was up there. This stuff that I found so superficial—the cheerleading, the nice clothes, the country club—it all made her *genuinely* happy. I saw it now.

The referee whistled for halftime, and everyone got up to go pee and grab food. I stayed put in my seat, not wanting to miss a single thing.

The football team jogged off the field and Jamie got up to join them. Again, I hoped for a backwards glance, anything to signal that he was thinking about me. But I got nothing.

A few minutes into halftime, the homecoming courts from both schools came out, driven out in their floats. But after the first couple floats, I noticed something. The princesses were accompanied by older men—not the princes.

Their dads.

I felt a sharp pang in my chest. *Who would be with Priscilla?* I knew that Halmoni wasn't coming. And none of the other girls seemed to be coming out with their moms anyway. God, what regressive quaintness was this?! It wasn't like they were walking down the freaking aisle! Shades of the country club brunch had me sweaty. Then Priscilla came out—wearing her cheerleading uniform, but her hair was out of its pony, instead falling over her shoulders in perfect ringlets. She was cradling a bouquet of white roses, perched on a palm tree–framed throne with her tiara twinkling in the stadium lights. Beautiful and untouchable. And alone.

Maybe it was my imagination, but I felt a hush go over the football field. And it had the stink of *pity*. Priscilla's smile never faltered but I saw a tenseness in her shoulders, a slight push up toward her ears that indicated a defensive posture.

This was *my mom*.

Without a second's thought, my backpack still on, I ran down the track toward Priscilla's float. I saw the surprised expressions of the cheerleading team, the marching band, the people in the stands, and the girls in the floats ahead of Priscilla. When I reached her, her smile turned into an open-mouthed "Huh?"

I grabbed the edge of the truck bed and awkwardly pulled myself over it, landing in a pile at her feet.

"What are you *doing*?" Priscilla asked, her voice high and *deeply* confused.

I scrambled up next to her, my butt perched daintily on the edge of her armrest. "I am here to be your chaperone, young lady."

The driver barely glanced at us and kept the snail's pace of the float moving forward.

Priscilla was so stunned that she was speechless.

"As your campaign manager, I think I earned this privilege, don't you?" I said, not looking at her but at the crowds, waving at them beatifically.

She was silent, and when I finally had the nerve to look at her, she looked like she might cry.

Oh my god. Nooooo! I couldn't make her cry twice in one day.

But she blinked her tears back and smiled. "You're so weird." And then she turned her megawatt smile at the crowds again, waving and being queenly. With that one proclamation, I knew that she understood what I was doing. And that she was grateful. Something that was felt rather than said. Like we were family.

We drove around the stadium at sloth speed, the marching band playing some heavy saxophone cheesiness, and when we reached the tunnel toward the locker rooms, I saw the football team hovering, ready to run back onto the field.

And finally, *finally*, I made eye contact with Jamie, who was leaning against the fence. The look he gave me then—it zapped me to my core. He knew why I was in that car. When we got close to him, he lifted his hand up to his chest, right over his heart. His eyes warm, his expression soft—the distance from earlier gone. My cheeks burned but I smiled at him, giving him my best beauty pageant wave. His face cracked into a huge smile, as if he couldn't help it.

After the parade o' floats, Principal Barrett walked to the middle of the football field with a microphone. "Good evening, North Foothill Coyotes and our guests, the Lone Pine Titans!" Everyone cheered but in a bit of a lackluster, forced way. I found my way back to my seat, clapping politely. "I just wanted to talk to everyone about why we're all gathered here today. Homecoming is a tradition that we've held here at North Foothill for over seventy years. For as long as there were alumni for this school, we've devoted an entire week to welcome them back. It is a literal homecoming for anyone who has walked through these halls as a student."

Wow. Legit *never knew* that's what homecoming meant.

"It's when the past comes to the present. And let me tell you, youngsters, no memories that you have will ever be as vivid as these years. The people you know, every relationship you've formed—they'll never leave you. Ten, twenty, thirty years from now."

I searched the lineup on the field for Jamie. There he was, number 28. And it was like my eyeballs, my thoughts, called out to him. He turned his head slightly, his profile lit up by the stadium lights. His hair damp and curled against his forehead. Then he turned completely to look at me.

Yeah, we wouldn't ever forget this.

"Okay, back to the game! Don't forget to join us tonight for the homecoming dance here at the gym!" Everyone clapped and the football players ran onto the field, giving Principal Barrett high fives along the way.

The ref blew his whistle again and the game immediately started up. Jamie sat back on the bench.

Almost immediately after the game started, there was a roar from the crowd. My head snapped back to the game. The Titans had just made a touchdown. *Damn!*

My heart was in my throat as I watched them play—a smash of bodies, a figure darting through, running like lightning, a ball being passed in a smooth arc high above, a whistle blown—it felt like a lifetime as I watched the game go on. And through it all, Jamie sat on the bench, his elbows on his knees and his chin propped on his hands as he watched Teddy intently. He would jump up at times and yell, cheering him on.

Finally, in the fourth quarter, we scored—but it was a field goal. Which meant yet another tie, this time 17–17. But the relief was short-lived, because Lone Pine also made a field goal—giving them the lead at 20–17. With one freaking minute left on the clock.

"COME ON!" I yelled, pounding my feet on the stands.

A guy behind me muttered, "What a psycho."

I ignored him, my eyes riveted on the field. "WIN THIS FREAKING GAME!"

The Coyotes were now on the Titans' thirty-yard line. The woman next to me yelled, "Come on, go for the field goal! We'll get them in overtime!" I agreed wholeheartedly. If the Coyotes went for the field goal, they would keep it completely out of Teddy's hands.

Suddenly, a whistle was blown, and the Coyotes coach turned and looked at the bench. "Mendoza! You're in!"

My breath caught. Jamie got up quickly, fumbling with his helmet.

Holy shit. This was great—this meant they were going for the field goal. I clenched my hands, still worried because Jamie had so much riding on this game.

The coach yelled for him again and Jamie ran to him in a hurry. Teddy was also standing next to the coach, his hands on his hips as Jamie bent in to hear the coach's words. Suddenly his head snapped up and I saw his entire body tense.

Shit. What now?

He nodded robotically and then looked over at me, finding me in the crowd instantly, as if he had known where I'd been the entire time. Intense affection coursed through me, and I tried to give him an encouraging smile before he ran onto the field, but my palms were instantly sweaty. Something was wrong.

Shit, shit, shit.

thirty-four

thirty-four

homecoming day

As suspected, Jamie set himself up for the field goal, crouching down and holding the ball in place. The kicker jogged over and the two of them exchanged quick high fives, while Teddy took his spot on the line with the rest of the team.

The crowd grew quiet as the kicker stepped back, taking a breath before running toward the ball. But then, in a moment of pure déjà vu, I saw the kicker veer to the side at the same moment Jamie stood up.

Oh my god. It was the trick play. Jamie had to do the damned trick play. Which meant—he had to *pass the ball.* To . . .

Teddy. Teddy was in the end zone, ready to catch that pass. His hands were thrown up, waving to show Jamie he was open.

"Ohmyyyyygoddddd," I couldn't help but groan, clutching the sides of my face as I watched Jamie hold the ball up in the air, his arm poised, his eyes on Teddy. Lone Pine players started rushing him immediately and the kicker blocked one of them with a full-body tackle, buying Jamie about half a second.

As I held my breath, as every muscle in my body stilled, Jamie, all six foot three of him, let go of the ball. It soared through the air, high above the heads of the linebackers, spiraling like it was blessed by Coach Taylor himself.

A perfect arc that then landed directly into Teddy's outstretched hands.

The silence immediately exploded into cheers, into stomping feet. I thought that was it but the team immediately got back into kicking formation. Jamie held the ball, the kicker kicked it, and it soared between the goal posts. The announcer's voice yelled, "And the Coyotes *win it* with a game-winning touchdown by Teddy Quintero! Twenty-four to twenty-one!"

Everyone in the stands went absolutely wild and rushed the field. I ran with them, my vision laser-focused on one person. Whatever obstacle had been between us, it was gone now. I didn't care about any of it anymore.

And Jamie didn't either. He met me on the edge of the field just as I ran on—and there was nothing else I could do but jump straight into his arms. He was sweaty and hot and covered in dirt and grass, but he lifted me up high off the ground and I screamed, so loud that my voice cracked, "*YOU DID IT!*"

I was suspended there—in the air, in his arms, and in time—forever. My happiness and relief for him crashed over me until I was laughing and crying at the same time. I slid down from his grasp, his pads and jersey catching my jacket. When I finally looked at him, his dark eyes were wet. He was taking huge, gulping breaths, totally shaken.

I went to wipe his tears off his face and he caught my hand and pressed his mouth into my palm. "I'm sorry."

"It's okay—I get it, I totally get it," I said, getting teary, too.

He kept his lips pressed to my hand when he looked into my eyes. "Find me, okay? Find me in the future. We're going to remember each other, I know it."

I wasn't laughing anymore. I was barely able to breathe.

"Promise?" he asked. I nodded. He let go of my hand, of my body, and turned to hug Teddy. Fierce and hard. Said something into his ear.

Teddy couldn't stop smiling, his lean face stretched to accommodate the bigness of it. I wished for him the best future he could possibly have. Not just for Jamie's sake, but for his. And then I got distracted because something in Jamie's pants was glowing.

His phone. *Holy shit.*

It must have vibrated, too, because he startled and reached for it. Everyone was on the field now and it was so chaotic that no one noticed him looking into the screen of a device that wouldn't be invented for another decade.

He looked up at me and nodded. We ran off the field together, him much faster than me. I heard Priscilla call out my name and I turned to her as I ran. "I'll see you at the dance!" I could feel the million questions from her open-mouthed stare.

When I turned back, I saw that Jamie was waiting for me, his hand outstretched. I grabbed it and we ran to the front of the school together, as natural as if we'd been doing it forever.

The teal hatchback was parked in front, idling, with the exhaust gathering around it in a dense cloud.

Jamie and I stopped in our tracks.

"Throwback." My voice was almost a whisper—oddly reverent of the cursed rideshare that had brought us here.

We looked at each other, our hands still clasped, our breathing hard and uneven.

"Did you get a notification or something?" I asked.

He nodded. "Yeah. It said I completed my mission, and my ride was here."

We stared at said ride. With the cloud of exhaust shrouding the car, I could barely make out the silhouette of Marge. I couldn't tell if I found her menacing or comforting or both.

"Okay. It's your time, Jamie." I smiled, even though it was harder than anything. "I'm so relieved for you. For Teddy."

He started chewing on his bottom lip in this way that made me think he was trying not to cry again, and I just wouldn't be able to handle it if he did. I'd probably start sobbing for the next thirty years.

"Why is this so hard?" he asked.

We had only known each other for one measly week. But now that it was time to say goodbye, the pull of wanting to stay together was as strong as gravity. I squeezed his hand. "You don't belong here. I don't belong here. We need to go home."

He blinked and swallowed hard. "Yeah." And then he pushed his glasses up with a single index finger, a nervous habit, I realized at that moment. "Good luck with your mom, Samantha. I'll . . . I'll be thinking of you."

It was kind and also kind of smoldering. "Thank you, and good luck with Teddy. I hope this all works out for him and your family in the future," I said, my insides melting. "Also, hey, don't look for me yet. Wait for *me* to find *you*, all right?"

He hesitated for a moment, and I grabbed his shoulders with both hands. "I mean it. It'll mess things up. And I don't want you to see me as a fugly sophomore anyway."

He laughed then and pulled me into a tight hug. "Right. Wouldn't want to scare you with my cool senior vibes."

A honk came from the car, the passenger side window rolled down, and Marge yelled, "I'm leaving in ten seconds!"

Jamie cursed under his breath, then brushed his lips over my cheek. A kind-of-but-not-really kiss. A ghost of something more intense. Or a foreshadowing. "See you on the flip side," he said, voice close to my ear.

Then he ran to the car, sliding into the back seat, his tall frame in football gear immediately filling up the small space. He looked straight ahead, not making eye contact with me, and I kept a smile on my face until the car turned a corner, out of view.

I stood alone, the sound of the football game behind me, the evening air metallic with the promise of a storm.

thirty-five

thirty-five

homecoming day

After everyone left the game, I ducked into the girls' locker room to get ready for the dance. I turned the lights on, and the rows of lockers and benches were lit in a sudden garish wash of white. I shook Pricilla's dress out of my backpack and was relieved to see it wasn't too wrinkled.

There was something grim about the empty locker room and harsh lighting as I did my hair and makeup in complete silence. After a while I felt like throwing myself off a cliff, so I took a risk and started playing some music. Thank god I believed in downloading actual albums over streaming. When I hit play, my battery started draining immediately, but I felt good about tonight. I was going to go back home. It was like proof of faith by playing music.

When a moody track by Billie Eilish filled the locker room, I kept replaying the image of Jamie driving off into the night fog as I brushed a streak of glittery eyeshadow across my eyelid.

I blinked and stared back at my own face. *I'll be thinking of you.*

I fumbled for some drugstore mascara, my mouth open ever so slightly as I applied it. *Find me in the future.*

My cheeks were already pink as I brushed on a dusty rose powder onto my cheekbones. I needed to *stop*. Suddenly, a memory came over me. When I was little, I loved watching my mom put on makeup. I would sit on her bed and watch, entranced, as she sat at her vanity, gently patting her face with her products. Everything she did was intentional and calming.

For the five hundredth time that day, I felt my eyes prick with tears. Everything from the past few hours seemed to catch up with me in this locker room. I thought of saying bye to Jamie, at having to say bye to Priscilla soon.

A few days ago, I would have chopped off my own arm to go back to my timeline. And now I found myself hating having to say goodbye to it all. Inexplicably, I'd grown fond of this time period—so foreign yet a needed blank slate for me. It was here that I felt good about school. Clear-eyed about Curren. And it's here I became friends with my mother.

After a while, I could hear the DJ setting up in the gym.

This was it.

The gym was thumping with music and strobe lights flashed through the dark.

I was one of the first ones there, so I headed to the drink table where losers of time immemorial hung out at school dances. A few teachers and chaperones approached me kindly to chat and I endured the awkwardness valiantly. Eventually people trickled in as I sat at a table with my third drink. I kept my eye on the entrance until I saw Priscilla and her crew walk in. She was holding Neil's hand with an orchid corsage on her wrist, a swirl of silver ribbons trailing down. Her dress was ice-blue satin, the delicate spaghetti straps and full skirt giving her very real princess vibes.

She saw me and waved, grinning. Abandoning my plastic cup of 7 Up, I walked over to her. "Hi! You look great!"

And she did. Her hair was curled into perfect ringlets, her makeup was flawless, and her dress fit her perfectly. Halmoni had come through.

"I'll go get us drinks," Neil said, eager to have something to do that wasn't witnessing two girls talking about things.

"A proper date," I said.

"Oh, god. What are you going to criticize now?" Priscilla asked with a frown.

"Actually, nothing. He seems . . . fine tonight."

"He's tall," she said with a shrug. "We'll look good in our dance photos."

"Jesus," I said with a laugh.

Her face lit up then. "Hey! Let's take one, too. I'll pay."

I was about to agree to it, when it occurred to me that it was a very bad idea. "Oh, um, no, that's okay."

She tugged on my arm. "Come on!"

Shiiiiiiit! I laughed. "I hate photos. I'm so unphotogenic." Vanity she would understand.

"You look good! Let's do it," Priscilla said firmly, dragging me to the photo area near the back of the gym.

How was I going to get out of this? Priscilla couldn't have a photo of me—one day it might occur to her that I looked exactly like a friend she knew back in high school.

No one was in line for photos. *God damn!*

The smudgy-paint photo backdrop somehow complemented Priscilla's blue dress. She stood in front of it, waiting for me impatiently. Panic filled me but I found myself, as in the future, unable to push back against my mother. She had us standing back-to-back, Charlie's Angels style.

"Put your hands on your hips; it'll make your upper arms look less flabby." Priscilla poked me with her elbow.

"I personally love when my arms look flabby," I muttered. But I moved my arms into the requested position. When the photographer called out "One, two, *three*," I shot my hand out and covered the bottom half of my face. I did it so quickly that Priscilla didn't notice. The photographer peered over at me, his mouth opening to say something, but I shook my head at him.

"There's Neil with our drinks," I said, pulling Priscilla away. Neil was, indeed, standing in the middle of the gym holding drinks. I took a tentative sip. Yup. Not spiked. This was going to be a long night.

Deidre and company eventually found us, and I hung back as they talked shit as usual, but louder and in formal wear. Sweat started to pool under my arms. It wasn't the heat, although it wasn't exactly fresh and breezy in there. It was that every minute that passed brought me closer to the homecoming queen announcement.

Marge, that weirdo, wouldn't ever let me get *stuck back in time*, right? If only Jamie were actually from the same time as me—he'd be able to know if I made it back. As it was, he'd have to wait two years to see if my plan worked.

A song came on then that made everyone literally scream and drop everything and run to the dance floor. Once I could hear the song, I smiled. "Nuthin' but a 'G' Thang." Some things about high school dances were timeless. I watched this group of suburban kids sing and rap along, feeling ownership over a song they didn't actually understand.

But there was something nice about it anyway. It was weird to know that when I went back home, these kids would all be thirty years older. What I was seeing now . . . maybe these weren't their best years. For some people, high school was just this obstacle they had to get through before living their real lives. I imagined that some of these people who lived in the margins, in obscurity, would grow up to do awesome things. To be themselves. To thrive outside of the social norms of 1995.

But others . . . I don't know. Maybe these would be their glory days.

I watched Priscilla glow in the middle of the dance floor, a huge smile on her face as she danced—happy and so comfortable in her skin. But always contained and in complete control.

Why do you care about stupid things?

My own words to her echoed in my mind as I watched her dance, as I felt myself care so much about her winning homecoming queen. I didn't know if high school was Mom's glory days. I certainly hoped not. But I understood why it was important to her.

And then Priscilla looked straight at me and waved me over, mouthing, "Dance!" I put my drink down and walked to the dance floor, passing by people freaking low on the gym floor. Wow, a little early for that, but whatever. When I reached Priscilla she did this goofy wave of her hands, drawing me to her. I laughed at the surprising absurdity of it. My mom was many things, but playful was not one of them.

For many songs, we danced. Shimmied, clapped, and spun around. At one point, we bumped into Sung and Jennifer on the dance floor. And there was something about dance floors that neutralized everything—in our sweaty, giddy states we just danced together. Free from the social lines that separated us. I even threw my arm around Sung and jumped up and down to "Blister in the Sun" with him. Time passed and it stayed still. I tried to be in it every second, to appreciate every last minute I'd have with Priscilla as herself. Not as my mother. Not as a wife. Not as a woman who had expectations for me. But as someone who was excited to spend a night dancing with her friends.

When Principal Barrett finished his embarrassing dance and tapped the mic before announcing the homecoming king and queen, I felt Priscilla's hand reach out for my own. My heart beat so hard I thought she'd be able to feel it in my palms.

And it was the weirdest thing. Suddenly, the shape of my desire for her to win changed—from this thing that determined my fate, to one that determined her happiness. Whether that happiness would go the distance, sustain itself for more than a few hours or days, I didn't know. But it didn't matter. I wanted it for her.

The center of the gym lit up in colorful spotlights and Principal Barrett held up a piece of paper. "First up, our homecoming king is . . ." A drumroll played off the speakers. "Neil Harper!" Cheers rang in the crowd as Neil, chest puffed up, strolled up to Principal Barrett. A girl with an elaborate updo handed him a red velvet crown, like one you'd find on a cartoon king. He wore it at a rakish angle, all swagger. For Priscilla's sake, I refrained from barfing.

"And now, for the winner of the homecoming queen crown . . ." Another drumroll. I squeezed Priscilla's hand and she looked over at me with a nervous smile. Principal Barrett paused and looked into the audience. "With one of the tightest races I've ever seen as principal—Priscilla Jo!"

A scream shook loose from my soul. Completely out of my control and so incredibly loud that people around us made faces and clutched their ears. But I didn't care. And Priscilla didn't care either—she reached over, and we hugged, jumping up and down. We did it. Holy shit. HOLY SHIT!

"Congratulations!" I cried, my smile huge.

She shook her head, amazed by it all. "I can't believe it!"

"Believe it!"

And then her hand was leaving mine, the crowd pulling her away from me. I watched her with a lump in my throat—knowing this was probably the last time I would see my teenaged mother. When she walked past Sung and Jennifer, Sung cupped his hands over his mouth and whooped. She flashed them the biggest, most beautiful smile I'd ever seen on her, and Sung looked like he'd been physically stunned.

The girl onstage handed Priscilla her bouquet and a sparkly, jeweled crown. It sat on her head perfectly, like she was born to wear it.

Her smile was big enough to light up the entire world. Her happiness couldn't be contained. I felt my chest constrict with pride, and relief unraveled from there to my entire body. We did it. *She* did it. When I glanced at Jennifer and a still-stunned Sung in the crowd, I knew that I had helped make it happen.

Then I saw Steph in the crowd, her candy-pink dress tight, her hair straightened into a shimmering cascade down her back. We made eye contact, and I mouthed, "Thank you." And even though she was clearly crestfallen, she smiled at me. Steph wasn't too bad. I'd have to make sure Priscilla eased up on her.

As confetti poured down from the ceiling, I reached for my phone, turning it on and waiting for the message.

Except it wasn't there.

Maybe there was a delay. I should wait in the front of the school, like Jamie did. I took one last look at Priscilla, beaming in her crown, and felt peace come over me. All was right in the world. I gave a silent goodbye while dashing out the door. *See you in the future, Mom.*

It was freezing outside, and my breath came out in visible puffs as I ran, taking the stairs two at a time. But when I reached the entrance, the street was completely empty. The air was heavy with fog, the streetlights glowing in diffused balls.

Where was she? I glanced down at my phone again. Nothing.

I stared out into the road, willing the car to come careening around the corner dramatically. My arms broke out in goosebumps, and I rubbed them for warmth, the minutes ticking by.

But the car never came. Instead, people started spilling out of the gym—the dance was over. My heart sank into the depths of my body. *Why isn't Marge here? Why the hell am* I *still here?* People moved around me, everyone flushed and happy after the dance. But I watched it all on mute, in slow-motion, not hearing anything over the roaring freak-out in my own brain.

"Sam!"

The familiar voice shook me out of my paralysis. Priscilla's arm was hooked through Neil's, her crown still perched perfectly on her head. The picture of high school royalty. "Where were you?" she asked with a laugh, still euphoric from the win.

I tried to look normal. "Oh, just needed some fresh air. Congrats, by the way! You did it!"

She grinned. "With your help." She shook her head. "Thanks, Sam." She came in close for a hug. Awkward and stiff because hugs were probably so outside of her brand. But I hugged her back, with a fierce sincerity that probably made her very uncomfortable. I was scared, and it was good to have my mom near, in any form.

When she pulled away, she frowned. "You're ice cold," she said. "Neil, let Sam borrow your jacket."

He sighed deeply but shrugged out of his jacket anyway. I held my hand up in protest. "No, no, it's okay!" I looked at Priscilla carefully then. Did *anything* change? This was it, right? Winning homecoming queen?

"Sam, just wear the jacket, you're turning like a weird purple color," she said firmly.

And yet.

She acted the same. I didn't know what I was expecting. Some profound softening of the heart? A visible warmth in her matter-of-fact, survivor armor?

"You're coming to Deidre's, right?" she asked as I draped Neil's cologne-scented jacket over my shoulders. Right, there was an after-party. An after-party that I hadn't thought about because I had assumed there was no way in hell I would still be here for it.

I tried to blink away the tears threatening to spill down my face. "Um, I'm not sure . . ."

"Come on! It'll be fun! We need to celebrate!"

And because she looked so happy and excited to hang out with me, I nodded. "Okay, sure."

"Ride with us!"

Too worried to care about third-wheeling it, I accepted the offer. We got into an SUV and drove to Deidre's house, up windy hillside streets lined with tall trees and pleasant gas lamp streetlights. Raindrops fell on the windows as I watched the dark houses pass. *Am I stuck here? What the hell else could my mission be?*

thirty-six

thirty-six

homecoming day

Hell is having to be at a house party while you wonder whether or not you fucked up the chance to go back to your own timeline.

My bottle of beer was warm in my hand, and it sloshed on my dress when some guy bumped into me.

"Whoops," he slurred, staggering down the stairs. I stared after him, hoping to see him trip and tumble, knocking other people down like bowling pins.

Alas. He made it. I leaned back against my post at the top of the stairs. It was a good spot to passively watch the party below. After taking a celebratory vodka shot with Priscilla, I had wandered, letting her enjoy the party without having to babysit me. I needed that alone time—to strategize about what the hell I needed to do.

My phone was useless as usual, and it was now perilously low on battery power. Eight percent. I tried calling 911 again. *Operator? Please airlift me out of 1995, thanks.*

A commotion at the front door snapped me out of my self-pity. I walked over to the second-story banister, pushing myself against it to see what was going on downstairs. A loud voice pierced through. "Priscilla!"

Oh. No. It was Halmoni.

"*Priscilla!*" she yelled again, this time entering the foyer. Her hair was up in its French twist, and she was wearing a large gray coat over some loose pants and plastic slides. Exuding a fury I had never witnessed before.

"Is that her *mom*?" someone said with incredulity. As if the idea of someone's *mother* existing outside of their own home was the craziest shit they'd ever contemplated. I made my way down the stairs, past the people staring and laughing, hoping to calm her down somehow. Before I reached the foyer, I saw Priscilla pushing through the crowd.

Her face was beet red, and not from drinking. Unlike me, she didn't get flushed when she drank. Her crown was crooked now, her hair a little less than perfect. She stopped in front of Halmoni and said in a low voice, "What are you *doing* here?"

"*Doing here?*" Halmoni yelled. "What we're doing is leaving. *Now.*"

People started laughing again. And I saw the humiliation in Priscilla's eyes. In her clenched fists, her tense shoulders. I thought she'd fight it, be stubborn, and tell Halmoni off. It's what Priscilla would do to anyone who embarrassed her in the future. Everything she did was to avoid this sort of public messiness.

But she followed her out the door.

"*Move,*" I said to a couple of laughing guys as I shoved past them. When I got to the bottom of the stairs, I ran into Deidre giggling into her Solo cup, not a flicker of concern for her so-called friend.

"Her mom's crazy," she said with a derisive snort.

I stopped in my tracks. "Hey, Deidre?" I walked up to her slowly.

She raised her eyebrows and tried not to laugh. "Uh, yeah?"

I grabbed her cup from her and poured the drink on her stupid, perfect hair. "When you've gotta go, you've gotta go, right?"

She turned red as she sputtered through the beer pouring down her face, and when I ran out the front door, I heard her shout, "You *bitch*!"

I turned with both of my middle fingers held up. "Don't fuck with an Aries!"

It was pouring rain out. I stood on the porch, watching Halmoni and Priscilla as they walked to Halmoni's car, parked haphazardly on the street. A little face peeked out from the front seat. Grace. I was about to step down and do, I don't know, *something*, when Priscilla stopped on the front lawn.

"Umma, I *told* you where I was going to be tonight!" she shouted, her hair and dress getting soaked.

Halmoni wheeled around. "*You're* shouting at *me* right now? I thought you were going to a sleepover with Deidre. You didn't say it was a party! You know how I find out? Through Paul's mom at Bible study tonight! She was shocked I didn't know. Do you know how embarrassing it was for Umma to realize that you lied to me? That you're spending time with all these bad kids?"

Priscilla laughed. Hollow and mean. "They're not *bad kids*. They're *normal kids*."

"They're trash," Halmoni said in Korean. I blinked. That was *harsh*. "Only trash people let their kids do stuff like this. Focus on nonsense, do bad things. Dances and homecoming and all this. I let you go far enough. It's over now."

"It's not useless *to me*. Why don't you care about what matters *to me*?" Priscilla's voice cracked, and her lower lip trembled. I recognized the anguish and frustration behind her words, echoes of fights with my mom.

"Because I know better than you!" Halmoni yelled. It made Priscilla flinch, reel back, protecting herself.

My mom never yelled. I always thought it was because she had no emotions. But maybe it was to protect us from them.

"Don't you even want to know if I won homecoming queen or not?" she asked, her voice small and completely miserable.

Halmoni looked at her, her arms folded, her clothing getting soaked by the rain as well. "Looks like you won, wearing that cheap crown."

I felt that like a punch to the gut. It didn't make any sense to me, to see Halmoni so punishing, so hard-edged.

Priscilla was silent for a second. "Yeah, I won. Thanks for caring."

"I care about your *future*," Halmoni said, starting to walk toward the car again. "Focusing on the things that really matter. That's my job as a parent. Not supporting everything you want to do. You think this is worth crying about? There are bigger problems in the world, Priscilla! You are so ungrateful for everything you have."

Those words hit me hard. That criticism, that accusation, was so familiar. I understood then. This was it, the big fight. I felt it in the air—a heaviness that foreshadowed something life-changing. It was the feeling in the car the morning I fought with Mom.

"*Everything I have?*" Priscilla's voice pierced through the rain. "You mean, like how I work for *free*?"

Halmoni scowled. "What? Are you complaining even after I hired Sam to help you?"

"Yeah! I'm complaining! God forbid I have *opinions*!" Priscilla cried. "Yeah, so *finally* you hired someone to help. But I still work Saturdays and you still expect me to do *everything* at home."

I could see the guilt and anger flitting across Halmoni's features. I thought of how she told me on my first day, "I know I ask too much of her." And here it was—proof of her fears.

A light bulb went off for Priscilla. "I was offered a job. At the country club. Like, a real one that *pays*. Maybe I'll go do that instead of working for you. That way I won't be such a financial burden anymore."

An awful expression came over Halmoni's face then—one of betrayal and hurt so deep it gutted me. "You're a bad daughter," she said. Devastating in its calm delivery. Then she walked to the car.

It was like she had hit Priscilla. Priscilla blinked, her face streaked with rain and tears. Watching my mom stand on the wet grass alone, in a dress that was so beautiful only minutes before, was one of the saddest things I'd ever seen. How you could go from being so incredibly happy to feeling like you were completely worthless?

A similar scene flashed through my mind like lightning: my mom and me, standing in the rain in the mall parking lot. *I hate you.* My mom's expression then. And I regretted it. I really regretted ever saying that to my mother.

Suddenly I knew why I was sent back here. It wasn't to prevent this fight. This fight was inevitable.

I was here to help them *after*.

But before I could say anything, Priscilla got into the car, and they drove off.

• • •

A frantic downhill sprint in the rain and one bus ride later, I was standing in front of Priscilla's apartment. I doubled over with my hands on my knees to take a breath, getting increasingly soaked by the rain. I couldn't believe I had made it here so fast. With every minute that passed, I felt the battery drain from my phone. Felt the relationship between my mom and grandmother disintegrating.

Hi, Halmoni. This may or may not be my last recording to you. I really hope it's not. But in case it is, I hope everyone knows that I tried my best. And I love you.

Two fucking percent. I turned my phone off, praying that my piece of crap battery didn't drain regardless.

I took the elevator up to the third floor, trying to squeeze the water out of my hair when the doors opened, and I almost ran straight into Halmoni. She was clutching her car keys and still wearing her coat.

"Sammy?" She startled. "What are you doing here? It's late."

It was. Where was she going?

I held the door open so she could get in and I could step out. "I . . . um, I wanted to give Priscilla her wallet. She forgot it at the party."

She frowned. "Hmm. Okay. How are you getting home?"

"My dad drove me, he's waiting outside." The lies, they were so easy. "Where are you going?" I knew it was nosy.

Her eyes wouldn't meet mine, looking at the panel of buttons in the elevator instead. "I have to finish work. I had lots of work this weekend; it's why I couldn't come to this homecoming thing. But I wish I did, so that I could keep an eye on Priscilla." She did look at me, then, sternly. "Sammy, do your umma and appa know you also go to these parties?"

I never had to lie about going to a party. My parents gave me a lot of freedom with my social life, always encouraging me to get out of my room more. In fact, I always felt a little loserly whenever they pushed for me to go out with friends, like I wasn't meeting some popular-kid quota of leaving the home. "Yes, they do."

"And they are okay with it?"

"Yes." I was almost challenging her.

She looked at me with narrowed eyes.

"You kids think we're strict with you because we are selfish and unfair, that we want to control you. To raise children who we can brag to others about. Priscilla always says this. But you know, we do all this . . . only for you." Halmoni's voice cracked, her hand balled into a fist as she tapped her chest. "How nice it must be to just support everything your children want. That is . . . that is *luxury.* Like a Prada handbag I do not have."

I blinked back tears, too. Because I felt the raw desire in her words, how hard this was. How she was hoping *all this* would end up rewarding her daughters, in a country where she didn't feel like she belonged. Hoping that they would belong, but also hoping that they wouldn't be lost to her in that exchange.

The elevator began to buzz loudly—we'd been hovering around its open doors too long.

Halmoni looked at me, her eyes brimming with tears, "I react so strongly to these things because I can't . . . I can't lose her, too." My heart cracked in half, the shadow of my grandfather's death hovering over us. She continued, "And it feels like she's further and further away every day."

I shook my head, against the elevator buzzing, against what Halmoni was saying. "You won't. You won't lose her if you try and understand her. You'll always be her mother." The buzzing became unbearably loud then—a screech that could have shattered glass.

"Go, go," Halmoni said with a wave, drying her eyes. "Priscilla's at home and your dad's waiting."

I let go of the door and felt a sharp pain in my chest. Would this be the last time I spoke to Halmoni? It felt like too huge a moment to be rushed in such a mundane way.

As the doors closed, I saw her face—a strange look of understanding passing over her features, her eyebrows drawn together, her eyes sparked with a sort of *recognition.*

I smiled, forcing myself not to cry. "Thank you, Mrs. Jo. And . . . see you soon."

The doors shut before she could answer, and I let out an epic exhale. God, I needed to get back home.

As I walked toward Priscilla's apartment, the sounds of dishes being washed, of TV being watched, echoed through the courtyard. And then I saw her—sitting on the little step by her front door, her shiny blue dress pooled around her, her palms pressed into her eyes.

I hesitated. Would she feel embarrassed that I was seeing her like this?

But she looked up, sensing my presence before I could say anything. Like she always would. "Sam?"

"Hi," I said with a feeble wave. "Um. Sorry to bother you. I just . . . well, I saw the fight with your mom and wanted to make sure you were okay."

Her mascara had run down her face from crying. "How embarrassing."

She was quiet as she wiped her face with her hands, her back now straight and full of pride.

I sat down across from her, on the ground. "Sorry your night ended like this."

Another tear ran down her cheek and she laughed while she brushed it away. "It's okay. Why are you sorry? It's not your fault."

"It's not your fault, either."

She looked up, her eyes smudged with dark makeup. "What?"

"It's not your fault your mom doesn't get you." What would I have wanted to hear when I fought with my mom?

I took a deep breath. "Trust me when I say that I know what that feels like. How you want to scream into your pillow some nights. How you feel like you live on a different planet from your mom. How it seems like she doesn't care about your feelings, just her own hang-ups."

Priscilla looked at me curiously. "But you seem like you have really cool parents. They let you do whatever you want."

I laughed. "No, they don't let me do whatever I want. And . . . up until now, I didn't realize how lucky I am."

Because my life was this: My mom sitting at the kitchen table with me every night, making sure I didn't leave until I figured out which theorem worked. Grilling friends' parents before a sleepover. Grounding me for leaving my new phone in the locker room. Snapping my blinds open on Saturday mornings to get me out of bed for soccer games. My mom. She was always there. Pushing me to do things that made me uncomfortable, to challenge me. All with the same hope that my grandmother had for her, just shaped differently, evolved into something new.

My eyes filled with tears, too. "Your mom just wants you to be happy. It's just that, her idea of what that looks like is different from yours. And that's okay. It *sucks*, but it's okay. And I get it. I understand more than you know." More than I did before, more than a week ago. Because *I* had changed. Because not only did traveling back to see my teenage mom help me understand *her*, it also made me understand *myself*. And what really mattered. "Your mom loves you." It was so simple and obvious, but I knew what it meant to hear those words said out loud.

Priscilla looked at me, and for a glitchy second, it felt like *Mom* looking at me. Or maybe I was projecting. I wanted her to hear the words from *me*, her daughter. But all I could hope for in this moment was that Mom felt seen, that she wasn't alone, that this gave her tools for the future, left spaces for softness, for putting aside her armor sometimes.

She gave me a sad smile. "Thanks, Sam. You know . . . it's so strange. I feel like you got here at just the right time."

My phone buzzed in my pocket.

Oh my god.

I did it. *I did it*. I *fucking* did it.

I reached over and gave her a tight hug, my tears falling into her hair. "I'm really glad we met."

"Me too." Priscilla pulled back to look at me. "I know it all went to shit, but thank you again for helping me with the campaign. I really couldn't have won without you. I still don't get why you were so nice to me, why you helped me so much, but . . . well, I've learned to stop asking questions. I've just come to accept that you're totally weird."

I laughed, swiping at my tears. "Such a benevolent queen." Then I remembered something. "And hey, Steph really did us a solid. Lay off of her, okay? She's not that bad."

Priscilla looked like she was going to argue when my phone vibrated again.

"I have to go," I said standing up. "Promise me you'll be cool to Steph."

Priscilla rolled her eyes. "Okay, okay."

I took a mental photograph of teenaged Priscilla rolling her eyes at me in a homecoming gown. I was going to miss her so much. "Congrats on winning homecoming queen. No one deserves it more than you."

Priscilla gave me an odd look. "Why are you so . . . drama right now?"

My laughter rang through the courtyard. "Never change, Priscilla."

She waved and I turned, wiping my tears away. Then I got in the elevator, finally ready to go home.

thirty-seven

thirty-seven

"Did you have a good time?"

I stared at the back of Marge's head. "Are you fucking kidding me?"

"No need for profanity."

"You're lucky I'm not suing you."

"You can't sue a magical rideshare."

The car sped through intersections, the scenery blurring in the rain. I clutched my seat belt. "Slow down! You're going to kill me before I make it back."

"I have a force field protecting us," Marge said as she cranked up the heat.

I leaned forward. "Wait. Really?"

"Haha."

I frowned and leaned back. "Listen, I have no idea how any of this works. You sent me *back in time*. So, no need for *mockery*, okay?"

"So many of you don't know how to properly show your gratitude," she said mildly as she took a turn at the bottom of the hill. "Your, ah, *friend* Jamie also had a few things to say to me."

My breathing hitched. "Jamie? Did he get back okay?"

She didn't answer. The rattling of the car filled the silence.

"Marge!"

"Every passenger's journey is private, Sam. That's how this works." And before I could ask how it worked, she braked hard. "Here we are."

What the hell? I looked out the window. We were at my house. It was daylight. The rain had stopped. "How . . ." My voice trailed off as I looked at the absolute *normalness* of it all. The giant sycamore, the lavender bushes, the white Spanish-style house and its pretty sage-green door. It felt incredibly weird that nothing was weird.

I was back.

Just like that.

"You're welcome." Marge's smirk was visible in the rearview mirror.

"That's it? I'm back?" I stayed seated, suddenly nervous. Scared.

"Yup."

"How much time has passed?" I asked, pulling out my phone. The data signal popped up. The date and time were . . .

"None. It's the same exact time that I picked you up." Marge reached around and unlocked my door. "Now, go. I have other rides."

I took off my seat belt but didn't move. "I don't know if I'm ready."

"Too bad." The car started to creep forward, and I yelped, reaching for the door.

When I got out and shut the door, Marge rolled down her window and threw me a peace sign. "Good luck, Sam. Thanks so much for using Throwback's services."

A low cackle was the last thing I heard before she drove away.

What in the hell?

I stood outside for a second, taking everything in, the whiplash of coming back making me feel dizzy for a second. Despite my rage at Marge, I realized something. I had done it. I had figured it out—everything I had done, everything I had hoped for the past week was *right*.

I pumped my arms into the air and yelled, "Fuck, yes!"

Then I realized I was cold.

Shit. The dress.

I knew for Mom, thirty years had passed. She might not remember this dress. But my mom also kept track of her clothes like normal people kept track of their medical histories. As I walked up to my house, I pulled the bobby pins out of my hair and tried to rub the glitter off my eyelids.

I snuck around to the side, obscured by a jasmine hedge as I peeked into the kitchen window.

It was empty. I glanced at my phone. It had only been ten minutes since our fight so she must still have been driving.

As soon as I was inside, I ran upstairs to my room, worried that Mom would come home any second. I peeled the dress off and stuffed it under a pile of laundry in my hamper. Then I paused and reached into the hamper again. Shook out the dress and rolled it up neatly. Hid it in the bottom of my sweater drawer.

It was vintage, after all.

I caught my harried reflection in the hallway mirror, and I tried to tidy up my hair so Mom wouldn't think I had been jumped on the way home. As I wiped the last trace of glitter from my cheek, something caught my eye.

Under the mirror, there was a long console table cluttered with family photos. This was the one place my mom allowed photos. She said photos around a house were "tacky." Here were all the baby photos of me and Julian. Wedding photos of my parents. Family portraits through the years.

But that wasn't what caught my eye.

I grabbed the tasteful silver frame that held all of Mom's older photos—she and Grace as kids, an old black-and-white photo of my grandparents in Korea. Mom's senior portrait. And in one of the oval spaces was the photo of Mom and me. At the homecoming dance.

Me in the red dress, covering half my face with my hand comically while Mom posed seriously next to me.

Oh my god. It all actually happened. I traced the photo with my fingertip. This was just a few hours ago for me. But there was Mom—a teenager. I stared hard at myself. Yeah, it was near impossible to make out my face. Just a winged eyebrow, a peep of glitter-lined eye. I was scrutinizing my face in the mirror, making sure I looked different enough from the photo, when my phone buzzed.

I glanced down and saw a group text from my mom to my family.

She woke up! Come by when you can.

I stared at the text for several seconds before I could process it. And then when it did finally register, I felt everything inside of me unclench—it was like my insides had been tied up in knots since the day Halmoni was in the hospital. Even through the time travel, through all the insanity of the past week, I had been holding this terror inside of me.

Wild excitement coursed through me as I grabbed a jacket and portable phone charger, pulled my shoes on, and flew out the kitchen door. Halfway to the garage, I remembered that my car wasn't working.

So, I ran down the street, to the nearest bus stop—an option that would have never occurred to me before. And it wasn't until I was seated on the bus, headed to the hospital, that I realized that my mom had used an exclamation point in her text.

thirty-eight

thirty-eight

When I reached Halmoni's hospital room, there was a flurry of activity outside her door that made me immediately nervous. Was she okay? Did something happen between Mom's text and me getting here?

But a second later, my mom popped out of the room with a huge smile on her face as she shook a doctor's hand and thanked him profusely. Relief shot through me.

Then my mom looked up and saw me.

I was nervous to see Mom for a lot of reasons. But at the top of my list was her recognizing me as Sam from the past.

Her hair was still damp from our fight in the rain. Her sunglasses perched on top of her head. Her cream silk shirt still flawless somehow, tucked into her high-waisted dark jeans.

And I felt intense happiness take over all other concerns. This was *my mom*. I was really, truly back home.

"Samantha?" She looked surprised. "Were you able to leave school?"

I tried to keep the overwhelming emotions at bay. "I actually didn't go. I saw your message before I got there. I just really wanted to see Halmoni."

A second passed where I thought she might get pissed that I had ditched school, but she nodded instead. In fact, Mom looked how I felt—extremely relieved, like a boulder the size of a skyscraper had been lifted off of her. "Well, the doctors and nurses just finished checking on her. Let's go in."

I felt light-headed seeing Halmoni in the hospital bed, still hooked up to machines, but *awake*. She was sitting up, just a little, and her eyes were clear and focused when she spotted me.

"Sammy." She smiled, subdued but unmistakably happy.

I burst into tears, wailing like a little kid.

"Yah! I'm not dead, why are you crying?" Halmoni scolded.

And even though that made me laugh, I couldn't stop crying. Everything was just *too much*. Relief and happiness but also complete exhaustion at the roller coaster I'd been on for the past week.

I felt a hand on my shoulder, a gentle squeeze. "Go over and say hi," Mom said.

I looked at her with surprised, wet eyes. Maybe it was my imagination, but something felt so familiar about this version of Mom. It was different but familiar. And I realized why. She was reminding me of Priscilla.

But I didn't have much time to think about it. I stepped over to Halmoni's bed, reaching for her hand. She held it tight. "Hi, Halmoni."

"Hi, Sammy." Her eyes were bright. "Halmoni's sorry she made you worry."

"You should be sorry," I said with a laugh. "Clearly, all of this is your fault."

"It *is* my fault," she said, her voice serious now. "I didn't tell you about my heart."

Those words landed hard—the unintentional subtext almost knocking me over. Seeing Halmoni as a struggling single mother made me appreciate everything about the grandmother I loved: her good humor, her utter contentment with her life, and most of all, it made me appreciate everything I had—all the things my mother built because of the opportunities my grandmother gave her. All the layers of it.

I leaned forward and gave her a tentative hug, aware of her fragile state. "I forgive you."

She gave me a funny look then. "Hmm. How long was I in coma?"

"Just one day." How was that even possible?

"Interesting," she murmured, her eyes roving across my face. "I must have dreamed about you, Sammy. I feel like you've been with me the entire time."

I thought of the last time I saw her, the expression on her face before the elevator doors had closed. How she seemed, against all logic, to have recognized me. Maybe it was because my connection to Halmoni was so strong—that it transcended time. It was some kind of magic I would never understand.

A nurse came in then, rapping on the door. "Hi, all. We have to give Mrs. Jo some rest. She's been through a lot. But you can come visit again in a few hours."

My mother frowned at the nurse, and I waited for her to give the nurse an earful, but instead she looked at Halmoni. "Is that okay with you, Umma? I can stay in the lobby and wait."

Halmoni shook her head. "No, no. It's okay. Go home and come later. I will just sleep."

Mom hesitated before picking up her purse from a chair. "All right. But call me when you wake up. I'll bring some food. The stuff here is atrocious."

Ah, there was the mom I knew.

But then she glanced at the nurse. "Sorry."

The nurse shrugged. "Oh, I agree."

And then, Mom did something that astonished me. She leaned over Halmoni and kissed her forehead. "Be back soon."

I stared at them, waiting for Halmoni to have a second heart attack. But she just nodded, as if Mom being affectionate were the most normal thing in the world. Something unfurled inside my chest. Maybe . . .

Mom and I walked down the hall to the elevators, the din of the hospital surrounding us. The last time I was here, it was the ambient sound of a horror movie. Now, all I felt was immense gratitude for all the machines and people in here who had helped Halmoni get better.

Both our phones vibrated with messages from Julian and Dad. Julian sent a boatload of celebratory emojis, and Dad said he would come to the hospital during his lunch break. I smiled, realizing how much I had missed my entire family.

As we stood waiting for the elevator, I glanced at Mom. A week had passed for me since our fight, but Mom was freshly out of it.

"Mom?"

She glanced at me, her eyes tired but relieved. "Yes?"

"I wanted to talk to you. About . . . our fight."

Her expression was inscrutable. And I felt a sense of loss just then—at how less opaque she used to be in the past. I thought of the last time I had seen her. Both of us real and vulnerable and sad to say goodbye. Where was that girl? My voice sounded small when I said, "I'm sorry about what I said earlier."

Still nothing.

It was hard for me to look at her and I dropped my gaze down to my boots. I stared at the fat laces against the black leather, tracing their lines with my eyes. "I was feeling really sad and scared about Halmoni and probably took it out on you. But I know that's not an excuse. I shouldn't have shouted and said I hated you." I glanced up at her. She hadn't moved an inch.

"Because it's not true." My voice clogged with tears. "It's just sometimes, I feel like . . . I feel like there's this huge *thing* between us that makes it hard to understand what the other is saying. And it's been growing bigger and bigger, and now it feels impossible to move." Tears dropped onto my shirt. *Sweet Jesus, here we go again.*

A movement made me look up. Mom turned toward me, and her hand reached out and brushed the hair out of my eyes. "Samantha, I know you don't really hate me. Just like I didn't hate my mom when I used to yell that at her."

I wiped at my eyes. "Really?"

"Yes."

I waited for more—an apology for the things she said. But it didn't come.

The pang of disappointment was harsh. She hadn't changed. Somehow, I hadn't changed our relationship. Maybe . . . maybe when I traveled to the past, it was just *me* that was supposed to change. And I had. Because even with my mom not doing exactly what I hoped she would do, her response didn't fill me with despair or frustration.

I knew why she was like this now, why she kept her emotions so locked up. And I never knew it before—that this steely strength which seemed so cold was necessary for her back then. It kept her from falling apart under all the weight of her family's dreams. It didn't completely erase my frustrations with her, but it helped. It reminded me that not everything was about me. That my mom existed beyond being my mom.

"Okay, thanks for listening," I took a deep breath. "Also, do you think you can drop me off at school?"

"Sure," Mom said as the elevator doors opened. I glanced at her as I stepped inside. No lecture about asking for a ride?

She paused. "How did you get here?"

"The bus."

"The *bus*?" Her voice an incredulous yelp.

I laughed. "Yeah, the bus. I like the bus."

She gawked at me. "What? Who likes the bus? I swear to god. You remind me so much of her, sometimes."

I froze. "Who?"

"You know who I'm talking about," she muttered as she stepped into the elevator. "Your namesake."

The doors closed and Mom hit the button for the ground floor, but I wouldn't let it drop. I thought of the Samantha jar in Priscilla's bedroom. "Wasn't I named after that doll?"

"A doll?" Mom looked offended. "Of course not. You're named after my friend. I've told you this a million times."

I swallowed. The photo upstairs. Mom remembered me. She carried something of our friendship all the way to the future. It wasn't imagined. The enormity of that was so mind-boggling that I was silent all the way down.

"What happened to her again?" I asked when I could finally speak. We were outside now, the rain gone and the morning sun warm as we walked across the parking lot.

"You know, it's really strange, but I don't remember," she said in a bemused voice. "She had to move, again, I think. Some kind of family emergency according to the school. Yeah, it was that weird new counselor, Marge something-or-other, that told us."

MARGE? "And . . . you lost touch?" I asked, curiosity pushing me into risky territory.

"Yeah, Marge said she moved overseas somewhere. We didn't have a way of contacting each other then." She smiled fondly as she pulled out her keys. "I haven't thought about her in a long time. I hope she's doing okay."

I didn't respond because I was pretty sure I would confess to time travel and break some sort of rule that would tear the fabric of reality apart or something. So, I just sent her a silent message: *Yeah, Mom. She's okay.*

When the car started, music started blasting. Mom turned the volume down. "Sorry."

"Mom, are you playing . . . *BTS*?"

She put on her sunglasses. "Uh, yes? Samantha, did you hit your head on something? How can you not recognize my boys?"

MY BOYS?

She shook her head as we pulled out of the parking lot. "Did you know that someone at work offered me two thousand dollars for our concert tickets? People are *desperate* since they have such limited US shows this year."

Concert tickets. To BTS. Both of us? I . . .

"We're so lucky that Mrs. Jo can always get us these great seats."

I swung around so fast that I almost hit my head on Mom's. "*Mrs. Jo?*"

Mom looked at me askance. "Uh, yeah? Are you okay?"

"Mm-hmm!" I tried to stay calm. "You mean Mrs. Jo . . . who lives in Halmoni's old folks' home, right? The one with dementia?"

Mom looked perplexed. "Dementia? Oh, yeah. She has some mild signs of it, but she's been managing it for years. Being as fabulously wealthy as she is, she can afford the best medical care money can buy."

My note had worked. My smile was wobbly as I kept my eyes on the road ahead. "Oh, glad to hear that."

As BTS continued to play in the background, Mom drove me to school, tapping her hands on the steering wheel to the music. I thought of us dancing at homecoming. And I finally made up my mind about something I had been thinking about my entire trip to the past.

"Mom?"

"Yes?"

I took a deep breath. "I want to go to the dance and keep running for homecoming queen. You're right. If I got this far; I might as well go all the way."

Something sparked in her eyes, and I saw it. I saw the old Priscilla, excited, in her element. "Really? Are you sure?"

"Yes, and . . . can you help me pick out a dress?"

She rolled her eyes. "Of course. If I left it up to you, you'd wear an ironic sweatsuit."

Never change, Mom.

We pulled up to school and I was about to open the door when Mom touched my shoulder.

The morning sunlight surrounded Mom in a soft light. She looked at me for a second, her eyes searching my face. Curious with a hint of affection that I hadn't seen in a long time. "You don't have to run for queen, you know. I know my reaction earlier was . . . unfair. Sometimes, when I'm worried, I'm not the kindest person. I know that."

I didn't move a muscle. I probably stopped breathing.

Not noticing, she continued, "I know how scared you were for Halmoni. And I'm so sorry for making it worse. I was scared about Halmoni, too. And that's not an excuse, either. Not an excuse for not understanding you sometimes. You deserve to be understood."

A sob wrenched out of me and while she didn't hug me exactly, she did place her hands gently on my shoulders. "I'm really sorry," she said softly.

The years-long tension that had unfurled in the hospital room was unraveling in me so fast that I couldn't make sense of any of it. Was I happy or sad or relieved or shocked? Maybe everything all at once. All I could focus on was the feel of my mom's firm grasp on me. Her reassuring voice. "And you know, you're wrong. You don't disappoint me and Dad. I know it sucks to be Julian's little sister." I laughed, snot coming out of my nose. "We don't expect you to be Julian. In fact, we're really glad you're not. That would just be too much."

I looked up at her, hopeful. "I know you guys want me to be more focused, though. But I'm just not that certain about my life yet."

Her eyes were serious, and for once, I felt like she was truly listening to me. "Okay. That's okay. I'm sorry, Samantha, it's just that we want you to find something that drives you, so that you can do something you love." She paused, and her expression shifted, as if coming to a troubling realization. Her laugh was low and bitter when she said, "I always thought I would be different from my mom, but god, I find myself doing the same stuff to you. This terrible Korean-mom pressure."

I shook my head. "You don't, really." And she really didn't. It was clear to me now that my mom was trying her best to break from the dynamic she had with her mom. But that didn't mean her approach with me was perfect. It was all just . . . "It's just hard."

My mom took a second before saying slowly, "The way that I'm like your grandmother is that everything I do, I do it to make you happy. But I realize that sometimes we have different ideas of what that means."

They were the words I had said to her just hours before. Hearing them repeated sucked all the air out of me.

She kept going. "I'm going to try and reconcile those two things. Okay?"

I nodded, wiping my nose. "Okay. I will, too."

She rubbed my arm. "I'm always here."

And then the unraveling stopped. It reached its end. The coiled tension that had built over the past few years—all of it relaxed.

"I know," I said, trying to smile through the chaos of my feelings.

"Now, go to school," she said as she unlocked the doors. "I'll pick you up right after so we can visit Halmoni again."

And I knew she would. All those sleepovers when I got homesick? The person who picked me up, every time, whether it was midnight or three a.m., was my mom. My mom had always been there for me. Even if I hadn't always seen it.

thirty-nine

thirty-nine

When I got to school, morning break had just started. I walked through the hall, staring at everyone and everything, not quite believing that at any second Priscilla wouldn't come up behind me with an exasperated comment about my hair.

I passed by a table set up with a sign that said "REFORM HOMECOMING COURT"—the colors written in rainbow colors. A guy behind the table shouted out, "Hey, Sam! Be a part of the solution and not the problem!"

I was definitely back. I gave a thumbs-up. "Don't worry—I'm on it!"

When I reached my locker, I felt a poke in my back. I turned quickly and saw Val, standing there as if everything was normal.

Relief washed over me so powerfully that it was visceral—like walking into an air-conditioned room on a hot day. I tried not to cry as I threw my arms around Val.

"Are you okay? What's wrong?" They pulled away to take a good look at my face. "Is it your grandma?"

I shook my head. "No, it's just . . . I've been through a lot since we last talked. But also! My grandma woke up this morning!"

Val's face broke out into a huge grin, and they hugged me. "Oh my god! I'm so, so glad!"

"Thanks, me too." I gave them an extra hard squeeze. A week without my best friend had been brutal. There was so much I wanted to tell them—*everything*, really. But I wasn't sure if I could. And I had a couple of pressing matters at hand.

"Hey, have you seen Curren?" I asked, sweeping my eyes through the hallway. No sign of him. He was probably still mad at me for that text.

Val shook their head. "Not this morning. He's probably out in the quad."

I tossed my stuff into my locker and shut it. "I have to go talk to him. See you at lunch?"

The quad was bustling with everyone scarfing down last-minute snacks before third period. It took me a second to adjust to the small differences from the quad of 1995, to see completely different sets of humans scattered around.

I spotted Curren standing under a tree, scrolling through his phone with a few of our friends nearby, sunglasses on, hair artfully mussed. I thought of the way Jamie's hair felt as it sifted through my fingers, then took a deep breath.

"Hey."

Curren looked up from his phone. "Hey."

"Can we talk in private?"

He tilted his head. "In private?" It was slightly mocking, and I realized how sick I was of his brand of humor—repeating things with a smirk, as if that were clever in any way.

"Yeah." I headed to a quiet spot nearby before he could respond. When he followed me there, I said, "Here's the thing. I think we should break up."

My heart pounded as Curren just stood there, frozen.

"What?" he asked finally. "Is this because of the donuts?"

Oh my god. "No, it's not the donuts."

I looked at his face—that beautiful face—and thought of how my stomach used to flip when I saw it. How I used to spend hours just staring at it, loving it. Loving when it was focused only on me. Not believing that this face could love me back.

"I'm sorry. I know that you're probably surprised." I tried to keep my voice steady. To keep going. "It's just . . . something's changed. In me."

He drew close. "Are you serious, Sam?"

I braced myself for the overwhelming feeling of his presence—how just being close to him could send every part of me into some Mercury-in-retrograde malfunction.

But it never came. I was clear-headed—about him and so many things. "I am. Serious. We've been fighting a lot, too, you know? I can't be the only one who's noticed."

He ran his hands through his hair, a gesture that used to make me feel religious. "Yeah. But I didn't think it was anything we couldn't get over."

He spoke as if he were in a daze. And it occurred to me that he'd probably never been dumped before.

"I don't want to become one of those couples that fights all the time and stay together just because breaking up is hard," I said. "I'm sorry, Curren."

He nodded, his shoulders sagging. "To be honest, I guess I'd been feeling it, too. I just . . . wait, is your grandmother . . . ?" His voice trailed off, his expression worried.

I shook my head. "Oh! Halmoni came out of her coma this morning!"

He looked genuinely relieved. "Oh, man. Thank god! I'm so, so glad for you." His hand clasped mine and he pulled me in for a hug.

I smiled into his shoulder. "Thanks, Curren. Thanks, bruh."

He groaned. "Too soon to call me bruh."

The warning bell rang, and he looked hard at me. "Well, see you around, Sam."

I tried to smile, tasting the bittersweetness of it all in the back of my throat. "Yeah, see you."

As he walked off to class, I headed to English. People were filing in, and Mr. Finn was at his desk, clicking on his mouse, looking the proper age again. I went straight to him.

"Mr. Finn?"

He looked up, graying hair and all. "Hi, Sam." But I could see it now—a shadow of his former hot self.

"Hi. So, I'm sorry I don't have it written down, but I know what my senior project is going to be. Can I just tell you right now?" I clasped my hands nervously.

Leaning back in his chair, he said, "Okay."

"So, I want to produce a podcast about my family." Jamie had said it offhand, but his words after our presentation had been stewing in my brain.

He remained straight-faced and motioned for me to continue. *Geez.*

"I'm going to document my grandmother's journey from Korea to here, and then my mom's life in America—she also went to school here. Priscilla Jo, do you remember her?"

"Priscilla Jo? Not only is she present at every parent teacher conference, but she was also my student a lifetime ago," Mr. Finn said with an amused expression. "Anyone who meets Priscilla remembers her."

I nodded. "Right? So, um, then the podcast is going to explore how their experiences inform my own life. It's essentially about what it means to have a dream in this country that claims to be the promised land. And what that dream means to whoever you pass it down to, to your children who are the beneficiaries of your lived experiences. What ends up happening the further removed you are from the struggles to survive here. What gets saved and what gets lost with each generation."

My words tumbled over each other, spilling out on their own. This idea was still half-formed but feeling tactile and real the more I explained it out loud. Talking about it for the first time made me kind of feel like throwing up, actually, and I was breaking out into a cold sweat. Is this what people felt like when they shared their ideas with the world? Fucking awful.

I took a deep breath. "It's essentially about how the past never leaves you. For better or for worse."

I aged one thousand years as I waited for Mr. Finn to respond. He straightened in his chair. "Well, Sam. This is what I've been waiting for. It sounds incredible. I'm really excited to hear it."

"Really?" I felt my anxiety recede immediately. The weightlessness after—it was the best feeling ever.

"Yes, really," he said. "I knew you had something like this in you."

"You did?" I was incapable of any original words. I had used all of them.

He chuckled. "I did. Do you think I'd give you a hard time if I didn't think you had something to say?"

"I—I don't know," I said, embarrassed. "To be honest, I wasn't sure I had anything to say."

"Well, I'm glad you're finding your voice," he said with a smile. "Now, go sit. Class is about to start."

I walked to my seat, practically floating. For the first time ever, the world felt opened up to me, with infinite possibilities I had never seen before. It felt like I finally had the space to figure out who I really was—separate from my family, and Curren, and everyone else. And it was the single best feeling in the entire world.

forty

forty

nine days later: homecoming 2025

I felt an intense wave of déjà vu. The smell of the gym mixed with everyone's hair products. The heavy vibrations of the bass. The giddiness and optimism in the air as people clustered in groups, looking at each other's formal wear.

My second homecoming dance in a week.

Val, in their sleek black jumpsuit, tugged on my arm. "Let's go take pictures!" We had decided to nix dates this year and just go with each other, which was always more fun anyway. I had spent the week lobbying hard for my homecoming queen campaign, using all my social currency to make my case—and for a gender-neutral homecoming court as well. I had no idea if it would work or not. I think people were mostly confused by my sudden zeal for the homecoming crown. Unlike 1995, no one else really campaigned.

Thinking about the past and Jamie had been unavoidable. But the week had been so nuts that I barely had time to wrap my head around the whole other-guy-ness of it all. Or maybe that's what I told myself. Part of me knew . . . I was waiting for him to find me. Not because of some outdated notion of chivalry or anything, but because I was a little scared to go looking for him. What if, when he came back to 2023, he realized he didn't actually like me? That it was all just heightened emotions during a stressful time? So, I had avoided it, which had been easy with all the homecoming hoopla.

"No embarrassing poses," I said firmly as Val and I stood in front of the lush tropical plant display in the photo booth. The theme this year was "Welcome to the Jungle." Again, *why*? The theme was written out in neon-green light set on the backdrop, framed by the foliage. Very Insta-worthy.

Val and I made various silly and deadpan faces as the photographer snapped away. When we were done, we looked at the photos on the photographer's iPad, swiping through to make selections. The luxury of digital.

"Your dress just, like, *pops*," Val said, pointing at me on the screen. I agreed. I was wearing a gauzy hot-pink dress with shiny black platform boots. My hair was slicked back, short and sleek. "Like Linda Evangelista," my mom had said approvingly. We had gone through about one million dresses the past week because the Venn diagram overlap between Mom's taste and mine was like a teeny tiny sliver. But both of us knew this was *the dress* when we saw it. The best part was it was vintage, but *fancy* vintage so that my mom could live.

When we made our way to the dance floor, I saw Curren enter the gym, taking his time, his gait relaxed. He was wearing a tight-fitting suit, à la early Beatles, and had a camera slung around his neck, of course. Looking at him without my smitten-girlfriend filter, I realized so much of Curren was self-conscious and practiced—that what I thought was confidence was actually bravado. I felt relief for the billionth time this week that I no longer had to squash my little irritations with him. Now that our lives weren't intertwined anymore, they no longer bothered me. And we were actually totally fine. In fact, we were so fine that I wondered how long we'd both been ready to break up before I actually did it. I think we had been more into the idea of being a couple than actually *being* together. We exchanged friendly waves, and then Val and I hit the dance floor with our friends.

A few seconds in, the music changed, and I couldn't believe it. It was "Insane in the Brain." I started cracking up and Val looked at me weird.

"It's a good song!" I yelled.

"I *guess*!" they yelled back.

My dress had the perfect flounce for dancing. While I was twirling away, I felt a hand tap my shoulder. I turned. "Hi, Mom!" I shouted.

Even in her grown-up finery—a flawlessly tailored lavender wrap dress and silver pumps—Mom managed to look like a surly teenager when she made a face at the volume of my voice. "Samantha!"

There was a group of adults by the beverage table, all dressed up and wearing sashes with various years printed on them, like my mom's. Former homecoming royalty and their families were invited to visit the dance this year since it was the one hundredth anniversary of North Foothill High's founding.

I glanced at Mom's glittery "1995" sash. *Wild.* "Are Dad and Julian here?"

Julian had come home this week to visit Halmoni.

She nodded. "Yeah, they're both hiding in a corner somewhere. Dad almost didn't come. This is his nightmare." Unlike Mom, Dad hated high school and had been extremely unpopular. Apparently, it's because he had a metal phase?

"Are you nervous?" she asked me, pulling me away from the speakers so we didn't have to yell.

I took some time to answer. Compared to Mom's homecoming, this was a breeze. Literally, life-changing stakes versus zero stakes. But, I realized, seeing Mom buzzing with nervous energy, I did actually care. It would be nice to win; it would make Mom happy. Although, I knew now, she wasn't putting that pressure on me—that her own shit was her own shit.

"Kind of?" I said, truthfully. "It's just been . . . a long couple weeks."

Mom nodded. "Yeah, with Halmoni."

I just smiled in response. *Right.*

"Oh, there they are!" Mom waved to Dad and Julian across the room. They came over, both wearing suits and looking deeply uncomfortable—Dad dealing with whatever metal demons, and Julian just at his usual discomfort level. I swatted his arm. "Thanks for coming, you look nice." More than a few people had glanced at my hot-in-that-preppy-way brother.

He shrugged. "Mom said I had to come."

Mom sighed. "I didn't say you *had* to. But it's nice for all of us to support Samantha."

"Of course," Dad said quickly. I knew Mom had strong-armed them, but it was still nice.

"Let me see your makeup," Mom said as she reached over to brush my hair out of my face but then stopped, realizing my hair was slicked back. "Habit, I guess," she said.

Fixing my hair was one of many little things that my mom had always done—things I had managed to forget while I was so fixated on what had started to change between us. Everything was in proper focus since I had gotten back from the past, like I was wearing the right prescription glasses for once.

The music stopped then, and someone made a loud airhorn sound. After the laughing stopped, our student body president,

Leona Kazeminy, stepped onto the stage. She tapped the microphone with her long, glittery fingernail. "Good evening, North Foothill High!"

Some dickhead yelled, "Good evening!" in a British accent in response.

Leona rolled her eyes. "Wow, cutting edge. *Anyway*, as you all know it's the hundredth anniversary of North Foothill's founding. That means this is the hundredth homecoming dance!" She paused for awe that never came. "In celebration, this year I'd like to welcome all the former alumni who have been crowned king and queen in the past!" She started clapping, making a face at the audience like "Clap, assholes." We did, and I watched as my mom and a bunch of other people walked up onstage to stand with Leona. She ran a roll call with everyone's crowning years, and when Mom's name came up, my family cheered. I gave a loud whistle, and saw my mom visibly cringe. *Ha, embarrassing Priscilla since 1995. Love this for myself.*

"And now," Leona said into the mic, "it's time to announce this year's homecoming royalty!" A pause. "And given this year's protests about the gendered, heteronormative practice of crowning a king and queen, the North Foothill student government has decided to remove all requirements of gender from the homecoming court qualifications." A loud cheer went up, this time genuine. Principal Wang nudged Leona. She continued, "So without further ado . . ."

Val appeared at my side, giving my arm a squeeze. They looked at me with a huge grin. "Eee!"

I rolled my eyes. "Nice try at excitement."

They shrugged. "Seemed like I was supposed to do that."

"I appreciate it."

A drumroll blared over the speakers, and then Leona opened an envelope dramatically. Such a theater kid.

Mom looked for me in the crowd and I smiled at her when we made eye contact. She waved crossed fingers at me.

"Our homecoming queen this year is Zella Sussman!" A cheer went up as Zella, the water polo captain in a pink tux and amazing mohawk, walked up to the stage to receive her crown and flowers. A tiny thread of disappointment wove through me as I clapped for her. I saw Mom clapping politely, but I knew she was disappointed, too.

Leona opened the other envelope with a flourish, her hand making an exaggerated gesture. "And this year's *other* homecoming queen is . . . Samantha Kang!"

Val screamed. I jumped in shock. "What the hell?"

They covered their mouth and looked distressed. "Sorry, I guess I *am* excited?"

I laughed and hugged them, Dad, and Julian before I made my way to the stage, people congratulating me along the way. When I got up there, Mom handed me my bouquet and set the crown on my head. She was beaming. "Congratulations, Samantha!"

"Thanks, Mom." And then, something about her ecstatic expression gave me an idea.

I stepped up to the microphone, surprising Leona. "Sorry, I just need a second," I said to her quietly, then spoke into the microphone. "Thanks, everyone, for voting for me," I glanced at my mom, who looked confused. "I especially want to thank my mom. She's the real queen. Always."

I stepped away from the mic and Mom engulfed me into a fierce hug. "Thank *you*, Sam." *Sam. She called me Sam.* And like Halmoni in the hospital, she paused to pull back and look at me with a perplexed expression. "It's really strange, something about tonight feels so familiar."

Before I could respond, Leona bellowed, "*Back to the music, North Foothill!*"

Mom covered her ears. "On that note, I think it's time for us to leave so that you kids can enjoy the night."

We found Dad and Julian, who both looked ready to bust out of there. After giving me a congratulatory kiss on the cheek, Dad headed out to bring the car around and Mom went to go grab her bag from the coatroom.

Julian smiled at me. "I knew you'd win."

"What? How?"

He shrugged. "You're always good at this kind of stuff. People just like you."

Julian never bullshitted anyone; in fact, I wasn't sure he was capable of it. But I didn't know what to do with a compliment from him, so I just shrugged and said, "Not everyone."

He sighed. "Yes, everyone, Sam. It was this huge relief for Mom when you were born, to finally have a kid who could charm people. I've . . . I've always been really envious of that."

I almost stuck my fingers in my ears to squeakily clean them out. "Envious of *me*?"

"Yes, of course," he said. I wanted to argue, but stopped when I saw Julian's expression. I realized that maybe I wasn't the only one who felt like I couldn't live up to Mom's expectations.

Mom rushed back, holding her coat and bag. "Okay, Julian, let's head out. Dad's waiting."

I crushed Julian into a hug. "Hey, I'm glad you're home."

His voice was muffled in my hair. "I'm glad, too."

"And when I get back, I'll show you how to beat the Yiga Clan Hideout."

Mom smiled at us, pleased to see her two children showing affection to each other. "Have a wonderful time, Samantha, and just text me when you're headed home, okay? And only take a rideshare if you're with Val. The news stories about all the weird drivers lately have been extremely upsetting."

You have no idea, Mom.

As my family walked out of the gym, Julian stopped and gave me a weirdly sneaky look. "Hey, Sam—you might want to save your first dance for someone special."

I stared at him. "What?"

Julian lifted his chin, his eyes focused on something behind me. "Someone's here to see you."

forty-one

forty-one

Everything stilled. The lights, the music, the entire dance. I turned—slowly—trying to wish it into reality.

And there, across the gym, was Jamie.

He looked . . . *so good.* Wearing a dark blue suit with a pin-striped shirt, no tie. The brown skin of his throat peeking through the unbuttoned collar. His hair was a little shorter than I remembered, but still thicker than anything, and parted so deeply onto the side that a lock of it fell into his eyes.

His eyes. He wasn't wearing glasses!

I looked to Julian sharply. *What*?

He grinned at my surprise—a shit-eating older brother grin. "You've never met my roommate. For some reason, he *really* wanted to meet you." And before I could stop him, he rushed out to join Mom and Dad.

With the entire world muted around me, I walked over to Jamie. Everything was a blur except him. Our eyes never left each other's, and I saw his face break out into a slow, knowing smile.

When I reached him, I just stood there for a second, unable to believe what I was seeing.

"Hi, Samantha," he finally said. That low, measured voice. I loved that voice. It was quiet and confident—a real confidence that came from knowing exactly who he was. And who he was was pretty wonderful.

"Hi," I managed to say. "My brother just said the weirdest thing—"

A dark flush crept up Jamie's neck. "Okay so hear me out. I ended up going to Yale."

I couldn't help it, I squealed. Like *squealed*. "Oh, my god! Congratulations!"

He bit back a smile, pleased as hell. "Thank you. Um, so yeah. I met him at orientation and when I found out who he was, I requested to room with him." His eyes darted up to mine, dark and nervous. "Sorry to be creepy. But I had to find out how you were doing. It was my way of catching up with you without breaking my promise not to seek you out until after you traveled back."

It could have been creepy, but I knew that if I had been in his position, I would have been equally creepy. If not creepier—let's be honest.

I shook my head. "No, I'm glad you found me. By whatever means necessary."

He fumbled in his jacket pocket. "I have, um . . ." A corsage, made of gorgeous pink and peach-tinted dahlias. "Maybe you already have one—"

I held my wrist out. "No, I don't!"

His hands were steady and elegant as he slid the corsage over my wrist. I stared down at it for a second before I dropped my bouquet and fell into him with a crush, wrapping my arms around his solid frame.

I felt his laughter on the top of my head. "You're welcome."

His scent surrounded me, familiar and incredibly heady. I breathed him in before responding. "You found me."

"I did."

"You waited for me."

We pulled back, our faces still so close, his dark eyes so focused on mine. "I did. I'm a good listener."

I laughed. "You are."

He touched my crown. "Looks like you won."

"Oh. Yeah. Ha. It . . . it made my mom happy. I guess everything kind of worked out, in its own weird way."

Jamie let out a huff of laughter. "Same. Very much same."

And then a shyness dropped over his eyes, and he stepped away. It took everything in me not to jump him. I clasped my hands to keep them away from him. "I want to know everything. There's so much to talk about."

"Yeah," he said. "There is."

A slow jam came on, and the dance floor dispersed, making room for swaying couples. People crowded around us, pushing us closer. But Jamie kept his distance, looking away. "So, did you come to the dance with Curren, or . . ."

Oh. *Oh.*

"We broke up," I blurted out. It was loud. My face flushed.

His eyes flew up to mine. "You did?"

My cheeks were hot when I laughed. "Yeah, it was like . . . almost the first thing I did."

Both of us were dying, not looking at each other, feeling rigor mortis set into our limbs, unable to move. The entire world could have reached an apocalyptic end, and we'd still have been rooted in those spots.

I let out a huge breath. "But you know? No pressure!" *Really believable, Sam.* "It was something I should have done a long time ago. I just . . . I didn't know it until, until . . ."

"You traveled back in time?" I could hear the smile in his voice, and it made me look up at him. His thoughtful, handsome face.

"Yeah," I said, stepping closer to him, the feeling returning to my limbs. "And until I met you."

Our faces were inches apart. I could count his eyelashes. "I like you, and unless I'm misinterpreting you waiting for me for two years and low-key stalking me through my brother, I think maybe you also—"

The rest of my words were lost when he pulled me against him, his hand pushing up the back of my neck, into my hair, as his lips met mine. And—like everything else with Jamie—the kiss was good. Soft and urgent and everything I had imagined for the past week.

When we pulled apart, he didn't look shy anymore. He looked incredibly happy—a little flushed and dazed, but happy. He looked how I felt.

I took his hand. "Want to dance?"

He linked his fingers through mine. "I'd love to."

And then time stopped standing still. The lights, the music—everything came alive around us. And we were finally right where we were supposed to be.

The entire future stretched out before us.

acknowledgments

The entire world changed while I wrote this book—in ways universal and personal. As I wrote a book about mothers, I became one myself. And I was only able to finish this book with the help of *so many* people.

Thank you to Faye Bender—for helping me change course, for pushing me to dream big, for your quiet strength that felt like steel when I was unsure. You're who I want to be when I grow up.

Thank you to all of The Book Group.

Tiffany Liao—I adore you. Thank you for understanding everything about this story, from the mom feels to the nineties fashion to the way Priscilla takes off her shoes. It was such a privilege to work with you on this book, and it's one million times better for it.

Endless thanks to the entire Zando team, including Molly Stern, Sarah Schneider, TJ Ohler, Andrew Rein, Allegra Green, Nathalie Ramirez, Anna Hall, Amelia Olsen, Chloe Texier-Rose, and Sara Hayet. I'm so honored to be a part of this big adventure.

Thanks, also, to Kemi Mai Willan, Jeanne Tao, Aubrey Khan, Rachel Kowal, Natalie C. Sousa, and Lindsey Andrews.

Thank you, always, to Mary Pender and the entire UTA team, for making movie magic and championing my voice. So excited for all that's ahead.

There were lots of people who have no idea they helped shape this book and who will never know. Podcasts kept me going during lockdown, pregnancy, and newborn days. Thank you to my pod friends at *Forever35* (Kate Spencer and Doree Shafrir), *The Empire Film Podcast*, *Blank Check*, *Pod Save America*, *Still Processing*, and *You're Wrong About*. And, yes, Michelle Obama.

Thank you to Robert Zemeckis and Bob Gale for making my favorite movie of all time. Thank you to Cathy Park Hong, who made me rethink this book and crystallized into brilliant words the simmering rage I've been feeling my entire life.

Thank you to Kate Lao Shaffner for US government inspiration. Derick Tsai for TCMC. Cody Tucker, for everything.

All the readers, librarians, teachers, and booksellers who have supported my books over the past decade. I am so, so grateful.

How would I have survived being a new mom without other new moms? Much love to Olivia Abtahi, Rachelle Cruz, Cassandra Fulton, Celia Lee, Britta Lundin, Samantha Mabry, Isabel Quintero, Jill Russell, Jen Wang, and Brenna Yovanoff.

Love and gratitude to my Wednesday writers: Julie Buxbaum, Anna Carey, Sarah Mlynowski, Rebecca Serle, Jen Smith, and Siobhan Vivian. Very special thanks to Adele Griffin.

My friends/colleagues/lifelines: Sumayyah Daud, Laurie Devore, Kate Hart, Michelle Krys, Amy Lukavics, Diya Mishra, Zan Romanoff, Courtney Summers, Elissa Sussman, Kara Thomas, and Kaitlin Ward. Thank you for, well, you know. *All* of it.

For the early reads, invaluable support, and brainstorming every step of the way—and gold standard friendships: Sarah Enni, Morgan Matson, and Veronica Roth. Hawaii forever.

I was lucky to have help with childcare when so many others didn't. Thank you so much to my sister Christine Goo, cousin Elaine Koo, and Maralee Kent for taking care of the most precious person so that I could write this book.

Thank you to all my family: Appelhans, Appelwats, Peterhans. My grandfathers, cousins, and uncles . . . 고모부, you will be missed.

My grandmothers:
To 외할머니, who left North Korea not knowing she would never see her family again, raised six children, immigrated to the US, and worked as a seamstress before helping raise her thirteen Korean American grandkids. Her kimchi and sujebi was the best, and she always kept the door open when she was expecting us.

To 할머니, who was raised by her own grandmother during the Japanese occupation, who immigrated to the US and learned to speak English by way of soap operas, who loved driving in Los Angeles. She taught me how to pick out the best fruit at the grocery store and knit my Barbies' scratchy sweaters.

I miss you both.

To my aunts, several of whom owned dry cleaners in the eighties and nineties. Who ran their own businesses. Who worked as designers, nurses, and bankers. Who raised their children and cooked every single meal. All in a country so far from home. You are all legendary, and I'm so grateful to have been raised by, and around, all of you.

To my mom, who came to America as a journalist and retired as a bank executive. Who reshaped her dreams so that I could pursue mine. Who has been essential in helping raise her first grandchild during a pandemic. Thank you for everything you've done—and do—every day for all of us. I'm a grateful daughter who had to write an entire book to show you the magnitude of my love and appreciation.

To my husband, Chris, and my son, Alexander. Thank you for expanding my definition of love beyond anything I could have ever imagined. The future is ours.

about the author

about the author

MAURENE GOO is the author of several acclaimed books for young adults, including *I Believe in a Thing Called Love* and *Somewhere Only We Know*. She's also written for Marvel's *Silk* series. She lives and writes in Los Angeles with her husband, son, and cats.

Follow Maurene on Twitter
and Instagram @maurenegoo

Visit maurenegoo.com

LFG CLASS OF 25!
xx SAM